Also by Rachael Stewart

Surprise Reunion with His Cinderella
Beauty and the Reclusive Millionaire

Claiming the Ferrington Empire miniseries

Secrets Behind the Billionaire's Return

Also by Jennifer Faye

Wedding Bells at Lake Como miniseries

Bound by a Ring and a Secret
Falling for Her Convenient Groom

Greek Paradise Escape miniseries

Greek Heir to Claim Her Heart

Discover more at millsandboon.co.uk.

THE BILLIONAIRE BEHIND THE HEADLINES

RACHAEL STEWART

IT STARTED WITH A ROYAL KISS

JENNIFER FAYE

MILLS & BOON

First published in Great Britain 2022
by Mills & Boon, an imprint of HarperCollins*Publishers* Ltd,
1 London Bridge Street, London, SE1 9GF

www.harpercollins.co.uk

HarperCollins*Publishers*
1st Floor, Watermarque Building,
Ringsend Road, Dublin 4, Ireland

The Billionaire Behind the Headlines © 2022 Rachael Stewart

It Started with a Royal Kiss © 2022 Jennifer F. Stroka

ISBN: 978-0-263-30222-6

07/22

MIX
Paper from
responsible sources
FSC® C007454

This book is produced from independently certified FSC™ paper
to ensure responsible forest management.
For more information visit www.harpercollins.co.uk/green.

Printed and Bound in Spain using 100% Renewable Electricity
at CPI Black Print, Barcelona

THE BILLIONAIRE BEHIND THE HEADLINES

RACHAEL STEWART

MILLS & BOON

For Bree and Sarah,
founders of The Categorically Romance Podcast.

Thank you for sharing your love of romance
with the world and bringing so much joy to readers,
authors, editors and publishers alike.

You ladies ROCK! Keep being you!

Rachael

xxx

CHAPTER ONE

'BREE! BREE! YOU need to come here!'

Resisting the urge to roll her eyes, Bree set her spatula down and cleaned her hands on her apron. Whatever it was, it wasn't going to be important, but ignoring Angel was never easy. Ignoring the ever-increasing rabble outside her best friend Felicity's B & B even less so.

Taking a steadying breath, she left the sanctuary of the kitchen for the bar where her charge for the day—Felicity's sixteen-year-old daughter, Angel—was pressed up against the window.

'Aren't you supposed to be helping me with the baking?'

'Just look at them!' Angel flung her hands at the glass, her blue eyes bright. 'I know we're a tourist trap and we get the odd travel journalist but this…this is something else.'

Something else, indeed…

'You sure we shouldn't be out there talking—'

'Absolutely not.'

Angel frowned. 'But it could be great for business. Just think of the extra punters we could attract for the B & B if we name-drop—'

'No.'

'Shouldn't we at least call Mum and see what—?'

'We're not disturbing your mum.'

Angel's eyes started to dance, her frown morphing into a grin. 'You think there's something there, too, then? Between them, I mean… Mum and that guy she's gone off with.'

Something was definitely there and, though it felt inappropriate to confirm it, Bree couldn't stop the hint of a smile. Her friend certainly deserved the happiness of something being there with the man from her past who had checked into the B & B the night before…though the fact the horde

of reporters outside were also here for that same man was
a worry.

'That's not for us to say, honey.'

'Yeah, right! You'd be the first to—'

Bree widened her gaze and Angel promptly zipped up,
the girl's attention going back to the scene outdoors.

'What did you say they were asking about again, Bree?'

'Some article on someone in the area.'

'Some special someone if it's bringing this many of them
here… You sure we can't let them in?'

'Absolutely not.'

'The bar would get amazing trade.'

And her friend would have her head for it. No matter
how much money it put in the till.

But surely the press was wrong—a simple case of mistaken identity. The guy they were after was Sebastian Dubois. A billionaire hotel mogul who rarely surfaced from
his ivory tower and had no reason whatsoever to visit teeny,
tiny, poky Elmdale. Their village.

Not Sebastian Ferrington, returning heir to the local estate, current B & B guest and Felicity's date for the day.

Yet the press had been doing their hardest to gain access
to the B & B for the last few hours and their numbers were
steadily growing, hungry to catch a glimpse of him and refusing to believe he wasn't here.

And just like that the banging on the front door started
up once more…

'I said we're closed!'

'We won't take up much of your time!' someone called.

'You won't take up any of it,' she murmured.

Maybe she should ring Felicity, just to warn her. But the
woman had sounded distracted enough when she'd asked
her to cover the B & B for the day. And that was before the
media circus had descended.

She'd never asked Bree to look after the B & B for a

whole day before. Never even taken a holiday in all the time Bree had known her. Three years and counting. Every day was a work day and she deserved a day off with the hot guy from her past.

The hot guy who had definitely been called Ferrington. Not Dubois.

And though Felicity hadn't admitted it, the colour in her cheeks had certainly hinted at a romantic past.

But Dubois? No, the press was wrong.

You could run a quick Internet search...

'Absolutely not.'

Angel's eyes narrowed on her. 'What?'

'Nothing.' She really needed to stop speaking her thoughts out loud when she was stressed. Maybe she should've taken a closer look at the picture the third inter-fering journalist had tried to ram under her nose, but she'd been too outraged by their attempt to gain access via the private door to the rear of the building to give it the time of day. 'Right, never mind all this nonsense, we have muf-fins to bake.'

She started to move off when the roar of an approaching engine set the windows rattling.

'Oh, my God!' Angel was back up against the glass, mouth agape.

Slowly, Bree turned. 'What now?'

'If this new arrival is a reporter, I'm changing my mind about career paths.'

'Why?'

'Why?' The engine purred as it came to a stop, then revved some more as it progressed, likely navigating through the masses. 'Because they're driving a mean Porsche and the press are all over them. Check it out!'

Bree rolled her eyes, walking up behind Angel and know-ing that her twenty-eight years should mean she knew bet-ter than to get sucked in by all the drama. Sure enough, the low-slung vehicle was causing the frenzy to build before their eyes, the press parting to make way for the car but staying close.

Who on earth could it be now?

She sighed and backed away, grateful the doors were locked and the chaos was safely on the other side.

'Come on, love, we have muffins to prep. Whatever that is, it's none of our business.'

'But, Bree, whoever that is, they have to be important.'

'Not to us and the muffins we're supposed to be cooking. Plus, there's the mojito mix to test.'

Now she had Angel's attention. 'You're going to let me have some?'

'You can have a sip.'

Angel glanced longingly back at the window and the excitement on the other side. Bree got it. This was the most exciting thing to happen in Elmdale in…well, for ever.

'Can't I just—?'

'No, love. While your mother isn't here, I'm in charge and we're staying well away from whatever that is.'

Because the more the frenzy built, the more she doubted her own conviction…

And if she was the one who was wrong, and Sebastian Ferrington and Dubois were one and the same—well, then they'd all be necking mojitos soon enough.

'You coming?' she called back to Angel as she entered the hall.

'Yeah, I'm— Wait! Bree, you need to see this.'

'If I hear that phrase again, I'll—'

'But, Bree, the guy in the Porsche, you're not going to believe who it is…'

Shaking her head, she returned to the window and peered through the lace curtain. 'I really don't think— You've got to be kidding me!'

'See!'

She did see. Though she couldn't believe it. The man leaning out of the gunmetal-grey Porsche was instantly recognisable. His wild mop of blond hair with its defiant fringe that fell over one eye was the stuff of teenage dreams, his chiselled jaw and trademark grin, too. A grin that was currently lighting up the entire pavement along with her insides.

She let out a curse and slapped her hand over her mouth.

Way to go, swearing in front of a minor!

'It is him, isn't it?' Angel asked.

Bree shook her head dumbly.

'This is un-freaking-believable!' Angel took the words right out of Bree's mouth as she raced to the check-in desk, rummaging about before rushing back seconds later, a magazine in her hand. 'It *is* him. Look!'

She slammed the magazine up against the window, palm holding it in place as her eyes pinned the very real man in question.

Bree looked at the magazine cover, looked at him, looked at the magazine and back again, not that she needed the comparison. It was undeniable. But him, here?

The Theo Dubois. World's rich list, hot list, on everyone's list, Theo Dubois!

It wasn't just the press confused about which Sebastian was staying here, it appeared his brother was, too.

Unless…

'I need to tell Iona…' Angel was racing off.

'Where are you going?'

'To get my phone, she's never going to believe this.'

'No…' Bree said, staring at him as he flirted with the press, feeding their frenzy. 'I don't suppose she is.'

The Internet search Bree had been putting off now felt like a mighty fine idea.

Heading back into the kitchen, she gave the mojito mix she'd been preparing earlier a stir and unlocked her tablet…

Still, it felt like snooping. But being abreast of the facts was to be prepared and she owed it to Felicity to get up to speed. Likely, her friend would already know all there was to know after her day out with Sebastian but…

She tapped in 'Sebastian Dubois' and hit 'search'. Clicking through the images, she had her answer in seconds. Shots taken mostly from a distance filled her tablet but even from that angle she could see that Ferrington and Dubois were one and the same.

She checked the recent headlines, too.

Is the Recluse Out of Hiding?

Does it Take a Family Inheritance to Get the Man Back into the Land of the Living—

'What you looking at?'

She spun on the spot to see Angel trying to glance over her shoulder. 'Nothing.'

Not that Angel would have cared. Bree did though. She didn't like the idea of Internet stalking someone. Enough of that happened on social media, something else she wasn't quite au fait with and avoided at all costs. She didn't need to have her face rubbed in everyone else's successes day in, day out. Marriage, kids, family. All things she'd dreamed of having by this point…

She grabbed a spatula and went back to the baking. Baking was safe, reassuring, methodical. She was folding in the flour when the banging started up on the front door once more.

'I'll go!' Angel lowered her phone, mid-text message.

'No, you won't.' Clutching the bowl to her chest, she stormed into the bar area. 'For the love of God, knock on that door again and I'll have you with my spatula.'

Angel giggled behind her. 'You tell them, Bree.'

Banging suddenly started up at the back door, joining

the thunderous knocking at the front and the shouts she didn't bother trying to decipher. Spinning away, she headed back to the kitchen. She wasn't even across the threshold when she heard someone at the rear door once more, playing with the handle.

'You have to be kidding me.'

She was already approaching the door, spatula raised, all fire as she prepared to stand their invader down—even beat them down, if necessary. This was getting out of hand. Maybe she ought to call the police.

'The B & B is closed, and the press is not welcome!' she shouted through the wood. 'Take your questions elsewhere!'

No response…other than what sounded like a key turning in the heavy lock. What on earth? Could journalists pick a lock? Would they really sink that low?

'Bree Johansson?' The door opened a crack.

And now they had her name? Unless it wasn't the press at all… She swallowed down the nerves, raised her chin. 'Depends. Who's asking?'

The door swung open and there, filling the rear entrance, was the magazine cover model himself in all his very real, sex-god glory.

'Oh, God.'

He cocked a brow and her cheeks burned. Had she said it out loud? Called him out as a sex god to his face?

She swallowed with a squeak. 'I told you we were closed.'

He's Sebastian's brother. Act normal. Just…act…normal. And polite!

'I'm not the press and I'm not here to check in.'

'No?' Her heart was threatening to leap out of her chest, her brain struggling to function over the burn. 'Just breaking and entering, then?'

His grin lifted to one side and he combed one big, strong hand through his floppy blond locks, his pale blue T-shirt straining as his muscles flexed. 'Is it breaking and entering if one's been told where the spare key is?'

His scent—warm, male, musky and hot!—filled the space between them as he lifted said key to show it to her and she wet her suddenly dry mouth.

'How did you…?'

'My brother told me where it was. And Flick told him. They're on their way back now.'

'Oh, my God!' Angel skidded up behind Bree. 'You're the brother?'

His grin cracked both cheeks now, his blue eyes dancing as he took in Angel. 'For my sins. And you are?'

'The daughter.'

Some of the laughter left his face, his words slow and drawn out as his brows drew together. 'Flick's…daughter?'

'For my sins.'

'Angel!' Bree admonished.

'What? He said it first.'

'I did.' He dragged his eyes from Angel's to hers, but there was no mistaking the shock. Something had him suddenly off kilter. Not even the rebuilding of his grin could conceal it completely. 'Now, if you'd be so kind as to lower the cooking utensil, I'll turn around and get this door locked again because I don't know about you ladies, but I'd really appreciate putting the barrier back in place. I fancy my chances better being on this side of the door…though maybe not.'

He eyed Bree's raised hand, which was still brandishing the spatula, and she snapped it down, grateful that her deep brown skin would keep much of her heated flush hidden.

'Of course.' She swallowed. 'You do that and…come join us in the kitchen. We're testing mojitos—' One sexy brow quirked up and, remembering Angel's age, she hurried to add, 'Mojito muffins, not cocktails!'

'Mojito muffins, you say.'

'Don't they sound delish?' Angel piped up.

'I can't say it's something I've ever sampled before, and I've sampled a lot.'

'I bet you have.' Bree bit her lips together, her eyes flaring—her cheeks, too.

Think before you speak it, Bree.

She turned away, resisting the temptation to bury her head in her mixing bowl.

'Our Bree works at the bakery across the way.' Angel pulled Bree back to face him, her arm tucked in Bree's. 'She's amazing! Once you taste her goods, I promise you'll be hooked.'

If ever there was a time for the ground to open up and swallow her, it was right now. Angel seemed unaware of the innuendo but everything about the sparkle in the infamous playboy's eyes as she disengaged herself from the giddy teenager said he wasn't.

Please, please, please hurry up, Felicity, it's supposed to be the muffins baking...not my entire body...

Theo locked the door and turned back to see Angel still standing there, her starstruck gaze something he was accustomed to. His own sense of being struck dumb, less so.

But he was.

Angel had to be around sixteen. The same length of time he and his brother had been away. The same length of time Sebastian and Flick's relationship had been over. Which would mean...would suggest...but she couldn't be...could she?

She swept her long brown hair back from her face, her smile revealing dimples that looked an awful lot like...

'You don't look much like your brother, you know.'

'Don't I?'

'Angel!' The call came from the kitchen and the fiery

piece of skirt he was also struggling to adjust to, though for an entirely different reason.

'I think you're wanted.'

'I think we both are.' She grinned. 'Come on.'

He sucked in a breath, grateful that this one was devoid of the vanilla sweetness he'd been engulfed in when the spatula had been raised to his head and a pair of blazing brown eyes had pinned him to the spot, her teasing pink lips full and pursed into a very unimpressed pout.

Bree hadn't been starstruck.

In fact, he'd feared for one second that she might kick him back out, forcing him to wait outside with the wolves for Sebastian and Flick to return. And though her dress and its brightly coloured pattern had given off warm and inviting vibes, he had the impression the striking woman wearing it would sooner see him gone.

And that disturbed him more than he'd care to admit.

'So, mojito muffins are a thing?' He paused on the threshold, not wanting to invade what instinctively felt like her domain.

Her eyes reached his across the room, her sudden smile taking his breath away. 'They are now.'

'What can I do?' Angel asked.

Bree looked to the girl, her skirt sashaying as she moved about the kitchen with ease, all curves and action, and he was entranced. She passed Angel a bowl. 'Grate those limes into there, love.'

'Do I get to taste the cocktail first?'

Bree laughed, resecuring her long black hair into a knot high on her head that highlighted the length of her neck, the angle of her cheekbones. 'A sip, and I mean a sip.'

He chuckled and leaned into the doorframe, settling in to watch them work as Bree flicked him a look.

'You want to take a seat, Mr Dubois?'

'Mr Dubois?' He chuckled some more. He wasn't Mr to

anyone, not his employees and not the press who'd learned over time to drop the respectful address. 'Theo, please. And no, I'm more than happy standing.'

She gave a shrug. 'Suit yourself.'

He planned to, he just didn't expect to be told to and his grin grew. 'I've been sat long enough already.'

'Long drive?'

'Very.'

She caught his eye once more, her warm brown depths sucking him in. The journey must have left him more tired than he thought because he didn't want to notice any woman in the way he was noticing her. He was done with the opposite sex for the time being. Ten minutes ago, he likely would have said for good. But there was something about the curvaceous and fiery woman before him that he couldn't quite ignore.

'How far is very?'

'Hmm?'

'The journey?' She didn't look at him now as she worked and he cleared his throat, forced his attention on the far less provocative—the ingredients all lined up on the side.

'I'm not sure, precisely. I guess it's around five hundred miles from Paris. I wasn't paying that much attention.'

'You drove from Paris?' Angel blurted. 'In one go?'

'I did.'

'That must have taken you…' Angel's eyes went to the ceiling as though doing the maths and then she shrugged. 'I've no idea but it must have taken for ever.'

'I made good time thanks to the Eurotunnel.'

'But you must be exhausted?' Bree said, her eyes working their magic once more as he caught on their concerned depths and couldn't let go.

'I'm fine.'

She didn't look as if she believed him and he wondered

whether she could see past his polished veneer to the truth beneath.

She'd attribute it to his drive though. To fatigue.

But the real reason cut far deeper, left him unable to sleep, unable to settle…and had ultimately seen him racing out of Paris as though a herd of wild animals were nipping at his heels.

There'd been no herd though, just an ex.

An ex who'd turned his life on its head and now he was left waiting for the story to break. The story that had more roots in fiction than fact. But the press wouldn't care.

'Are you sure?' Angel piped up. 'We have rooms free, you're more than welcome to—'

'I think he'd rather see his brother first, Angel.' Bree's concerned gaze shifted from him to Angel, her expression urging the girl to leave well alone.

'I would. I also make the worst spectator so put me to work, I'd like to help.'

Plus, keeping occupied kept his thoughts off his ex, Tanya, and his eyes off Bree.

'You can call your brother and warn him about the crazies outside. He might be used to all that attention, but Felicity won't be.'

'The crazies?' He laughed. 'Don't worry, he knows, he'll have warned her.' He pushed away from the doorframe. 'So what makes a muffin a mojito muffin?'

He came up behind her, the vanilla scent reaching him once more and transporting him back to his teenage years in Paris, working in the patisserie. It was comforting and strangely alluring, and he stuffed his hands in his pockets as he fought the urge to start helping before being invited.

Her eyes lit up as she flashed him a wicked smile. 'Now, that's a trade secret.'

'Ah, of course.'

'Nah, not really.' She gave a soft laugh, her attention

back on the bowl as she mixed. 'You just throw in every-thing you'd expect from a classic mojito, save for the ice and soda water.'

'So, it gets the rum?'

'Absolutely…put it down, Angel.'

He turned to see Angel, straw in mouth, slurping at what he assumed was the cocktail mixture, and shook his head. 'Do you often make cocktails so early in the day?'

Another laugh. 'No. That's for taste testing alongside the baked variations.'

'Gotcha.' He looked down at her and told his pulse to stop racing as her eyes connected with his. 'So, can I help?'

She frowned. 'You really want to help bake?'

'Yes.' He chuckled. 'I really want to help bake. Is that so hard to believe?'

She looked at him a second longer; shook her head. 'Okay, you can tackle the drizzle.'

'Drizzle it is!'

She directed and he followed, happy to be in the kitchen, happy to be useful, happy to be occupied and out of his thoughts…

'I'm sorry about earlier.' Her apology broke through the easy flow of instructions.

'What for?'

'Threatening you with a spatula.'

His laugh was heartfelt. 'Terrifying things, spatulas.'

'They can be in the right hands.'

'Or the wrong ones.' They shared a grin and he felt his shoulders ease, his eyes going back to the pan as he stirred the drizzle, careful not to let it boil as she had warned. 'In either case, it's fine.'

'It isn't. Not really. But I'd already had a reporter try and break through that way earlier and I figured you were just another one going too far to get a story from us.'

He sent her a quick look, admiration firing in his veins.

'For the record, I, for one, am glad you're in your friend's corner. My brother will be, too. You weren't just looking out for her and the B & B, but...'

His eyes drifted to Angel and the more he looked at her, the more he was putting two and two together and coming up with an accurate four. His brother would definitely be grateful.

'But?' Bree prompted and he realised he'd left the sentence hanging, the truth hitting home that he was...he was an uncle.

He assumed Angel didn't know his brother was her father, else her greeting would have been something else entirely. But Bree? Was that why she was so protective of the girl? He wasn't sure. She struck him as the kind to protect her from the chaos regardless of whether she knew Angel would be at the heart of the gossip or not.

And that would come...as soon as the press pieced it all together.

Hell, maybe he didn't need to worry about the media storm brewing courtesy of his ex if she were to dish the dirt. His brother looked as if he was about to fill the tabloids all by himself.

'You sure you don't want to take a lie down?' Bree tried again as Angel's phone started to ring and the girl rushed out into the hall to answer it, leaving them alone.

'And miss out on sampling these babies?' He eyed the mixture she was scooping into the awaiting muffin tray and mustered his trusty front. A front that had been cracking ever since he'd learned the truth of Tanya's cruel ploy. 'No way.'

CHAPTER TWO

BREE WASN'T SURE what shocked her more, the fact that Theo Dubois was baking in the kitchen with her; or the fact that Theo Dubois was baking at all.

He wasn't a spare part in the kitchen, clumsy or unaccustomed to it.

And darn if it wasn't sexy seeing those big capable hands at work, those muscles flexing beneath his tight blue T-shirt, the look of concentration on his face…

He was almost as delicious as the scent of muffin batch number one, which was currently baking. Almost.

And she really wished Angel would get her phone call over with and get back in here. Bree's neglected libido needed a chaperone and pronto!

'Is this Annie's old recipe?'

'Hmm?'

Concentrate, Bree, before you sound like the goofy airhead you often portray!

He gestured to the dough he was now rolling out. His new task—shortbread. Something she often made for Felicity when her best friend was under the cosh and today felt like one of those days. 'Flick's grandmother, Annie. Is it her shortbread recipe?'

'Oh, yes, yes, it is.' She nodded as if he needed the extra affirmation and wanted to slap herself. She was getting far too hot and bothered and it had nothing to do with the oven heat. 'How did you know?'

'Annie used to make it all the time for her B & B guests and if I happened to be passing, she'd rope me in to help.'

'She'd rope you in…?' She felt distracted. Too busy watching him move the rolling pin back and forth beneath his palms. Hypnotised by the movement of the well-honed muscles in his forearms bunching...

You're gawping!

She snapped her eyes away.

Focus on your muffins, Bree!

And now even that seemed to have a double meaning—eek!

'What was that?'

'What?' She couldn't look at him. Had she eeked aloud? Oh, God.

'You sound surprised?'

'Do I?'

He looked at her, curiosity sparking in his depths as her cheeks burned beneath his scrutiny. 'Yes. You seem surprised that I used to bake...'

'Sorry, I shouldn't be,' she rushed out, refocusing on their conversation and her muffins. Actual muffins. And not the heat blooming through her middle. 'Though I can't imagine it being the most thrilling task for a teen with more exciting things to be doing...'

His chuckle was low. 'More exciting is debatable.'

'Really? You're telling me that teenage Theo Dubois found excitement helping out in Annie's kitchen.'

'It was Ferrington then...'

Of course, it would have been, and she knew a tale existed there. Not that she would pry. It was none of her business...none at all... Still...

She bit her cheek.

'And I absolutely did. The payoff was well worth it.'

She gave him a quick smile. 'When you got to eat them, you mean?'

'Yup.'

It was her turn to laugh and she shook her head. 'You're full of surprises.'

'Why?'

'You really have to ask?'

'I really have to.' He turned and leaned against the counter, folding his arms and smudging flour onto his once pristine T-shirt. Flour looked good on him…though it was the biceps bulging that truly had her mouth watering. *Eyes up, Bree.*

'You're not going to expand?'

'You're Theo Dubois!'

He laughed harder and his pecs rippled. 'Guilty as charged. Once a Ferrington, now a Dubois. That's me. Still, I don't get it.'

'But now you're here, in our small Yorkshire village, baking in this kitchen like it's the most natural thing in the world.'

'Well, we all need to eat.'

'But you're…you're on the world's top ten sexiest billionaires list.' *Oh, God, did you really have to say that out loud?* 'And you must have people that do this kind of stuff for you now,' she hurried to add to take the focus off the sex and on the everyday, but his eyes were dancing, his grin lifting to one side.

'Been reading up on me?'

'No. Not at all. Not really. Not me.'

Both brows lifted. 'Because you would never read that kind of stuff.'

'Hell, no.' *Gee, you could have been a little more delicate, Bree.*

She opened her mouth to take it back, to soften it, but his hearty laughter filled the room and she swore her bare palms were hot enough to bake a muffin within them.

'I'm sorry you find reading about me so distasteful, Bree.'

'I don't… It's not… That's not…' She wiped her palms down her apron. He was teasing her. She could see it in his face, in the way his mesmerising blue eyes danced, and she pursed her lips. 'If you must know, it was the headline on the magazine Angel was flashing about just before you stepped inside. You were on the cover and…and I couldn't miss it.'

'That so?'

She tried to go back to muffin mixture number two but could feel his eyes on her, the air crackling with a tension that she'd put there. Because there was no way this was two-sided; it was all her and her stupid libido. Why did he have to be even better looking in the flesh? And all self-assured and arrogant with it?

Get back to neutral territory. The past. Annie. Baking.

'So, you used to bake with Annie?'

'I did.'

'How did that work out?'

'About as well as you'd expect…you obviously knew her well.'

'I only knew her a short while—she sadly passed away a year after I came to the village—but she's one of those people you get the measure of fairly quickly.'

'She certainly had a knack for getting you to do exactly what she wanted in the kitchen and out of it.'

'Exactly.'

'And to be honest, I needed that kind of authority in my life. She looked out for me, took me under her wing, so to speak.'

Bree could hear the soft sincerity in his tone and, scared that he would zip up, she stayed quiet, focused on what her hands were doing as her ears stayed attuned to him.

'Truth is, I was a bit of a tearaway in my youth but Annie was one of the few who saw my inner potential. Baking was how she coaxed me into talking it out as opposed to…'

'As opposed to?'

'Lashing out.'

She looked up into his eyes and caught a glimpse of the boy he'd once been.

'I can't imagine you being a fighter.' She couldn't. His eyes were too friendly, his grin too infectious…though no one could deny he had the body for a boxing ring. She waved a hand at him, cursing the heat too quick to swirl within her. 'Aside from all the bulk, of course.'

He gave another low chuckle. 'You should have seen me back then; I was all skin and bone.'

She cocked a brow. 'Really?'

'Unrecognisable, baby.' He sent her a wink loaded with mischief and a swarm of butterflies took flight inside. His ability to swing from sober to teasing, keeping her on her toes and her heart rate unsteady.

She looked away, busying herself with sliding the tray of muffins into the oven. 'If you say so.'

'No lie.' He followed her lead and went back to the job she had assigned, rolling out the dough with practised ease. 'What you see before you now took years of work.'

'And plenty of women,' she muttered quietly, her ears on fire as she prayed he hadn't heard her. She really needed to get a grip on her out-of-control tongue that seemed to be so much worse for his presence.

It was none of her business that he was a renowned playboy. He was a grown man and if women were willing to flock to him with his reputation, then more fool them.

Though now she was in his orbit, witnessing his charismatic appeal up close and personal, she was frustrated to admit she was as susceptible as the flock.

'I was sad to learn of Annie's passing.'

She stilled, the quiet emotion in his voice catching her unawares, the switch from jest to…to something so much deeper, so raw and heartfelt.

'Her loss hit the whole village hard.'

'I can imagine. She was as much a part of the landscape as the building itself. Feels strange being here without her.' He continued to roll out the dough, the move measured, controlled, therapeutic. 'Can't be easy for Flick either, looking after this place alone.'

'She gets help from Angel and the villagers.'

'Like you?'

'It works both ways.' She shifted, uncomfortable to have the focus back on her as she racked her brain for something else to make. A safe conversation to start. 'How does it feel to be back?'

'In Elmdale?'

She nodded. 'You've been gone a long time…'

His eyes drifted to the doorway, a crease teasing between his brows. 'Over sixteen years.'

She frowned. Where had he gone to? His expression was all distant and… Oh! She swallowed a squeak, her eyes widening. Angel was sixteen. Sebastian and Felicity… Angel. Her head was racing, pieces falling into place as her skin thrummed with the dawning realisation that Sebastian could be…more than likely was…

Theo started to turn back to her and she looked away, rushed out, 'That is a long time.'

'It is, though some things don't change. The village looks just the same.'

'The village yes, but the people…'

Like your secret niece!

She sucked her lips in, sensed him eyeing her peculiarly.

'Indeed…' He brushed his forearm over his brow, his eyes releasing her from their probing stare as he went back to the dough, marking it out just as Annie would have done. 'Anyway, I wouldn't say I'm back. Not really. It's more of a flying visit…'

'You're not sticking around?'

'I'm not sure what I'm doing.'

Curiouser and curiouser. The simple statement seeming to mean so much more and making her want to dig deeper. Though wouldn't his intent to leave change when his brother learned of Angel? Was Felicity breaking the news to Sebastian that very day?

Now you're getting carried away. You don't even know for sure that Sebastian is her father. And if you keep disappearing off into your head like this, you'll add fuel to Theo's already roused suspicions and it's not your place!

'Well, right now,' she declared, all smiles, 'you're baking shortbread.'

He grinned, the tenson behind his eyes easing, and her heart skipped a beat. 'True.'

Breathe, Bree! Keep the conversation flowing...

'Bringing back memories of way back when?'

'You could say that.'

'Must be strange though.'

'What is?'

'Being back here, whether it's a flying visit or not. This is Elmdale. Quiet, sleepy Elmdale. The sights you must be used to, the company...'

'I don't know.' He turned to look at her. 'It's really not all it's cracked up to be.'

No. She could believe that. She'd take Elmdale over her old life in London any day of the week. It surprised her that he should feel the same though.

'You mean the life the press portrays you as living isn't so very—' she struggled to find the right word and he raised his brows at her '—full, after all.'

He gave a short laugh. 'Full? That's one word for it.'

'And another would be…?' she pressed, unable to stop herself.

'Tiresome. Monotonous. Intense. Chaotic. Public. Very, very public.' He pricked the shortbread with a fork, emphasising each syllable, and she frowned at his tensed-up back.

'Sounds…tough.'

'But hey, when you've got all the money in the world, you have no right to complain, right?'

She frowned deeper, his false bravado digging beneath her shield.

'So, the mantle of baking the daily shortbread now falls to you, then?'

He was changing the subject, clearly uncomfortable discussing his return, and she could sense something was playing on his mind. Was he worried about the attention their return had stirred up?

Was he worried about the impact it would have on Angel if what she suspected was true and Sebastian was the girl's father?

He turned when she said nothing and she looked away again.

It's none of your business...

'Not quite daily, no. I make it when—' She listened out for Angel's continued voice in the hallway, making sure she was still properly distracted before admitting, 'I make it when Felicity needs it. You know, a comfort thing.'

'And you figure with that rabble outside, she's going to need it.'

'Precisely.'

He grimaced. 'Yeah, it's not what my brother or I would have wanted. I'm sorry for that.'

She shrugged. 'It's hardly your fault the press has nothing better to do.'

'True.' He gave her his full grin once more, his eyes warm and dizzying as he subjected her to their full intensity. 'You're a good friend, you know that?'

'I try to be.'

'Doing this when you already have your bakery to run, that's a big deal.'

'Oh, no, I don't own it. My aunt does. I just work there.'

He nodded. 'Is that what brought you to the village?'

'Yes.'

'Where were you before?'

'I—' Her gaze caught on the dusting of flour on his cheek. Flour she shouldn't want to sweep away but the urge was there, tingling at her fingertips. And his eyes…he was looking at her as though she was someone worthy of being desired, wanted…

'You?' he pressed softly.

She shook her head, looked away from the spark she must be reading wrong. 'I'm from London.'

She swallowed the little niggle in her throat. It had been three years since she'd left the city; she should be over it now. But not thinking about her old life and being over it wasn't one and the same. And she really didn't want to think about it now.

'That's quite the change, London to Elmdale. They couldn't be more different.'

She tried for a nonchalant shrug. 'My aunt was sick, the family bakery needed help. Mum and Dad have a life in Scotland, their own shop to run, so I answered the SOS.'

'A good niece as well as a good friend. Seems London's loss is Elmdale's gain.'

'I suppose it is.'

'You suppose?'

'You make me sound like a saint.'

'You're the one looking after the B & B for your friend on what I assume is your day off. You're the one baking shortbread for that same friend to cheer her up. You're the niece who left London to help her family when they needed you… How's your aunt now?'

A smile fluttered about her lips. 'Much better, thank you.'

'And yet, you're still here. You don't miss the city life, the buzz…'

She snorted. 'Hardly.'

He went quiet and she snuck a peek at him, a peek that she couldn't quit. She'd thought his brother hot, but Theo… with his grin, his overlong hair, and that look in his eye as he held her gaze, her libido was well and truly out of its box and wouldn't go back in.

Maybe it was time to bury her unfaithful ex and London in some wild Yorkshire fun. Only everyone knew everyone's business in Elmdale and casual flings were not the done thing…and really, she wasn't ready to commit to anything more.

But everything about Theo was casual and the way he was looking at her…was it possible this wasn't one-sided after all?

'Quick! Quick! Turn on the TV!' Angel came rushing in, already snatching the remote before anyone else could locate it. 'We're all over the local news!'

Bree frowned. The news?

Surely there had to be more important things going on in the world than…

'Viewers, it's true. The billionaire hotel moguls have been spotted in our very own village of Elmdale and are creating quite the stir,' came the newsreader's smooth Yorkshire tone. 'Rumour has it that the infamous recluse Sebastian Dubois is none other than Sebastian Ferrington, the missing heir to the Ferrington empire. Ever since Lord Ferrington passed away over a year ago, the estate itself has sat empty. Now the brothers are back to stake their claim and sources close to the company have revealed that Elmdale will soon be home to a new luxury spa resort, the latest addition to the worldwide Dubois hotel chain. That's right, folks, the Ferrington Estate will be reborn as a luxury spa retreat with all the features fans have come to expect of the elite hotel chain. Our reporter, Sally-Anne, is there now catching up with the locals. What's the news on the ground, Sally-Anne?'

'That's right, Lucy. Theo Dubois himself has not long disappeared into the B & B behind me, the same B & B Sebastian himself is reported to have stayed at last night and, as you can imagine, their return has sparked a mixed response. Nadine here owns the local restaurant, Adam & Eve's—you think this is good news for the village, Nadine?'

'Absolutely I do! It'll be great for the area, bringing in more visitors and helping the local economy, which of course includes, as you mentioned, Adam & Eve's right here in Elmdale.' Nadine beamed down the lens of the camera. 'As well as its sister restaurant, Romeo & Juliet, just down the road. If you're looking for somewhere that goes the extra romantic mile, you can count on one of my restaurants to deliver on every level.'

Angel choked on a laugh. 'Trust Nadine to turn this into an advert.'

'It's an opportunity not to be wasted,' Bree commented, her mind awash with this development. So, they weren't back, just as Theo had said they weren't. They were here to convert the estate into a hotel…

'That's not what you were saying about the B & B earlier when I wanted to go outside and speak to them.'

'No. But that's different.' That had been about keeping Angel away from the tenacious tongues of the press and all the questions. Questions she hadn't until now considered might relate to Felicity's daughter being the billionaire mogul's secret daughter.

'Not all the residents are in agreement however,' Sally-Anne piped up, 'and Nadine is definitely in the minority. We caught up with the local pub landlord, Martin, earlier and he had this to say…'

Bree turned, her eyes finding Theo's as the questions raced. Some she could ask, some she certainly couldn't. 'Is it true? Is that what you intend to do?'

'It was the plan, yes.'

'But—'

She was cut off by the elevated sound of the crowd outside and Theo started. 'That'll be Sebastian returning with Flick. I'd best go clear the way. You guys stay here.'

She nodded dumbly.

'This is totally rad, Bree! Can you believe it? Real live billionaires, here under our roof, and one of them taking a shine to Mum…it's so bizarre!'

Absent-mindedly, she nodded. 'Yes. Very bizarre.'

She needed to talk to Felicity, like yesterday. Never mind the potential hotel landing on their doorstep, if Sebastian was Angel's father, there were bigger fish to fry…

'Who's frying fish?'

'Huh?' She refocused on Angel and the girl's bemused frown. 'No frying, only muddling.'

'Muddling?'

'The mojito needs more mint.' She moved quickly, eager to avoid another mishap courtesy of her wild tongue, but she couldn't stop her gaze drifting back to the door and the empty space left by Theo.

Whatever the future held, would he really come and go again just as swiftly?

She couldn't deny the tiny stab of disappointment as she mashed the mint, taking it out on the fresh green leaves. Theo had intrigued her. There was so much more behind the pretty face the press portrayed—hell, he himself portrayed when he was all grins and winks and innuendo.

And now she'd had a sampling of the real him, she wanted to know it all.

Every last drop.

Or maybe that was the mojito talking?

She eyed the drink and winced. Not the wisest of choices when she needed to keep her wits about her with the press frenzy outside.

She heard the outer door open, the noise upping with it, and grimaced.

Then again, maybe it was the perfect choice.

She plopped the mint into the glass Angel had been sampling earlier and raised it, 'Bottoms up!'

'Your timing couldn't be better, bro…' Theo muttered to himself, tugging open the door and plastering his grin in place, barely flinching at the press closing in, the camera clicks, the chaos…because it was chaos, his entire life. He hadn't been lying to Bree.

The flicker of a frown caught between his brows. No, he'd been far too honest. And he was never that with a stranger. Hell, he was hardly that with the people that knew him well, but something about those big brown eyes, the scent of baking, the warm aura that seemed to follow her about, had him practically spilling his guts.

It was uncharacteristic and disarming.

Or maybe it was stepping into Annie's kitchen that had done it, the old and familiar colliding with the very new and very…appealing.

It wasn't just the newsfeed his brother had rescued him from, but the spell Bree had unwittingly cast, too. Hot off the back of Tanya it was the last thing he needed…or maybe it was everything he needed. Bree and Tanya were as different as night and day, fire and ice…

And Bree had certainly put enough fire in his veins to ease the chill of Paris.

He raked a hand through his hair, took a breath and strode out. Using his body as a shield, he cleared the way to the car and rapped on the passenger window. Flick spun to face him, her dark ponytail flicking out, her blue eyes wide as her cheeks flushed pink and her mouth formed a startled 'o'.

He widened his grin in apology for scaring her and gestured to the door handle, waiting for his brother to unlock it. His brother who, if he wasn't much mistaken, had been laughing. He couldn't remember the last time his brother had laughed, let alone at a situation that would normally demand a far graver response. It was usually Theo doing the smiling for the press and his brother cursing their entire existence.

Not that he had time to question it now. Not with the press closing in and unassuming Flick at the heart of it.

The lock sounded and he pulled open the door, careful to put his body between her and the crowd with their stream of never-ending questions:

'Theo, Theo! Are you back to stay?'

'Why change your name?'

'What's the story with the estate?'

'Are the rumours about Dubois and the estate true?'

Sebastian cringed. 'Get her inside, Theo.'

'Oh, I'm on it.'

'What rumours?' Flick frowned at Theo as he helped her out of the car, his palm on her back as he urged her forward.

'Don't worry,' he said into her ear, 'it's us they want.'

'For now,' his brother grumbled as he came up behind them, ensuring she was protected from all sides as they strode forward.

The second they were inside, Sebastian turned to the pressing rabble. 'You'll be getting nothing more from us today.'

He closed the door on the escalating voices and Theo was about to comment on their persistence when his brother's posture stopped him. His head was bowed to the door, his palm pressed into the wood. He looked…broken.

The king of cool and aloof, to laughter…to this?

Theo knew it had to be about Angel, the shock of it, and now the press breathing down their necks…

Flick shifted beside him, her pallor giving her an ethereal quality that had Theo straightening up, his smile returning. One of them needed to keep their cool in front of her, and if it wasn't going to be Sebastian…

The man himself came alive then, blowing out a breath

and combing a hand through his hair as he turned to face them. 'How long have they been hounding the place for?'

'They arrived just before lunch according to the fiery skirt out front.'

'Fiery skirt?' Flick choked over the reference. 'You mean Bree?'

'Aye, that's the one.' Okay, so maybe he shouldn't have used that term, but he meant it in all the right ways, positive ways, complimentary to a fault. He rubbed the back of his neck. 'How to make an entrance, hey? I turn up outside and that lot circle me like a pack of vultures, then one step inside and she was on me. She knows how to protect those she cares about; I'll say that for her.'

He threw a wink Flick's way and saw a flush of colour reach her cheeks—better, much better.

'And before you ask, brother, I gave her my good side, best behaviour and all that jazz, Scout's honour.'

'You were never a Scout.' Flick seemed to respond on autopilot, her eyes still sporting the rabbit-caught-in-the-headlights look.

'Ooh, harsh!' Theo grinned, his lively front returning. 'But you've got me.'

'I'm going to check on Angel…and Bree,' she said quietly. 'Where are they?'

'In the kitchen—' he nudged his chin in their direction '—baking up a storm.'

'Thanks.'

His brother watched her go, his eyes tormented, his hands fisted at his sides.

Interesting.

'What's up with you?'

Sebastian flicked him a look, flexing his fists as he caught Theo's gaze upon them. 'You don't want to know.'

Theo folded his arms and leaned into the wall, his frown and attention wholly on his brother. He'd known something was up when he'd spoken to him on the phone the night before, had attributed it to the estate and their nasty past, but now he knew about Angel—well, at least suspected—he knew it ran far deeper.

'Oh, I most definitely *do* want to know. Why do you think I'm here a day earlier than planned?'

Sebastian eyed him, his own gaze narrowing. 'I think that has more to do with whatever you're running from.'

His brother wasn't entirely wrong, but... 'This isn't about me; this is about you. Now spill.'

Sebastian blew out a breath, shook his head, forking his hand back through his hair.

'Hell, bro, I've not seen you this agitated in—'

'She's mine.'

Theo bit the corner of his mouth. 'I know.'

'You do?'

'I suspected it. She looks like you, and with her age, your history with Flick...it didn't take much to piece it together.'

Sebastian looked grey. 'I hated the old man enough when we were forced to leave Elmdale and I had to leave Flick behind, but to know I left her... I left her with...'

He couldn't finish and Theo's world spun. It wasn't just the old man's fault. Yes, their grandfather's cruelty had seen them run, but if he hadn't—if Theo hadn't wound him up so severely that night...if he hadn't... 'I'm so sorry, Sebastian.'

'Why are you sorry? You didn't abandon her.'

'That night...you wouldn't have...we wouldn't have left like we did if I hadn't made him so angry.'

Sebastian was shaking his head. 'This isn't your fault. I could have reached out to her over the years, found out about Angel. This isn't on you.'

And yet, Theo felt the sickening weight of it. He'd screwed his brother's life up, good and proper. He couldn't believe he'd been offloading on Bree, flirting even, when the reality of what he'd done all those years ago should have been hitting home.

But you hadn't known for sure that she was Sebastian's daughter. You hadn't known for sure that your actions had stripped him of all those years of fatherhood. You hadn't known the consequences of your actions...

But he sure did now.

'Seriously, Theo, whatever you're thinking, stop it. This is my mess and I'll fix it. And right now, my biggest priority is protecting them from that lot out there. Can you imagine what they'll do when they get wind of this?'

Theo cursed, forcing his mind to function over the churn of guilt. He needed to help his brother in the present, not lose himself in the past that he couldn't change.

'Well, you can't stay here, not with that lot camped outside. And it won't take much for them to piece things together the way I did. It'll only take a few hints from the villagers and they'll be all over the story, whether they have proof or not.'

'I know.'

'And you need to break it to Angel before they do.'

'I know.' Sebastian's hands were back in his hair, messing up its usual pristine state. 'But where do we go? I can't expect Flick to leave the B & B unmanned, she has guests.'

'Leave that bit to me.'

'Really?'

'Bro, it's the least I can do, and you know you can trust me with this. What we don't know about hospitality isn't worth knowing, right?'

Sebastian didn't look convinced.

'Look, Bree is just next door. You can reassure Flick that she'll keep me in check.'

'A woman, keep you in check? You sure about that?'

'You obviously haven't met her.'

Sebastian's strained glance went to the kitchen doorway, to the hint of conversation beyond, and Theo reached out to grip his shoulder. 'It'll be okay. Just get them out of here and you and Flick can control how and when Angel learns of…of you.'

'But where?'

'You know where.'

Sebastian shook his head.

'You've been to the estate today; you know it's ready for you and you'll have all the protection you need. Go and talk it through with Flick and I'll sort the rest. I can have the guards at the gates within the hour and Maddie is just waiting for the call to get set up over there. She's already going out of her mind with boredom.'

'Once a housekeeper, always a housekeeper.'

'You got that right.'

'Okay. Let's get the wheels in motion.'

Theo nodded and without thinking, tugged Sebastian in for a hug. 'A belated congratulations, big brother! Angel might not realise it yet, but she's a lucky girl to have you. They both are.'

Sebastian snorted against him. 'I really don't think they see it that way.'

'They will, eventually.' He released him, his trusty grin back in place. 'Believe me.'

His brother managed the smallest of smiles. 'So, you going to tell me what brought you from Paris?'

'All in good time, bro.' Or maybe never… His chest tightened as he fended off the pain of the very recent past. 'Right now, it's not important.'

'But you—'

A sharp rap on the rear door silenced him as they both looked to it, the shout that followed making them both grimace. 'Miss Gardner! Felicity! It's the *White Rose Press*. We'll pay good money for an exclusive!'

'Saved by the press,' Theo muttered, pulling his phone

from his pocket. 'Security first, and then I'll get on to Maddie. You talk to Flick.'

Theo placed the call as his brother entered the kitchen. He issued instructions rapid-fire, eager to back up his brother who, by the sounds of it, couldn't convince Flick to talk to him in private. No matter how much Bree and Angel were encouraging her to do so…

And then it wasn't them he could hear but the piped voice of another resident on the TV, 'We don't want no poncy hotel on our doorstep! We're quite happy just the way things are. Back in my day, the estate was a huge part of our community, our traditions. It would have been good to see some of that return. Not this…this…'

'Luxury spa?' the reporter provided as Theo headed for the kitchen, ready to back his brother up.

'Aye. It's a disgrace. His grandfather was a disgrace and now he's—'

The TV went quiet—muted or turned off, Theo didn't know—but the damage had been done. Sebastian had been labelled a disgrace; worse, he'd been slammed into the same box as their grandfather and if his brother hadn't been shaken before that would have tipped him over the edge.

The shrill ring of the oven timer rang out.

'That'll be the muffins, Angel!' Theo could tell that Bree was forcing her tone to remain light. 'An experimental batch of mojito muffins—I'll bring one out with your tea, so long as they taste good enough.'

'Someone say muffins?' He made his presence known, leaning against the doorframe behind his brother and feigning calm, just like Bree. 'If you need a guinea pig to taste test, I'm all yours.'

Angel laughed and Bree choked, her cheeks aglow, but Flick, she looked as if she'd seen a ghost.

If there'd ever been a time to step up for his brother, it was now. For years, his brother had sheltered him, protected him. It was payback time and he sure as hell wasn't going to screw this up.

He would do everything in his power to make sure Sebastian had the time he needed to look after his newfound family, free of interference from the outside world. And that included ensuring that the B & B ran like clockwork in their absence.

Bree would help him; he knew that well enough. The woman would do anything for her friend.

He just had to make sure he kept his basic urges under control where said friend was concerned. Old Theo would have followed his nose—or, rather, another part of his anatomy—new Theo had lived and learned and would do better.

He owed it to his brother and he needed to make amends. He couldn't give Sebastian the years he'd lost with Angel, but he could make this transition as smooth as possible.

He would not mess this up.

CHAPTER THREE

BREE LIFTED THE blind on the bakery window.

The sun was on the rise, peeking out behind the church spire, the skies were clear, promising another glorious day, and the streets were still deserted. A marked contrast to the chaos of the previous day, the night even. Though it was nothing compared to how it would be when the world learned that Angel was Sebastian's daughter...something Felicity had confided in her the second they had been alone.

Now the newfound family were safely ensconced on the Ferrington Estate, out of harm's way—or rather the press's reach—while they broke the news to Angel.

It had been quite the day but if Theo had found the news unsettling, he hadn't shown it. Doing everything he could to reassure Felicity that the B & B would be in safe hands— his hands—in her absence.

Which put him right across the road from Bree for however long he was needed.

Her heart fluttered, his proximity enough to set her body into a little tizz of its own. It had been undeniably impressive and undeniably surreal watching as he'd taken charge of the situation the previous day. Helping Sebastian, Felicity and Angel leave without being intercepted. Calling in his own team of muscle to stand guard at the B & B and assist with escorting a rather bemused family of five, the B & B's current guests, back inside after their day out.

Guests who would now have the infamous Theo Dubois looking after their every whim.

Lucky family...

'What was that, love?'

She spun to see her aunt behind her, the blind clattering back into position. There went her big mouth again.

'Nothing.' She smoothed her palms down her skirt. 'Is that the last of the order for the B & B?'

'Yup.' Her aunt slid the basket onto the side and swept a stray grey curl back under her hairnet. 'Is it still quiet out there?'

'For the moment, it's the perfect time to run this lot over. I'll just grab my jacket.'

'Oh, no, you don't, I've got this one.'

'Since when do you do the morning deliveries?'

'Since trouble moved in next door.'

Bree frowned at her. 'Trouble?'

'Yes!' She wagged a finger. 'That Theo Dubois thinks he's God's gift to women and you'd do well to steer clear.'

Bree couldn't contain her laugh, nervous or otherwise. 'And you think I'd be his type?'

'I think any woman is his type.'

'Aunt Clara, you can't say that!'

'I can and I will. One of the benefits of getting to sixty is saying what you want, when you want.'

'And don't I know it.' Her uncle came out from the back with pastries to fill the display by the till. 'Never mind your aunt, Bree, she's just protecting your innocence.'

Now she really did laugh. 'My innocence? Pull the other one.'

They both exchanged a look that went deeper than jest and inwardly, she cringed. She didn't need them pitying her or protecting her or pondering her single status any more than she was herself.

She strode forward to sweep up the basket. 'I'm more than capable of looking after myself, and you both know it.'

Jacket forgotten, she hurried for the door, her escape.

'We know, love, but men like that, they have their cunning way of making one forget good sense,' her aunt called after her. 'Why, just last week he dumped his latest squeeze, that supermodel, you know the one…she was the face of that perfume—Tanya… Tanya…'

'Bedingfield?'

Her uncle instantly coloured as her aunt glared at him, fist on hip. 'You can't remember our wedding anniversary, but you can remember the surname of a woman half your age.'

'Only because someone makes me watch the celebrity news.'

'Well, anyway,' her aunt continued, 'he dumped her the night of some big catwalk event in Paris. Poor woman was so traumatised she bailed on the show.'

Bree rolled her eyes at the door before glancing back at her aunt. 'I really wouldn't believe everything you read.'

'I don't. But you can't tell me it doesn't ring true. I mean, look at the man.'

Her aunt gestured to the small pile of magazines they kept by the door for people to peruse while waiting on orders. Someone had clearly had a good rummage and brought all the Theo editions to the top.

'You shouldn't judge a book by its cover either,' Bree said gently.

And with that she exited the bakery, her aunt's and uncle's eyes boring into her back. Three years and they hadn't forgotten. Three years and she was still the vulnerable ex-city girl who'd been taken for a mug by her fiancé and run away. Yes, she'd come to help, that was no lie, but they hadn't been blind to her heartbreak.

Well, she was a mug no more and Theo was the most exciting thing to happen in Elmdale in the three years she'd been here. It didn't hurt to enjoy the view a little…so long as that was all she was doing.

The wind whipped up around her, the lack of cloud cover making it a sunny but biting temp and she wished she hadn't been so quick to leave without her coat. By the time she'd covered the short distance to the B & B's rear access door she swore her lips were blue.

She slid her key into the lock and paused. She had warned Theo she'd be across early with the order but maybe she should have warned him it would be just before seven. To her that was positively late, but then she worked in a bakery where anything after five was considered a lie-in. She didn't want to startle him, but neither could she call out and risk waking the guests.

She opted for stealth, opening the door quietly and tip-toeing her way to the kitchen, but she needn't have worried. Someone was up. The inviting scent of fresh coffee lingered in the air and there was a strange tap-tap-tapping coming from the bar area.

Her curiosity almost took out the sudden hive of activity in her stomach. She was nervous. Or was it excitement? A bit of both...

He's just a man, an everyday man, Bree. Get a grip. Ha!

She had to cover her mouth to stop the blurt of laughter erupting.

Theo was no everyday man and that was the problem.

And no, she wasn't referring to his celeb status, she was referring to everything else. The way he made her feel included.

Smoothing down her hair, which had been twisted under a net all morning and was happily trying to make up for it, she made for the bar and the continued tap-tap-tapping.

What she wasn't prepared for was the sight of him crouched under the bar, his jean-clad behind proffered up to her in greeting.

She swallowed a squeak. 'Hubba-hubba!'

The behind launched into the air, his head colliding with the underside of the bar causing a curse to erupt from his lips. Oh, God, she'd spoken aloud...again.

'Bree!' He rubbed the back of his head as he straightened to face her. 'You scared me.'

'Hi! Morning! Sorry.'

He lifted his hands to his ears and beneath his hair pulled out two tiny earbuds. 'Not your fault, I was listening to music, then I caught a glimpse of bright red shoes and that was it.'

He was listening to music…*thank heaven.*

'What are you…erm…doing?'

He gestured behind him. 'One of the pumps was misbehaving last night; thought I'd take a look.'

'Oh, right.' She frowned from it to him. 'Are you qualified to do that?'

And there it was, the cocky grin to one side that made her stomach swoop. 'I'm a jack of all trades.'

Her brows rose. 'And a master of none?'

'Oh, I'm a master of them all, believe me.'

Including getting women into bed, the glint in his eye was telling her. She could almost hear Aunt Clara saying it in her ear, too.

And then he laughed. 'Sorry. Kidding. Couldn't resist. But yeah, I know my way around a bar. A bathroom. A kitchen. A car. Pretty much anything. The benefit of working numerous jobs in hospitality when I was young.'

All honing his craft with his hands…

Shut up, mind!

'Where does the car come into the whole hospitality bit?'

'That was more of a hobby and a necessity. Besides, I was never one for paying someone to fix what I could readily do myself given the skills.'

She nodded, her mind conjuring up images of him seminaked, shirt off and tucked into the belt of his jeans, oil streaked across his…

She wet her lips.

'Bree?'

'Huh?'

Oh, God, woman! Stop ogling and do your job!

His face shone with bemusement. 'I was asking if everything is okay? Despite the goosebumps you're looking a little...flushed?'

She looked down and sure enough *everything* was alert to the cold. Could this moment get any worse?

Just be thankful he thinks it's all down to the cold.

She cleared her throat, drowning out the inner voice. 'It's a stunning morning, I didn't think to throw on a coat.' She scanned the room, looking at anything but his invigorating presence, willing her internal body temp to cool. 'Is everything okay here?'

'Running like clockwork...well, save for this pump, and the boiler had a moment this morning.'

'Oh, yeah. Felicity had Bill take a look at it yesterday morning; he was waiting on a part.'

'Right, well, I gave it a figurative kick but if you can pass me his details, I'll find out what's what.'

'Err, you might want to leave Bill to me.'

He was cleaning off some piece of metal with a cloth but paused, his brow wrinkling beneath his fringe. 'Why?'

'Bill's kind of in the we-don't-need-no-fancy-hotel camp.'

Realisation dawned in his striking blue eyes. 'It's like that, is it?'

''Fraid so.'

'Even if the boiler is for the benefit of the B & B and Flick.'

'Best let me liaise with him...just to be on the safe side.'

'I can hold my own with Bill, don't you worry.'

'I don't doubt it for a second.'

He laughed. 'Thank you, I think. Though, if I'm honest, the entire thing needs a complete upgrade.'

'I think Felicity knows that, but they don't exactly come cheap.'

And why was she standing here discussing boiler upgrades when they could be talking about far more exciting things…like how he managed to keep his body in such amazing condition and run a hotel empire?

His grin widened and she had the horrible feeling he could read every one of her salacious thoughts because she was sure she hadn't said any of that out loud…or had she?

A bubble of panic hiccupped through her. Maybe she should let her aunt come next time!

'Don't worry, I'll see it sorted.'

She started. 'See what sorted?'

'The boiler. A new one if necessary.'

'You will? Just like that?'

He nodded. 'Just like that.'

She had the urge to put her foot down, turn down his over-generous offer, but this was Theo Dubois the billionaire—he could afford it and it wasn't as if his brother didn't owe Felicity. Still…

'Maybe run it by her first because, as generous as it is, it feels an itty bit weird, you just moving in here and revamping the place.'

'I'd hardly call a new boiler a revamp. I'm not talking about giving the place a facelift, just modernising the hidden fixtures.'

'But still.'

'I'll check first, don't worry.'

'So…how come you're looking at the pump and not getting someone in to do it?'

He placed the metal thing down and lifted another, his eyes on it rather than her as he cleaned it off. 'I like to keep busy. I figure while I'm here I'll do what I can.'

'And you can't think of more entertaining things to be doing?'

He laughed, his eyes reaching hers now. 'Are you offering?'

She'd walked right into that one, and if it weren't for the sudden fire in his gaze, she'd have laughed it off, anything but… 'What did you have in mind?'

Bree!

And then the mood shifted so suddenly she felt as if the ground itself had moved beneath her.

'It's probably best I keep that thought to myself.' He turned away from her and her body begged him to come back.

She gave a soft laugh, disappointment and something far more painful cutting deep. Of course he wasn't serious about flirting with her. She'd been getting carried away on the possibility and more fool her. 'Fair enough.'

She hesitated on the spot, not quite ready to leave but knowing she had no reason to stay. More than that, she no longer felt welcome.

'Right, well, I'll leave you to it.' She gestured to the kitchen even though he had his back to her. 'I left the breakfast order on the side for the O'Briens. The sandwiches, sausage rolls and jam doughnuts for their picnic lunch are there, too. Any problems just call me. My number's stuck on the fridge.'

He half turned, his fingers forking through his wayward blond locks as his eyes lifted to hers and he gave her an uncertain smile—was it apologetic, bashful, something else? It certainly wasn't cocky and just like that the hurt, the disappointment, the inferiority complex evaporated—how could one smile do all of that? And leave her weak at the knees?

'I will.'

She nodded and forced her legs to move. Time to go…

'Bree?'

She swallowed, turned back slowly. 'Yes.'

'Thank you. I really appreciate it.'

Oh, God, that smile, those eyes…
Swallow. Speak.
'You're welcome.'

Theo watched her go, a fire in his gut and a stern word in his head.
Get a hold on it.
What was wrong with him?

Bree was a good woman. Kind-hearted. Soft on the inside, bubbly on the outside. Absolutely not for him and still, he couldn't get his body to obey—his mouth, either, it would appear.

He was supposed to be on a break.

A self-enforced break. No more women. No more partying. No more anything.

And certainly not with someone who deserved far better and would look for more where there wasn't more to give.

Not to mention she was Felicity's best friend—messy, messy, *messy*.

He had a responsibility to his brother; he had a debt to repay…

But everything about her appealed. Her big brown eyes so quick to dance, her broad smile that lit up her face, her luscious curves, and her brightly coloured clothes that set off her rich, dark skin.

She was trouble. He was *in* trouble. If he couldn't keep a lid on it and stick to the task at hand—helping his brother and his newfound family.

His phone buzzed in his pocket and he pulled it out, his gut tightening at the message on the screen. It was from Tanya.

I'm sorry. Can we talk? Xx

A chill ran through him, prickling at his skin. Sorry didn't cut it.

Was it possible to grieve something that never existed in the first place? Or was it simply anger that had his blood running cold? Anger that he'd been taken for a fool. Anger that he'd been duped in the worst possible way. Anger that she'd turned his entire life on its head and left him questioning everything.

He shoved the phone back in his pocket. Hell, maybe he should thank Tanya, she'd at least done what he hadn't been able to and got his body to stand down, his thoughts of Bree taken out by Tanya and her thoughtless act.

He dragged in a breath and faced off the dodgy pump. A simple problem, a practical one and one that would keep his head occupied and his body out of trouble.

'Mr Dubois?'

Startled, he spun on his heel. 'Huh?'

There was no one…and then movement low down caught his eye. Peeking around the corner was the little O'Brien girl, a soft bunny dangling from her hand, her hair mussed up from sleep.

'Hey, Becca, isn't it?'

One pudgy hand shoved her fringe out of her eyes as she gave a nod and stepped closer.

'Does your mum know you're up and about?'

'I couldn't sleep.'

Not quite an answer. He looked past her but couldn't see anyone…or hear anyone, for that matter.

'She's poorly. So is Daddy. And Archie. And Sam.'

He frowned down at her. 'Oh, dear, what's wrong?'

'Poorly tum-tums. Mummy says it was the fish but Daddy says it was her driving.'

He bit back a laugh and held out his hand. 'Come on, the lovely lady from the bakery has just delivered the morning pastries. How about we get you one and then we go and check on your family and see whether I can help?'

She gave another nod, her hand slipping into his and he

felt her trust in him warm his chilled heart. But she didn't move, she was too busy staring up at him, her eyes narrowed. 'What is it?'

She nipped her lip. 'Are you really famous? My mum says that all those people outside were after you.'

He gave a chuckle. 'I'm sort of famous.'

She gave him a gappy grin and his gut gave a sudden twist. Perhaps spending what was supposed to be breathing space after Tanya's stunt in a family-centric B & B wasn't the wisest of choices.

But you don't have a choice, you have to make amends.

'Now, what do you fancy?' He pushed aside the unease and threw his focus into her, lifting her up onto the kitchen counter and taking off the gingham cloth that covered the tray Bree had delivered.

Becca's eyes were like saucers as she took in all the food. So much goodness that his own neglected stomach growled.

Becca giggled up at him. 'I think your tum-tum needs something, too.'

'Yeah. You're probably right there.' He smiled at her. 'So, what will it be?'

She hummed as she made a big show of deliberating and then she pointed at a Danish pastry, its glaze and custard centre the obvious choice for a kid with a sweet tooth.

'Good choice.'

He lifted a paper napkin from the side and used it to take up the pastry, handing it to her. 'Now let's go and—'

'Oh!'

He spun to see Bree in the doorway, open-mouthed. 'Bree!'

Her eyes drifted from Becca in his arms—her bunny flopping over his shoulder, the pastry in her hand—and then to him and for some reason, his cheeks started to burn.

'So sorry, I forgot to ask if there was anything you wanted bringing over for lunch, to save you having to dash out. I wasn't expecting a little stowaway.' Her eyes returned to Becca, her smile softening—her eyes, too. 'You're up early, little miss.'

'Apparently her family aren't too well. I was just on my way to check on them and take her back up before she's missed.'

'Oh, no, what's wrong?'

'It sounds like a stomach bug.'

'There's a lot going round. Why don't I pop up and you guys stay here? If Becca's still feeling okay, it makes sense for her to avoid it as much as poss.'

'True. But I thought you needed to get back.'

'I do, but I can check on them first, the shop doesn't start filling up till eight.'

'Okay, so long as you're sure.'

'I'll be right back.'

'Well, you heard the lady—' he set Becca back down '—you get to sit here and enjoy my scintillating company a little while longer.'

She giggled over a mouthful. 'Sinter-what?'

He caught Bree's laugh in the distance and felt his own chest dance with it, his smile growing, and then his eyes went back to Becca and his brow wrinkled. What exactly did one do to entertain a child? He had zero experience.

'You fancy some eggs? Sausages? Bacon?' Cooking was his go-to in any stressful situation and being left with a... 'How old are you?'

She sat up straight. 'Five.'

Okay, being left with a five-year-old definitely constituted one.

'So, what does a five-year-old like for breakfast?' Because he hadn't a clue, other than that a Danish pastry could never be considered adequate.

'Sausages.'

He started to move. 'Great.'

'And egg and soldiers.'

'Egg and what now?' His eyes were back on her. Was it a joke? Was he supposed to laugh?

'Soldiers!' She looked at him bug-eyed, mouth agape. 'You don't know what egg and soldiers are?'

'Err, no, I can't say that I do.'

'You chop the head off the egg and stick your sticks of toast in…and sausage. I like to dip the sausage.'

'Right, egg and soldiers. On it.'

He searched the cupboards while she fed bunny and herself the pastry. He'd got to grips with the location of most things and was just setting the water to boil when Bree reappeared.

'How are they?'

'Not good.' She grimaced, adding softly, 'They were pretty upset that you'd left your room, Becca.'

The little girl pouted. 'I didn't want to wake them.'

'I know, honey.' She stroked a stray blonde curl behind the girl's ear. 'And I've told them you're safe and sound down here with Uncle Theo and me, but you shouldn't go wandering on your own, okay?'

The little girl nodded but Theo was still reeling from the 'Uncle Theo and me' when she turned to him. 'Have you seen any paracetamol or ibuprofen? Her mum's running a temperature and I'm sure Felicity will have some here somewhere.'

'Sure. It's just here.' He'd spotted the collection of medicines earlier and reached up into the cupboard behind him, pulling out a packet and passing it to her. 'What else can we do?'

'It'll be good for them to have water on hand, but I don't think they'll be up for anything more for a while. They're in the family room currently but I wonder if it would be better to give them the room next door, too, so they have more bathrooms and space?'

'Of course. I can sort all that. Hadn't you better get back?'

She hesitated, looking from Becca to him. 'You sure you're going to be okay?'

He gave her his trusty grin. 'Oh, ye of little faith.'

'Not at all, it's just…this isn't quite what you signed up for.'

'Is life ever?' That was a little deep—too deep.

'I guess not.' So was her response, the look in her eye reminiscent of when he'd touched on her life in London. 'But I'll be back as soon as I can. I've given the O'Briens my number so they can text for any supplies they may need. I don't think they'll be going anywhere for a couple of days at least.'

'That's very kind, thank you.'

'No problem.'

They shared a look, an understanding, neither of them wanting the O'Briens to suffer and miss out on their holiday but knowing fate had other ideas.

'Uncle Theo, please can I have another?' The small plea came from the little girl between them.

'Sure.' He reached in with a fresh napkin and grabbed another pastry from the pile of goodies. 'At least there's nothing wrong with your appetite; perhaps much of this won't go to waste after all.'

'Of course, the picnic! I'll take it back.'

'It's okay, it saves me having to think about food for the next couple of days.'

'You're going to eat it?'

'Is that a problem? I'll pay for it.'

Suddenly all he wanted was Bree, a bottle of beer, the contents of the basket and an entire evening to feast on it… and her.

Not happening.

'No. No, of course it's not…so, I'll see you at ten. I'll come earlier if I can.' She flashed a concerned look at Becca and he got it. The little girl was okay now, but for how long. 'I'm going to take this medicine up to your family and I'm sure they will all be right as rain in no time. But you have an important job to do until then, okay?'

'I do?' Becca stared up at her.

'Yup. You need to keep an eye on this one for me and make sure he behaves himself. I believe he can be a bit of a monkey at times and he has to be on best behaviour to look after your family and this B & B for my very special friend.'

'A monkey?' Becca giggled and Theo blushed—actually blushed.

'Yup. Can you do that do you think?'

'Me and Bertie cert'nly can.' She lifted her bunny up and sat proud.

'You superstars.' Bree grinned from them to him. 'I'll see you all later.'

A shell-shocked Theo raised a weak hand and gave an equally weak, 'Bye.'

And then it truly struck him. He was alone and in charge of a five-year-old.

Give him a B & B, a multibillion-pound corporation, a failing enterprise to whip into shape, no problem. But a real, live five-year-old...

What could possibly go wrong?

CHAPTER FOUR

IT WAS CLOSER to lunch by the time Bree made it back across the road. The morning rush had defied the usual pattern as the press returned in their droves, adding to the local and normal tourist footfall.

She practically fell through the rear door as the men Theo had employed to keep the rabble out were back on guard and had to clear her a passage through the crowd that was hungry for a sneak peek of Theo and any insider gossip they could get.

But she wasn't talking. No one was.

Unless it was to add their two pennies' worth to the rumours of the luxury resort landing and speculate over the reason behind the heirs of Ferrington disappearing all those years ago…which she couldn't deny intrigued her, too. But it was none of her business, nor was the article about him that her aunt had tried to shove under her nose when she'd returned that morning.

Her aunt who was clearly convinced that Theo was a pastry order away from leading her niece astray.

Bree wished. She was rapidly coming to the conclusion that a brief hot fling could do her the world of good. She sighed the idea away and zeroed in on Becca's laugh coming from the bar area. The sound was contagious, teasing at her own lips as she tiptoed forward. It wasn't as if she wanted to creep up unawares and spy on them, more that she hoped for another unguarded moment like she'd witnessed that morning.

Okay, so that was kind of like spying, but the surprising sight of Theo with the little girl had done something inexplicably gooey to her insides, the scene only adding to her conviction that there was so much more to Theo Dubois than what the world saw.

And she liked what she saw. A lot.

'What do you mean that looks nothing like the Easter bunny? It's quite obviously a bunny and these are his Easter eggs.'

She rounded the corner to see them hunched over the table before the unlit fireplace, papers and crayons strewn everywhere, Becca's elbows in the middle of the table, her knees on the chair as she shook her head.

'No. His ears are too small.'

'Too small?'

'Yes!'

'You show me.'

Becca caught her lip in her teeth and started to draw as Theo watched her, his expression easy. He looked comfortable, relaxed, and Becca was clearly in her element. 'See!'

He grinned. 'Ah! I do see!'

Suddenly his eyes lifted to hers and the entire room seemed to tilt on its axis.

'Bree! You're back.'

It took a second for her to stabilise, another for her to find her voice. 'Looks like you're having fun.'

'If by fun, you mean having your artwork ripped to pieces by a five-year-old then, yes, that's exactly what's happening.'

She laughed, closing the distance between them and peering down at the table and the many, many drawings. 'I'm so sorry I took longer than I thought.'

'Hey, no need to apologise. As promised, Becca has kept me in check.'

'I have, Aunt Bree!'

'So I see...' She gave the little girl a smile before her eyes drifted back to Theo. He looked far too at home with a crayon in his hand and his hair all wayward. Less cover model, more father of the year.

Oh, wow, Bree. Engage the brakes!

'I'm afraid I can't stop long either…' Good job, too, if she couldn't get her mind or body in check. 'The bakery has never been so busy.'

'Aah, now at least that's one perk to my presence.'

'Just one?' Her disobedient libido could think of so many more…

'Aye. Those reporters will be grazing here for days, not to mention the tourists adding a stop in Elmdale now that the news is out that I'm here.'

'Oh, to be so popular!' she teased, yet his eyes didn't look amused, they looked strained and shadowed. Something she'd glimpsed before but had put down to travel fatigue and the shock of having a niece. Now she wasn't so sure. 'Is everything okay?'

He blinked and the look was gone. 'Absolutely!' He gave Becca a nudge. 'We're having a great time, aren't we, kiddo?'

Becca gave him a happy grin, which she then turned on Bree. 'I'm teaching Uncle Theo how to draw.'

'You are?' When she'd asked if things were okay, she'd meant with him, and he knew it, too. But she got that he might not want to talk about anything too deep in front of the little girl. She focused on the drawings rather than the distracting and somewhat haunted artist. 'Wow, that's a pretty good…cat?'

Theo groaned as Becca laughed. 'See, I told you it looked nothing like the Easter bunny, Uncle Theo.'

'Nothing's a bit harsh. You could at least soften the blow a little—there's only so much a guy's ego can take. Especially when being ganged up on by two women.'

Bree laughed, unable to stop her eyes from finding his, and the sound stuttered to a stop. Something sparked to life in the blueness of his, something warm and appreciative, something so very akin to the fire she felt inside.

But you're not his type. Remember.

If she'd needed any more proof of that then her aunt had handed it to her, in the form of magazine after magazine, every article on his personal life proving the man had a type…and it wasn't her.

He liked his women well poised and statuesque. Tall, slim, all hard angles and perfect hair. Preferably blonde.

Definitely not her, and yet that look in his eye…the fire in his depths, the way his mouth parted, and his eyes dropped to her own.

'Oh, I think you have plenty enough to start with.'

Oh, God, was that really her voice, all husky and needy?

'Plenty of ego?'

She nodded and his grin darkened, made her pulse skip.

'Is that so?'

Another nod, as though she was egging him on, urging him into crossing an invisible line.

'What's an ego?'

They both looked down to find Becca between them, staring up at them, her brows drawn together.

'Good question, sweetheart!' Bree looked to him. 'Uncle Theo, you have more experience in this area than me, would you care to explain while I put the kettle on?'

Grinning, she walked away, happy to land him in it, even more happy to gain some much-needed space. She'd only been in his company again mere minutes, and she was already confusing fantasy with reality once more.

Her aunt wasn't wrong. Theo was dangerous…but not in the way her aunt believed.

She'd never risk giving the guy her heart, but chances were that given the opportunity she'd explore that mouth of his, that body, that mind…she'd just be careful not to go back for seconds, or thirds.

She wouldn't be needy.

Leon had labelled her as needy.

She'd preferred the term lonely.

One couldn't be lonely in Elmdale though. It was like one big happy family and one she felt very much a part of now. She was happy. Content. Or she had been until he'd lit this spark in her that she wasn't quite sure how to put out.

Other than to do the obvious and run with it. Just once.

She filled the kettle and tapped it on, her back suddenly warm and prickly, and she knew he was behind her even before she turned.

'So, you think I have plenty?' He was leaning against the doorframe, those biceps bulging as he crossed his arms, his charcoal T-shirt clinging indecently to his torso. Didn't the man own any clothes that fitted properly?

You're purposely missing the point of a slim-fit tee, Bree...

'Where's Becca?'

'Watching her favourite cartoon. And don't change the subject.'

'I wasn't.'

'No?' His eyes were dancing, the air alive with tease and the fact that they were now alone.

Fantasy once again overtaking reality, she fired back, 'Are you saying you don't?'

'Have an ego?' He chuckled, the low and rumbling sound making her insides quiver. She clenched her body against the sensation, raised her chin. 'I prefer to call it confidence.'

'Ego, confidence, surely they're one and the same.'

'Not at all.' He stepped towards her. 'Ego is all about self-interest. Seeking approval, recognition, constant validation to always be seen as "right".'

Her lips parted but she struggled to breathe let alone speak, her words so very hushed. 'And you're none of that?'

'No.' He was upon her now, looming tall, his blue eyes

blazing, his scent…oh, God, he smelled delicious. She leaned her hands into the worktop behind her, anchoring her body as she resisted the urge to lean closer. 'I'm confident in my own ability, I believe in my skills…but then I have good reason to.'

She inhaled deeply, her chest lifting into his. Time to play him at his own game…

'Of course.' She batted her eyelashes, cocked her head to the side. 'I'm sure women often fall over themselves to flatter you all the time and tell you you're the best they've ever had.'

'Are you goading me, Bree?'

'*Moi?* I wouldn't dare.'

His eyes flashed, his cheeks streaked with colour, and the tension in his body was palpable. He was holding back, exercising restraint, because for some reason unbeknownst to her, he wanted her. He really did.

She could never hope to hold his attention for ever, but she had it now and the power of it flooded her veins, the rush of endorphins euphoric.

'But I think you should prove it to me—' shallow breath '—show me just how good you are, and in return I promise to be honest.'

His chuckle rumbled through his chest, reverberating against her breasts, sending heat rushing to their peaks, her belly molten…

'Because you wouldn't waste meaningless platitudes on me.'

'Absolutely not.'

'You'd say it how it is?'

'I would.'

'You're an intriguing woman, Bree.'

'Now who's wasting platitudes?'

He shook his head, his mouth mere inches from her own. 'I say it how it is, too, Bree. And if I say you're intriguing—'

he gripped the counter either side of her, the sides of his hands brushing electrifyingly against hers '—I mean it.'

She wet her lips. In for a penny... 'Intriguing enough to kiss?'

His jaw pulsed, the muscles in his arms flexing. 'More than.'

'So why don't you?'

Something shifted in his gaze, something deep, meaningful, but when he opened his mouth, it was gone, replaced by the tease, the front. 'Because we have company.'

'Not right now we don't.'

'One thing I've learned in my very limited experience with a five-year-old is that they have a very short attention span, and if I start kissing you right now, I'm not going to want to stop—not for anyone or anything.'

Her breath shuddered out of her, the thrilling promise of his words vibrating through her. 'Later, then?'

She watched his throat bob, watched his eyes flicker with so much and yet, he didn't move, didn't respond, his well-honed body staying taut as the kettle hit a rolling boil behind her, its sudden click off punctuating the silence.

'Saved by the kettle,' he murmured.

Not really. She'd gladly neglect the kettle for the promise that had been in his eye but she knew the moment was over.

For now, at least.

She forced herself to turn, her body brushing his as she moved, and he backed away.

'Do you have enough time to join us for lunch?'

'Huh?' She glanced back at him.

His grin was lopsided as he gestured to the basket of food. 'Just like my ego, we have plenty of it...'

She laughed, her chest lifting so completely, the tension with it. 'I can spare some time over a cuppa, and then I really should be getting back.'

'Tonight, then? Dinner here? I'll cook...'

'Don't you have guests?'

'The only one up for dining is five and I'll make sure she eats beforehand.'

There was a strange look in his eye, as if he was warring with the offer he was making. As if he knew it was a bad idea but was making it anyway.

Not so dissimilar to the battle she had under way inside. Common sense telling her this was outrageous; Aunt Clara's voice, too. But she wasn't daft enough to look for more. All she wanted was to end three years of abstinence with a man she trusted to make good on his promise.

She fully understood her own hesitancy but what was Theo's problem? This was the norm for him. Bed 'em and forget 'em, as her Aunt Clara had so eloquently put it.

Couldn't he just do that with her?

She smiled at him, her decision made. 'I'll bring dessert.'

'I'll bring dessert.'

Her response and the tentative smile that had accompanied it had replayed over and over in his mind for the remainder of the day. While they'd sat with Becca and had lunch. While he'd ferried drinks and dry toast upstairs, changed beds, kicked the boiler again...

Even intermittent messages from Tanya had failed to tame his thoughts where Bree was concerned.

I'll bring dessert... He knew exactly what he wanted for dessert and it wasn't of the food variety. And he shouldn't be wanting it. Only he couldn't seem to stop himself.

Bree was different. He knew that was the crux of it. There was so much about her that excited him. Her kind and thoughtful nature wrapped up in a body made for sin was a combination he'd yet to come up against. The world he moved in, the women within it...they wanted his money and his fame and, hell, his body, too.

He knew he looked good and that wasn't his ego talking—it was fact. He worked hard to maintain his appearance; it didn't come for free. It took blood, sweat, and tears.

What had started as a necessity—to outrun everyone and be the toughest—had become a force of habit. And he had no objections to being treated as a sex object. He didn't want anything serious—he was incapable of serious—and so long as the women he dated knew the score, all was well.

Only Tanya had gone in for more…gone in for more and lied to get it.

And now he was supposed to be helping his brother and clearing his head in the process. Not getting embroiled in some reckless love affair with Flick's best friend.

Yet he was the one inviting Bree for dinner with a promise of more hanging in the air between them…

Would she have expectations like Tanya?

Would she be foolish enough to want more from him?

Surely not. She was good, kind, and so unbelievably sexy. He should be trying to make her run the other way. Instead he was lighting candles ready for their dinner together.

'They're pretty.' Becca gave a yawn as she eyed the table and its cluster of tea lights.

'You think she'll like them?'

She gave a swift nod, hugging her bunny and a book close to her chest. 'Definitely.'

'You ready for that bedtime story now?'

'Uh-huh!'

'We'll read it here and then I'll take you up to bed so we don't disturb the others, okay?'

She nodded and he picked her up, taking her over to the bay window and the cushioned seat built into the alcove. The curtains were drawn, the soft light coming from the copper wall lights and the lit fire enough to read by.

He opened the book and she scooted in closer, rested her head into the crook of his arm and he lifted it automatically wrapping it around her as he read, surprised at how easy it felt, surprised all the more by her ready acceptance of him.

She was softly snoring four pages in and still he read, not wanting to rouse her too soon, not ready to stop either. There was something so normal about it, soothing right down to his bones as he relaxed into the seat. It was a sensation he couldn't remember feeling before. So peaceful and content.

'I think she's gone.'

He started at Bree's hushed tone, his eyes lifting to find her in the doorway, and his cheeks flushed. He felt exposed and vulnerable, which was ridiculous. He'd just been reading a bedtime story, nothing more. She didn't know how deeply it had got to him. He was going soft. Losing his mind. Elmdale had given him some weird personality transplant and he needed to shake it off.

'I think I've exhausted her.'

'You've exhausted yourself, too, I imagine.' She gave him a small smile that lit him up from within. The appreciation he could spy there, the warmth, the compassion...

It wasn't the same heat that had assaulted them in the kitchen, the heat that never took much provoking to become a full-blown flame. It was deeper, more meaningful...and it touched him.

God, get a grip, man.

He started to shift and she tiptoed forward. 'Wait, let me help.'

She took the bunny and the book and pulled the table back to clear his path. 'Now you can carry her. I'll run ahead and clear the way. Which room is she in?'

'She's with her mother in the room to the right of the family one.'

She nodded. 'Good shout.'

He followed her lead, her hair swaying hypnotically before him, the long black waves trailing down her back and drawing his eyes lower…to her hips and that…

No, don't look at her behind.

He tried not to look, he honestly did, but as soon as they hit the stairs it was there at eye level, her red dress cinched in at the waist and sashaying as she climbed. He'd never seen anything more delicious or arousing. Her curves were going to be the death of him.

Bree tapped lightly on the door to the bedroom and waited for Becca's mother to call out. She peeped inside. 'We've brought Becca to bed.'

She turned to him and reached out to take the little girl from his arms. 'I'll tuck her in, you go and freshen up.'

He handed her over and ran his hands through his hair—did he really look that beat?

And there she was looking fresh as a daisy and he knew full well her day had been non-stop thanks to the chaos his presence had stirred up.

He hit the small room he was using for his stay and tugged off his tee, tossed it aside and headed for the sink. A quick wash. A bit of aftershave. A new shirt. Good as new.

Well, almost. He ran his fingers through his hair, his fringe refusing to stay back as it curled over his right eye, and gave up. He would do.

And if he didn't get a move on, the lasagne he'd prepared wouldn't be fit for anyone.

And why was he worrying so much?

He reached for his phone and stopped. Leave it. No distractions. No outside world. Just him and Bree.

His gut gave a weird little wriggle—were they… nerves?

He dated all the time and never got a hint of the wriggles.

Correction, you know how to date a certain type of woman and that woman isn't Bree. She's an unknown entity.

Not that this was a date…not at all…
What is it, then?
Crickets.
Helpful.
Not.

CHAPTER FIVE

'IT SMELLS INCREDIBLE in here.'

Bree entered the kitchen, breathing in the aromas and trying not to lose herself in the charismatic presence that was Theo Dubois in the kitchen.

This man just made it impossible to think platonic thoughts. If everyone had a superpower, that would be his. The thought made her laugh and his eyes shot to hers. 'Something funny?'

'No, not at all.'

His eyes narrowed on hers, his lips quirking up. 'Way to go in making a man relax.'

She smiled her sweetest smile. 'How can I help?'

'You can go and sit at the table in the bar—it's all ready for you. I took the liberty of choosing a red, but feel free to grab something else if you'd prefer.'

'Red's perfect. Can I take anything through with me?'

'There's the garlic bread on the side.' He gestured to a china dish containing a plaited garlic bread, fresh steam rising from the sliced pieces.

'Did you make this?' She lifted it off the side, the delicious scent of garlic and butter invading her senses, and she gave an appreciative hum, her lashes fluttering.

'I did. But it's been a while so go easy on me, won't you?'

'Like I did with the drawing?'

He pulled a face and she laughed some more.

'Yeah, just like with the drawing.'

'Well, this looks amazing and smells it, too.'

'Hopefully, it will taste just as good. Becca helped. It seems cooking is the one job she doesn't get bored of…'

'You cooked together?'

'We did plenty—drawing, baking, watching TV, reading…' He opened the oven and lifted out a rectangular dish, its contents covered with a bubbling layer of cheese. 'She even constructed this baby with me, my mother's classic lasagne.'

'Wow. You really have been busy. I'm feeling quite spoilt.'

He grinned as he slid the dish on the side and grabbed a knife. 'I will admit my motives weren't quite so altruistic. I did have to keep her busy, too.'

She gave a soft laugh, unable to keep her awe out of it. It was easy to forget who he was when he was like this, easy to believe this was a normal everyday date, with a normal everyday man that one could let their heart…

Oh, no, no, no, don't go there, Bree! Remember your aunt's warning. Remember who he is and what this is—a bit of fun. Temporary. He's not a man looking to settle down and get all homely, content in Elmdale. He's rugged round the edges, good with his hands, yes, but he's not a man to fall head over heels for, he's a man to wear them for…one night only.

Her bright red stilettos clipped the floor as she made her way back into the bar and spied for the first time the round table set for dinner before the fireplace. An intimate dinner for two… Her heart stuttered in her chest.

Just because he's lit a few candles, it doesn't mean more…

She set the bread down and poured the wine he'd already opened, swift to lift her own glass to her lips and take a sip. And another.

What are you doing, Bree?

Five years ago, she would have dived headlong into dinner and more, not caring what tomorrow held. But that was pre-Leon, full of the carefree London vibe, confident and sassy.

Now though…

She was different. Leon had changed her. Elmdale had changed her. She wasn't so sure who the real Bree was any more... Miss Wary or Sassy?

The former wanted to run and keep her heart protected. The latter wanted to throw caution to the wind and succumb to the wild heat he sparked within her.

'I hope it's okay.' Theo appeared, tray in oven mitts, his cheeks flushed from the kitchen, his hair doing its own thing and it was a beat before she could breathe, another before she could speak.

'If the smell is anything to go by, it's going to be delicious.'

'Take a seat.'

She did, watching him beneath her lashes as he set the dish down between them and started to serve her a slice. 'Help yourself to salad. I wasn't sure what you preferred, and Becca insisted on using every serving bowl the kitchen possessed. So now you have an array to choose from and nothing tainted by something else. Apparently, it's very icky to let the tomato juice run onto the cucumber.'

She laughed. 'Oh, the wisdom of children.'

She dished out a selection of everything and waited for him to do the same, lifting her glass to him when he was done. 'To the chef, or chefs.'

He smiled across the table at her, his face softened by the candlelight, his eyes glittering with gold. 'To the beautiful baker who makes the best jam doughnuts I've ever tasted.'

Another soft laugh. 'I can't take the credit for those, I'm afraid, they're my aunt's work. The sausage rolls are more my speciality.'

He pressed a palm to his chest. 'Ah, a woman after my own heart.'

Her stomach did its thing and swooped, her heart danced, her wary mind screamed...

'The press has one thing right.'

'Oh, yeah, and what's that?'

'You could charm the knickers off a nun.'

He spluttered over his wine. 'They said that?'

She laughed into her glass, loving the sparkle in his eye. 'Well, not the nun bit, I added that for effect…though I can believe it possible.'

He chuckled, shook his head. 'You overestimate my powers of persuasion, Bree.'

She held his gaze, the chemistry drawing them together, pulsing in the air.

'In either case, there's only one kind of woman I'm interested in right now and it's not the veiled variety.'

Her smile lifted to one side, her heart receiving the compliment far too readily.

'And now we should eat before this gets cold.' He changed the subject swiftly, his gaze lowering to his plate as he took up his cutlery and, slowly, she did the same, trying to find her appetite amidst all the butterflies.

She needn't have worried; one mouthful and she was in food heaven, eager for more. The taste explosion was so divine she hummed around a mouthful.

'You like it?'

She covered her mouth, swallowed. 'I love it.'

'Nice to know I haven't lost my touch.' He smiled at her, but there was something almost wistful in his tone, in his gaze…she tried to guess at its source.

'Your mum clearly knows how to make a good sauce.'

His smile faltered. 'She did. She passed away a few years ago.'

'Oh, Theo! I'm so sorry.' She reached across the table, not enough to touch him but enough to feel that little bit closer. Curse her big mouth! 'What happened?'

'Cancer.'

She felt her eyes prick at the rawness in his voice, the obvious pain. 'I can't imagine losing my parents. They live in Scotland so I don't see them as much as I should, but just knowing that they're there on the other end of the phone...' She gave a sad smile. 'I'm so sorry.'

'It is what it is. Sebastian and I tried everything, flew in the best specialists, anything to get a different result but...' He studied his wine glass, his fingers toying with its base. 'She didn't tell us she was sick for a long time—didn't tell anyone—so by the time she did...well, there was nothing that could be done.'

He sounded guilty. As if he were somehow to blame for his mother not confiding in them. 'I imagine she didn't want you worrying about her.'

'She was our mother.' His eyes shot to hers. 'We should have been given the opportunity to worry, to save her, to support her.'

She leaned forward, covered his fingers with her own. 'You were there for her, whether you think you were or not, and she made that choice. It was hers to make. You can't blame yourself for something you had no control over.'

His lashes flickered, his breath shuddering past his lips. 'I've never—I've never thought of it like that. And who knows why I'm coming out with all this now? I'm sorry.'

She gave him a watery smile. 'Don't apologise. Please. I'm glad you can open up to me. It sounds like you needed it.'

'Bree...' He shook his head, looked at her with eyes that widened and sparkled with so much. 'You are incredible.'

'Incredible. Intriguing. I'm racking up these compliments.' She was purposely lightening the mood. 'What's next? Another "I"?'

'I can drop in an "intelligent" if you like.'

She gave a laugh. 'Okay, okay, let's not get ahead of ourselves.'

'If the cap fits...'

'Well, if we're dishing out compliments, you, Theo Dubois, are more than just a pretty face.'

'Is that so?'

'Yup, you're also a great cook! And judging by this dish, I take it you still cook a lot?'

'Not as much as I like. In fact, hardly ever. Most of my evenings are taken up with networking dinners, parties, events…'

'Most nights? Wow! Don't you ever get tired of it?'

'It's the nature of the beast. It's what I do being the face of Dubois. I network, I attend charity fundraisers, I'm always on the list somewhere in the hope that I'll attend.'

'Sounds unrelenting.'

He gave a shrug. 'It's my life.'

'Don't you ever want to press pause?'

A soft scoff. 'Now, there's an idea… Is that what you're doing? Living here instead of London. Pressing pause on your life.'

Her mouth quirked to one side. 'I don't think you can compare my city days to your life now.'

'I don't know. I get the sense we're kindred spirits of a sort.'

She chuckled low. 'Kindred spirits?'

'Yes. Playing at being all calm and countryfied when really we're just city slickers waiting for the party to descend.'

She laughed harder now. 'I think you may be play-acting, Mr Dubois, world's sexiest billionaire bachelor enjoying his time as a countryfied homemaker, but me, I'm just Bree.'

'Well, just Bree, you're a breath of fresh air and whatever kept you here in Elmdale, I for one am grateful as it puts you here now.'

The warmth in her chest spread, her pulse kicking up a notch. 'It's not that bad, you know… Elmdale, I mean.'

'I know.'

'Do you?'

He nodded, resting his head on his hands as he leaned in towards her. 'I'll let you into a little secret.'

She leaned in, too, her voice all breathy as she murmured, 'Is this going to be X-rated, because if so, maybe we should save it for dessert?'

His grin was worth every salacious word.

'For your information, Bree Johansson, I was just going to say that I like it here. I'm glad I came back. I like the landscape. I like the quiet…well, save for the press, but they'll clear out eventually. And I like the community—'

'Save for when they're threatening to see you and your brother off with pitchforks.'

He laughed. 'Except for that. But it's more than all that…' Sincerity thickened his voice now. 'I like how I feel when I'm doing stuff. Physical stuff.'

'Stuff?' she repeated dumbly, trying to get her brain to stop conjuring up all the wonderful, magnificent things that could entail.

'Making myself useful. Fixing things. Working.'

'Surely you work hard earning all those billions?'

'You'd be surprised.' He leaned back in his seat. 'When you get to the heights we have, you have people you trust to get the work done.'

'Is that how you have the time to do this now? Help Flick out, take care of the B & B.'

He nodded.

'Like a knight in shining armour, coming to the rescue…' She was only semi-teasing because in any fairy tale, any movie, Theo would aesthetically fit the part. With his mop of golden hair, piercing blue eyes and all that muscle…all he'd need was the costume and the white horse.

'Hardly. That's more Sebastian's role. I'm just his willing aid. Plus… I owe him.' The last was grave, taking some of the spark out of his gaze and though she wanted to understand why, she knew she'd already probed enough into his life, into the real him, and she was in danger of forgetting what this night was about.

'Well, whatever the case, I, for one, am grateful.'

'You are?'

'Yes.' She poured her gratitude into her smile. 'It's been a long time since I've let my hair down like this.'

'Me, too.'

'Ha! You just admitted to partying every night.'

'Social networking and projecting the image of Theo Dubois is a full-time job; it's exhausting.'

'How can it be exhausting if you're just being you?' she teased but the look that came over him was far too serious. 'Unless…you're projecting somebody else?'

'Who knows?' He tried to shrug it off, but she wasn't buying it. Not with that look still in his eye.

'Maybe you've been projecting it for so long, you've lost sight of who the real you is?'

'Perhaps.'

'Sounds to me like you need a time out, time away from everything.'

'That's kind of what this is. Time to reflect, take stock and re-evaluate what I want from life.'

They shared a look, a look that raced with so many questions. Was that what this meal was about? Was she just a part of his reset? An opportunity to sample something different…

And if she was, was she really okay with that?

'God, just listen to me, I sound so pitiful.' He shook his hair out, sat straighter, dragging her back from the painful abyss she was about to topple into. 'Please ignore me, Bree, I have no right to burden you with any of that. I don't know what's got into me. I'm fully aware of how lucky—'

'I don't want to ignore you.' She spoke from the heart, unable to stop herself and unable to stand by and have him dismiss his feelings so readily. 'I want to know the real you.'

His eyes held hers—one beat, two…

'You don't, Bree.' His voice was quiet. 'I can promise you that.'

'Why not?'

'You know my reputation.'

'I know what the press has to say about you. But I want to hear it from you.'

'What, that I'm a player?'

Always was, always would be…wasn't that what Tanya had thrown at him, wasn't that what he'd always told himself, too? Was it his front talking, or the real him deep down? Ultimately, actions spoke louder than words and there'd been plenty of action on his part.

'If you think that's the most important thing to know about you…'

Bree's brown eyes were soft in the candlelight, her smile small and sympathetic and it irked him. Made his skin crawl on the inside. He didn't want that look from her. He wanted the fire back, the flirtation, the fun.

He shook his head, choked on a laugh. 'It probably is for you.'

'But is that you talking, or the press?'

'Both.' He threw back some wine. She was burrowing beneath his defences, and he had no idea how to stop her, or how to stop himself from letting her. 'Look, Bree, I re-alised a long time ago that settling down, getting serious, wasn't for me.'

She forked up some lasagne, chewing it over as her eyes narrowed on him.

'Is this you trying to warn me off, or are you just being honest?'

His lips quirked—she was so direct. No beating around the bush, easing in gently, coaxing out the truth in a roundabout way with a demure smile, a flutter of the lashes, a twirl of hair around a finger...

'Again, both.'

'So, the great Theo Dubois truly is a sworn billionaire bachelor?'

Her eyes sparkled and her tease was ripe in her face. He wanted to kiss her. Kiss her for being so blunt, kiss her to see what those cherry-red lips tasted like, run his hands over those luscious curves and coax more than just a tease from her lips.

Much as the food had succeeded in doing. Every hum of appreciation and closing of the eyes as she savoured a mouthful, had made him decidedly uncomfortable below the waist...even the tricky nature of their conversation couldn't smother it.

'Do I take your silence as confirmation, or...?'

'Hmm?'

She laughed, the sound a heady tinkle. 'Have I spilt something?'

She patted her chest, looked down and he forced his eyes to stay up, to meet hers when they returned. 'Not at all. You're just quite the distraction.'

She wet her lips, sipped her wine. 'If you say so.'

'Oh, I do.'

She shook her head, her smile bashful as she drew her hair over one shoulder.

'So, tell me, how old are you?'

He started. 'Why?'

'It's all part of me piecing the real you together.'

'And my age is important.'

'It's as good a place to start as any.'

He shook his head, 'I meant what I said, Bree. I really wouldn't try too hard, you might not like what you find.'

Her eyes narrowed. 'For a man so well liked in the

media—playboy antics aside—you don't think very highly of yourself, do you?'

Something twisted deep inside him and he tried to laugh. 'Does anybody?'

Her frown deepened. 'I may not like everything about myself, but I certainly think I'm a good person. I care for those around me, I look out for them. I like to think I'm kind, thoughtful. I have a weakness for cheese and don't let me loose with cinnamon swirls. I should probably eat less, exercise more and I definitely need a holiday, but, other than that, I don't think I'm all that bad.'

His smile grew as her critique rolled off the tongue, the bubbly, unashamed Bree in full flight now and only increasing his appreciation of her.

'Your turn.'

'What?'

'What do you like about yourself?'

'I have a good head for business.'

'Stating the obvious.'

'Indeed.'

'And?' She waved her wine glass at him. 'What else?'

'And as we've already discussed, I've received no complaints in the bedroom department.' He was aiming for distraction; she was aiming for the truth…and she wasn't going to let him get away with it if the purse to her lips was anything to go by.

'I'll have to take your word for that. What else?'

He toyed with his wine glass, his recent past coming to the fore. Tanya and her lie in all its painful glory.

'Need me to help you out?'

He lifted his gaze to hers in question.

'What about the charity you and your brother run? Isn't that something to be proud of?'

'Ms Johansson…' a smile teased at his lips, a hint of

Bree's warmth taking out the chill '...have you been reading up on me? Intentionally, this time?'

Her cheeks glowed. 'I may have had the smallest amount of time this afternoon to do a quick search online... I had to make sure I was safe to dine with you. You are, after all, virtually a stranger.'

'I suppose I am.' Though sitting with her, in the quiet of the evening, alone with the connection continuing to thrum between them, strangers wasn't how he saw them... 'What else did you discover?'

'That the charity provides shelters all over the world to help people escaping domestic abuse and just the other night you attended a gala in Paris where you raised a record-breaking amount.'

His smile was full now, pride filling his chest. 'We did.'

'What inspired you?'

'To set up the charity?'

She nodded and his eyes narrowed. 'Do you know much about my childhood?'

'How could—?' She swallowed as his brows lifted. 'Okay, so, yes, this is Elmdale and people talk but I only know a little from Felicity. It sounds like your family suffered plenty of loss in a short space of time. First your grandmother, then your father so soon after...it must have been hard for you all.'

The sympathy was back in her gaze but not even Bree could take the edge off the chill within, not this time. Not when thoughts of his past, the estate, and his grandfather were at the fore.

'Not for the reasons you're thinking. My grandfather wasn't a very nice man. In fact, my father wasn't either, though we didn't find that out until long after he'd passed.' He looked to the windows as if he could somehow see the Ferrington Estate in the distance, along with all the pain it harboured. 'They liked to communicate in fists...or, in my grandfather's case, a cane.'

She gave a small gasp, her eyes widening and watering in one. 'That's horrific.'

He gave a chilling laugh. 'I don't know, I think he just saw it as the way of things. He was a born and bred public-school boy, accustomed to the kind of discipline dished out by your stereotypical headmaster.'

'But—but how could he?'

'Relatively easily by all counts.' He tried to reassure her with a smile. 'Don't let it upset you. I got over it a long time ago.'

'And your father, he...'

His stomach lurched and he shook his head. 'No. He only ever beat my mother. And only ever behind closed doors.'

'Oh, Theo. That's awful.'

'We didn't realise until we left...' His eyes went back to the window as he relived the horror of that night. 'He'd been my idol. I'd looked up to him. When he died, I went off the rails, lashing out, getting up to no good...'

'Hence Annie taking you under her wing.'

He nodded. 'Annie, my brother, my mother, they all tried. But I was a law unto myself and that night, I'd been out late. My curfew was ten and I just had to push my luck. My grandfather had already threatened to have us shipped off to boarding school, taken away from Mum, and when I came home late, he was in a rage, his cane at the ready.'

He could see Bree shaking her head on the periphery of his vision, but he couldn't look at her, not with the sickening churn in his gut.

'When he went to strike me, Mum got in the way. My brother—'

'He was there?'

Another nod, the nausea rising and making his voice raw. 'Sebastian lost it. Mum was on the floor, bleeding, and

I was shocked still, so he did what he had to and came to our defence. Our grandfather took a nasty hit. He deserved it but it wasn't pretty and Sebastian hates himself for what happened. Hates himself even more now that he knows how much deeper the consequences of that night go.'

'You mean, Angel growing up without her father?'

He nodded, finally looking back at her. 'Don't you see, Bree? If I hadn't been the way I was, that night may never have happened and Sebastian and Flick wouldn't have broken up, Angel would have had her father, my brother wouldn't have missed out on all those years he can never get back…'

The confession was killing him but he had to get it out. He had to make her see him for the man he was.

'Is that what you meant when you said you owe him?'

Another nod. 'Not that this in any way can make up for what I did and what he lost because of it.'

'But it wasn't your fault, Theo. If it hadn't happened that night, it would have happened some other time. From what you've said, living with your grandfather was no kind of life for any of you.'

'I guess that's true.'

'And if we're totally honest, Sebastian could have come back for Felicity at some point. I know he didn't know about the pregnancy and Angel, but if he'd loved her that much, he could have returned.'

It was something he'd thought himself since arriving, but the repercussions of that night went far deeper for Sebastian. His brother had been a model citizen—studious, kind, generous, thoughtful. That night had broken him, changed him for ever. Theo got that he wouldn't want Flick to see that side of him—hell, Sebastian had hated it enough that Theo and his mother had witnessed it.

'It wasn't that straightforward. In the beginning, my grandfather was still a threat. He had connections, powerful ones. He could have had us taken from her permanently and we lived in fear for a long time. And after…things had moved on, life had changed us.'

He gave her the partial truth, keeping the specifics of his brother's mental fallout to himself. It wasn't his place to comment on it, but he did hope that now they were back, now that Sebastian had Flick and Angel in his life, his brother would start to live again and put the past to rest.

'So that's why you changed your name?'

'Yes.' His chest eased, grateful that she didn't press him any further on his brother's delayed return. 'We fled to France and stayed with a friend of my mother's. She ran a B & B just outside Paris. If it hadn't been for her, we would have had nowhere to turn.'

'Hence the charity…' Her eyes sparked with realisation. 'Making sure people in the same situation have a place to run to and feel safe?'

'Yes.'

'That's admirable.'

'It was my brother's idea.'

'That may be, but you're the face of it; isn't that something to be proud of?'

'Proud?' He laughed. 'You really are determined, aren't you?'

'Determined?'

'To make me see some good in me.'

'Of course.'

'Even with my dating record?'

It was her turn to laugh. 'Will you stop with the dating record? It's not going to put me off.'

His grin broadened, the alien sense of pride swelling unchecked within his chest. How often did he feel as if he garnered attention for the right reasons, fulfilling reasons?

'But on a serious note, is that truly how you see yourself in five, ten years? Living alone. Single and happy?'

And just like that the pleasing sensation died.

Two weeks ago, he was heading for it all, a wife, a child. All things he'd never dared imagine before—never dared want—but fate, or so he thought, had handed him an alternative path.

Until Tanya's lie had been outed and everything he'd believed, everything he'd thought of as a future, had been obliterated.

It was one thing to never want to be a father, another entirely to have it thrust on him. And then, at the very moment he had come to accept it, come to yearn for it even, it had been ripped away.

Though could it truly be ripped away if the pregnancy had always been a lie?

He didn't know. Just as he didn't know where the fake Theo ended, and the real Theo began.

The only thing he knew right now that was tangible and trustworthy was Bree.

And if his dating record hadn't put her off, was it possible she didn't care that there was no future here?

No promises. No commitment.

Just this.

CHAPTER SIX

THE LONGER THEO took to answer, the more she regretted asking.

She was about to change tack when he spoke up.

'I tend not to dwell on the future when it comes to my personal life. In business, it always makes sense to know where you're heading, to know what your goal is and make sure you reach it. But in my personal life, I've learned to take each day as it comes.'

'Sounds…' she searched for the right word '…exciting.'

'You don't sound like you're excited by it.'

'To be honest, I quite like it.' She smiled as she thought about how liberating it must be not to worry about the future, not to wonder if the right person was just around the corner, not to worry about the biological clock ticking away and just be. Easier said than done when Aunt Clara was very much aware of her age and reminded her often enough. 'And I can respect it. So long as the women you see know the score and want the same, who's to judge?'

'Precisely.'

'So, we're agreed.'

His eyes narrowed on her, his lips quirked around his wine glass. 'Agreed?'

'That this thing between us is as temporary as your presence in Elmdale?'

He opened his mouth, closed it again. Frowned.

'Don't look so stunned.' She gave a pitched laugh, her nerves getting the better of her. Maybe she'd gone too far. Maybe she'd called the entire thing wrong—the chemistry, the desire she'd glimpsed looking back at her…no, no she couldn't have. He just wasn't convinced about her view on it all.

'I'll have you know, I'm a contemporary woman with a contemporary outlook on life. I don't need a man to complete me. They have their…uses.' She gave him a slow smile, resisted a wink. 'But I don't need to hanker after one, all loved up and foolish with it.'

'Wow.' He sat back in his chair. 'The carefree and caring Bree sees love as foolish. I never would have thought it.'

'Not in all cases.' Her stomach twitched—she'd played the fool once; she'd be a lot more careful before she'd dare go there again. 'But sometimes, in certain circumstances, with certain individuals.'

'Agreed.' He nodded. 'So, you're not looking for love, I'm not looking for love—you know what I'd call this evening in that case?'

Her lips pursed together in an amused smile. 'No, you tell me.'

'Perfect.'

Her smile grew with her confidence. 'I'll drink to that.'

'Me, too.'

God, his eyes were sexy, the chiselled cut to his jaw, too, the way the grooves deepened either side of his mouth when he smiled, even his throat and his Adam's apple that bobbed as he swallowed. She itched to reach across, drag his mouth to hers and end this meal with the best possible dessert.

She lowered her glass, the gentle clink as it hit the table all the more pronounced for the sizzling silence between them. She traced the base with her fingers, trying to steady her pulse enough to eat and failing miserably. A change in conversation, that was what they needed…a platonic direction…at least until she'd done his wonderful meal justice.

'So, what do you make of your brother's situation—do you think they'll be okay?'

'My brother will do everything in his power to make sure they are.' His loyalty and love for his brother blazed in the blue of his eyes. 'The press may have me pegged right, but Sebastian…they haven't got a clue.'

'What do you mean?'

'Tarring him with the same brush as our grandfather was a low move, even by their standards.'

She grimaced. 'After all you've said about him, that must have stung.'

'Aye, the old man may be dead, but his legacy still has the power to hurt.' He lowered his gaze to his plate as he placed his cutlery together, signifying he was done. 'Even when it comes via the press.'

'You must be well versed in ignoring what they have to say.'

'I am. Sebastian not so much. He's lived his life in hiding for so long, but now he's out there and when the press learns of his fatherhood status, they'll be all over them like a rash.'

'Knowing Felicity and Angel like I do, they'll cope. They're stronger than they look. And like you say, they have Sebastian to look out for them now. I imagine he'll park his own feelings to look after theirs.'

He gave a soft grunt, the hint of a smile returning. 'He's the best protector there is.'

'And he also has you here to help him.'

'True.'

'Does that mean you'll stay a while?'

'Until I'm no longer needed, yes.'

'And then back to… Paris?'

His jaw pulsed, the sudden tension in his body palpable, but all he said was, 'Maybe. What about you? Any plans to return to the big city?'

And just like that the tension crossed the table, his innocent question as powerful and unwelcome as an ice-cold shower. 'Not particularly.'

'How come? You don't strike me as the kind to be content in the country.'

'I don't?'

'Or maybe it's more that you stand out a little in Elmdale.'

She gave an amused frown, her discomfort momentarily forgotten. 'Stand out?'

'You're so bright and exuberant, full of style, a class act…'

'A class act?' she spluttered.

'Absolutely. There's definitely a city vibe about you.'

'And that's a compliment?'

'Yes.'

She gave a dubious laugh. 'You really are the charmer.'

'I know. Sorry, is it too much?'

'If I thought you truly wanted an answer to that question, I'd give it honestly…'

'I do. Honestly.'

She laughed fully now, his wide-eyed sincerity tickling her. 'In which case, yes, it is a little too much…'

Because she wasn't used to it. Genuine compliments or teasing ones or anything in between. Even in the early days with Leon they'd been scarce and admitting it felt like revealing too much, weakening too much, falling in deeper with whatever this was.

'I'm afraid it was a necessary weapon in my arsenal when I was younger to make up for my many misdemeanours and now—' he shrugged '—now it comes a little too naturally.'

'And just look where it has got you, Mr…what was it? Number three on the world's sexiest list?'

His laugh was so deep and, true to his label, sexy. 'I think you'll find I was second only to Damien Black and with a name like that how could I possibly come first?'

'I don't think it's the name voters were concerned with.'

'You think?' He cocked a brow, his expression an exact replica of one he'd worn on more than one magazine cover, and she laughed all the more.

'Definitely.'

'And now you're using your flattery to avoid giving me a straight answer. Why don't you want to return to London?'

She should have known he wouldn't let it go and she toyed with her food as she mulled it over. Just how much to admit to. She didn't want to relive her London days but neither did she want to feel ashamed of them or in some way to blame for what happened. They'd shaped her into the woman she was today, and she'd learned from her mistakes.

She knew when to trust and when to keep on walking.

And you should be walking now...

She ignored the warning and admitted, 'I'd outgrown my life there. I was ready to move on and when my family called, I was more than happy to have a purpose, something to leave for and...'

Her voice trailed away with her thoughts, her memories...

'And?'

Her eyes met his, their inquisitive light leaving her feeling exposed, raw. 'And lose myself in.'

He studied her intently. 'What is it about us, Bree, that we both need to lose ourselves in something else?'

This time she was ready to admit it, knew she wouldn't be judged. 'I split with my ex.'

He tilted his head to the side. 'Divorced?'

'No, thank heaven. We were engaged but I saw the light before the aisle, so to speak. What about you? Why do you think you do it?'

'You haven't worked that out already? I'm a cliché, Bree. Unhappy childhood, unhappy adult. Unwilling to commit, but more than willing to project a front that makes me irresistible to the masses.'

He was teasing, she knew he was, but she also saw the truth in it. 'And I'm not a cliché? A city girl escaping to the country in the hopes it will heal her heart?'

'Does it need healing?'

An unexpected wedge formed in her throat, the sincerity of his question momentarily flooring her. 'It did. Once upon a time.'

'But not any more?'

She shook her head. 'No.'

He scanned her face, looking for a lie she was sure, a crack in her armour. 'I'm glad to hear it.'

'And I'm glad you're glad…but I really don't want to talk about him when I could be enjoying you.' She nipped her lip on her bold statement, held her breath on his response.

'You'll hear no argument from me, Bree, but if my brother asks, I didn't seduce you, attempt to seduce you or anything between—is that agreed?'

'Agreed. I'll take full responsibility.'

'Now that hardly feels fair.'

'Doesn't it? You haven't seen what I have in mind yet… wait until you see dessert.'

His eyes danced in the low light as they travelled over her, his smile a sexy tilt. 'Which is?'

'Patience, Mr Dubois. All will be revealed.'

He chuckled. 'Promises, promises.'

A nervous flutter rose up within her. One minute she was fine, high on his attention, his flattery…the next, demons instilled by her ex would come to life, telling her to run a mile.

You're not his type. You're all lumps and bumps. You're not worthy.

The last riled her though. She knew she was worthy. With the right man. And though Theo Dubois would never be that man, he could give her the boost she needed, right now.

A boost she somehow sensed he needed in return, regardless of the charismatic grin he projected to tell the world otherwise.

'Can I help?'

He came up behind her in the kitchen, the scent of something sweet on the air and this time it wasn't all Bree.

'No, it's all ready. I'm just reheating the sauce.'

'Mmm, it smells good.' He leaned over her shoulder to see what was bubbling gently in the pan. 'Toffee sauce?'

'My aunt's recipe. The best sticky toffee pudding you've ever tasted—the best dessert even.'

'Is that a promise?'

'It's a guarantee.'

She angled her face up to him, her nose only inches from his own and he knew what he wanted to taste, and it wasn't the pudding.

'You should go and sit down. It's my turn to wait on you.'

But neither stirred other than her hand tending the sauce in the pan.

'Bree?' He dragged his teeth over his bottom lip and she tracked the movement, her soft inhalation making her nostrils flare.

'Uh-huh?'

'You know I want to kiss you right now.'

'Uh-huh.'

'But I'm not convinced I'll want to stop.'

Her lashes lifted, her gaze connected with his. 'Who said anything about stopping?'

It was all the provocation he needed and he tugged her to him, his mouth claiming hers in a kiss that he couldn't tame, couldn't soften. She tasted of toffee and wine, all sweet and warm and utterly addictive.

Her whimper filled his ears, her body filled his arms, his hold tight as he sought to feel every inch of her against him. He loved her softness, her heat, her mouth. God, her mouth. He caught her bottom lip in his teeth, the briefest of nips as her hands lifted to his hair, tugging him closer.

'You're wrong.'

She whispered a confused, 'What about?'

'It can't be the best dessert.'

'No?'

'No.'

'And why's that?'

He lowered his hands to her waist, her heat permeating his palms and making him desperate to feel beneath, to strip her of every layer and trace every curve. 'Because you are.'

Her laugh was deep, throaty. 'Why don't we put that to the test?'

'What do you have in mind?'

'Close your eyes.'

He frowned. 'Close my eyes?'

'Yes.' She peeled his hands away and he huffed out a protest that only served to make her smile. 'I want you focusing solely on your taste buds.'

Dutifully, he did as she asked. 'Was that supposed to turn me on?'

He sensed her smile, the slightest of draughts as she shook her head and turned away. He could hear the oven opening, felt its warmth and risked the tiniest of peeks, unable to resist a glimpse of her bending forward. She really did have the most appealing—

'Eyes closed!'

Busted. He squeezed them shut. 'I told you I was something of a rule breaker.'

He heard her laugh, heard her move around before him, the clink of cutlery on china, the scoop of a spoon and the scrape of a pan. Steam rose beneath his nose, the delicious scent of caramelised sugar and cream rising with it. His mouth was watering, his palms itching to reach for her once more.

'Open up.'

He parted his lips, closing them when the spoon brushed against his tongue and every taste bud zinged to life. She slid the spoon from his mouth as a groan rumbled through him. It was incredible, a mouthful of ecstasy, warm sponge cake with chewy toffee pieces and hot sauce. He savoured the lot before swallowing it down.

'You're right, that is sensational.'

'Told you…' He heard the spoon scrape the bowl once more. 'Now try this…'

He opened his mouth again. This time he got the cake and sauce with something cold and vanilla-flavoured…the contrast so satisfying, he was in food heaven.

'The ice cream is home-made too.'

'Your aunt's?'

'No. Mine.'

He opened his eyes to find her watching him, pleasure alive in her vibrant brown eyes, in the flush to her deep brown skin, too. Even her lips were parted as though savouring his every reaction. 'Does it often turn you on feeding people?'

Her sudden laugh choked out of her. 'Who said anything about being…?'

She didn't get to finish, he was already devouring her lips, swallowing her words and her surprised gasp. High on the remnants of the dessert and her, all her.

'You denying it?'

She gave a breathy, 'No.'

He broke away, took the bowl and spoon from her hand. 'My turn…eyes closed.'

Her lashes fluttered, a second's hesitation—what was she thinking? 'You going to feed me, or shall I take what I want?'

'Oh, no, I'm definitely feeding you…but you need to close your eyes first.'

She laughed softly.

'I'm serious. Eyes closed or no pudding.'

She nipped her upper lip, stifling another laugh, he was sure, and then her lashes closed, their dark crescent shape sweeping over her cheeks that were rounded with her smile and he had the deepest urge to kiss both, to cup both, but first…

'Open up.' He filled the spoon with a mix of everything, almost overloading it. 'Wider.'

A thrill ran through his body as he watched her do as he asked, her lips still stained red from her lipstick now round and waiting… When had he last wanted anyone like this?

Never.

He ignored the repercussions of the answer his mind so readily gave and focused on easing the spoon inside. Her eyes widened behind her lashes, her hum around the spoon filled with surprise, her mouth trying to smile and chew in one.

And he loved every second, every sound she made, every move of her mouth, her throat as she swallowed, finding himself doing the same though his own mouth was empty… save for the moisture her response had evoked.

'I'm not sure whether to be offended—' slowly she opened her eyes to look up at him '—or pleased that you gave me such a mouthful.'

'Call it novel.'

'Novel?'

'Most women I date wouldn't dare glance at the dessert menu, let alone devour anything on it.'

Her brows drew together. 'Must suck to be them.'

'I think it does.'

'And yet, you date them anyway.'

'Sometimes it's easier to do what is expected of me, rather than what I'd like.'

'And what is it you'd like?'

He grinned. 'To sample the entire dessert menu and go back for seconds.'

'But think of your figure.' She gave him a look of mock horror.

'That's what the gym is for…and the bedroom.'

'Now that I could definitely get on board with—the bedroom, not the gym.'

And there it was, that connection, that ease, that electric current that already had him placing the bowl on the side and pulling her to him.

She looped her arms around his neck and he bowed to kiss her but she leaned away. 'Who was right?'

'What about?'

Her eyes danced as she looked up at him, her fingers toying with the hair at his nape. 'The best dessert?'

He lowered his mouth to hers, caught her up in a kiss that had him sampling both her and the lingering sweetness of the dessert. 'We were both right.'

'How can that be?'

'Because you and that dessert make the best there is.'

Her laugh was breathy and soft, her kiss deep and provocative. 'I've decided I was wrong earlier though.'

'You have?' He was lifting her against him, deepening their kiss, his hands hungry as they travelled down her back, to her round behind that felt so luscious in his grip. 'What about?'

'You're not too much at all.'

It was his turn to chuckle. 'Thank heaven, because I won't be held accountable for all the compliments about to spill from this mouth of mine.'

She giggled more as he started for the door, taking her with him. 'Where are we going?'

'To bed…unless you have any objections.' He gazed down into her eyes and felt his entire body pulse with the lustful heat reflecting back at him.

'None, though if my aunt Clara asks, I was helping with Becca.'

'Deal.'

CHAPTER SEVEN

'THAT WAS…' BREE stared at the ceiling, a hand resting between her bare breasts, her neck resting on Theo's outstretched arm.

'Something else?' Theo suggested, eyes also on the ceiling, his head resting in his hand.

'Quite.' She smiled and looked up at him, her breath catching. The evidence of their lovemaking was plain to see—mussed-up hair, flushed cheekbones, and a light sheen. Not to mention the way his eyes sparkled in the low light of the bedside lamp.

My God. It had been something else. He was something else. Caring, attentive, he'd made her feel it was all about her and she couldn't remember ever having someone pay so much attention to every part of her.

Her toes wriggled as she recalled it all in detail, hoping to keep the memory alive long after his departure to wherever he was heading… Would it be Paris?

She recalled his tension when she'd brought up his potential return earlier and, in the relaxed aftermath of what they'd just shared, she wondered whether to broach it again. She wanted to understand, she wanted to be the ear she felt he lacked elsewhere…no matter how fleeting this would be for them, it was special. At least to her…

'Is Paris your home these days? I assumed but…'

He gave a hum in confirmation, the noise reverberating through her ear and, encouraged, she snuggled in closer, her sigh wistful.

'It must be amazing to live there.'

Another shrug, his arm beneath her curling around to stroke the hair from her face, the gesture so natural and easy. Did he even know he was doing it?

'I guess we always take for granted what we see every day, though even I admit the view of the Eiffel Tower from my apartment never gets old.'

'I bet. I'd love to see it.'

'My apartment?' It rumbled out of him, full of tease.

'The tower, cheeky!' She gave him a playful shove, met his gaze and saw his sudden frown.

'You've never been?'

'Don't look so surprised, not everyone's been to Paris, you know.'

'But I would have thought…it's just a short hop by train, when you were in London it would have been—'

'Easy, I know.'

'So why didn't you?'

Okay, so this wasn't quite going as she planned. He was learning more about her than the other way around, but it felt good to just talk…

'My ex travelled a lot with work—city-hopping was a regular thing for him—so our weekends tended to be quiet and holidays revolved around a beach and a good book.'

'But if you'd always wanted to go, surely he could have made an exception? Just for a few days…'

She gave a soft scoff. 'Hardly. I think he couldn't think of anything worse to do with his precious free time.'

'Selfish fool,' he growled and her lips quirked with the rush of warmth his defence of her triggered.

'Not really. In hindsight I don't think I ever pushed hard enough for what I wanted. I was too focused on what made him happy. The curse of being a born people-pleaser.'

'Aah, yes, happy, smiley Bree, always sacrificing her own happiness for the sake of others—I can believe it.'

'Oi.' She dug him in the ribs, sensing he was teasing her, and he chuckled.

'You think I'm joking? Anyway, it doesn't explain why you didn't go after you split.'

'You mean, go on my own?'

'Yes.'

'To the city of love?' She looked at him askance, but he merely shrugged.

And didn't he have a point? She'd had the money, the opportunity, the freedom over her own diary…

'I guess the romantic in me was saving it to do with someone special. And to be honest, the last few years I've been so busy with the bakery and making a home here, I've not thought much about holidays.'

'Are you telling me you haven't had a holiday in—how many years have you been here?'

'Three.'

'Oh, wow, Bree. Everyone needs a break once in a while.'

'I've had breaks. Sort of.'

'And what's a break for you?'

'I have Tuesdays off, and Sundays.'

'But a holiday—a real break?'

She scoured her brain. 'I did take one shortly after my aunt returned to work, but it was more because they made me than wanting to.'

'Where did you go?'

'Barcelona.'

'Nice.'

'It was okay.'

'Just okay?'

She shrugged, ignoring the way her tummy twisted with the truth. 'The weather wasn't great and, to be honest, I found travelling alone just gave me too much time to think.'

His body stiffened beneath her, his caress through her hair stalling. 'About your ex?'

'How did you guess?'

'What went wrong? Other than him being a selfish ar—'

'Theo!' She shook her head but laughed all the same; it was the best medicine after all. 'I don't know what went wrong. One day we were fine, or at least I thought we were, the next he came home from work, told me he didn't think it was working out.'

'Just like that?'

'Pretty much. Of course, I then found out he'd been seeing someone at work. She was everything I wasn't. Tall, slim, blonde…'

He wrapped her in his arms, held her closer. 'I'm sorry he put you through that.'

'I'm not, not any more. He actually did me a favour. They both did.'

He kissed the tip of her head. 'What makes you say that?'

'I'd spent so much time trying to please him, to behave how I thought he wanted me to, I'd stopped thinking about what I wanted, what I liked and didn't.'

'Like city breaks instead of beaches?'

She gave a soft laugh. 'Exactly.'

'It must have hurt though.'

Her stomach gave a little roll, her voice cracking. 'It did, yeah. From a very young age I'd had my life mapped out—a degree, a good job, marriage, kids. I was so focused on ticking boxes I didn't stop to think whether I was happy, whether they were the right kind of boxes. The job was dire, the marriage ended at the engagement stage and kids…well, I need the right man first.'

'What was the job?'

'I was a business analyst.'

'Sounds far too serious for the Bree I know and…admire.' Her heart gave a tiny leap, didn't matter that it was mostly tease, that it didn't mean anything deeper…

'It was. Coming to my aunt's rescue was a godsend on so many levels. I needed to get away from him and the city, and she needed me. I'm much happier now.'

'And what about the future—the marriage, kids?'

She snuggled in closer. She didn't feel the need to lie.

'Hopefully that'll come one day, when I feel ready to be that vulnerable again.'

'And that's what makes you better than me. I'm not sure I could come back from that kind of betrayal and still be open to it all.'

'What choice do I have? I could be bitter and let what happened drive the rest of my life or I can move on and be free of it, live my life taking each day as it comes…which sounds an awful lot like someone else I know.' She squeezed him and kissed one naked pec as he gave a soft chuckle.

'Yet somehow when it comes from you it sounds so much healthier.'

She rose up, her palms pressing into his chest as she looked down at him. 'If you think your outlook isn't healthy, doesn't that already show you're ready to make changes for the better?'

His jaw pulsed, his eyes narrowed and then he looked away, a thousand shadows chasing over his face and she sought to catch and understand every one.

'I thought I was ready.'

'You thought?'

He sensed her frown, rather than saw it. His eyes were on the ceiling, his thoughts on the recent past and the chill it sent running through his veins.

'I… I wasn't lying when I said I never had any intention of settling down, of being—' he cleared his throat '—a family man.'

'I didn't think you were.'

He looked down at her, stroked her hair out of her face, but his eyes only saw the past and Tanya. 'I thought the girl I was seeing was on the same page. Nothing serious, just the odd…'

'Hook up?'

How could she talk about his casual attitude to sex so

easily? She was so warm, so compassionate, a woman who desired her own family one day, and yet here she was looking at him, understanding him, not judging him…not yet anyway.

'But she wanted more?'

'Apparently so.' He looked back to the ceiling 'We'd been seeing each other over the past year, mainly when our paths crossed, if we were in the same city, the occasional function where a plus one was required…'

'What happened?'

He swallowed to clear his throat, but nothing could ease the tightness in his chest. 'She told me she was pregnant.'

Her body froze beneath his palm, her 'No' a gasp.

'At first, I didn't believe it was mine… I'm always safe. Always.'

'But…'

'She threw some stats at me, condom failure rates, dates, cried a little, then a lot…' It didn't sound as if it was him talking, his voice sounded distant, too thick, too raw. 'It wasn't pretty.'

'I'm sure it must have been a huge shock for her, too.' He could hear the ice creeping into her tone, the judgement, the distance building even if the space between them wasn't.

'If she'd been telling the truth.'

'What do you mean?'

He couldn't answer.

'She was lying? About being pregnant?'

His smile was as cold as he felt inside. 'Unreal, right?'

'But…no, surely not…' Her brow furrowed, her entire face screwed up in disbelief. 'You can't fake a pregnancy.'

'Turns out you can, if you try hard enough…or your man is gullible enough.'

'But what could she possibly have hoped to achieve?'

'A ring on her finger, me in her life. Turns out we hadn't been on the same page at all.'

'But to lie to you?'

'She knew certain things about my past, enough to know why I wouldn't settle down, why I could never be that guy, and she used all that against me. She knew I wouldn't want a child of mine to grow up without a father, a stable home...'

Bree shook her head. 'I can't get my head around it. I can't.'

'That's because you're a good person, Bree. Honest, caring, thoughtful. You wouldn't be capable of it but Tanya... she knew what she was doing. What she wanted.'

Her eyes widened, her voice whisper-soft. 'Tanya Bedingfield, the model?'

'One and the same.'

Her throat bobbed, her lashes lowered and he wanted to lift her chin, make her look at him, keep the bond building that eased the pain of Tanya's recent betrayal.

'Bree?'

'She's very beautiful.'

'On the outside, yes.'

'The press think you abandoned her, broke her heart.'

'The press can think and say what they like.'

'But don't you want to put them straight?'

'What's the point? It would only add fuel to the fire, make them dig deeper, ask more questions, harass us both. I'm just grateful that news of the phantom pregnancy hasn't broken.'

'Phantom pregnancy...' she repeated softly. 'How could she possibly have hoped to get away with it?'

'I think she hoped a miscarriage would explain it away when the time was right.'

'But that's—'

'Cruel? Twisted? Messed up?'

'All of the above.'

'It wasn't my proudest moment when I learned that she lied to me. But then neither was my initial reaction to the pregnancy. On some level, I guess I deserved what came next.'

'No one deserves to be treated like that!'

'I'd love to have your conviction.'

She studied him quietly and then, 'How did you find out?'

'That it wasn't real?'

She nodded.

'I came home earlier than planned, I wanted to surprise her. She'd been suffering with morning sickness and I'd been doing everything I could to make things right, to make her and the baby feel wanted, anything to make up for my earlier behaviour. Anyway, the housekeeper was there with a package.'

'A package?'

'Tampons.'

'What?'

He gave a shrug, 'She had everything delivered in, it wasn't unusual, but for a pregnant lady to be buying tampons... I panicked, worrying about her and the baby. Such an idiot, right?'

'No, Theo! How could you have possibly known?'

'I should have known in that moment, instead I was reeling and she went along with it, so relieved that I had gone down that path. But as soon as I suggested the hospital, getting her checked out, she started backtracking, making excuses, insisting she do it alone and it just didn't add up. That's when I knew.'

'You must have been devastated. The child you thought you had, the baby...'

He forced a shrug. 'It never was.'

'Still...'

'Leave it, Bree. Please. I don't want to talk any more of her, of...of it. I'd rather spend this time in other ways...'

He pulled her against him, grateful that she yielded to

him, her warm, inviting mouth moving willingly against his own. 'This is better, is it not?'

She broke their kiss, her lashes lowering as she gave a soft exhale. 'It is…but I need to leave soon.'

Chilling disappointment chased the heat through his system. 'I knew I shouldn't have said anything.'

'No.' Her eyes shot to his. 'No, I'm glad you told me, that you trust me with it, but I—I have to get back to the bakery…or rather bed.'

'This bed is perfectly big enough for the two of us.'

'It is, but I have to be up in a few hours and I'd rather not face the Spanish Inquisition by returning in the morning.'

'Your aunt?'

'The very same. And I'd hate to interrupt your beauty sleep by making my exit at four-thirty.'

'Aah, the joy of running a bakery… I'd forgotten how harsh the working hours can be.'

'And you'd know all about them because…'

'Because I worked in my fair share when I was a teen.'

She shook her head, her expression flitting between awe, curiosity, and something else, something he couldn't identify.

'You going to come back and visit tomorrow?'

'I'll come back every day until the O'Briens are better.'

'You don't have to. I'm more than capable of playing nurse.'

She laughed. 'Now, there's a delightful picture… I'll have to keep coming back just to witness it.'

He laughed with her, grateful that the mood had lifted so completely and they were back to as they were. 'Is that a promise?'

'It is and, besides, I promised Felicity I'd keep you in check.'

'Ah, so you did…'

She rolled away from him and he fought the urge to pull

her back, respecting her decision and telling himself it was wise anyway. Better to keep some distance than slip into habits that could be difficult to shift and readily lead into expectations. Expectations like Tanya herself had formed.

Though as he watched Bree slip back into her dress the urge persisted regardless.

She turned to look back at him, a hand sweeping through her dark hair, which was now wild from his attentions. 'See you tomorrow.'

He started to move off the bed. 'I'll walk you out.'

'Don't be silly—I have a key. I'll see myself out. Besides, you make a delicious parting image just as you are.'

He rested back, his grin lifting with the lightness in his chest. Had he ever met a woman more perfect?

'In that case, who am I to argue?'

Her soft laughter followed her out, kept him smiling long after her departure and filled his dreams too.

Bree was perfect.

Too perfect for a reprobate like him.

But they were on the same page. This was temporary— out of this world, but temporary. And so long as they remained in agreement, where was the harm?

CHAPTER EIGHT

'WHAT'S WITH THE huge grin?'

Bree eyed Theo suspiciously as he sauntered back into the kitchen. She was already salivating and not over the sweet mix Theo had her stirring on the stove. It was Saturday, forty-eight hours since they'd first succumbed to the pull between them and, instead of feeling in some way sated, she yearned for him top to toe.

'That was Sebastian just checking in.'

'Come to check we haven't burned the place down?'

'Something like that.'

'And you're grinning because…'

'Because my brother is having something of a moment.'

'A moment?'

'An epiphany, I reckon.'

She grinned with him, her eyes going back to the pan as the mixture started to turn into a ball. 'What kind of epiphany?'

'The kind that suggests he might be sticking around.' He came up behind her, his hand lowering to cover hers stirring away and moving in synch.

'I should hope so, he has a daughter to get to know.' She felt his heat permeate her back, resisted the urge to lean back into him and succumb to the other ideas that never seemed too far from her mind when she was in his presence. None of them would do with Becca colouring in at the centre island behind them.

'That he does, and that looks pretty ready to me.' He slipped his hand between her and the stove to turn off the heat and she felt her entire body burn with the brush of his fingers, her eyes colliding with his and reading the same thoughts simmering back at her.

'What's next?' she breathed.

'The eggs.'

She nodded, but her head was on her heart. Aunt Clara was right, Theo Dubois was trouble. And the more she got to know him, the more that trouble grew.

It was a good thing he would be leaving soon, out of sight, out of mind—unless…if his brother was sticking around, did that mean he would be, too?

And where did that leave her safety net—his imminent departure?

'What about you?' She swallowed the bubble of nerves. 'What will you do if Sebastian decides to stay?'

'Funny that, my brother asked the same question.'

'Great minds…'

He gave a soft laugh. 'Yeah, well, I'm no closer to an answer. Paris is calling and I have things I need to take care of there, but now…' His eyes caught on hers, so much passing between them.

'Now?' she prompted softly, and his eyes flickered.

He took a drawn-out breath before lowering his gaze. 'Now we need to add the eggs…'

'Eggs?' Not what she was expecting to hear…

'Ooh, eggs!' Becca blurted, saving Bree from her sudden funk. 'Can I crack them?'

She turned and smiled at the little girl.

'Sure!' Theo was already crossing the kitchen to lift her from the stool and bring her to the counter. 'You remember how I showed you?'

She nodded emphatically, her eyes sparkling, her smile lighting up the entire room. He pulled another stool out and set it before the stove, lifting her onto it and standing behind her in case she should slip.

Bree took in the protective gesture with a smile. 'You make a good team.'

Becca beamed. 'We made breakfast for Mummy and

Daddy.' Then she frowned. 'They couldn't eat much of it though.'

'I'm sure they thought it was very tasty.'

'They did, but I don't think their poorly tummies did.'

'Well, I'm sure with you looking after them they will be much better soon.'

Bree smiled up at Theo, loving the bond he'd so readily formed with the little girl. Couldn't he see for himself what a great father he'd make? How much love he had to offer given the chance?

She hated Tanya for what she'd done, opening his mind to the possibility, only to crush the dream before it became a reality.

'Right, you ready, kiddo?' He handed an egg to Becca, who took it gingerly. 'You drop it in, and Bree will stir.'

Bree took up the spoon and watched as he helped Becca crack the egg into the pan.

'Thank you, honey.' She stirred the mixture, her thoughts going back to their conversation and Sebastian's potential intent to stay. 'What will it mean for your plans for the estate, the hotel, if he stays?'

'I'm not sure. I think he's re-evaluating everything right now. I don't think he ever saw himself returning to Elmdale, let alone as a family man. It's going to take some adjustment.'

He could have been talking about himself, too, she knew. Yet watching him with Becca, seeing how good he was with her…and he'd already admitted that he was glad to be back in Elmdale, that he liked being here.

'But you think he will?' she pressed, trying to ignore the worrying direction of her thoughts, the race to her pulse, the spark of hope flickering to life even though she knew it was unwise. Theo could do what he liked. Live wherever he liked. She shouldn't want him to stay. Sebastian, yes. For her friend and their daughter's sake, yes. But his brother…

'If he knows what's good for him…' He flashed her a quick smile, his attention returning to Becca and the second egg. 'And it makes sense to keep the estate as a family home. It's on Flick's doorstep, the perfect base for him to explore what the future holds without the pressure of having to find somewhere to live.'

'And what about you?'

Bree! What are you doing?

'What about me?' He passed Becca the egg. 'Wait until Bree has it all mixed in, kiddo, and then you can crack this one.'

'Will you stay at the estate for a bit?'

He laughed. 'Not while they're getting reacquainted. I know my brother and that spark in his eye hasn't existed in a long time. I'm giving them all the space they need while that exists.'

Her lips quirked as she read between the lines, her laugh soft. 'Wise, very wise.'

'As for the future… I don't know. Paris feels less like home when I think of Sebastian moving back here.'

'They say home is where the heart is.'

Again, he caught her eye, again the connection resurfaced, and she found herself drowning in those captivating blue eyes, wanting to ask so much more, beg for so much more…

'Can I crack it now?'

Saved by Becca!

Again!

'Sure.' She stepped back as Theo helped with the egg, creating space though it wasn't enough, not for her heart.

'Can I have a go at stirring, too?' Becca wiped her fingers off on her dress and reached for the spoon.

'Of course, you can.'

She scooted back in as the little girl took over and Theo moved away. 'I'll prep the pastry bag.'

'Okay.' She watched him go, missing the warmth of his body beside her and knowing her intent to keep her heart out of their relationship had failed miserably.

Did she regret what they'd shared though?

No. Absolutely not.

It was a high price to pay but worth the future pain, surely?

'I've been thinking…' He turned to look at her, something about his expression making her panicked heart skip a beat.

'A dangerous pastime for you,' she tried to tease.

His chuckle was edgy, the hand raking through his hair even more so. Was he nervous? What could possibly make him…?

'Very funny. But if you quit with the teasing, I was thinking about heading back to Paris the week after next.'

Disappointment swamped her, her smile faltering. 'You w-were?'

'I have a meeting to attend but…well…' His hand was back in his hair, uncertainty enhancing his boyish charm as his eyes failed to meet hers. 'I wondered if you might… I thought you could… I thought you might…'

'Theo Dubois—' she pursed her lips, bemused '—are you tongue-tied?'

A bashful grin. 'I think I might be.'

Becca looked at him, her frown confused. 'You have a tie in your tongue?'

They both laughed. 'Something like that.' He looked at Bree properly. 'I thought it would be an opportunity for you to come with me. My treat. As friends. Just two people, in Paris, eating out, drinking, relaxing. I can show you the sights and you're long overdue a holiday and if your aunt can spare you…'

His cheeks flushed deeper with every word and, heaven help her, Bree's heart was trying to leap out of her chest.

As friends. He'd qualified it, made it clear it didn't mean anything more, but he'd listened to her. He knew how much she wanted to go, knew how much she didn't want to do it alone, but to do it with him? Was that even wise?

And who on earth proposed such a trip when they'd known you less than a week? Or was that just the way it went in his jet-set world where money was no object and the entire world really was your playground?

'No rush to decide now, but the offer is there. I have a spare room. You'd have your own space. I know how much you want to see the Eiffel Tower and it can be my way of saying thank you.'

'For what?' was all she could manage as the offer truly hit home. That it wasn't some joke or figment of her over-active imagination.

'I daren't say in front of this one.'

'Theo!'

His grin widened. 'Okay. Okay. For helping me out. Keeping me sane. Reminding me of how much fun it is to bake. To talk it out. To take pleasure in the simple things again.'

'The simple things?' she repeated, brows lifting.

'Not that you are simple by any stretch of the imagination.'

It should have had her laughing, taking his joke and brushing it off, instead she was caught up in the heat firing behind his eyes, the genuine gratitude. Had it helped him heal a little? Talking it out with her? Just as he had helped her to move on, to realise her own worth, her own appeal…to go after what she wanted and not live in fear of the consequences.

'Are you going to kiss now?' Their eyes shot to Becca, her blue eyes big and round as she looked up at them.

'Absolutely not,' Bree blurted, taking the bag Theo had

sourced and opening it. 'You're going to scoop the mixture into here for me and then we're going to get these *chouquettes* in the oven before this mix is over-mixed!'

'Spoilsport,' Theo muttered and she poked him in the ribs.

'Behave! You told me these French fancies were quick and easy to make.'

'They are…when you don't get distracted.'

She smiled. At least she wasn't alone in the distraction.

The panic perhaps, but the distraction…no, they were both well and truly lost in that.

And Paris. Could she? Did she dare?

Aunt Clara would have kittens and then some.

But there was no denying the appeal…

Who better to share Paris with than the man who had made her heart beat again?

The man who had made it beat but was only going to be around for the short term…

And then what?

When she'd left London and Leon behind, she'd had to find herself all over again. And she loved her new life, her new home, the new her…and with Theo, she felt confident, happy, in control of taking what she wanted.

But when he left…would she still feel the same, or would she be back to square one, her heart torn in two and all alone?

No. She would never be alone. She had her family, her friends, she had Elmdale…

It was enough pre-Theo; it would be enough again.

It had to be.

Theo had well and truly lost it.

He didn't know whether to blame Tanya, Elmdale, his brother or the little girl currently piping little mounds of dough onto the baking sheet Bree had prepared for her. They were a tag team in the kitchen, him and his little shadow, and he'd miss her when her family checked out.

You'll miss Bree more though. The true cause of your impulsive invitation to Paris.

Because he knew their time was coming to an end. Soon the O'Briens would leave and then there would be no reason for Bree to keep calling by. The B & B would be empty, he'd have served his purpose and fulfilled his promise to his brother.

And then Paris had struck him—Paris and Bree's dream to go there.

The perfect excuse to spend more time together.

No commitment, no promises, just more time.

But to what end?

'Theo?' Bree nudged him back to reality. 'Becca's asking if she can sprinkle on the sugar.'

'Oh, yeah, sure!' He picked up the bowl of crushed sugar cubes. 'Go for it. You'd normally use pearl sugar, but this is the next best thing and you'll hardly notice a difference.'

'A bit hard to notice the difference when I've never had one before...' She helped Becca with the bowl as the girl scooped out the sugar.

'You've never had a *chouquette*?'

'Never been to Paris, never had a *chouquette*. Are you trying to rub it in?'

'Absolutely not.'

'And you will go to Paris, Aunt Bree. Uncle Theo is going to take you.' Becca stated it so matter-of-factly and he couldn't help but smile. If ever he needed an eager accomplice in his master plan, he had unwittingly gained one.

'If Aunt Bree agrees...' the woman herself murmured,

her eyes alive with spark as she looked at him and shook her head.

'If Aunt Bree knows what's good for her, she will.'

'You know, Uncle Theo can be frustratingly annoying when he wants to be.'

'Annoying. Why?' Becca's frown of confusion made a return. 'When my brother's being annoying it's because he pulls my hair. Does Uncle Theo pull your hair?'

Bree's face was a picture. He had. Once. And the memory had heat streaking through his limbs, hers, too, if her glow and stifled choke was anything to go by.

'I'll just get these in the oven,' she blurted.

'Great idea. And you, little miss, can show me the masterpiece you've been working on.'

He swung her down, cherishing the little giggle of delight she gave.

Yes, he'd miss Becca and their time together. She made him feel good about himself, made him feel like a better person. Just like Bree. He enjoyed his time with the two of them. Getting more out of a simple baking session than he had in the boardroom in a long time.

If ever.

Maybe some of his brother's surprising happiness was starting to rub off on him.

And maybe this has more to do with Bree than you care to admit?

'This is Bree in the bakery,' Becca was saying, waving a hand at the picture before her of a woman in a brightly coloured dress with the biggest smile and even bigger flounce of black hair.

'And this is you...' She pointed to a triangular-shaped guy with the most ridiculously sized blond quiff and another big grin.

'Bree is perfect, but I'm not quite sure about—'

'Oh, yes, that's definitely you.' It was Bree who spoke, her eyes on the image but her laughter all for him.

'You think?'

She nodded, her eyes alive, her mouth begging to be kissed.

'Right, munchkin!' He nudged Becca towards the doorway. 'I think you best run upstairs and check if your mum and dad would like anything bringing up.'

'Oh, I did promise, didn't I?'

'You did.' Off she hopped and he watched her go, quiet, contemplative.

'If I didn't know any better, I'd say you were getting quite attached to that little girl.'

He shook his head, his smile goofy. 'It's been an eye-opening week, I'll admit that.'

'Eye-opening enough to realise you deserve more from your life?'

His gaze sharpened, his intent to kiss her as soon as they were alone falling by the wayside.

'Come on, Theo. You put on this front, this laissez-faire playboy attitude, but you're so much more than that.'

'No, Bree. I'm not. You ask Tanya. You ask any other woman that I've dated.'

'You can tell yourself that all you like.'

'I'm telling you.'

She stepped towards him, hooked her hands into his hair and his heart skittered. 'You can tell me all you like, but your actions tell a different story...'

And before he could utter a denial, she was kissing him. Kissing him with so much passion, so much care, and he was lost in it. The all-consuming fire that rushed his veins, the feeling of belonging unlike anything he had ever known. 'What are you trying to do to me, Bree?'

'I like to think I'm showing you another way.'

'Well, let me show you another. Let me show you Paris and all its delights. Let me spoil you for a change.'

She chuckled against his lips. 'You sell it so well.'

'And you deserve it, so it's a win-win.'

'I'll think about it…so long as you agree to think about how different your future could look if you stopped obsessing with the past.'

'Don't, Bree.'

'Don't what?'

'Don't make us a cliché.'

She frowned up at him, her hands frozen in his hair. 'What does that mean?'

'I'm a playboy. You're a kind-hearted country—' she raised her brows and the corners of his mouth twitched up '—ex-city girl. You can't fix me and we're not about to run off into the sunset together.'

She gave the slightest flinch. 'I didn't say we were.'

'That look in your eye says otherwise.'

'For your information, that look in my eye is telling you I think you're worth more than you give yourself credit for. It tells you I'm pinching myself to have been invited to come to Paris with you. That it doesn't feel real and it's a lot to take in. It says nothing more.'

'You sure about that?'

'Positive.' Her fingers were once more moving, the tension in her body dissipating beneath his palms. 'So, you can tell that ego you claim not to have to stand down, and I'm thinking about it.'

'Thinking about it?'

She nodded. 'I'll think about coming to Paris.'

'Well, in that case, while you're thinking about it, think about this and how much better it could be with the Eiffel Tower as your backdrop.'

And then he kissed her as deeply as she would permit,

burying the moment of panic with what felt safe and sure—the chemistry, the passion, the connection.

She knew who he was, he'd never promised more.

No hearts would be broken, there were no promises to keep, implied or otherwise...

And who are you trying to convince?

CHAPTER NINE

'ARE YOU SURE you're okay?' Bree asked her friend for the umpteenth time. Felicity had arrived at the bakery just after closing with a face that demanded an interrogation and indicated a strong need for coffee. Neither woman had suggested the more obvious choice of an alcoholic beverage at the B & B's bar, both having their own reasons to avoid said establishment, but both staring at the building across the way as if they could readily teleport there any second.

Longing. That was what Felicity's expression looked like.

For what, Bree wanted to understand.

She knew her own dilemma and it was six foot three of gorgeous male hunk.

Perhaps Felicity's dilemma wasn't so different…but the impression Theo had given of his brother's relationship with her friend had been quite encouraging.

Whereas Theo and Bree…she'd successfully avoided any alone time with him since Sunday. The day the O'Briens had checked out. It was now Tuesday. Almost two days without any one-on-one time as she sought to keep a clear head and considered his Paris proposition. She deserved a bleeding medal.

'I slept with him.'

Bree choked on her coffee, her eyes widening over her mug as Felicity's confession chimed with her own secret. 'Not what I was expecting to hear just yet.'

She understood her own impatience to jump Theo, but Felicity had always been the level-headed one. Steady, measured, never one to act without thinking it through properly. Unlike Bree and her equally uncontrollable mouth.

'No?' Felicity looked back at her, a semi-smile on her

face. 'The day I left with him you were all about me getting my end away.'

She screwed her face up. 'I was, wasn't I? But then you were very much "no way". What changed?'

'Everything…and nothing.' Felicity dropped her head into her hands with a groan and Bree reached across the table.

'Hey, what happened?'

'I was an idiot,' she mumbled. 'Despite all the warning signs, my better judgement, I let him in again.'

'Oh, honey.' Bree rounded the table and scooted up next to her on the bench, put her arm around her.

'How could I be so stupid, Bree?' She shook her head. 'To fall for him all over again when I know we can't work.'

'Who says you can't?'

'I do. He does. We both do.'

'Was the sex that bad?' she teased, already regretting their choice of coffee over alcohol.

'No, the sex was…the sex was amazing! But he'd already made his feelings clear, that this isn't about love for him. It's about sex, duty, money and all the stuff I couldn't care less for…'

'I don't know,' Bree said, with the same hint of tease. 'Good sex isn't all that easy to come by.'

'Bree!'

'Sorry. Too soon?'

Her friend shook her head, her smile watery. 'You're— oh, God, what is that guy doing?'

Bree spun to see what had caught her friend's eye. There was a guy in a boiler suit approaching the B & B and Theo was there waiting to greet him, decked out in jeans and a sweater. A sweater that fitted his build like his many, many tees—far too snugly.

'I think that might be the boiler man.'

'The boiler man?'

Bree looked back at her. 'You didn't know?'

'Know what?'

She winced. 'I think Theo has designs on getting a new system installed. He thinks the old one is on its way out and wanted to do something nice…for you.'

'Nice?' Her head was back in her hands. 'What is it with these Ferrington—Dubois—men that they think they can simply splash their cash about and all will be right with the world?'

'I guess it is kind of sweet that he wants to help. And Bill was saying the thing could do with an upgrade. There's only so much magic he can work. And let's face it, they can spare the cash, right?'

'I've had enough of Sebastian throwing his money at me and Angel.'

'This isn't Sebastian, this is Theo, and…' Bree shrugged. 'I don't know, I feel like he needs to do this. He…he feels the weight of what went down all those years ago and wants to make amends.'

Felicity's eyes narrowed. 'You know what happened, don't you?'

'If you mean the fight…' Felicity nodded. 'He feels terrible, hon. He thinks it's his fault Sebastian had to step in…'

'And hurt their grandfather?'

'Yes. You should have seen him, Felicity. When he told me. The guilt… He feels like he owes Sebastian, owes all of you for the years you missed out on.'

'But it wasn't his fault.'

'I know, I told him but…maybe just let him have this, yeah?' She gestured across the way to where the men were heading back inside. 'Let him help and clear his conscience a little. The man needs it.'

'Oh, my God.'

'Oh, my God, what?'

'You've…you've really got the hots for him, haven't you?'

She brazened it out with a smile. 'Me and almost the entire female population.'

Felicity was shaking her head. 'Not you though. You told me he didn't have you fooled, you made me think you were impervious to his Dubois charm, you...you... Oh, man, I've been so selfish, caught up in my own drama when I should have been looking out for you.'

'Hey, don't be so dramatic! I fancy him, that's all. And when you get to know him, it's hard not to fall...just a little.'

Felicity was staring at her as if she'd grown two heads and she hurried on.

'He's a good guy. Sweet and thoughtful beneath all that arrogance and the body chiselled from granite, not to mention the cover-model grin.'

Felicity was still shaking her head. Her expression not too dissimilar to the one Aunt Clara wore every time Bree said she was popping to the B & B or Theo nipped into the bakery for some extra food when they all knew the O'Briens had been too sick to eat.

Aunt Clara wasn't blind, and neither was Felicity.

'You know his reputation, Bree!'

'I do. But I'm surprised you do when just last week you didn't know him from Adam.'

'I've had time to read up since then—about him and his brother—and I don't like it, Bree. You look as caught up as me and that's not a good thing. We don't even know how long they'll stick around once that hotel is up and running.'

Wait. Felicity didn't know that Sebastian was reconsidering his options on that score? Well, she could hardly say anything. It wasn't her place. Maybe Theo had misunderstood his brother's intentions. Or maybe Sebastian didn't want to say anything until it was a done deal.

In either case, she was sure about one thing...

'I hardly think Sebastian is going to do another disappearing act, not now he has you and Angel.'

'Angel. He has Angel. Not me.'

'Right, of course. But that man isn't about to abandon you again, honey. I know it.'

Her friend made a non-committal sound, her eyes drifting back to the B & B.

'It'll be okay, Felicity. Whatever happens, he'll make sure you're taken care of, that you both are.'

'I don't want to be taken care of. I want— Gah! It doesn't matter, ignore me.' She turned to look back at Bree. 'I'm more worried about you now. It's enough to have my head all over the place but if Sebastian's return brings misery your way, too, I won't forgive myself.'

'There's nothing to forgive. I'm a big girl, capable of choosing whom I sleep with.'

Felicity's eyes bugged out of her head. 'You've *slept* with him?'

Bree looked to the open door into the back where the stairs led up to the flat above and the living room where her aunt and uncle were catching up on the soaps. 'Easy. Aunt Clara would shoot me if she knew.'

'She'd shoot him first, I bet!'

They both laughed and Bree lowered her voice. 'Anyway, you're hardly one to talk. Sebastian's been back in your life just as long and you've already slept with him.'

'But we have history, a daughter…'

Bree stared her down. 'And you've not seen him in sixteen years.'

'Fair point.' Felicity gave a muted laugh. 'What a pair we are.'

'A pair that were long overdue some excitement in the bedroom, I reckon, and for that I'm grateful to you for bringing these hunks our way.'

Her friend laughed all the more. 'How can you say that, Bree?'

'Because aside from the weight you're carrying around,

there's a spring in your step and that's all down to him. I know because I have it, too.'

'But what are we going to do?'

'Keep our hearts protected and our heads in the game. Take what they're willing to give, enjoy it and move on at the end of it.'

'You make it sound so easy.'

'Isn't it?'

Felicity's eyes drifted back to her B & B. 'I'm really not so sure.'

'That's because you have history and you have Angel. You must protect her as much as yourself. It complicates things.'

'Perhaps. But what about you? Do you know where you stand with him?'

'One hundred per cent.'

'Which is?'

'We're friends. Kind of. Friends with benefits.'

'And you're happy.'

'Oh, believe me, he makes sure I'm happy.'

Her friend giggled. 'Why do I feel like I need to put my hands over my ears at this point?'

They laughed together, and the sound trickled off as Bree sobered up and looked to her friend of three years who was now closer than any sister could be.

'But seriously, honey, don't you waste any more time worrying about me. I know what I'm getting into, or out of, rather, and the ball is in my court.'

'It is?'

She nodded. 'He's invited me to Paris with him.'

'Paris? When?'

'Week after next.'

'And? Are you going?'

'I think I should.'

'You think?'

Bree shrugged, sipping her coffee as she tried to understand the gripe to her gut when she thought of going. She understood the excitement, the thrilling race to her pulse when she considered staying in his apartment, maybe even sharing his bed—they'd spent enough time in his B & B bed, after all—and with the Eiffel Tower as her promised backdrop, too. Just wow!

But the confidence she was trying to project to Felicity had its cracks, her heart, too, and she knew how vulnerable she was. She wasn't stupid or naïve on that score.

'I haven't asked Aunt Clara if they can do without me yet and I don't want to leave them in the lurch. Not when there's still the extra traffic pushing through.'

Felicity grimaced. 'The draw of the Dubois brothers.'

'Indeed.'

'But you know they'd be glad to see you take a break. They've been on at you for ever about how you need a proper holiday.'

'Which is pretty much what Theo said.'

Felicity's eyes narrowed on her. 'So, the ball is in your court, you know he's not offering anything long term, but he is offering you a free trip to Paris. And you still haven't agreed?'

Bree nodded. 'That about sums it up.'

'So, what am I missing?' Then her eyes sparked to life. 'Oh, wait! I get it! You're letting him stew a little. Playing hard to get.'

That was exactly what she was doing. Leaving him to stew on his offer and not jumping on the opportunity as her body wanted to. It paid to be a little restrained where Theo was concerned. It gave her time to keep her emotions in check and her heart locked away.

Locked away? Yeah, right.

'I like it, Bree.' Felicity picked up her mug in both hands, positioned it beneath her chin but didn't drink, her eyes turning distant once more. 'Playing hard to get beats another trip to Brokenheartsville, for sure.'

'Amen to that.'

'Are you avoiding me?'

Bree started. She'd been so deep in thought she hadn't even heard the tinkle of the bakery door opening but Theo's deep and sexy rumble had the power to break through anything. Her common sense most of all.

She swept her hair back from her face and knew she was sporting something of a sweaty glow. She'd been steam-cleaning the floor for the last hour, twice as long as it needed, nowhere near long enough to get him out of her head.

And here he was...

'Theo!'

'At your service.' He leaned back on the door, everything about him cool and relaxed save for those piercing blue eyes that were scrutinising her so closely she felt stripped bare, her vulnerabilities laid out ready for him to stamp all over them.

She smiled brightly. 'You here to help me clean?'

'I was thinking of serving you in other ways, but now the B & B is empty I can certainly return the favour and lend a hand here.'

Even when flirting, he had to be nice. Why couldn't he flirt and be evil? Maintain a bit of balance. Help her to keep him at a distance, the kind of distance she'd been trying all the more to maintain since her chat with Felicity two days ago.

'That's not necessary.'

'Which one? The helping you clean or...'

His eyes trailed over her and her whole body burned with a lascivious heat. He opened his mouth to provide the detail and she shook her head, her voice as sharp as the pang down low. 'Shh! My aunt will hear you.'

He eased away from the door, his eyes flitting to the hallway and back to her as he closed the distance between them, his hand closing around hers on the mop.

'I've missed you, Bree.'

She wet her lips, looked up into his eyes that were far too sincere and far too disarming. 'It's only been a few days.'

'But I've seen you every day since my arrival, then the O'Briens check out on Sunday and you stop calling by. I'm starting to think you were using me to get to Becca.'

She gave a laugh, pitched with her racing pulse. 'You got me.'

'I hope so, because the alternative is too depressing to even consider.'

She frowned. 'The alternative?'

He reached up to cup her cheek and her heart soared at the simple touch. 'That you're afraid to be alone with me.'

She gave a breathless laugh. 'Don't be ridiculous.'

'Is it ridiculous? Or did my invitation to Paris scare you off so entirely?'

'Of course not.' She tried to sound steady, determined, unbroken. 'I've been busy here, and without the O'Briens to look after, you didn't need me on hand any more.'

'But that's where you're wrong…'

His chest was against hers, his body so close, his power over her impossible to fight, to resist. Her head was swimming, her mouth was dry and her limbs were giving in, her body folding into his. She wanted him to kiss her, wanted it so badly she could feel her eyes pleading with him as her lips parted. 'I am?'

He nodded, his head lowering. 'I do need you on hand to tend to this fire inside me. You've entranced me, Bree, and I'm—'

'What in the devil?'

They leapt apart, their eyes snapping to the hallway as they both declared in unison, 'Aunt Clara!'

It would have been funny to hear him say it if it hadn't been for her aunt's murderous expression, her hands fisted on her hips. 'So, this is what's been keeping you down here, or rather who...'

Theo raked a hand through his hair. 'I'm sorry for keeping her. I just wanted to offer my help in return for all the hours Bree has chipped in at the B & B.'

Aunt Clara's eyes narrowed. 'Really?'

'Absolutely.'

'Well, you're a bit late, we closed over an hour ago.'

'And I figured I could offer my services cleaning up, any heavy lifting, I'm even a dab hand at the DIY. Bree can testify to that.'

'I can.' Bree nodded and then wanted to slap herself. Why was she even helping him in this silly endeavour? The last thing she needed was Aunt Clara and Theo under the same roof for any length of time.

'Well, if you're a fan of a good roast, you can help us with dinner.' Her uncle appeared waving the metaphorical white flag and sending all of their jaws dropping to the floor. 'I think Clara thought we were hosting Christmas eight months early judging by the volume of food upstairs.'

Theo was the first to recover, his grin full of his infamous charm. 'Is that what smells so good?'

'Sure is.'

Both Bree and Aunt Clara gaped at the men. They couldn't be serious.

Bree tried for an easy smile. 'I'm sure Theo has better things to be doing with his time.'

'Not in the slightest,' the man himself said. 'I'd love to join you, so long as you ladies are happy to have me?'

'But... Aunt Clara?'

Bree looked at the woman in question, who blustered and

boiled and then shook her head and threw her hands in the air. 'Fine! Just you be sure none of those sneaky reporters try and weasel their way in again. Why, just this morning one tried to play the friend-of-the-friend card and I'm not having it. I'm not.'

She glanced beyond the glass to illustrate her point and frowned at the quiet streets.

'As you can see, they've all cleared off. I think they've had their pickings for now.'

Until they realised that his brother, Sebastian Dubois, the reclusive billionaire, was not only out of hiding but a father...and he'd found out sixteen years after the fact.

Bree shook off the thought. 'It's hardly his fault though, Aunt Clara; he can't control the reporters any more than we can.'

Her aunt harrumphed and her uncle stepped in. 'You see, Clara, the guy is well overdue a break and now the excess of food won't go to waste. I put money on the big guy being able to put away plenty. You eaten today, lad?'

'Not since breakfast, I've been busy cleaning the B & B before I leave tomorrow.'

'You're leaving?' Cold washed over her and she winced at the disappointment in her voice, winced even more when Theo's far too astute gaze landed on her, his mouth quirking just a little.

'I am. The guests have all checked out and my services are no longer required.'

'You're going back to Paris?' But he'd said the week after next, not tomorrow!

'Via the Ferrington Estate, yes. I figure I'll spend a couple of days there first, catch up with my brother and then it's back to Paris.'

She stared at him, wishing her body would quit pining. He wasn't even gone yet and his absence had triggered a pang so deep it took her aunt Clara's exclamation to snap her out of it.

'Fabulous!' She clapped her hands together. 'Well, in that case let's make sure we give you a proper send-off! *Bon voyage* and all that *je ne sais pas*!'

'I think she means *quoi*,' Bree murmured as her aunt bustled out of the kitchen and her uncle chuckled.

'Don't you worry about her, love, she's a big softy really. As for you…' he nodded towards Theo '…just make sure you compliment her cooking and you'll be reet as rain.'

'If you're sure,' Theo said.

'Never been more.' He pounded Theo's back and encouraged him forward in one. 'But if we stand here any longer it'll go cold and I, for one, hate a skin on the gravy.'

Theo chuckled. 'Me, too.'

'Me, three,' Bree muttered, shoving the mop in the cupboard and following them up, all the while trying to ignore how much she cared about his sudden departure…not that it was all that sudden. He'd always said the week after next, only she'd thought he'd meant the back end of the week, not the start.

She found him waiting at the top of the stairs. 'Ladies first.'

She shook her head at the laughter in his eyes. What did it take to push Theo Dubois out of his comfort zone? Because dinner with her family certainly felt as if it should…

'Don't you ever lose your cool?' she asked under her breath as her uncle joined her aunt in the kitchen.

'I think you do that enough for the both of us.'

'What's that supposed to mean?'

'Hey, I don't mean it in a bad way. That first day I met you, you were on fire defending Flick's property. In fact, I might have referred to you as a fiery skirt…'

A laugh choked out of her. 'You didn't!'

'I did. And since then, all I've seen is passion. You're overflowing with it, and that's no bad thing.'

And there he went again, layering the flattery with what should have been a negative and, darn it, she was swooning, her knees softening, her limbs all warm and…oh, God, he was going to kiss her. He was leaning in and then his lips were against hers, the shock of it maximising the thrill and then he was gone and she was swallowing back a groan.

'Now we best go join them before your aunt joins us. I really don't fancy my chances if we're caught a second time round…'

A true family dinner…

This was a first for Theo. A first since he'd left the Ferrington Estate behind, its controlling patriarch and all the misery his grandfather had dished out daily.

And even then, he couldn't recall a family dinner where love and conversation prevailed, and bitterness and reprimand were saved for another time. As a lad, he'd become so used to dining with his grandfather's retribution hanging over him that food and discomfort had come hand in hand.

Until he'd hit Paris, of course. And then it had been about freedom, and crafting, and losing himself in whatever task his hands could deliver.

But here, with Bree's family, even under her aunt's careful scrutiny, he felt relaxed. Happy. Love as evident as the abundance of food on the table. He knew her aunt's animosity stemmed from just that—her love for her niece—and he got it. He totally got it. But he couldn't stay away.

It wasn't as if he hadn't tried, wanting to give her the space she so obviously needed, but just knowing she was here within reach had seen him visiting the bakery multiple times over the past few days. Always under the guise of buying extra for the B & B, but the only thing benefitting had been his waistline and not in a good way. There was only so much weight exercise could shift and if he didn't get this hankering under control, it wasn't just the baked goods he'd be buying, it would be new jeans, too!

Paris was the end game.

If he could get her to agree to Paris, he could drop the ruse. He'd have the trip on the horizon, something to look forward to and then they'd have some real time together. No interference from family members, friends, the B & B, the bakery…just them.

A proper break together and then a parting of ways, and life would go back to how it was…

'It must be a pleasant relief to have the press gone?' her uncle said to him around a mouthful, tugging him from his thoughts. 'Though I have to admit it's been great for business. We haven't been able to keep up with demand this week.'

'I'm sorry for the disruption we've brought to the village.' Theo filled his fork with an array of veg and turkey. 'It certainly wasn't our intention when we came to stir up such a fuss.'

He popped the food into his mouth and gave a hum of appreciation. It was delicious. Homely and satisfying. When was the last time he'd had a proper roast? Too long ago…

Aunt Clara caught his eye, the hint of a smile touching her lips. He'd done something right. At last.

'Ah, but you came back, and for Felicity it's the best thing you could have done,' her uncle was saying. 'Whether you go down the road of this hotel or not, the unfinished business between your brother and that lovely woman needed addressing.'

Theo's eyes narrowed, his brain racing—did he know Sebastian was Angel's father? Did they all know?

Hell, everyone knew everyone's business in Elmdale so it stood to reason they would at least suspect it, but nobody had said anything to the press. Or if they had, the press had yet to speculate on it publicly.

'I agree. I've not seen my brother this happy in a long time.'

Her aunt and uncle exchanged a look, the smallest of smiles. He hoped he hadn't painted too rosy a picture without any solid evidence…but he'd felt the need to say something upbeat.

'So, what will you do?' Aunt Clara piped up, throwing the focus on him, and he almost choked on his turkey. 'You going to plonk the resort on our doorstep and then leave us to pick up the pieces in the community?'

'Clara!'

'What, Alf? It's true, isn't it?'

So much for being upbeat…

'I understand that there are concerns but we believe it has the potential to bring more money into Elmdale, raise its profile, attract more visitors… You've already seen a boost in trade, but this would be a sustained one.'

'It's not all about the money, young man.'

He took in the woman's sharpened gaze, could practically see her fluffing up her feathers to protect her brood. This wasn't about the village, the hotel, this was about Felicity and Bree and the risk he and his brother posed to their happiness.

He shifted in his seat, trying to come up with a response that didn't sound dismissive or, worse, as if he didn't care. Because he did. Too much.

'The man has a point, Clara.' Her uncle came to his rescue. 'You can't deny the amount we've put through our tills this week. It'll set us up until the May break for sure.'

She snorted into her wine glass, her eyes not leaving Theo's. 'You and your brother can put a positive spin on it all you like but what if your presence has other consequences? That poor girl has lost her grandmother, brought up her daughter single-handed and now what? Heaven knows what promises he's feeding her and who knows whether he'll stick to them when the past proves he's capable of leaving her high and dry…no offence.'

No offence and yet he felt as if she was throwing those words at him, too. Was that what she thought he was doing? Turning up here, luring Bree out with a load of empty promises that would eventually rip her apart?

He felt the colour drain from his face, his eyes flitting to Bree—did she think the same?

'Aunt Clara, whatever happens with Sebastian and Felicity it's none of our business, but from what I can tell, the man is trying to do what's right. For Felicity and Angel. Let's not be so quick to judge, yeah?'

She gave Theo an apologetic smile and he tried to return it but inside his gut writhed. He tried to focus on the conversation, tried to keep it on Sebastian. 'My brother is a good man, the best, he will take care of them. I can you promise you that.'

'And I reckon it will all work itself out,' her uncle declared. 'Given time and freedom away from the press interfering. Mark my words, brighter days are coming.'

Bree gave a pitched laugh. 'And now you sound like a TV ad, Uncle.'

Alf shrugged. 'If the phrase fits…now eat else it will be Christmas by the time we get to dessert!'

Theo managed a laugh, her uncle putting him at ease as quick as her aunt had him on hot coals. And then there was Bree. Her face aglow, her eyes bright, her cheeks round with her smile…and his chest ached.

Would she say 'yes' to Paris?

After her aunt's obvious warning, he wasn't so sure and two hours later, finally alone in the flat's tiny kitchen, he asked, 'Will you come with me?'

She turned to look at him, dishcloth in hand, her eyes… wary. She nipped her bottom lip and went back to the dish she was cleaning. 'I'm still thinking about it.'

'What's there to think about, Bree?' She passed him the dish to dry but her gaze didn't reach his. 'You're long over-due a holiday and the press are calming down. When I clear out, most will likely leave, and the bakery will quieten down for a period…'

Until the news broke about Angel's true father, sure, but there was time before that happened. He hoped.

'I know. I just…' She stopped washing and met his eye. 'Doesn't it feel weird to you, going away together when we're not…you know…?'

They eyed the open doorway, absorbed her aunt and un-cle's easy conversation coming from the living area before looking back at each other. He resisted the urge to reach out and stroke a stray curl behind her ear, to coax her into accepting the one way he knew how…

'Can't we just be friends, Bree, enjoying a holiday and maybe enjoying a lot more on the side?'

She laughed, the light sound music to his ears. He loved her laugh. He loved her smile. And he'd missed it so much over the past week. Missed it more than he wanted to admit.

'It's hardly a holiday for you when you live there.'

'It is if I'm touring the sights and seeing it all through your eyes.'

She studied him quietly, so much racing over her ex-pression.

'Please, Bree. Life's too short to live it for others.'

'I'm not.'

'You are. You did it with your ex and you're doing it now, helping your family, Felicity, making sure everyone else is happy.'

'Is that really so bad?'

'It is if you're not going after what you want, too. You need some balance, Bree.'

'And is that what you have? Balance?'

His chest panged as she hit her mark. 'This isn't about me right now, it's about you. Come to Paris, see the city you dreamed of, let me give you that happiness. Do it for you, no one else.'

She gave a semi-smile. 'Says the man pleading with me for my company.'

'Who's pleading?' He blushed as she shoved him. 'Okay, yes, I'm pleading. But this is as much about me wanting to see you do something for yourself as it is me wanting you there.' And he realised the truth of it. He cared about her too much to simply walk away and let her carry on living her life for others.

'Okay.'

It was so sudden, so unexpected he had to repeat it back at her. 'Okay?'

'I'll come.' She smiled, her brown eyes shining up at him, and warmth exploded in his chest, his heart fit to burst.

'You will?'

'Yes!' She flicked her cloth at him and he threw caution to the wind, clasping the end of it and using it to tug her to him, but before he could capture her lips she pressed her palm into his chest. 'On one condition.'

'Which is?'

'You come out of your brother's shadow.'

His brows drew together, his laugh gruff. 'I think you'll find I'm the one in the limelight and he's…'

She was shaking her head. 'That's not what I mean. You seem to think your brother is better than you. Looking up to him, being proud of him, is one thing, but the way you talk about him, it's more than that.'

He hooked his hands into the back pockets of her jeans

and held her to him as he admitted, 'He's a better man than me.'

She shook her head, holding his gaze. 'Why?'

'Because he saved me when I needed saving. Without him, I don't know where I'd be now. I was trouble and he was the fixer. And I don't mean that in the assassin kind of a way,' he added to try and lighten the sudden intensity, the opening of a wound that he had put there and it had never quite healed.

She gave a soft laugh but the sincerity was still there in her gaze, and it was tightening up his chest, making his insides squirm.

'Was. He was the fixer. You were trouble.'

'Okay. Okay. You don't need to rub it in.'

'You're missing the point.' She reached up, her fingers finding the hair at the nape of his neck, toying with it, a move she often did, a move he often craved. The touch, the contact, the bond. 'It's past tense. In the past. You've worked so hard to make up for those years, to be a good man, to give back. You've paid your dues. Why can't you acknowledge that you're your brother's equal now?'

'Are you sure you've read up on me properly? Because those articles, even the ones about my charity efforts, will give you an insight into my darker side.'

He waggled his eyebrows, knew he was being deliberately obtuse, but he needed this conversation over. He needed to kiss her and forget the turmoil she'd stirred up. She was the only person to have ever bothered to look so deep. She was the only person he had ever dared give enough away to. Save for Sebastian and that was different. His brother had been there through it all, lived it with him, but Bree…

He hadn't given her a rose-tinted view either. She'd got it warts and all. And still she cared. The look in her eye sucking the very air from his lungs.

'I don't care what the press say about you, Theo. I only know what I've seen with my own eyes, and you're better than you think you are, better than they make you out to be, and if I'm coming to Paris, you're agreeing that you'll take the blinkers off and see you for you.'

'Bree, I don't need a therapist.'

'I didn't say you did…'

'But the suggestion is there.'

'Perhaps…'

He shook his head, his hold around her pulsing. 'I worked through my past a long time ago. I'm over it.'

'You think you are, but it's still there, the mark—'

'The mark I deserve to bear.'

'And that's where I think you're wrong, and I intend to prove it to you.'

The unease within had goosebumps spreading across his skin, alarm bells ringing in his head. This wasn't what he wanted. Paris, yes. Bree, yes. Therapy, hell no.

'You can't fix—'

She cut off his denial with her kiss. It was soft, coaxing, the warmth rushing through his body disproportionate to the pressure of her kiss. 'We'll see.'

'I was wrong about you, Bree,' he murmured against her mouth, the tension in his body uncoiling with the heat of her kiss, the gentle pressure of her curves against him.

'In what way?'

'You're devious.'

'Devious?'

'Using your unique powers of persuasion to render me helpless to your suggestion.'

You mean, using your own sneaky tactics against you… clever woman.

'We'll see about that. When do we leave?'

'Tuesday? It's already your day off so your aunt and uncle only have to arrange cover for a few more days.'

She nipped his bottom lip, igniting his veins. 'How long are you proposing we go for?'

'A week?'

She laughed, her fingers twisting in his hair as a thousand flutters came alive in his gut.

'That might be pushing it. Five nights? I can be back at work for Monday.'

'But Paris is a big place, there's a lot to show you…that I want to show you.'

'Five nights,' she insisted. 'That gives us plenty of time for me to work my magic on you.'

'Speaking of which…'

He spun her towards the counter, pressed her back against it and kissed her, cherishing every muted whimper she gave, every ragged breath she took, her nails that raked down his back as she clung to him for more…

If it meant more of this, he would bow down to her every demand and then some.

Famous last words…

CHAPTER TEN

'To you and Sebastian.'

Bree clinked her champagne flute against Felicity's as they sat before the fire in the B & B's bar.

It was Monday, almost a week since their chat in the café, a few days since Theo had joined her family for dinner, and everything had changed—between Sebastian and Felicity at least. She knew Theo had played a hand in bringing his brother and her best friend together and she couldn't be more proud or more fearful of where her heart was heading.

'I still feel like I need to pinch myself, Bree. Two weeks ago, I never thought I'd see him again and now...'

Felicity smiled, her cheeks all rosy, the glow nothing to do with the heat of the roaring fire and everything to do with the man standing at the bar, deep in conversation with his brother.

'And now you're getting married.' Bree eyed the ring on her friend's finger, a sapphire solitaire surrounded by diamonds. 'And that's one incredible ring.'

Felicity held her hand out, her eyes bright as she took it in. 'It's been in the Ferrington family for generations, traditionally passed down to the first male born to give to his betrothed.'

They both fell quiet, and she sensed her friend was lost in the same thought.

'Does it feel strange with their history?' Bree glanced in the direction of the bar and the two men that had come to mean so much to them. Whatever they were discussing it had them both looking far too serious...

'You mean his parents?'

Bree looked back at her. 'His grandfather, too. The entire Ferrington legacy seems to be riddled with pain.'

'I know. But that's all in the past. We get to change the future, right? Make the estate a home once more, create a past that Angel can be proud of...'

Bree smiled softly. 'So, it's really happening? He's going to reclaim the Ferrington Estate for himself and make it your home rather than a hotel.'

'Yes.'

'I'm so happy for you, honey. For you and Angel.' She smiled wide, desperately trying to bury the kick of envy as she yearned for the same. 'Who would have thought two weeks ago that you'd be getting married and I'm about to be whisked away to Paris by a sexy celeb with more money than I could ever see in my lifetime? Lucky us, hey?'

'Bree...?' Felicity's eyes narrowed. 'You sound...weird—is everything okay?'

'Okay?' *Too pitched, Bree.* 'Why shouldn't it be?' *Better. Much better.*

'Because those words that just came out of your mouth had your usual oomph dialled up to a thousand.'

'Oomph?' She tried to laugh.

'You know what I mean. Is there something you're not telling me?'

Bree's eyes were back on Theo and he chose that moment to turn, his eyes lighting on her, his mouth quirking up. The room fell away; it was just them and a whole heap of excitement and nerves and happiness and panic. Sebastian was saying something but Theo's attention was all on her and her body revelled in it, her disobedient heart, too.

'Oh, my goodness, Bree.' Felicity leaned in close, her voice hushed. 'You've fallen for him, haven't you?'

Her eyes snapped back to Felicity's, ice rushing through her veins as she gave a choked laugh. 'Don't be silly! Just because you're all loved up and happy, don't be projecting it onto me.'

Felicity simply stared at her. Hard.

Bree gave another edgy giggle. 'Come on, honey. As if I would be so stupid.'

'You say that but…'

'Look, I know he's not after a relationship. I know he's not the settling-down sort. I know…' Her shoulders sagged as she resigned herself to the truth. She couldn't lie to Felicity. 'I know all of this but…but…'

Her throat closed over and her friend's gaze softened. 'But you've fallen for him?'

'Messed up, right?'

Felicity's head tilted to the side as she gave her a small smile. 'Not really. Look what happened to me.'

'And you look great on it. The risk paid off, so to speak.'

Felicity looked to her man and the brother beside him. 'You know, there's nothing to say Theo doesn't feel the same way you do. You're a pretty special human being, Bree. If anyone could crack his playboy shell, it's you.'

Bree shook her head. 'Don't.'

'Don't what?'

'Put that hope there.'

'Do you not think it's possible?'

'I choose not to think about it and that way I can't kid myself.'

'But he's taking you to Paris, you're sleeping together…'

'And we've made an agreement to move on after.'

'You have?'

'Kind of.'

'Kind of?'

'To use his words, I am not going to "make us a cliché".'

Felicity snorted into her glass. 'What's that supposed to mean?'

'You know, the whole playboy meets girl next door and suddenly he's head over heels in love, mending his ways, golden halo and all that jazz.'

'He said that?'

'Thereabouts.'

Felicity raised her brows and took a healthy sip of her drink. 'Well, maybe, just maybe, the man doth protest too much. Hmm?'

'And maybe, just maybe, you've had one too many glasses of fizz.'

But what if Felicity was right? What if for all Theo spoke of clichés and being a playboy and being unfixable…he was actually falling for her, too?

Was his heart just as disobedient as her own and refusing to listen to his head?

It was possible—wasn't it?

'So come on, you going to tell me what's really going on between you?'

Theo dragged his eyes from Bree. 'There's nothing to tell.'

Liar. You're pining for her and she's only sitting across the same room as you.

No, not pining. His ears were burning, that was all. Convinced as he was that they were talking about him, or more specifically his relationship with Bree, and now his brother wanted to go there, too.

Sebastian scoffed. 'Pull the other one.'

'Look, just cos you're all loved up—which is great, by the way, and I'm super happy for you—don't be looking for more here. There isn't anything to see.'

'I wasn't. I was just asking you to be straight with me.' His brother eyed him over his pint. 'She's Flick's best mate. The idea of you leaving and us having to pick up the pieces is worrying to say the least.'

Anger fired in his blood. 'Geez, thanks, bro.'

'Can you blame me for thinking it? You hardly have a reputation for anything else and it's obvious you've been sleeping together.'

Theo bristled even more and yet…

'She knows what we're about.'

'And what exactly is that?'

'Fun, brother. Bare, naked fun. Nothing more. Nothing less.'

'You sure about that?'

Theo's brows drew together, his grip tightening around his pint as his heart did a weird little jig of its own. The image of his future life without Bree was as unwelcome as this conversation. 'Why wouldn't I be?'

His brother fell silent, studying him as the fire crackled in the grate and the women laughed…and then he said, 'Not so long ago you told me it was good to see that spark back in my eye, Theo, that I had the sign of a life on the horizon. A proper one.'

'I did. Not sure what that has to do with me and Bree now though.'

Theo thought back to his very recent trip to the estate. Hot off the back of his dinner with Bree's family he'd been in a weird head space, keen to get back on an even keel, to feel like himself again and sure of his intentions, so he'd sought out the grounding companionship of his brother and the estate, their shared past.

Instead, he'd found himself landing in the thick of a huge fall-out between Flick and Sebastian. A fall-out caused by the repercussions of that fateful night sixteen years ago and he'd buried his own insecurities to give his brother the long overdue pep talk he needed.

He'd been the one dishing out the advice, helping Sebastian see past it all to the goodness inside him. He'd been the one telling his brother to look to the future and not let the past get in the way of a life with Felicity.

And look at them now. He'd played his part in their reconciliation, in the ring now on Flick's finger, maybe he was coming out of his brother's shadow, after all. Maybe Bree had been right to give him that nudge.

'I must admit, I was surprised to have you go all big brother on me.'

Theo raised his brows. 'Big brother?'

'Yes. I've never seen you so serious. Dishing out the advice, talking relationship sense...'

'God, you really are piling on the compliments today.'

'You know what I mean, Theo. And something tells me it has a lot to do with Bree. She's been good for you.'

He gave a dismissive snort but it landed flat. Bree *was* good for him. She saw him as no other woman had before—her positivity, her encouragement, her kindness and understanding... He could feel it chipping away at the surface, already fooling him into believing it, too, and in such a short space of time.

'Snort all you like, Theo. I'm telling you, I see it in you, too.'

Was his brother in his head? 'See what?'

'The spark, a happy future on the horizon, a life with a woman—'

Theo's laugh was harsh enough to cut Sebastian off. He couldn't bear to hear it, to have that future teased before him once more. He leaned back against the bar, his eyes finding Bree of their own accord. Her ebony hair, glinting gold in the firelight, her brown eyes, too, and that smile—it lit him from the inside out.

Even if he did have feelings for Bree, he knew she deserved better. Someone who could give her the marriage and the children she dreamed of, and that man wasn't him.

He turned away as the image tried to tease its way back in. Of the two of them, a child much like Becca between them holding their hands, smiling up at them.

That just wasn't him.

Tanya had proved so spectacularly that he didn't deserve that to be him.

'Come on, Theo, don't tell me you can't see it, too?'

'Brother, as far as I'm concerned that loved-up heart of yours is as deluded as it ever was. I'm happy for you and Flick—Angel, too—really truly happy, but don't try and thrust that on me.'

'I'm not.'

Theo raised his brows at him, would have snorted again, too, if he weren't taking in beer.

'Take your own advice, little bro, don't pass up the best thing that's ever happened to you because of the past and some misguided belief that you're not good enough.'

Now he did snort, mainly to fend off the pinch in his chest. 'You're the best thing that ever happened to me, Sebastian, and I'll spend the rest of my life making it up to you.'

'Theo, will you stop? What I did was no more than any brother would have done. And you've spent more than enough years trying to make up for it all. Why can't you see that?'

'Because I'll always be the screw-up and you'll for ever be the saint, dear brother, and there's no getting away from that.'

'There is, you just need to see it for yourself.'

And now his brother sounded so much like Bree it was crippling him. He downed his pint, trying to fill the vacuous chill inside but it was no use. He craved the warmth that only Bree could bring. Craved it even though he knew it wasn't fair.

Unless...were they both right? Was he the one that was wrong? So blinded by his past he couldn't see straight?

'I love you, little brother—' Sebastian wasn't giving up '—and it's high time you started to love yourself.'

CHAPTER ELEVEN

BREE HAD TO keep reminding herself to close her mouth.

But when everything around her filled her with wonder, it was too easy to forget.

From the moment she'd stepped on the private jet, she'd been swept up in another world. Theo's world. And she was in awe. Of Theo, of his private jet and fancy car complete with driver, of the amazing city itself...

'I would have driven us,' he'd said when she'd raised her brow at the sleek black car and driver dressed in livery, 'but this way, I get to give you the attention you deserve.'

She'd laughed it off, trying hard to downplay the remark that had given her heart a dangerous boost. Laughed even more when he'd made the driver take the long way round just so she could get a sneak peek of the sights he would take her to over the coming days, even persevered through the traffic to navigate the Arc de Triomphe twice over so that she could gaze up at one of the city's most infamous monuments...

But now they were at his apartment building and her insides were alive with nerves. She tried to focus on her surroundings, the luxurious mix of old and new. Brass and glass. Rich wood and glossy floors, antique paintings and tapestries. Marble pillars and patterned rugs. It was so un-Theo and yet, all him.

And he was clearly at home, the staff welcoming him with warm smiles that readily extended to her as he ushered her through the foyer to the glass elevator that took them to the top floor. His penthouse. His home. And as the lift doors opened, she could barely contain her gasp.

'Theo! This is incredible.'

Not that she was looking at the room.

She was vaguely aware of the marble floor, the clean

lines, the dark furniture…but what held her gaze was the view beyond the wall of glass. The fairy lights twinkling in the carefully manicured rooftop garden, the plunge pool and double-bed cabana, and as its backdrop, just as Theo had promised, the Eiffel Tower itself. Lit up as dusk befell the city, its golden light reaching up into the sky, it was just as she'd imagined. Stunning and romantic.

She walked towards it, her mouth open once again, and heard Theo give a soft chuckle.

'I promised you the view.'

She glanced at him. 'You promised me something else with the view as the backdrop.'

She was teasing him, grounding them, reminding herself that, as much as this was real, it was temporary… Her eyes went back to the view, drinking it in, counting her blessings for what she did have right now.

She sensed him come up behind her and refused to turn, not while she was wrestling with her emotions. It was true no one had ever done something like this for her and seeing Felicity so happy with Sebastian, it was hard not to wish for the same. To think it possible.

His arms wrapped around her middle and she sank back into him, her head resting against his chest, her hands upon his. 'It's truly beautiful here.'

'It's not the only thing that is.'

He turned her in his arms and she closed her eyes, tilted her head back to his kiss. Lost herself in what she knew she could readily give, her body, not her heart.

'I'm beginning to wish I hadn't booked a table for dinner.'

'We can always cancel.'

'No way. We only have five nights and I intend to make the most of every one.'

And he did. Over the next few days, he filled every hour with something. He took her to the Louvre, the Sacré-Coeur, gave her an inside peek at the restoration works on the fire-ravaged Notre-Dame, wandered the eighteenth-century Place de la Concorde plaza with its Egyptian obelisk and she lost herself in pondering the sights it had seen over the years. They did the length and breadth of the Champs-élysées, visiting cute little bars and restaurants. Brushed off the odd paparazzi with a ready smile and a swift introduction to her as his friend where necessary.

She'd asked if he was worried what they would print about her, to which he had said so long as she didn't mind, he couldn't care less. They knew what they were and that was all that mattered.

They knew what they were…

The phrase echoed around her mind as she readied herself for dinner. It was their last night together before she returned to Elmdale, to her own reality, and Theo would… what would Theo do?

She hadn't asked the question and he hadn't volunteered it.

And she knew she would have to. She needed to know before the night was over what tomorrow would bring. Was this to be it? The end?

A gentle rap on the bedroom door roused her and she frowned. It wasn't like Theo to knock, the ease with which they'd come to live together adding to her secret hope that this could be something more.

'Come in.'

A woman she didn't recognise entered, pristine in a crisp white suit, blonde hair perfectly coiffed and the kind of make-up that looked as if it took hours and a team to perfect. 'Mademoiselle Johansson, Monsieur Dubois requested that I tend to you this evening.'

Bree's frown deepened. 'He did?'

'If it is agreeable to you?'

She gave a soft laugh as her phone pinged from the bedside table. She reached over and checked the screen.

It was a message from the man himself:

Courtney works with the best, and you deserve the best. I hope you enjoy being pampered. I have some business to take care of but I'll pick you up at eight. T xx

She smiled at Courtney and told herself this was all fine. Perfectly acceptable. It meant nothing.

Only…it meant everything to her romantic heart that had watched *Pretty Woman* too many times to count.

She wrapped her robe tighter around her, clutched the collar. 'I'm all yours.'

'*Très bien!*' The woman spun on her stilettos and gestured to someone outside the room. 'Come, come.'

In trooped a team of four bringing a rail hung with dresses, a tall dresser on wheels, several bags… Bree gaped at it all.

'Do not worry.' Courtney gave her a smile that softened her ice-blue eyes. 'I am not as scary as I look. Think of me more as a facilitator to achieving the look your heart desires.'

Bree nodded, her heart still galloping away, her eyes still wide as she watched the team set up camp.

'But first, champagne. *Oui?*' And, as if by magic, in walked a maid with a trolley complete with glasses and champagne on ice.

'*Oui,*' Bree repeated numbly, wondering how on earth she could continue to be surprised by the man who had turned her world upside down in the space of a fortnight.

And how on earth she could hope to go back to life without him now that her heart knew how it felt to feel so full again.

Theo sat at the bar, a whisky in one hand, his phone in the other, staring at the simple reply.

Thank you xx

His business had been done and dusted an hour ago. He could have returned to the apartment, to her, instead he was propping up the bar trying to get his head on straight.

Seeing Bree discover Paris had been like watching a child in Lapland, her wide-eyed awe and excited gasps stripping him of his layers. Layers he depended on to keep his life predictable, steady...

If he didn't want for more, then he couldn't get hurt.

He'd dared to go there with Tanya and it had cost him dearly.

But Bree was nothing like Tanya, she was unlike anyone he'd ever known, and he wasn't ready to say goodbye to her yet. The 'goodbye' that was supposed to come tomorrow.

His brother's words revolved around his head, his heart...

Take your own advice, little bro, don't pass up the best thing that's ever happened to you because of the past and some misguided belief that you're not good enough.

But she was too good for him. Wasn't she?

Or was his brother right? Hell, was Bree right? She was the one telling him he was a better man than he gave himself credit for. Could they make this work? For real? Not just some temporary arrangement to satisfy an itch neither of them had intended to scratch but had done so all the same.

He threw back his drink, no closer to the answer but knowing he wasn't ready to say goodbye to her yet. And who said they had to? Who said they had to put a name to what this was between them?

It hadn't even been three weeks, for heaven's sake. Yes, Sebastian and Flick had agreed to marriage in that time, but they shared a past and a child.

This was different.

Bree was different and she hadn't asked him for more.

He simply had to propose an open arrangement, one where they could continue to see one another until...

Until what?

Until she met someone she truly wanted to be with. Someone who could offer the marriage and kids she so desired. Was it fair to ask her for more when he couldn't give her what she wanted deep down?

He pulled his dinner jacket off the back of his stool, thrust it on and righted his shoulders.

No, it wasn't fair and that was why tonight had to be it.

It *had* to be.

He strode into the lift, barely acknowledging the porter who had readied it for him. He stared up at the glass ceiling, counting his way to the top, telling himself it was the right thing to do.

It *was*.

The gentle lurch of the lift as it came to a stop tugged his gaze down and he sucked in a breath, stepped through the opening doors...and froze.

His heart launched into his throat, his knees threatened to buckle, the air stalled in his lungs. He wanted to grip something, anything, but there was nothing within reach.

Before him, in the centre of the living area, the twinkling Eiffel Tower as her backdrop, was Bree. Bree as he'd never seen her before. She wore a strapless red dress that hugged her curves all the way to the floor, the fabric parting over one thigh and teasing him with a glimpse of shimmering leg and strappy gold heels. Her hair had been twisted up high, strands falling to frame her face, teasing at her bare shoulders. The carefully applied make-up highlighted every stunning feature in her face, features he had come to adore, her cheekbones, her brown eyes, her smile...

'Bree.' He breathed out her name, long and slow.

He didn't know which way was up, how his life had

ever felt full without her in it, how he could possibly let her go tomorrow and not know when he might see her again.

'Is it too much?' She lowered her thick dark lashes, suddenly hesitant, a hand lifting to pat her hair. He wanted to hide her away, keep her all to himself, and what a crime that would be when the world should see just how beautiful she was. *She* should see how beautiful she was.

Beautiful both inside and out.

He cringed, he was so full of clichés now, but nothing else would come, nothing that could do her justice.

'You're starting to worry me.' She shifted from one gold stiletto to the other. 'I can change, it's not—'

'No!' He rushed forward, stopped as her eyes widened into his. 'Sorry, I'm just—Bree, you look perfect. Stunning. Breathtaking.'

Slowly, her cherry-red lips curved up into a smile. 'Yet you look like you've seen a ghost.'

'Not at all. You just…you rendered me speechless for a moment. It's not a usual occurrence for me.'

'Courtney outdid herself, I think.'

'No. This is all you, Bree.'

She went to contradict him and he shook his head. 'Don't. Take the compliment. Own it.'

She gave a soft laugh. 'So, you do like?'

Like? Like was the weakest, most inadequate word ever for the woman before him…

'I love…'

Her lashes flickered over brown eyes that shone, the dark angled eye make-up making them ever more vibrant, ever more captivating…or was it his rash word choice that had put that look there?

Too late now…

'Are you going to come any closer?'

His feet felt heavy, weighed down by lead, as though stepping forward would be crossing a line into accepting something more. Something greater than what he'd let his heart feel his entire life. And yet, his heart raced with it anyway.

'Didn't your mother ever teach you it's rude to keep a lady waiting?'

And just like that he was crossing the room, great strides that had him before her in seconds and reaching for her hand. He pulled her to him gently.

'I don't dare touch your hair. Or your dress. Or your face...' His free hand was hovering close but not close enough.

She pouted up at him, her brown eyes striking out. 'Then where's the fun?'

He gave a low chuckle, swept his lips over hers and felt his entire body come alive, his entire world settle. Was this what it could be like every day if they continued as they were?

Was this the feeling that had put the spark back in his brother's eye, the genuine smile on his face?

Could he truly have it, too?

She broke away first. 'Didn't you say we needed to be leaving at eight?'

It was his turn to pout.

'Theo Dubois, are you pouting at me?'

'Maybe.'

She shook her head, the freed strands of hair flouncing about her shoulders and making him want to catch every one.

'Well, we'd best not keep the restaurant waiting.' Her smile was everything as she stepped past him, her fingers locked in his as she tugged him with her and he went. Gladly. Knowing in that moment he'd willingly follow her to the ends of the earth to keep this feeling for longer.

CHAPTER TWELVE

BREE FELT INCREDIBLE. She looked incredible, barely rec-
ognising herself when Courtney had turned her to face the
mirror and clapped her hands together and exclaimed, 'You
are a vision!'

A vision? Her?

She'd never felt her curves to be the height of fashion, her
size being touted as plus never really helping, but encased
in the exquisite satin that fitted her like a glove, she could
totally see the appeal. And her skin was radiant, her make-
up and hair divine…divine and pinned within an inch of
its life, which meant for a very long session before bed to
locate and remove every hairpin.

But judging by the look on Theo's face as he helped her
out of the car, he would be more than happy to strip her of
her clothing and every accessory later.

She smiled as a thrilling shiver ran through her, something he didn't miss.

'Are you cold?'

'No.' She straightened, kept her hand in his. 'But you
have that look in your eye.'

'Which look?'

'The one that says it's not food you're thinking of devouring.'

His dark chuckle sent another shiver running through her
and she wanted to kiss him, kiss him and drag him back
inside the car, back to the apartment and back to the bed
that held as much appeal as the entirety of Paris and all its
sights. He looked far too edible himself. His black jacket
and trousers fitted his frame intimately, his crisp white shirt
unbuttoned one too teasingly many at the collar, and his hair

had been smoothed back but for the one stray lock that insisted on falling forward.

'Hold that thought.' His lips claimed hers for the briefest kiss, long enough to make the heat spread through her limbs, but not so long as to ruin the glossy red lipstick she had just reapplied. 'Hungry?'

'Ravenous.'

Another chuckle told her he caught her true meaning and then he was leaning into the back of the car for her coat and wrapping it around her shoulders before leading her into an unassuming door down an even more unassuming back alley. 'Don't be fooled by the front. This way we avoid causing too much of a stir.'

She nodded, though she hadn't even thought to question it. He'd taken her to many quirky locations over the course of the week, often finding ways to avoid any lurking paparazzi and unwanted fan attention in the process.

He pushed open the door revealing a very dark, very narrow, and very unappealing corridor lit by small sconces in the wall. She felt as if she'd walked back in time.

'Where on earth are you taking me, Theo?' she murmured.

'You'll see.'

'Ah, Monsieur Dubois!' A man appeared—tall, dark and handsome, his smile bright and welcoming, his white shirt, unbuttoned waistcoat and dark trousers giving him a waiter vibe. 'It is good to see you again.'

'And you, Émile!' He shook the man's hand. 'How are you, buddy?'

'Better for seeing you again. It has been too long, my friend. And who is this?' Émile turned his sparkling brown eyes on her, his smile turning conspiratorial and making her want to giggle.

'émile meet Bree. I've known Émile and his family for

a long time. His parents actually gave me my first job in their kitchens.'

'And now he gets to dine at our tables.' He grinned at Theo before taking Bree's hand. 'It is a pleasure to meet you, *mademoiselle*. I hope we can please you tonight.'

'It's a pleasure to meet you, too.' She felt her cheeks warm as he dipped to kiss the tips of her knuckles. 'And I'm sure you will. Theo has yet to disappoint me when it comes to food.'

'Enough of your French charm.' Theo looked between them as Émile continued to hold her eye and her hand. 'She's spoken for.'

Her heart gave a little leap. Theo had said it in jest, yes, but still…

émile chuckled as he released her. 'As am I, more is the pity.' He gave her a wink that made her giggle more. 'The best always are. Come. Your table is ready.'

They followed him through the stone-walled corridor, past double doors to the left through which the clanking of dishes resonated, then onwards through an archway that led into a cosy room—navy wood-panelled walls with quirky portraits and wine bottles filling shelf upon shelf, some looking older than her. A handful of mahogany tables covered in ivory linen were intimately arranged with a lit candle and long-stemmed white rose at their heart.

It was a delight.

And they were the only ones there.

'This place is beautiful.'

Theo squeezed her hand. 'It's the city's best kept secret.'

'And we have it to ourselves?'

'For tonight.'

'I owed him a favour,' Émile explained, leading them to the table in the centre of the room and pulling out a chair. 'If you please.'

She lowered herself into it, feeling Theo's eyes on her the

whole time. Something had shifted between them. Something she couldn't put her finger on but it was there all the same, in his eyes, in the atmosphere that pulsed between them.

The second he had laid eyes on her that evening, she had felt it. Not just desire, but something else, something deeper, almost proprietorial...as if she was his.

And she wanted to be his.

She didn't want to leave tomorrow.

Yes, reality beckoned—the bakery, her job, her family—but she wanted Theo to be a part of it. Any lingering doubt over how she felt about him had evaporated the moment he had said, 'She's spoken for.'

Because there was no doubt in her mind now, she was in love with Theo Dubois and she wanted him to be hers.

'What?'

Theo waited until his friend had taken their order and left before saying it, unable to take the sparkle in her eye any longer without knowing what had put it there.

'Nothing.' She pursed her lips on a smile, reaching for her water glass.

'That look isn't nothing.'

Her eyes returned to his and he felt that same intense urge to reach for her, to hold her close. Only a table existed between them and even that was too much.

'I'm just pondering what you did to earn such a favour from Émile...'

'Aah...' He smiled, easing back into his seat. 'émile's fiancée is something of a water baby. He wanted to propose at sea and what better way than in the middle of the ocean with only the stars above for an audience?'

'Well, I know you couldn't gift him the stars, so...'

'I gave him the use of my yacht.'

Her smile glowed back at him. 'Your yacht?'

He shrugged. 'I wasn't using it.'

She gave a soft laugh, her eyes dancing in the candle-light. 'So, you just offered it up?'

'For a fortnight, not for ever, Bree.'

She shook her head. 'Of course, you did.'

The sommelier appeared with his favourite wine at the ready and he gave him a discreet nod, his eyes not leaving hers. She was still looking at him strangely—what was he missing?

The sommelier poured and he gave him his thanks, waited until they were alone again before lifting his glass in toast. 'To our time in Paris.'

She clinked her glass to his. 'To Paris.'

'I hope it's been everything you dreamed of?'

The look in her eye blazed deeper, her voice ever more husky, 'It's been everything and more, thank you, Theo. Really, truly.'

'No, thank you. Seeing it through your eyes has been as much a treat for me. It's too easy to forget how special your surroundings are when they're your every day.'

They sipped their wine, gazes locked together. Why did it feel as if she was desperate to say something? Or was it just him? Was it the fact that he wanted to ask her to stay? To commit to something other than nothing?

It was so easy to be around her, his body high on her every reaction. She found so much pleasure in everything, the buildings, the food, the people…and they loved her back. Instantly warming to her. There was no pretence, no snobbery, no superiority.

He'd been racing about Paris with her for days, barely pausing for more than a second and he knew why. Pausing gave him too much time to think, too much time to ponder the future, a future without her in it, a future he didn't want but didn't know how to change.

'Do you have to go back tomorrow?'

Her lashes flickered. 'I need to get back to the bakery.'

'But you have Tuesdays off anyway. It would only be an extra day without you; I'm sure they could survive. I'm sure if we asked, Felicity would even chip in, or I could get someone to cover.'

Her smile widened with every bumbled word. 'Is this you trying to tell me you don't want me to leave, Theo?'

'You tell me. You've always been able to read me so well.'

She searched his gaze and he didn't shy away, wanting her to see it all, every last chaotic thought.

'I'd love to stay, but I need to get back to my life, too. I'm not sure how long I can spend in your world without wanting to stay in it and I'm not sure that's a good thing. For either of us.'

'Why?'

'Because we want very different things.' She said it slowly, as if she wasn't so sure, and heck, neither was he any more.

'I don't know, Bree. I just know that when I'm with you, I never want to be without you.'

'And I you.' She wet her lips. 'But what of the future?'

'Why do we need to talk of the future? Why can't we live for the now?'

'Are you asking to see me again?'

'If I was, would you say yes?'

She took a slow sip of her wine. 'You're hard to say no to.'

'Funny, I could say the same about you.'

Their smiles were a mirror image, perhaps their thoughts, too. It wasn't an answer, but it wasn't an outright 'no' either and that gave him hope.

The meal was brought out seamlessly, Émile and his team outdoing themselves just as he had expected they would. Three courses of perfection made even more as he watched Bree enjoy every last mouthful, her appreciation teasing him more and more each time, the chocolate soufflé for dessert a true test of his patience...

'Did you enjoy that?'

She covered her mouth, her eyes aglow, cheeks too. 'Sorry, was I that obvious?'

He smiled. 'You've nothing to apologise for. It's a joy to dine with someone who actually eats rather than toys with her food.'

She lowered her cutlery to her plate. 'I'm afraid I have no willpower for that, but I may need a walk to help it all go down.'

He gave a soft chuckle. 'A stroll along the river and then bed?'

'Sounds perfect.'

Leaving Émile proved harder than he'd envisaged as he lost Bree to a conversation over how to ensure a soufflé kept its rise and rich, cloud-like texture. He was hopping from one foot to the other by the time he ushered her outside and Bree immediately started to laugh.

'What's so funny.'

'Do you need the toilet?'

He stilled, frowning down at her. 'No, what makes you say that?'

'Because you were doing the dance.'

'That was me trying to get you away from Émile so I could have you all to myself again.'

Her smile was as bright as the starry sky above, her eyes squinting as the chilling wind picked up around them. He reached out and drew her coat to her chin.

'Thank you for a lovely evening,' she whispered.

'It's not over yet...' He leaned in, kissed her softly. She tasted of chocolate, sweet and decadent, and suddenly a walk seemed like the worst idea in the world. A further delay he didn't need. 'You sure you want to take a walk in this?'

'My stomach is.'

He laughed and tucked her arm in his. 'In that case, we'd best move before I try and persuade you otherwise.'

'And how might you have done that?'

'I am a man of many talents…as you well know.'

She gave a blissful sigh. 'So true… I know I've said it already but thank you. I would actually go as far as to say this has been the best week of my life.'

'Really?' He looked down at her, a warmth unfurling deep within and contrasting with the very real chill around them.

'Don't let it go to your head, Theo. I don't fancy the ego conversation all over again.'

He chuckled. 'I wouldn't dare.'

'But you have taught me to slow down and take a moment just for me. To take pleasure in the not doing as much as the doing.'

'I feel the same.'

'Really?' Her eyes flicked to his, their depths disbelieving and bright. 'You've been eager to hop from one thing to the next all week.'

'Only to make sure you see everything…and to stop me contemplating the end of our trip. I meant what I said, Bree, I'm not ready for this to be over.'

She lowered her gaze and they moved quietly in step together, lost in their own thoughts.

'I lived my life at ninety miles an hour until I met you,' he admitted eventually. 'Always chasing the next big thing. With you I've taken time to just be. Whether it's baking in the kitchen, looking after Becca and the B & B, or seeing the sights of Paris through your enthralled gaze, I've been more present.' He laughed at himself, shook his head. 'Does that even make sense?'

She stopped walking. They were on the Pont Alexandre III bridge now, its bronze sculptures standing proud, the

Eiffel Tower glowing in the distance, the Grand Palais and Petit Palais, too. The River Seine reflected it all back at them and then there was Bree, her face softened by the glow of the art nouveau lamps that lined the bridge.

'It makes perfect sense.' She rested her palms on his chest, gazed up into his eyes and stole his breath. There was a reason this bridge was considered the most romantic of all in Paris but he'd never felt the full effect of its magic until now.

'I'm glad I've been able to give you that,' she murmured.

He hooked his arms around her, pulled her close. 'And me, you.'

He lowered his head, his lashes closing, his heart racing and—

'Theo!'

He jerked back, his eyes lifting to take in the woman standing a few feet away.

Oh, dear God, no…

CHAPTER THIRTEEN

BREE'S EYES SHOT OPEN.

Theo looked as if he'd seen a ghost, a real bona fide ghost this time. His skin was pale, his eyes were wide and he was looking past her at whoever had addressed him. He raked a hand through his hair, his arm around her tightening as he manoeuvred her to his side.

'I'm sorry,' he said under his breath.

'For what?' But his attention was on the woman she'd heard but hadn't seen...until now.

'Tanya.'

She knew it was her before he spoke. The stunning willowy blonde might as well have stepped from the page of a magazine. The man on her arm, much the same.

Anger swamped her. Anger at what the woman had done to Theo. Anger that she should ruin what had been such a perfect moment. Just when it felt as though they were getting somewhere. Somewhere good...

She took her cue from Theo, staying rigid and silent as Tanya gave a pitched giggle, her eyes drifting from Theo to Bree, where they sharpened, assessed, and dismissed her as readily as she would a piece of muck on her very expensive shoe. Then she swept forward, dragging her unsuspecting date with her.

'Fancy seeing you back in Paris so soon,' she purred, pressing her hands into Theo's shoulders. Bree felt him flinch beside her, his body tensing ever more as the woman leaned in to air-kiss his cheeks, thrusting her fur collar into Bree's face. 'And who is this...*delightful* person?'

She leaned back, her powerful perfume still lingering and making Bree's tummy roll, the roll continuing as an insipid smile touched the woman's lips.

'I'm Bree.'

'*Brreee*. What a lovely name. Isn't it a lovely name, Jonas?'

She turned to her man, whose smile felt far more genuine than his partner's, his arm wrapping back around Tanya as he gave them a courteous nod. 'It is. Lovely, indeed.'

'English, too, I presume?' Tanya intoned.

Bree nodded, her smile all for Theo as she palmed his chest. 'This is my first trip to Paris and Theo's been kind enough to show me the sights.'

'Has he now? Well, there isn't much about Paris that the infamous Theo Dubois doesn't know.' Bree hated the possessive, all-knowing look in the woman's eye. 'Still, I wasn't expecting you back here so soon...' Her eyes drifted from Theo to Bree again. 'And looking so happy and settled, too.'

'Paris is my home, Tanya.'

'Yes.' She seemed to visibly shake herself out of some thought or other. 'Yes, I suppose it is. Well, I guess we should let you get on. We have tickets to the theatre, and we don't want to be late, do we, Jonas?'

She didn't wait for Jonas to respond as she swept away, leaving a cloud of her perfume and an edge to the air.

'Well, that was awkward.' Bree shrugged her coat tighter around her. 'You okay?'

He dragged his eyes from Tanya's exiting form. 'Never better.'

'Really?'

'Don't let her get to you.'

'I wasn't.'

'I saw how she looked at you.'

'So? Thanks to you I've a clear view all the way to that ice-cold heart of hers and no amount of glitz and glamour or legs that go on for ever will make me feel any less than I am. Or any more for her than what she is.'

He laughed softly, his head shaking as he pulled her

to him, his eyes shining with admiration. 'I couldn't have phrased it any better.'

She went to him willingly, her hands lifting to his hair. 'Though now I understand the lack of press reports on us this week. I'm positive they've caught a snap or two, they've even questioned us, but no one has bothered to print anything.'

He frowned. 'You've been checking?'

'I think it pays to be up to speed and I'd rather know before Felicity, my aunt, or, heaven forbid, my own parents pull me up on it.'

'True. Though I'm still not sure what you mean.'

'Really? Isn't it obvious?'

'Not to me.'

'Well, clearly I'm not deemed press-worthy enough. I'm no match for the Tanyas of this world. Or you.'

He shook his head, his eyes pained. 'Bree, you're better, you're more than a match, you're—'

Her smile cut him off. It was big and bright and everything she wanted to give him in that moment. 'Theo, I don't care what the press thinks! And I thought you didn't either.'

'I don't, but for a second...'

'For a second, what...?'

He stared at her in wonder, his eyes raking over her face. 'You're amazing, Bree.'

'You may have already told me that.'

'Well, I'm telling you again.'

'Just promise me...' her tone turned grave with her continued concern '...you're okay?'

'I'm more than okay.' He pressed his forehead to hers. 'I'm only annoyed that she interrupted this.'

And then he was kissing her and, uncaring of their audience, she kissed him back with no thought as to whether Tanya could look back at any moment and see them, or any press lurking in the shadows might witness it. She simply cherished his attention and gave it back thrice over.

'Now can we go home and I can show you just how okay I am?'

Home. One simple word and it had her heart melting. It wasn't as if he were referring to it as being their home, but she could pretend.

Though if everything he'd said at dinner were true, he was willing to give this relationship a chance. Willing to see where it led. And didn't that mean it could be home one day? If she just agreed.

If she took that chance, that risk…as Felicity herself had done.

Surrounded by the glittering lights of Paris and the romantic ambience she'd fantasised about, she truly believed dreams could come true.

And hers was no exception.

Just promise me you're okay?

He ignored the voice of doubt, the erratic state of his pulse, the ants marching over his skin and having a party in his gut. Because he was okay.

He didn't love Tanya, he felt nothing for her now other than gut-wrenching sadness and anger. Part of him even pitied her, that she would stoop so low to keep him, that he'd made her that desperate.

But having Tanya, of all women, intrude on their moment.

Having her witness his joy.

He had the strangest sense of guilt. Guilt and desperation.

Guilt for the part he'd played in the woman's messed-up plan.

And desperation to forget it. To forget Tanya and the way she made him feel—the heartless playboy who needed to be tricked into marriage, into caring about more than just himself.

Desperation to forget it all in Bree. In the one person who made him feel like a better man—a good man—deserving of so much more than what he'd ever envisaged.

So desperate he hadn't let go of her hand.

Not during the walk to the car, the short ride home, the trip up to his apartment. And now they were in his living room and he was looking at her as if she could save him from himself.

'Can I get you a drink?'

Was that really his voice? So strained? So rough?

'I'd rather have you...' She stepped closer, released his hand to smooth her palms over his shoulders. 'If that's okay?'

He gave a soft huff, as if she needed to ask. 'It's music to my ears.'

He kissed her, walked her back to the bedroom without breaking the contact, their hands stripping one another of their clothing, a stumble here, a desperate groan there...

'You never said yes.'

'Hmm?' she murmured, her head arching back as he nuzzled her neck, teasing at the sensitive pulse point beneath her ear.

'To seeing one another more.' He reached down, lifted her bare thigh around his waist. Holding her there.

'Is that what you want?' She sounded as breathless as he felt, his growl of agreement reverberating through him.

'You make me feel good, Bree. This feels good.'

But for how long?

How long until she realises who you truly are and runs the other way?

He squeezed his eyes shut, let his hands worship her as his mind continued to race.

Sebastian thinks you deserve this. Bree thinks you deserve this.

Isn't it time you realised it, too?

He carried her to the bed, set her down on the crisp black sheets. 'I don't know what I did to deserve this, Bree, to deserve you...'

'I'd like to hope that you took the blinkers off and saw yourself as I see you...'

Had he?

Had she succeeded where others hadn't even deigned to try...aside from his brother?

She reached up, smoothed the frown from his brow. 'Now stop questioning it and make love to me, because you have me, Theo. You have all of me.'

He drowned in her words, her kiss...poured his soul into hers and lost where he ended and she began. The future opened up once more, filled with possibility. The kind of possibility Tanya had teased at and then ripped away so spectacularly.

Forget Tanya.

Bree wasn't her, and what they shared was something so very different. Something so pure and unique to Bree and all that she represented, all that she made him feel.

Was this what his brother had with Felicity? Was this what it felt like to—to love someone?

The answer was as powerful as the swoop to his gut, the pulse to his heart. He was in love with Bree. Loved her so much that a future without her felt devoid of colour, of warmth, of life...

'And you me, Bree.'

Emotion clogged his throat, the ache in his chest painfully acute as he kissed her and showed her with every caress just how much he loved her, how much he wanted to be with her always...how much he wished he could deserve her and maybe, given time, he would.

CHAPTER FOURTEEN

AND YOU ME...

Bree rolled over in bed, luxuriating in the warmth of the memory and the way her body throbbed in all the best places. Theo had been passionate, in both his words and his lovemaking, and judging by the way her cheeks ached, she'd been smiling in her sleep.

Was this really happening? Had she truly earned the heart of a sworn bachelor?

Theo and all his talk of clichés...

She gave a sleepy giggle, reaching for him and...froze. Theo?

Her eyes shot open. He was gone, his space cold. She shoved herself up, scanning the room. The clock said it was gone nine a.m., the half-open blinds revealing a grey mist outside. It was late for her but...

She tried to ignore the niggle of disappointment. Each day they'd woken with each other, roused each other, and this being her last day in Paris she'd hoped for the same.

Maybe he hadn't wanted to wake her? Maybe he wanted to treat her to breakfast in bed on their last morning?

Sweet but unnecessary. Her smile making a return, she pushed herself out of bed and stretched, smiling all the more as her body protested. She spied his shirt from the night before over the back of his wingback chair and slipped it on, buttoning it up as she went in search of him.

She found him standing before the glass in the living room, phone to his ear as he stared out. Even in low-slung lounge pants and a slim-fit tee he had her heart racing, her body wanting. How was it possible to want him again so soon and so intensely...the need an acute ache that had her pressing her palm to her belly?

'Just get rid of them!' She started at his tone, hushed but no less harsh. 'I want to be out of here within the hour, the jet's on standby and the car is to be sent round back, nobody is to—' And then he turned and spied her. 'I'll call you back.'

He gritted his teeth and strode for the coffee table, his eyes avoiding her as he tossed his phone down and snatched up the pile of newspapers strewn there.

Finally, he looked at her, but he was as grey as the world outside, his blue eyes muted. Something was very wrong.

'I'm sorry if I woke you.'

'You didn't.' She tried to smile, tried to ignore the icy trickle that ran down her spine, the growing sense of dread. 'You should have though.'

His response was to look away again. She took one step forward, opened her mouth…

'There's fresh coffee in the pot,' he bit out before she could speak, backing up a step. 'I've sent for some breakfast, too. I wasn't sure what you'd want so I ordered a selection.'

'Theo?' She twisted her hands in front of her, fighting the urge to reach for him. He wouldn't look at her. Could he not bear to?

'Theo?' she tried again.

Grudgingly his eyes came back to her, grazed over her top to toe, their burn intensified by their anguish. 'My clothes look good on you.'

It didn't sound like a good thing. It sounded like he hated it. Resented it even.

Her skin prickled with goosebumps as her breath shuddered through her. 'What's happened?'

His jaw pulsed, his grip around the newspapers tightening.

She hugged her arms around her middle, wishing she'd put on more layers, weren't wearing his clothes, weren't living through this moment right now…

'I need to get you out of here as soon as possible.'

Her throat threatened to close and she lifted her chin, dared another step that saw him backing up more.

'Why?'

He returned to the glass, to the gloomy world outside, the Eiffel Tower itself hidden within the mist.

'Theo, please, you're scaring me.'

'Because of this!' He tossed the papers on the ground between them. Each one had him on the cover. Some of the photos included her and some—she swallowed—Tanya. 'The morning news on the TV is much the same.'

She hunched down, lifted the first English one she could see and scanned the headline.

'Oh, my God!' Her hand soared to her throat, her eyes wide. 'They can't print this.' She glanced up at his rigid back. 'It isn't true.'

He didn't make a sound, didn't move. Had he even heard her? She riffled through the others, understanding enough of the Parisian ones to know they were all variations on the same...

Playboy Billionaire Dubois Dumps Supermodel After Miscarriage

Dubois Sinks to an All-Time Low

Supermodel Tanya Bedingfield Speaks Out

Playboy Billionaire Takes Unknown to Bed While Girlfriend Mourns Loss of Baby

She gasped over the last, bile rising as she clutched her stomach. 'They can't print this—this rubbish!'

'They can and they have.'

She launched to her feet, thrust the papers out. 'But it's not true, none of it.'

'That doesn't matter.' He sounded so cold, so shut off, so un-Theo.

'You have to put them straight, do a…do a press release or whatever it is you people do.'

He gave a scoff. 'It won't change anything.'

'Of course it will.'

'The damage is already done.'

'Theo! She lied to you, broke your heart…'

'She didn't break my heart, Bree.' He spun to face her, the most animated she'd seen him since she'd found him here.

'She did. She made you believe you were going to be a father; she gave you that hope for a future and then ripped it away.'

'I never wanted to be a father.'

'Because you don't think you deserve it, but you do! And you can say you never wanted it, but she painted that future for you and you didn't run. You promised her everything. You wanted that baby.'

God, he was so grey, so haunted, so broken. She wanted to run to him, hold him, anything…but a wall had gone up. An invisible shield that he didn't want her to cross.

'You did,' she said quietly. 'And you grieved it when it was taken from you, even though it was never real.'

He didn't move. Didn't say a word. But she knew she was right and she had to make him see it.

'You can't let her get away with this. This is some act of—of petty vengeance, jealousy. She saw us last night and this is her striking back, surely you can see that?'

'What does it matter why she did it? The fact is she has and I need to get you as far away from this media storm as possible.'

'As far away from you, you mean?'

He speared her with his gaze, lightning streaking in the

blue. 'You don't deserve this, Bree. The press is going to rip you apart. They'll hound you, your family, paint you out to be a monster right along with me. If you leave now I can try and contain it.'

'Contain it?' she choked out. 'You don't need to contain it. You need to set the world straight.'

He gave a harsh laugh. 'Tit for tat?'

'What's wrong with that?'

'Can you imagine what they'll do to her if I tell them she faked the pregnancy?'

'It's no less than she deserves.'

He shook his head. 'They'd have to believe me first.'

'They will believe you.'

'Why?'

'Because it's the truth.'

'Would you believe me if you didn't know me?'

She hesitated, the truth a sucker punch to the gut. But it was more that she couldn't believe any woman would be so cruel as to invent such a tale, not—

'See.'

'No, Theo, that's not—'

He was across the room in a flash, his hands in her hair, his forehead pressed to hers, his eyes blazing down, glistening with so much…love? And then he was kissing her, hard, desperate, and she clung to him, unable to resist, not wanting to, but then he was breaking away, sucking in a breath. 'I'm sorry.'

'Don't be sorry.' She wet her lips that thrummed from the pressure of his kiss. 'Just make this right.'

He choked out a laugh. 'Oh, Bree. Innocent, sweet, loving Bree.' He softened his hold, cupped her face, his thumbs sweeping across her cheeks that were suddenly damp. 'The world is so black and white in your eyes.'

Her blood fired, dizzy on his kiss, belittled by his words. 'Don't patronise me!'

'I'm not, I'm trying to tell you how it is. I'm trying to make you see.'

'See what?'

He spun away from her, flicked a hand in the air. 'That this is no world for you, that I never should have brought you into it, exposed you to it.'

Her gut rolled, her knees buckled and she forced them straight, gritted her teeth. 'You're breaking up with me?'

'There was never ever anything to break up.'

She was going to be sick. She shoved past him, stumbled forward. 'I need some air...'

She strode for the glass door and heard him come up behind her. 'Don't go—'

Too late she was pulling it open and the noise of the city hit her. Only it was different today. There was a crowd, there were people shouting...

She crept towards the bannister and Theo tried to grab her back. 'Don't!'

But she wouldn't listen, she was too caught up in reality. The cold, hard truth of what they were...or weren't, if she was to listen to him.

Gripping the railing, she leaned over, her hair tumbling forward, her heart with it. There was a swarm of reporters and cameramen below, all vying for position, and then there was a single clear shout from one woman that rose above the rest. Her finger pointed towards Bree and all eyes and lenses lifted in tune.

Bree's mouth parted a second before Theo yanked her back. 'I said don't.'

'Why? Are you embarrassed by me?'

'No. No. You know that's not what this is.'

'Do I?' She stormed back inside, straight for the bedroom, uncaring that he watched as she stripped off his shirt and shoved on the first clothes she could find—*her* clothes. The rest she started ramming into her suitcase.

'Please, Bree, I don't want you anywhere near this. You have to understand.'

'Understand?' Her laugh was bitter. 'Oh, I understand, all right. I'm a nobody and I'm dumped. All that talk of wanting to see where this went, of…of…'

'Do you truly want a hedonistic playboy for your partner?'

'No, Theo!' she flung at him. 'I want you and that's not you. Why can't you see that?'

He stared at her and she shook her head, her body sagging in surrender. It was over. There was no getting through to him. His decision was made and she wasn't going to stay a second more in the face of it.

She swept into the bathroom, gathering up her toiletries.

'They'll destroy you, Bree,' he said quietly from the doorway. 'Drag your name through the mud along with mine. I can't bear it. I never should have dragged you into my world.'

'You didn't drag me anywhere, Theo.' She shoved past him, back into the bedroom. 'I came because I wanted to be with you. I came because…' Her voice cracked but she knew she had to get it out, that, if she was leaving, she had to go knowing that she had been honest with him. 'I came because I fell in love with you. The real you.'

His mouth parted, his eyes flared and any colour that had returned to his face vanished.

She cursed. 'Is it really so awful to hear?'

He flinched.

'You know what?' She gave an erratic laugh, swiped the tears from her cheeks and shoved her toiletries into her case. 'Forget your jet and your fancy car; I can find my own way home.'

Now he moved, racing after her as she strode for the living room, case in hand. 'You can't go out there like this, not with them…' He grabbed her arm and she shrugged him off. 'Please, Bree, just let me get you to my car.'

'That's where you're wrong! I can do whatever the hell I like, and I'll do it as far away from you as I can get. Just as you desire.'

She found her handbag, slung it over her shoulder, and stormed to the lift, grateful to have it open as soon as she jabbed the button. She stepped inside and hit 'Ground'.

'Bree!'

He sounded so desperate, so lost, and for a second, for a brief senseless moment she thought he might say what she really needed to hear. She pressed the button to hold the doors and faced him. 'What?'

His eyes raked over her but nothing came. Just the storm raging in his eyes, his broken core, and part of her broke, too.

'Just do one thing for me, Theo?'

'Anything.'

'Please don't let her get away with this. Put the press straight and get your story across, show them the real you.'

She'd lived in her ex's shadow to her own detriment, but now she'd learned to shine and stand out from the crowd once more. With Theo, she'd taken control of her own heartbreak. She'd known it could come to this; she'd known the risks. Yes, she'd hoped she could change him as he had changed her. He'd made her go after her own dreams and desires, made her unafraid of asking for what she wanted above all else: him.

But he was too scared. She could see it in his eyes, in his pain, his torment.

And she'd never felt both so strong and so helpless at once.

She would survive this. Opening her heart up had been a risk but one that had brought her so much joy and changed her for the better.

What she couldn't bear was watching the man she loved being ripped apart from afar. To have him sit in the shadows of not only his brother but also Theo Dubois the celebrity, as portrayed by the press, by his ex…

And to have him here now, using that front as an excuse to push her away instead of admitting the truth.

'They'll believe what they want to believe.' He shook his head, his face defeated and reigniting her anger. 'It won't make a difference.'

'You sure about that or are you just too happy to hide behind the mask because tying yourself to me, committing to a future, hell, loving me, opens you up to a potential world of hurt? Real hurt rather than this fictional crap you seem so happy to live through.'

And with that she released the button on the doors and the lift took her away from him. She didn't care about the reporters, or the hotel staff, or the onlookers; she pushed her way through the lot and out of Theo's life.

For good.

Bree loved him.

No one aside from his mother and his brother had ever loved him. Not even Tanya had said those words, reaffirming his conviction that she'd been motivated by her desire for status and wealth.

Though he believed Bree had got one thing right. Tanya was reacting to what she'd witnessed on the bridge. It was the only explanation for her to have leaked the story to the press now. She'd wanted to ruin him, to ruin what he'd found with Bree.

But you were the one who let her do it. You were the one that let Tanya win and pushed Bree away. You. You. You.

He shook off the mental rant and grabbed his phone, spoke to his security detail to ensure that Bree had a team tracking her, keeping her safe from reporters and the public alike, and to report back as soon as she was safe at home.

He'd have to speak to Sebastian, too. He'd need help UK side to keep her shielded as much as possible. Her family, too.

And shouldn't you be doing the shielding, you fool?

But this *was* him protecting her. Keeping her safe from the screw-up he was. Using her to make him feel like a better man when in truth, he wasn't. And she would realise it soon enough when the stories kept on coming.

His phone started to ring in his hand, the sound so much sharper for the chilling silence Bree had left behind. He lifted it, the tiniest flicker of hope that it would be her—not that he should want it—and cursed. It wasn't Bree.

He lifted his gaze to the world outside as if it would somehow save him from the conversation he was about to have and sucked in a breath. Get it done.

Shoving the phone to his ear, he answered. 'I don't need to hear it, bro.'

'Hello to you, too, brother.'

'Can we skip ahead on the venting and talk—?'

'You know nothing about women if you think Flick is going to let me just skip ahead. What the hell happened? What's all this rubbish about you abandoning Tanya after she miscarried? Please tell me that isn't true.'

'Of course, it's not.' He sank into the sofa, his eyes unseeing on the coffee table and the papers that Bree had tossed back there as she'd raced from the room.

'Then why is she saying it?'

He blew out a breath, fell back against the cushions and stared at the ceiling. 'It's a long story.'

'Then give me the abridged version. Now.'

And so, he did. Summing it up, just as he had for Bree. Had it really only been a fortnight ago?

'She's not heartbroken,' he finished with. 'She's just upset that she saw me and Bree together last night.'

'How together?'

'Very.' He swallowed the sudden wedge in his throat,

the pang of what they'd had and what he'd now lost killing him from the inside out.

'Let me guess, she saw what Flick and I saw?'

'And what's that?'

'That you're in love, of course.'

The wedge returned, cutting off his ability to breathe.

'Theo? You there? What's—?'

'It's over, brother.'

Silence.

Then, 'What do you mean "It's over"? I know this news with Tanya is upsetting and distressing but—'

'I mean, I ended it. She's gone.'

'What? But why?'

'Because it wasn't going to work out and she didn't deserve to be stuck in the middle of this now.'

'And did you let her have an opinion on this?'

'Sebastian.'

'Don't Sebastian me, it wasn't so long ago you woke me up and gave me the talking-to I needed to fix my own love life.'

'You guys are different. You deserve each other.'

'And you deserve Bree!'

'I'm sure Flick wouldn't agree with you.'

'You'd be surprised.'

Theo scanned his very empty apartment, the sinking feeling in his chest deepening with every passing second. 'It doesn't matter now; she's gone.'

'So? Go get her back!'

'I can't.'

'Why can't you?'

'Because it will only delay the inevitable. It's only a matter of time before she sees the real me, the screw-up behind the grin. It's better to end it now, save her from all this, before…' Theo's chest spasmed, his head and his heart colliding.

'Before what?'

He couldn't answer.

'Before what, Theo? Say it.'

He swallowed but it was no good, the sickness was rising within him, the tightness intensifying in his chest.

'Before you fall in love with her?' his brother said softly.

'Yes,' he breathed.

'But you already are.'

'I know.' It was a choke now.

'And how does she feel about you?'

He heard Bree's words as clear as day, could conjure her up before him, her eyes bright, her tears falling. 'She says she loves me.'

'And you let her go?'

'What else could I do? She's in love with the idea of me, not—'

'For an intelligent guy, you can be so stupid at times.'

'Thanks for the understanding.'

'Have you listened to yourself? You've got your women confused! Tanya, yes, she was in love with the idea of you, the image. But Bree... I've never seen you more yourself than you've been around her. I mean it, Theo. You are good together and I believe that you're ready to settle down, not because you're older, or wiser, but because you've met the right woman and if you don't get over yourself and go after her, I'll be forced to come to you and sort you out in person.'

'Liar, you're not leaving Flick's side.'

'I'll bring her with me; Angel, too. Then you'll have them to deal with as well as me and if that idea doesn't put fear into you, I don't know what else will.'

'I don't know, Sebastian.' He forked his fingers through his hair, pressed his palm into his scalp. 'I have no track record of this. What if I make it worse? What if I break her heart?'

'I think you're missing the point.'

'Which is?'

'You've already broken it; your own, too. None of us can predict the future, Theo, but if you don't take this chance and go after her, you will lose her for ever. Is that really what you want?'

'No. God, no.'

He fisted his hand, pressed it to his mouth. How could he have been so stupid? Yes, he'd wanted to save her from the press frenzy, the pain of what was to come, the slander...he couldn't bear to have her name tainted with his.

But it was fear that had driven him to take control and end it now, fear and his love for her that had forced him to make a decision before it was made for him.

He moved quickly, his goodbye to his brother a blur as he threw on his jacket and grabbed his keys. He went straight to the basement and his motorbike. The helmet was his disguise, the transport perfect to weave in and out of traffic. His phone buzzed with a check-in from the security team tailing her. She was in a taxi heading for the airport. If he could just get to her, explain...

The engine reverberated beneath him as he shoved his helmet on.

He had time.

He could do this.

He emerged from the basement, a few stray members of the press were lingering but didn't give him more than a second's glance, and even if they had, he was already gone, speeding through the traffic. He had no idea which taxi she was in but so long as he headed for the airport, he'd reach her.

He would.

Traffic was heavy, noisy, but it was his heart pounding in his head that accompanied his race to the airport drop-off zone. It felt like an eternity but finally the terminal was in sight.

He swerved between the arrival cars, ignoring the shouts and the hoots. He needed to get to her. Where was she?

He peered through the windows of the taxis as he passed, uncaring at the looks he received in return...

Come on, Bree, where are you?

And then he saw her and the bike lurched beneath him. She was paying a cab driver, grabbing her luggage, turning away—

'Bree! Bree!' His voice was muffled beneath his helmet, and he flicked up the visor, tried again. 'Bree!'

But it was no good in the hustle and bustle of coaches, taxis, and people, too many people. He eased forward but she was getting further and further away. So close to the doors now. Cursing, he threw his bike up onto the kerb, tossed his helmet to the floor, and started to run. 'Bree!'

'Monsieur, monsieur!' Airport security raced towards him, gesticulating at the bike. *'Vous ne pouvez pas laisser votre moto ici!'*

But he wasn't listening, his entire focus was on the woman walking away so fast he swore she knew he was there. He waved down his own security detail as they made their presence known and moved to intercept her.

'Bree!'

She stuttered to a stop, her head turning just a little.

'Bree!' He slowed, gasping for air as relief coursed through him. She'd stopped. Thank God, she'd stopped.

She turned to face him full on, a confused frown tugging at her brow. 'Theo?'

He closed the gap between them, his hands reaching out to take hold of hers. They were limp in his grasp, her shock written in the wideness of her eyes, her pallor. 'What are you doing?'

'Monsieur...monsieur!'

Her eyes flitted to the security guards racing up behind

him and he turned, his hands raised, palms out. *'Pardon, s'il vous plaît. Juste une minute. S'il vous plaît.'*

The guards came to a standstill, looked to one another and gave a brief shrug, but their expressions remained grave as they permitted him a nod.

'Merci,' he rushed out, coming back to her, his hands returning to hers. He needed to hold her, to feel her in his grasp, within reach. Always within reach. 'Bree, I'm an idiot, a fool, please forgive me. I don't want this to be over. I just wanted to protect you and I was scared, so scared of losing you in the future that I—I ended it now. You were right. About everything.'

'And I'm supposed to believe you've changed your mind in the space of what—an hour?'

'Less than. I came after you almost as soon as you had gone. Sebastian rang and gave me a talking-to, he made me see sense, made me realise what I was losing.'

She was shaking her head, tugging away. 'I'm so glad your brother is capable of making you see what I can't.'

'No, Bree.' He caught her back to him. 'Please. That's not what I meant. Please. Don't go.'

She pulled away. 'It's too late, Theo. I want to believe you, I do, but… I can't be with a man that can tolerate the abuse like you do. I think on some level you believe you deserve it and I'm not sure I'm enough to convince you that you don't.'

'I know, Bree. I know, but I want to try. I want to give us a try…' He wet his lips, gripped the back of his neck as he took in her continued hesitancy. Why was this so hard? How could he convince her? There was nothing else for it but to wear his heart on his sleeve. And if she rejected him… His gut rolled. It was a chance he had to take.

'I love you, Bree. I truly do.'

She gave a choked sound, tears spiking in her eyes as she pressed her palm to her chest. 'And I love you, Theo.'

His heart soared as he stepped forward and then faltered. She wasn't smiling, coming closer, she looked more distant, more withdrawn.

He frowned. 'Bree?'

She backed away. 'Don't.'

'But, Bree…we love each other. Isn't that enough to make this work? To give me a second chance?'

'This morning, I would have thought so. If you'd said it to me this morning instead of pushing me away, I'd likely have fallen into your arms and said to hell with the rest.' She shook her head. 'But it isn't.' The tears rolled down her cheeks, their glistening trail crushing him with her words. 'You need to sort your life out. You need to take control of the narrative and deal with Tanya. You need to deal with you. And until you do, I can't trust your love for me.'

'But, Bree…'

'Please, Theo, we're gaining an audience and I've had enough of being on the stage for one day.'

She was right. They were. An audience filled with phones videoing, people murmuring, gossip spreading.

'And to use your own words, I won't be so naïve as to make us a romantic cliché. Goodbye, Theo.'

He watched her go, immobilised by grief, uncaring that he was a broken spectacle. Uncaring about anything or anyone but the woman walking away and taking his heart with her.

CHAPTER FIFTEEN

Three months later

'STARING AT IT isn't going to change what he's written.'

Bree lifted her gaze from the magazine to take in her friend's earnest expression. 'He didn't write it.'

'Come on, Bree! It's in every article…' Felicity picked up the stack of magazines she had collected over the past few months and dumped them on the coffee table between them. 'You know full well it's come from him. He's taking control of his life and Sebastian says he's never seen his brother so serious about anything…or anyone.'

'If that's the case, why hasn't he tried to reach me?'

'I could ask you the same. You have his number. You could have called.'

Felicity wasn't wrong, she could have. But…

'No. He needed time and space without me in it and I…'

'And you…?'

'I don't know. What if…what if all this…stuff—' she waved a hand at the articles '—is the press putting a positive spin on it? Everyone loves a Cinderella tale and they don't come more Cinders than yours truly. What if he's never going to be ready for a relationship? What if I'm the only one who still feels like this? What if I'm the last person he wants to see tomorrow?'

Felicity was shaking her head, her eyes sparkling, her lips quivering.

'I'm so glad my torment amuses you.'

'I'm sorry, honey, but you need to stop overthinking everything. When you see him tomorrow—'

'Tomorrow is your wedding day and the last occasion on earth I want impacted by this.'

'Don't be so ridiculous.'

'Felicity! He's Sebastian's best man and I'm your maid of honour. Tomorrow is about you, not us!'

'But if the time and place works…' Her friend shrugged. 'Seriously, honey, I can think of far worse wedding gifts than seeing the two of you happy and together again.'

Happy. Together. Her stomach flip-flopped and all the other reasons she hadn't called Theo raced through her mind.

It was all well and good Sebastian thinking his brother was making great strides in the right direction, but what if he wasn't? What if it was just another version of himself that Theo was projecting to appease his brother's concerns? What if the story the press was touting was just another Theo projection?

The man himself grinned up at her from the coffee table—that snile, those eyes…

Her pulse spiked and she looked away, snatching up her mojito to hide the gulp she couldn't quite suppress.

'Don't you snort at me, Bree Johansson.'

'It was more of a gulp.'

'Gulp, snort, whatever! There's hope for you both yet and I'm not giving up. You're the mystery woman all those magazines are talking about, the one that has captured his heart. As for Tanya Bedingfield, don't tell me you're not a little happy at her getting her comeuppance.'

Bree couldn't contain her smile at that. 'No, that much is true. He didn't out her though.'

'No…but he told the press there was more to that story if they looked hard enough and sure enough that housekeeper couldn't wait to spill the beans.'

'For the money they likely offered, the housekeeper would have said anything, I'm sure.'

'Yeah, well, the housekeeper's story corroborated what

Theo told you, and it wasn't just the tampons, there were the pregnancy tests she was buying for her too.'

'I still don't understand why Tanya didn't get them herself.'

'She'd never have been able to do it without being spotted, besides I imagine she was paying the housekeeper enough to keep quiet. That is until she lost it so completely.'

Bree grimaced. 'You mean the night she saw us?'

'Yup. She upset a lot of people on her rampage so it's no surprise all those tales have been leaked to the press. Sounds like she has quite the nasty streak. Heaven knows what Theo ever saw in her... Sorry.'

Bree waved her apology down. 'Don't be sorry. He's a grown man capable of making his own bad decisions.'

'Still, I do feel sorry for him.'

Bree sipped her cocktail, feeling her heart warm over his public exoneration, even as her chest ached with longing. 'I know.'

'It's nice that he didn't have to sink so low as to dish the dirt.'

'I guess. So where is he anyhow? Surely the best man should have been here this week ensuring everything runs smoothly tomorrow.'

Felicity's cheeks coloured—she was, quite literally, the blushing bride.

'He had some business to take care of but he's here now. He and Sebastian are having a quiet night in.'

'A quiet night at the manor, hey?' She tried to ignore the way her heart pulsed at the thought of him already so close. 'Sounds fun.'

'And fun is exactly what we should be having!' In came Angel, her arms laden with food, eye masks dangling from her elbow. 'But first we need a pic in our matching robes! They're so cute!'

Bree looked down at herself wrapped in baby pink satin,

a gold emblem labelling her as 'Maid of Honour' on her chest. Angel's was the same with 'Bridesmaid'. And Felicity's was white with, of course, 'Bride'.

'Cute? That's one word for it.' She forced a grin, determined to shift Theo from her mind and make the night one to remember for her friend. 'We need fizz for the pic. I'll crack open the champagne Sebastian sent over; you get the glasses, Angel.'

'Mojitos and champagne?' Felicity frowned. 'Do you think that's wise?'

'If you can't be a little wild the night before you tie yourself to a man for eternity, when can you?' Bree sprang to her feet as Angel giggled and Felicity stared at her almost empty mojito glass.

'Well, when you put it like that...'

'Will you stop?'

Theo glanced at his brother. 'Stop what?'

'Tugging at your collar. You're making me nervous.'

'You're not already nervous?'

His brother laughed, his shoulders shuddering with it. 'We're standing at the head of the aisle, on my wedding day, and you're the one breaking a sweat. There's something wrong with this picture.'

'Ahem.' The vicar cleared her throat, the music changed and the brothers stood to attention. 'If you can all be upstanding...'

'Here we go,' Theo murmured. 'You ready for this?'

'Are you?'

Sebastian gave him a grin and then they both turned, both froze, both gaped, and then came the smiles, slow and building. Theo's heart felt too big for his chest, pushing against his ribs as the warmth inside exploded. His first sight of Bree in far too long and she was...everything.

Radiant in gold, her dress shimmered against her rich

brown skin, her curves accented by the fishtail cut, her dark, silken locks twisted up high with diamantés glinting in the soft light of the church. And then their eyes met, and he forgot to breathe, he forgot his role, he forgot Angel behind and the all-important bride behind her. He only had eyes for Bree and hers were big and brown and shining right back at him.

He couldn't look away, his hands gripped one another before him, his body desperate to go to her and sweep her up into his arms, confess his all, and then she blinked, her gaze shifting to Sebastian and her smile filled her face and Theo's heart. His love for her pushing out all else as her shift in attention reminded him that he, too, had a job to perform.

He'd assured his brother he could get his best man duties right without attending the dress rehearsal and he knew what he had to do, he just hoped his fingers would stop trembling long enough to hand the rings over safely. He was nervous. Too nervous.

And not about the wedding, and his speech, but her and how she would receive him.

He was a man on a mission and he wanted to get to it as soon as possible.

He would have gone to her the night before, but that was one tradition Sebastian had insisted they stuck to, and he'd agreed.

Plus, the idea of coming to a wedding with a potentially fresh rejection hanging over him hadn't quite appealed. Though if Sebastian was to be believed, Bree had suffered just as much as he had the last few months.

Not that he wanted her to suffer, but it had to be a good sign…a sign that meant she would welcome what he had to say.

'Dearly beloved, we are gathered here today…'

He stood straighter, fixed his sights on the vicar and

shut down the rising turmoil within. There would be time for them later.

He hoped.

Oh, my God, stop staring, Bree!

Theo in jeans and tee—yum!

Theo in lounge pants and tee—totally edible!

Theo naked—hello, ovaries!

But Theo in a dark three-piece suit was…something else.

So much for rebuilding her defences before she saw him today.

She was a hot mess, a hot mess with a heart that couldn't seem to heal and a libido that had been sorely neglected the last three months.

This was not going to be a breeze. No matter how much Angel had told her it would be. But then again, listening to a sixteen-year-old when it came to matters of the heart was never wise. Particularly after several mojitos topped off with champagne.

Her head still hadn't forgiven her for the alcohol.

Just as her heart hadn't forgiven her for giving it away so readily when she should have known better.

She pulled her eyes from him and watched the ceremony proceed, her ears attuned to the words being said, her heart and body a buzzing hive of awareness all for him.

She just needed to focus. On the ceremony, not him.

But her eyes didn't agree, they kept drifting, eager to take in the cut of his suit over his broad shoulders, his hair curling over the collar, his strong jaw and straight nose, the hint of fringe that refused to stay put, and she clenched her hands around her bouquet. Tried to stare at the floral perfection in her lap, rather than the male perfection up front. But then he was stepping forward to offer the rings and she couldn't not look any more.

Her heart tripped over itself as he smiled and passed one

to Sebastian and then Felicity. She heard their vows, but she saw him. In all his perfection and imperfection.

She saw the recent press articles in her mind's eye, could repeat them word for word, his words of love, of regret…

You're the mystery woman all those magazines are talking about, the one that has captured his heart.

Her own heart fluttered and, as if sensing it, his eyes drifted to her.

Theo.

She felt his name breathe through her, felt her lips twitch into a smile, saw his own do the same, his blue eyes warming her from across the distance.

'You may now kiss the bride!'

She was jarred back into the moment as Sebastian swept Felicity into a kiss and the crowd roared, the villagers turning out en masse to celebrate the first marriage the Ferringtons had seen in years. All excited for the future now that they knew the hotel was no longer going ahead. That all the traditions they'd grown up with—annual galas, Christmas balls, charity events—were coming back to Elmdale courtesy of its new owners.

They stood to leave, the bride and groom taking the lead, and then Theo was offering out his arm to her as per his role and she went gladly. The second their bodies touched, a torch lit within her, blazing ever brighter as they stepped down the aisle.

'You're such a sight for sore eyes,' he murmured.

She gave a huff—half nerves, half disbelief—and kept her eyes ahead as the crowd either side of the aisle cheered and smiled on. 'Is that supposed to be a compliment?'

'Absolutely.'

And there he was, the Theo she had fallen in love with, the cheeky spark with the underlying sincerity, and she couldn't help looking up at him, couldn't help the continued flutter in her heart. She loved this man. Would always love him.

Regardless of what had happened, all that he had said, so much had happened since…

Yes, she'd got it second-hand via his brother and Felicity—through the darn press, too—but this time did the latter have it right? There was only one way to find out…

And then she'd know…in her heart she would know.

They stepped out of the church and the cameraman was upon them, demanding Theo's attention to help organise the photos but… He looked to where his brother and his radiant new wife were deep in conversation and made a decision.

It was selfish and Sebastian might crucify him for it later, but his gut feeling said his brother wouldn't. Sebastian had all his heart desired now. It was Theo's turn, and his brother would be the first to give his blessing. Wedding day or not.

'I think we're okay for a little while. Let them speak to the guests and then we'll get straight on it.'

'But we have lots of pictures to get through. I've been given a list…'

'And no one is going anywhere in a hurry. We have time and even the weather is playing ball; there's not a cloud in the sky.'

'But I—'

'Have all day and most of the evening to get all the shots you need.' Theo smiled his most charming smile. 'I just need a minute with this lovely lady and then I promise I'm all yours.' He looked to Bree, smiled down at her and felt his heart burst anew. 'Deal?'

Though he said the word to her, the photographer jumped to life. 'Of course, of course. You take all the time you need.'

Whether it was the suggestion of a scoop on Theo's love life, a picture he could sell himself for a fortune, or the look of desperate longing in Theo's eye, he didn't know, he was simply grateful that the photographer had moved on and to all intents and purposes they were alone.

'Bree...' It came out like a plea. Three months of being without her and he felt as if he was walking out of the dark again and into the light. 'God, Bree.'

She turned to face him and he reached to cup her face, his body softening as warmth seeped into his limbs when she didn't resist. Instead, her eyes lifted to his, their gazes connecting. 'What, Theo?'

'I've missed you.' He searched her gaze for the same. 'I've never known a pain like it.'

She wet her lips. 'You've been busy though, I see.'

He frowned and her face bloomed. 'I saw the articles, all of them, I reckon, thanks to your brother and Felicity.'

'Aah.' He gave a sheepish smile. 'I may have told them where to look but I had to get my message out to you.'

'And you couldn't do that yourself?'

Her voice was so whisper-soft he had to strain to hear her past his blood racing in his ears.

'I took your words to heart. You needed your space and so did I. I needed to get help before I could come to you and so I did.'

'Get help?'

He nodded. 'I've been seeing a therapist. It appears I not only have daddy issues, but also a whole heap of baggage thanks to my upbringing.'

She reached out then, her bouquet catching on his jacket as she slipped her hands beneath it. 'Has it helped?'

'I'd like to think so.' He raised his brows, grinned down at her. 'Turns out, it's all fixable...with a bit of hard graft.'

She gave a soft laugh. 'Something you're very good at.'

'The graft, yes...talking, not so much. But I'm getting better at it. Practice makes perfect.'

'So they say...'

'And it appears that talking about it to a stranger isn't the worst thing in the world.'

'No?'

'No. And now I'm here, not quite fixed, but getting there and...' He hesitated. This was it. The moment of truth.

'And?'

'And I'm sick of looking back. I want to look to the future.'

She tilted her head to the side, her eyes not leaving his. 'And what does that entail for you?'

'You, Bree. If you'll have me. I know I'm a risk, a long shot. I've spent the last two days in Scotland apologising to your parents for what I put you through and convincing them of my love for you and if you'll—'

'You've what?'

He shifted from one foot to the other. 'Look, I know your parents would have seen you in those pictures in Paris— half the world saw them—and I couldn't come back here, plead with you to give me another chance, without speaking to them first.'

'Are you kidding?'

'No. It must be hard enough for them to have you living so far away and what I did...what the press did...' He shuddered, unable to stop the cold running through him, the guilt.

'What did you tell them?'

'The truth. I told them I was head over heels in love with you and that I would like to date you with the intent to marry you—hopefully with their blessing—and I would spend the rest of my life doing everything within my power to make you happy.'

'You told them you would marry me?' she whispered, eyes wide. 'But...'

'Correction. I told them I would marry you if you would have me.'

'Have you?' She laughed soundlessly, head shaking.

'Yes.'

'This doesn't feel real.'

'Believe me, the nervous sweat I have going on tells me this is real.'

'You, Theo Dubois, have a nervous sweat on?'

'Yes, Bree! You broke me when you left, you broke me and I did everything I could to fix myself, to make sure that when I came back to you, I could promise you the world and my love for you, and you would believe me.'

She gave another laugh, her eyes glistening, her hands reaching up into his hair, bouquet and all.

'So, do you?'

'Do I what, Theo?'

'Believe me?'

'That you love me?'

'Yes.'

Her smile was electric. 'I believe you.'

He tugged her to him, his voice a growl. 'Thank God.'

'Wait!' She pressed a finger to his lips before he could kiss her, knowing she had to be completely open with him, she had to make him see what he had given her, too. 'Since we're being all confessional, you should know something.'

He frowned, his hands flexing on her hips. 'Do I want to hear this?'

'Yes!' She gave him a smile and a nudge with her hip. 'You're not the only one to have changed thanks to this, thanks to us. You changed me, Theo, you made me realise I can be whomever I want to be, I can go after what I want and though I may fear the repercussions, it doesn't mean I shouldn't do it. My heart wanted to keep you three months ago, but I wanted all of you—the real you—and that wasn't what you were offering. It took strength to walk away, and it takes strength to believe in us now, but it makes all the difference when we're both projecting the real version of ourselves. The one that makes us both happy because we're right for one another...just the way we are.'

He could feel tears spiking, the wedge in his throat threatening to cut off his airway.

'What?' A delightful frown creased up her brow as her eyes searched his. 'Why are you looking at me like that?'

'Because you, Bree Johansson, are the most amazing woman I have ever met and I want to slap myself silly for not seeing sense sooner. It would have saved us so much pain.'

'But you're here now and that's what matters. We needed that time.'

'And there you go again, talking so much sense.'

She reached up, brushed her lips against his, the contact thrilling him to the core. 'You ready to hear more?'

A smile tugged at his lips, his heart. 'I think so.'

His ears strained to listen, his eyes, too, as he refused to blink...

'I love you, Theo, always and for ever.'

He wanted to whoop. Instead, he swept her up into his arms and kissed her so sweetly, so passionately, throwing his all into a silent crowd-sensitive kiss, but he needn't have worried as an almighty cheer broke out around them.

'About time,' came Angel's voice.

'You're telling me,' came Flick.

'I'm proud of you, bro,' came Sebastian.

As for the crowd, they were grinning, they were clapping, the limelight shared between the two Ferrington couples for the moment at least.

'You know this wedding's going to be hard to beat, right?' Bree murmured.

'Don't worry, I'm used to living in my brother's shadow.' Her eyes snapped to his as she elbowed him.

'Hey, I was joking!'

'You better be!'

'Always, baby, unless it comes to my love for you, in

which case I am deadly serious.' And then he kissed her again, uncaring of their audience, uncaring of anything but the future that suddenly looked so bright and possible, because with Bree by his side he knew he could conquer anything.

His past, the press, his future.

He finally believed he deserved it all.

EPILOGUE

Two years later

'THEO FERRINGTON...' BREE drew circles over her man's naked chest, relishing the quiet morning after the celebrations that had run on way past midnight the day before. 'It has quite a ring to it.'

'I guess it was my name before so it feels quite natural now, and I couldn't not change it after Sebastian took the leap.'

'Well, I, for one, like it.'

He gave a soft huff. 'Good job you do, Mrs Ferrington.'

She giggled. 'Not quite twenty-four hours in and I'm loving the ring to that, too.'

'You are?'

'Oh, yes, it's so very *Dynasty*, you know.'

He chuckled beneath her, his chest vibrating against her cheek. 'And what does that make you, then? The rich and spoilt heiress, or the devious stepmum or the psychotic biological one?'

'Hey!' She shot up, her palm pressed between his pecs as they rippled with more laughter. 'What are you trying to say about me?'

'Nothing.' He gave her a lazy grin. 'Though you have to admit, you have to be a little foolish to fall in love with me.'

'Is that so?'

'It is.' He pulled her into him for a kiss, pausing an inch from her lips. 'But from what I hear, everyone's a little foolish when it comes to love.'

'Amen to that.' She kissed him, breaking away before she got too carried away to say what she needed to. 'You know, I'm not quite ready to leave Paris.'

'Who said anything about leaving Paris?'

'Well, I assumed, what with Sebastian and Flick all settled and you making such changes, like your name—' she was back to toying with his chest '—and I know my family are all there. Then there's Angel and I have a feeling another niece or nephew might be on the horizon…'

'You thought I'd want us to move there?'

She nodded and he gave her a bemused frown. 'Have you already forgotten that we own a private jet and can readily country hop? You don't have to leave Paris until you're ready to and, even then, we can come back as often as you like.'

'That's true.'

'Though when you said you wanted to honeymoon here, I was a little surprised.'

'Why?'

'Because we've spent so much time here over the last two years, I thought you'd be up for the Caribbean, the Maldives, somewhere hot and I'd get to enjoy you in next to nothing most of the time.'

'You're going to get to do that anyway.'

He gave an appreciative growl. 'I'm very glad to hear it.'

'And besides, why would I want to spend our honeymoon somewhere else when we fell in love here and—' she looked up into his eyes '—made a baby here?'

'Well, as you once pointed out to me, it is the city of— Wait!' His blue eyes widened. 'What did you say?'

She smiled as his arm around her pulsed. 'Bree, are we…? Are you—?'

She nodded, tears of happiness welling at the sight of his. 'I only found out yesterday morning and I would have told you, but we never had a quiet moment and then…well, when we got up here something else was on your mind and it was our wedding night, after all.'

'Bree!' He gave a choked chuckle. 'This is the best wedding gift ever.'

'And the two of you are mine.'

* * * * *

IT STARTED WITH
A ROYAL KISS

JENNIFER FAYE

MILLS & BOON

CHAPTER ONE

A PRINCE.

A genuine, sexy-as-all-get-out royal prince.

Indigo Castellanos swallowed hard. She couldn't believe she'd come face-to-face with Prince Istvan of Rydiania. She didn't want to be impressed—not at all—but she couldn't deny being a little bit awed by his mesmerizing blue eyes and tanned face. Just the memory of his shirtless body sent her traitorous heart racing.

She never in a million years thought they'd actually meet. When she'd taken this artist position at the Ludus Resort, she'd known the prince had ties to the private island. Still, it was a large resort—big enough to avoid certain people. Sure, the royal regatta was going on, but she'd mistakenly thought the prince would be too busy to attend. And if he did make an appearance, he wouldn't meander around the resort like some commoner.

And then, when she did meet him, she hadn't said a word. If staring into his bottomless eyes hadn't been bad enough, she'd been stunned into silence by his muscled chest and trim waist.

She gave herself a mental shake. None of that mattered. Not at all.

Nothing changed the fact that the prince came from the same family that had cast her father out of his homeland. But she didn't have time to think of that now. Besides, she didn't expect to see the prince again.

She perched on a stool beneath a great big red umbrella. Her bare, painted toes wiggled in the warm sand. She was so thankful for this job. It helped her care for her ailing mother. And she would do anything for her mother.

"Is she sitting in the right position?"

The woman's voice drew Indigo from her thoughts. She focused on the mother and young daughter in front of her. The girl was seated on a stool. "Um, yes. Why?"

"Because you were frowning." The mother didn't look happy.

"So sorry. Your daughter is just perfect." Indigo forced a reassuring smile to her lips. "The glare off the water is making it hard to see."

Indigo shifted her position on the stool. She couldn't afford to have her clients think she wasn't happy or they wouldn't continue to bring their children and family members to have her draw caricatures of them. And without the clients there would be no job—without a job, she wouldn't be able to pay the mounting medical bills.

She forced herself to concentrate on her work. Her art was what had gotten her through the tough times in her life, from her father's sudden death to her mother's collapse. Whereas some people lived charmed lives—Prince Istvan's handsome image came to mind—other people were not so fortunate. She didn't let the challenges stop her from striving for something better—from believing if she just kept trying, good things were awaiting her.

Minutes later, she finished the young girl's caricature and gently unclipped the paper from her easel. She handed it over to the mother, who didn't smile as she examined Indigo's work. She then held it out to her nine-year-old daughter and asked her opinion. The girl's eyes widened as a big smile puffed up her cheeks. And that was all Indigo needed to make her day. After all, it was as her father used to say: *it's the small things in life where you find the greatest reward.*

"Wait until I show my friends."

"Now what do you say?" the mother prompted.

The girl turned her attention to Indigo. "Thank you."

"You're welcome." In that moment, it didn't matter that Indigo was doing fun sketches instead of grand works of art.

The only thing that mattered was that she'd brought some happiness to this girl's life.

"May I see it?" a male voice asked.

Indigo turned her head, and once again, she was caught off guard by the handsome prince. Her heart started to pitter-patter as she stared at him. What were the chances of them accidentally running into each other again?

"Oh." The mother's hand flew to her chest. "Your Highness." The woman did a deep curtsy.

The young girl's eyes filled with confusion as her gaze moved between her mother and Prince Istvan. Then her mother gestured for her to do the same thing. While the girl did a semi curtsy, Indigo sat by and took in the scene.

Was the prince here to see the mother? Did they have some sort of business together? Because there was absolutely no way he was there to see her. Not a chance. The royals and the Castellanos no longer intermingled—by royal decree. The reminder set Indigo's back teeth grinding together.

The prince turned in her direction. His eyes widened in surprise. Was it because he wasn't expecting to run into her again so soon? Or was it that she wasn't falling all over herself in front of him doing a curtsy? She refused to bow to him.

She should say something, but her mouth had gone dry. Words lodged in the back of her throat. And her heart was beating out of control. What was wrong with her?

The prince turned his attention back to the drawing. "It's fabulous. And who would the pretty young woman in the drawing be?"

"That's me," the girl said proudly.

The prince made a big deal of holding the sketch up next to the young girl, and then his dark brows drew together as his gaze moved between her and the drawing. "So it is.

You're lucky to have such a lovely sketch." He returned the paper to the girl. "Enjoy your day."

The mother and daughter curtsied again. Then the mother reached in her bright orange-and-white beach bag. She withdrew her phone. With the consent of the prince, she took a selfie with him. Though the prince smiled for the picture, Indigo noticed how the smile did not go the whole way to his blue eyes.

After the woman repeatedly thanked him, she turned to Indigo. "How much do I owe you?"

"Nothing," Indigo said. "It's a courtesy of the resort."

"Oh." She dropped her phone in her bag. "Thank you." And then her attention returned to the prince. She curtsied again.

Indigo wondered if she'd looked that ridiculous the other day when she'd first met the prince. She hoped not. But she had been totally caught off guard.

She expected him to move on, but he didn't. His attention turned to her. "And so we meet again."

She swallowed hard. "Your Highness."

Quite honestly, she didn't know what to say to him. He certainly didn't want to hear anything she had to say about him or his family—about how they were cold and uncaring about whom they hurt in the name of the crown. No, it was best not to go there. She didn't think her boss would approve of her vocalizing her true feelings about the prince's family.

She glanced down at the blank page in front of her. She could feel the prince's gaze upon her. What was he thinking? Did he recognize her?

Impossible. She'd only been a very young child when her family had fled Rydiania. Back then she'd been scared and confused. She'd had no idea why they were leaving their home and everything they'd ever known to move to Greece—a land that she'd never visited, filled with people she did not know.

"Shall I sit here?" The prince's deep voice drew her from her troubled thoughts.

"If you like." In an effort not to stare at his tanned chest, she barely glanced at him. Though it was a huge temptation. Very tempting indeed. Instead she fussed over the blank sheet of paper on her easel, pretending to straighten it.

What did he want? Surely he wasn't going to take the time to flirt with her when she had no standing in his regal world. So if he wasn't there to flirt with her, why was he lingering?

Curiosity got the best of her. "Is there something I can do for you?"

He smiled at her, but the happiness didn't show in his eyes. It was though there was something nagging at him that he didn't want to share with her. She wondered what could weigh so heavily on a prince's mind.

"I would like you to draw me."

Her gaze lifted just in time to witness him crossing his arms over that perfectly sculpted chest. *Oh, my!* The breath stilled in her chest as she continued to drink in the sight of his tanned and toned body. She wondered if he spent all his free time in the gym. Because there was no way anyone looked as good as him without working at it.

Her attention slipped down over the corded muscles of his arms and landed on his six-pack abs. It wasn't until her gaze reached the waistband of his blue-and-white board shorts that she realized she shouldn't be staring.

"Will that be a problem?" His voice drew her attention back to his face.

This time when she stared into his eyes, she noticed a hint of amusement twinkling in his eyes. She'd been totally busted staring at him. Heat started in her chest and worked its way up her neck. What was she doing, checking out the enemy?

Just keep it together. You need to keep this job.

Her little pep talk calmed her down just a bit. She drew in a deep breath and slowly released it. "Surely you have better things to do—erm, more important things than to have me sketch you."

She couldn't believe she was brushing off an opportunity to sketch a prince. If her friends could see her now they'd probably rush her to the hospital, certain she'd lost her grip on reality. But Istvan wasn't just any prince.

"I'm right where I want to be. Go ahead. Draw me."

Indigo hesitated. If he was anyone else but a member of the Rydianian royal family, she'd have jumped at the opportunity.

She'd grown up hearing stories of how the royal family wasn't to be trusted—that they put the crown above all else, including love of family. Her father was never the same after the former king, Georgios, and those in service to him were cast out of the kingdom. How could they do something so heartless?

"Is there a problem?" The prince's gaze studied her.

Unless she wanted to reveal the truth and put her new position at the Ludus Resort in jeopardy, she'd best get on with her job. She just had to pretend he was like any other guest at the resort, but she feared she wasn't that good of an actress.

She swallowed hard. "I don't think my sketch would do you justice."

He arched a brow. "Are you refusing to draw me?"

She thought about it. How many times had this prince been denied something he wanted? She doubted it ever happened. Oh, how she'd like to be the first to do it. But even she wasn't that reckless.

"No." She grabbed her black brush pen. Then her gaze rose to meet his. "I just want you to understand that it won't be a conservative, traditional portrait."

"I understand. And I don't want it to be. Just pretend I'm

any other patron." He settled himself on the stool while his security staff fanned out around him.

He was most definitely not just any other person—not even close. And yet he didn't have a clue who she was or how his family had destroyed hers. She thought of telling him, but what would that accomplish?

As she lifted her hand to the page, she noticed its slight tremor. She told herself she could do this. After all, the sooner she finished the sketch, the sooner the prince would move on. And so she pressed the brush pen to the paper and set to work.

It was impossible to do her job without looking at him. Her fingers tingled with the temptation to reach out to the dark, loose curls scattered over the top of his head. The sides and back of his head were clipped short. His tanned face had an aristocratic look, with a straight nose that wasn't too big nor too small. Dark brows highlighted his intense blue eyes with dark lashes. And a close-trimmed mustache and goatee framed his kissable lips.

In order to do her job, she had to take in every tiny detail of the person in front of her and translate them onto paper. And normally that wasn't hard for her. But sketching the prince was going to be the biggest challenge of her career as her heart raced and her fingers refused to cooperate.

She glanced around at the finely dressed men with hulking biceps and dark sunglasses. They were facing away from Istvan and Indigo, as though they were giving them some privacy while protecting them from the rest of the world.

"Don't worry about them," Prince Istvan said as though he could read her thoughts. "They're here to make sure there are no unwanted disturbances."

Indigo kept moving the black brush pen over the page. On second thought, the prince was really a pleasure to sketch with his strong jawline and firm chin. And then there was the dimple in his left cheek. Under any other circumstances, she'd readily admit that he was the most handsome man she'd ever sketched. But she refused to acknowledge such a thing—not about a member of the Rydianian royal family.

Prince Istvan might not have had anything to do with her father's dismissal from his lifelong service to the royal family or his subsequent banishment from the country, but that didn't mean Istvan wasn't one of them—raised to be like the uncaring, unfeeling royals who had destroyed her family.

"Does it take you long to do a sketch?" His smooth, rich voice interrupted her thoughts.

"No."

"How long does it usually take?"

She wasn't sure what to make of him going out of his way to make small talk. "Five to ten minutes. It all depends on how much detail work I do."

"That's amazing. It would take me twice as long to draw a stick figure." He sent her a friendly smile that made his baby blues twinkle.

She ignored the way her stomach dipped as she returned her focus to the drawing. Why did he have to be the prince from Rydiania? Why couldn't he just be a random guest at the resort?

She smothered a sigh and focused on her work. She took pleasure in the fact that she didn't have to do a true sketch of the prince. Her job was to exaggerate certain characteristics. She chose to elongate his chin and emphasize his perfectly straight white front teeth. His hair was perfectly styled, as though not a strand would dare defy the prince. She would fix that by drawing his hair a bit longer and messier. And then she took some creative liberty and added a crown that was falling off to the side of his head. A little smile pulled at the corner of her lips. It definitely wasn't the image of a proper prince.

The man on the page was more approachable. He didn't take himself too seriously. And this prince wouldn't endorse the demise of innocent and loyal subjects. If only fiction was reality.

With the outline complete, she started to fill in the sketch with a bit of color. When she first took this job at the resort, she'd considered just doing black-and-white sketches, but she was partial to colors. And it didn't take her much more time.

When she focused on the prince's blue eyes, she had a problem combining the blues to get that intense color. Maybe she should have just done a plain light blue color like she would have done for any other person. But it was though his eyes held a challenge for her. How could she resist?

When she glanced at him, it was though he could see straight through her. She wondered what he thought when he looked at her. But then again, he was a royal, so he probably didn't even see her—not really. He most likely saw nothing more than someone who was there to serve him.

Indigo switched up color after color. Her hand moved rapidly over the paper. He became distracted with his phone. With his attention elsewhere, it was easier for her to finish her task.

"I see you've decided to get a caricature done," a female voice said.

Indigo paused to glance over her shoulder to find her boss approaching them. Hermione wore a warm smile. Indigo wondered if Hermione had a secret crush on the prince. It wouldn't be hard to imagine her with him.

But then again, Hermione was now sporting a large, sparkly diamond ring. And her fiancé was almost as handsome as the prince. Hermione and the prince made chitchat while Indigo continued to add more details to the sketch. At one point, she leaned back to take in the partial image. Her discerning gaze swept down over the page. She surprised herself. There wasn't one negative aspect of the sketch. How could that be?

No imperfection that had been exaggerated. No big front teeth sticking out. No bulbous nose. No pointy chin. Nothing but his hotness exaggerated on the page into a cute caricature. And the crown she'd added to make him look like a carefree prince—well, even that didn't look like a negative. In fact, it just upped his cute factor.

As Hermione moved on, Indigo was still puzzling over the image that lacked any of her normal exaggerations. Was this really how she saw him? Like some fun, easygoing and kind royal?

Obviously not. He was heir to the throne. He would do things just as they had been done before— stepping on loved ones and family for the good of the crown.

CHAPTER TWO

DID HE HAVE better things to do with his time? Yes.

Did he really care about the mounting messages on his phone? No.

Prince Istvan lifted his head and stared at the top of the young woman's head as she worked behind the easel. He shifted to the side to get a better view of her. Her long hair was pulled back into a ponytail that fell over her shoulder. His fingers tingled with the urge to comb their way through the dark, silky strands.

His gaze strayed to her gold name tag. Indigo. Such a pretty name for someone so strikingly beautiful.

His attention returned to her face. Lines formed between her fine brows as she concentrated on her work. A pert little nose led to heart-shaped lips that were just begging to be kissed. It was such a tempting idea.

Just then she glanced up. Their gazes caught and held, causing a warm sensation in his chest. Did she know he had been fantasizing about pulling her into his embrace? Without a word, her attention returned to the easel.

There was something about her that made him feel like they somehow knew each other, but as he searched his memory, he was certain if their paths had crossed he would have remembered her. She had an unforgettable natural beauty about her, from her big brown eyes with flecks of gold that made them twinkle to her pert nose and lush lips that tempted and teased.

But he didn't have time to be distracted. He had problems awaiting him back home. His father was reaching a point where his health was forcing him to step down from the throne. Istvan was expected to take on more and more royal duties in preparation for the transfer of power.

The problem was, the more responsibilities he took on, the more unhappy he became. It wasn't the work he didn't like—it was the lack of time he had to devote to his pet projects. He had taken under his wing the Arts for Children, Homes for All and his biggest project, We Care—a foundation to support sick children and their families. All such worthy causes, and all needed more attention than he could possibly give each of them once he ascended to the throne.

But with his name attached to the charities, more people stepped up to help. More people were willing to give of their time, energy and money. If he were to walk away now, the future of the foundations would be in jeopardy because they weren't designated as royal charities. To fall under the royal designation, each charity had to meet stringent criteria—including being established for a minimum of fifty years. His projects were still in their infancy. And quite honestly, he didn't want to walk away. It was good work—important work. The foundations put him in direct contact with the people of the kingdom in a way he never would have been if he'd secluded himself in the palace. How was he supposed to rule over people when he didn't know what was important to them?

He was quickly coming to the realization that his family was becoming antiquated. It was a sobering thought he didn't dare share with anyone.

What was wrong with him? He should feel like he was on top of the world, but as the day of his crowning approached, the more he felt himself withdrawing from his family.

He couldn't help but wonder if this was how his uncle felt before he'd abdicated the throne—not that Istvan was planning to do the same thing. He'd been young when it happened, but he clearly recalled the turmoil it'd caused his family. There couldn't be a repeat.

His phone started to ring. He withdrew it from his pocket. The caller ID said it was his eldest sister, Gisella. He could already guess what was on his sister's mind—royal business. She might not be the heir to the throne, but that didn't keep her from assuming an important place in the family business.

He could only imagine she was calling to admonish him for missing some meeting. He always heard the disapproving tone in her voice when he was away from the palace.

It wasn't like this trip had been spontaneous. It had been on his calendar for a year. He had the speed boat race tomorrow. And he intended to win. He wasn't going to let anyone ruin these few days of relaxation. He'd be back at the palace soon enough.

And so he pressed the ignore button on his phone. Whatever it was, it could wait.

"If you have somewhere else to be, I can finish this without you." The sweet, melodic voice drew him from his thoughts.

Istvan blinked and stared at the artist. "Excuse me. What did you say?"

"That I can finish this drawing without you and have it delivered."

"That won't be necessary." He forced a smile, reassuring her that everything was all right.

She looked at him for a moment longer but didn't say anything. It was impossible to tell what she was thinking behind those big brown eyes.

A few minutes later, the young woman released the white paper from the clips on the board. She grasped the paper and approached him. "Here you go."

He took the paper from her. He didn't know what he expected. Under normal circumstances, an artist would be very reserved in their work since he was, after all, a prince. So he supposed he expected something similar from Indigo.

But when he held the sketch out in front of him, he realized she'd treated him just like she had her other clients.

In fact, for a moment he didn't recognize himself. Instead of smiling, he was frowning in the sketch. Was that how she saw him?

But the seriousness of the frown was offset by a crown that was sliding down the side of his head as his eyes were upturned, trying to figure out what was going on. He noticed the details from his eyes and lashes to the pucker lines in his rather large bottom lip.

Had she really been that observant? She was able to translate his thoughts to paper. Because he'd been thinking of how unhappy he was with the restraints the crown would place upon his life. But a casual observer would never pick up on it. This woman was keenly observant.

"This is remarkable," he said.

Her fine brows momentarily lifted, as though she were truly surprised by his praise. "I'm glad you like it."

"I think it's amazing that you can do all this in just a matter of minutes. I wish I could do something like this."

"Have you ever tried?"

He shook his head. "No. But I'm sure any attempt I'd make would be a disaster."

"You'll never know until you give it a try."

Art had never been an important part of his upbringing. His lessons had consisted of the basics in grammar and math, but the emphasis had been on history, specifically the history of Rydiania, government and civics. There was no room in his busy schedule for sports or arts.

He wondered what he'd missed by not exploring the arts. Was he an undiscovered grand pianist? He immediately dismissed the idea. There was nothing wrong with the piano, but he had never been curious about it or drawn to it.

Perhaps he would have been good at playing the guitar—maybe he would have been the lead guitar player in a rock band. He struggled not to smile as he imagined his parents' horrified expressions if he'd wanted to go in that direction.

Indigo pursed her lips as her brows drew together. "You find the suggestion funny?"

Oh, no. He hadn't hidden his thoughts as well as he'd thought. "No. It's not that. I was thinking of my parents' reaction if I told them I was giving up the throne to pursue something in the arts field."

"Oh." Her lush lips smoothed out, and her brows parted. "I'm guessing they would absolutely hate the idea."

His brows rose. "You sound as though you know them."

She shook her head. "No. Not at all. I... I was just guessing about their response."

He nodded in understanding. Just then the head of his security detail stepped up and whispered in his ear. His sister was eager to reach him and not happy that he wasn't answering his phone.

Istvan cleared his throat. "I must go now. But I want to thank you for this...interesting drawing. I've never had one like it. How much do I owe you?"

Color bloomed in her cheeks. "Nothing. It's courtesy of the resort."

"But surely I can tip you."

She shook her head. "I am paid well."

"I see." He hesitated. This never happened to him. Most people asked many things of him. Some requests he could accomplish, but there were many other requests that were far beyond his power. But this beautiful woman wanted nothing from him. He was intrigued.

"Sir, we must go," his head of security reminded him.

Even here on his uncle's island, far removed from his kingdom, his life was still not his own. "Yes. I'm coming." He turned back to Indigo. "I must leave, but I just want to thank you for this drawing. It's truly unique."

Her cheeks pinkened. "You're welcome."

And with that he walked away. He was tempted to glance over his shoulder at the woman who treated him like any other human instead of the crown prince. Was she really that immune to his charms? Or was there something more? Some other reason she kept a wall up between them?

Buzz. Buzz.

He didn't have time to consider the answers to his mounting questions. Royal duty took precedence over everything. His jaw tightened as he reached for his phone.

He didn't have to check the caller ID to know who was at the other end of the phone call. Princess Gisella.

"Hello." He struggled to keep the irritation out of his voice.

"It's about time. I've been trying to reach you. You should have known it was important, because I do not like making phone calls."

"I was preoccupied." He knew she was expecting an apology for not jumping when she'd called, but he was tired of feeling like their roles were reversed—tired of Gisella always proving she was the most loyal to the crown. "What do you need?"

"You. Back here at once."

He restrained a sigh. This was not their first conversation about his whereabouts or her utter displeasure with him for visiting their uncle's island. "I'll return after the weekend. I have a race to participate in."

"You shouldn't be racing. It's dangerous. You can't take frivolous chances with your life. You're the crown prince. If something happened…"

"You'd step in and be an amazing queen."

"Don't say that. It's like tempting fate."

Laughter erupted from his throat. "Gisella, you do worry too much."

"Someone has to. You certainly don't."

"I'll be safe."

"Make sure you are. What about the visit from the Spanish delegation? The festival is this weekend, and you must make an appearance."

"I'm sure you can charm them."

Gisella sighed. "I can't always fill in for you. You are, after all, the crown prince."

"Maybe you should be. You enjoy all that pomp and circumstance."

"Istvan!" Gisella's voice took on a warning tone, telling him that he was going too far.

"Relax. I'm just giving you a hard time."

There was a strained pause. "See that you are here early. There's a cabinet meeting on Monday morning, and you are to attend with the king. And you have yet to sit for your portrait. It is needed not only for the palace, but it is also to be added to the currency."

And he had been dragging his feet. He didn't know how he felt about his face being on Rydiania's currency. Sure, it was only one denomination, while his father appeared on the rest. But still, it felt as though it were sealing his fate—hemming him into a life exactly like his parents'. The thought of being locked up in the palace for the rest of his life made him feel claustrophobic.

He'd much rather stay here on this sunny island with its colorful, fruity drinks and the most alluring artist. It was far more appealing than being cooped up with the royal painter for hours.

Suddenly a thought came to him. Perhaps sitting for the portrait didn't have to be as miserable as he'd been imagining. Perhaps it could be pleasurable.

Indigo's image came to mind. He wondered if she had any experience with personal portraits. He didn't know the answer, but it was something he planned to look into as soon as possible.

CHAPTER THREE

HIS VIVID BLUE eyes haunted her.

Later that afternoon, Indigo clipped a fresh paper to the easel. She couldn't stop thinking of the prince. He was not what she'd been expecting. Not at all.

Somehow she'd imagined him as a spoiled brat. He was not that. She'd expected him to be totally full of himself. He hadn't been. And she'd expected him to take himself too seriously—to the point where he wouldn't have been able to appreciate the sketch she'd done of him. And yet he'd genuinely seemed to like the silly sketch. What did that mean?

It would be so much easier to dislike the prince if he had some obvious negative qualities. But right now she was struggling to find something legitimate to dislike about him—other than his lineage.

As she bent over to retrieve a fresh pen from her large tote, she heard someone approaching. "Have a seat. I'll be right with you."

They didn't say a word, but she sensed their presence. She straightened, clipped the paper to the board and then glanced around it. She struggled not to gape when she found the prince sitting on the stool. Again.

Heat swirled in her chest. "Your Highness, you're back."

She noticed this time he was wearing a white T-shirt with the race logo on it. She felt an instant pang of disappointment at not getting another glimpse of his muscled chest. She swallowed hard.

When her gaze rose to meet his, she asked, "What can I do for you?"

"I would like to have another sketch done. I'm more than willing to compensate you."

"Another?" No one ever came back to her and requested a second sketch. "Did something happen to the first one?"

"No. Actually, I need another for a charity auction."

Charity? The prince? Really?

Nothing about the man sitting in front of her was like her father had warned her about the royal family. Istvan was not cold. He was not harsh. And he was not mean.

What was she supposed to make of this prince with his generous heart and dazzling smile that made her stomach dip? The only thing she knew was that the more time she spent with him, the more confused she became. It was best to keep her distance.

"Can't you use the sketch I already drew for you?"

"It can't be that one."

"Why? Was it too silly?" She'd been waiting for him to show his true colors.

He shook his head. "No. It was perfect. That's why I'm keeping it. I need another one for the auction."

"Something more serious?"

"Not at all. I enjoy your sense of humor. So have at it. I don't want any special treatment. You can do the same thing or something different. I don't care."

She inwardly groaned. What was it with this guy? He was making it impossible for her to dislike him. In fact, if she spent more time with him, she might fall for his azure-blue eyes and his sexy accent.

It was best to get this over with as quickly as possible. Indigo was certain that once she completed the sketch she wouldn't see the prince again.

In truth, she didn't need him to sit for her again. She had every detail of his handsome face memorized. She groaned inwardly.

The artist in her demanded she do something different than the first sketch. She never did duplicates of anything. Life was too short for repeats.

This time she decided to portray the prince in his royal world. She told herself it would be fun, but there was another reason—she needed a visual reminder that this man wasn't just another handsome face.

Her father had been obsessed with the royal family toward the end of his life. At the time, she couldn't understand why he went on and on about them. But as she grew older, she realized her father had considered his position as the king's secretary as much more than an occupation. To him, it was his life's calling—the position that had been handed down to him through the generations of his family's service to the royal family.

Not only had he been stripped of his calling, but he was then kicked out of the country like a traitor. It broke something in her father—something time and even love couldn't fix.

Indigo shoved the troubling thoughts to the back of her mind. Instead she focused on her work. She looked at the prince as little as possible, trying to work from memory. But she found herself questioning her memory time and again. Because it just wasn't possible for someone to look as good as him, from his high cheekbones to his strong chin to his perfectly straight nose.

And then there were his eyes. Oh, those eyes! She felt as though she were being drawn in every time their gazes connected. This time the prince wasn't distracted by his phone. This time his attention was solely on her. His unwavering gaze sent a current of awareness zipping through her veins.

She struggled to keep her hand from tremoring. That had never been a problem for her in the past. Why was she letting him get to her? He was just another guy. *Yeah, right.* He was anything but just another guy. And her traitorous body was well aware of it.

Her brush pen moved rapidly over the page. She forced

herself not to go too fast. After all, this was her art, and it deserved to be her best.

When at last she finished, she removed the page from the easel and handed it over. She wasn't sure what he'd think of her image. This sketch had him wearing a serious expression with his exaggerated chin slightly upturned as he wore his crooked crown and a royal cape, while holding a scepter in his hand.

He was quiet for a moment as he took in the image. "Is that how you really see me? Looking down on the world?"

He didn't sound pleased. It seemed her image had struck a nerve. She wasn't sure if it was a good thing—that he cared how the world saw him—or a bad thing, because he had the power to get her fired. She hadn't considered that dire consequence when she'd indulged her imagination.

It was best she try and smooth things out. She swallowed hard. "It's not how I see you. I don't even know you. I was just having some fun. If you give it back, I'll try again."

He stood, quietly staring at the image. "No. I will keep it."

"But if you don't like it—"

"Your art has a way of making one look at themselves in a totally different light." At last he smiled. "I like it." He paused and stared at the sketch a little longer. "I really like it."

"Are you sure?" It was in her best interest to make the prince happy, even if it was the last thing she wanted to do. She could imagine her father scolding her for placating the heir to the throne.

"I am positive. I will find a special spot for this."

Perhaps in the wastebasket? She kept the thought to herself. She'd already pushed her luck as far as she imagined it would go that day.

His gaze lifted and met hers. "Is this the only thing you do?"

"Excuse me?"

"Do you do other forms of artwork besides the sketches?"

She nodded. "I do. This is just a side job that I've picked up."

"You have more than one job?" He looked impressed.

"You have no idea."

In addition to her work at the resort, she was constantly adding to her collection of portraits. In her neighborhood, many of the residents were willing to pose for her. She was busy preparing for her first-ever gallery showing in Athens. It was a huge milestone. Plus, she helped care for her mother.

"I'd love to see some of your other work. Would that be possible? Do you have a website or something?"

She shook her head. "No website." But then she realized she'd taken a few photos of her latest pieces to show her agent. She pulled out her phone and pulled up the photos. "These are some recent pieces."

She wasn't sure why she was sharing any of this with him. It wasn't like they were friends—far from it. But it wasn't often she met someone who was interested in her work. And it felt good to be able to share it with him.

Her pieces were done in modern realism. There were paintings of her neighbors' daughters as they played, an older gentleman she'd met at the park and one of her mother. She painted what she saw and then gave the images her own interpretation.

Istvan paused on each photo. He was quiet as he studied them. She couldn't help but wonder what he was thinking. She wanted to ask, but she didn't dare. What if he hated them? As much as she tried to wear a tough outer shell, criticism still had a way of working past her well-laid defenses and planting a seed of doubt about her abilities.

But there was no way she was going to let him think his opinion mattered to her. Nothing could be further from the truth. She knew she was good at what she did. It wasn't her being conceited. It's what she'd been told by her agent, by clients and gallery owners. They were the people in the know.

She shifted her weight from one foot to the other. What was taking him so long? There were three photos for him to see. Unless he'd moved beyond those photos. Her chest tightened. Was he looking at her personal photos?

She moved slightly and craned her neck to get a glimpse of her phone. He was staring intently at the painting of her mother. Did he recognize her?

Indigo immediately scolded herself for overthinking things. There was no way he would recognize her. Her family had moved away from Rydiania when she was very little, so he couldn't have been much older. If he didn't recognize her mother, what was it about the painting that held his attention?

She glanced off to the side and noticed a rather lengthy line of customers had formed. She'd never had this much interest in her sketches since she'd arrived on the island. And then she realized what all the attention was about— the prince.

It was time to draw this conversation to an end. She cleared her throat. "Is there something else you need?"

He held her phone out to her. "These are good. No, they're great. You're very talented. So, then, why are you here doing caricatures?"

Because she needed the extra money to secure her mother a spot at the assisted living facility. But she wasn't about to reveal her struggles to the prince, who had no idea what it was to struggle for the things he wanted or needed.

"Work is work," she said.

He nodded as though he understood. "Thank you for sharing these with me. I see amazing things in your future." He turned as though to walk away, but then he turned back to her. "I was wondering if you'll be watching the race."

His inquiry caught her off guard. Why would he be interested in whether she'd be attending or not? Was he merely trying to make casual conversation? Or was it something more?

Was he flirting with her?

Laughter bubbled up inside her. She quickly stifled it. There was no way this handsome, eligible prince would be interested in her. Not a chance.

"I won't be able to attend. I have to work." She gestured to all the people lined up. The line kept growing. She really would have to work all day to get that many sketches completed.

"Surely they'll give you some time off to watch the race, since most every guest at the resort will probably be in attendance."

What she heard him say was that, being the prince, he was the center of the universe, so everyone would want to see what he was doing. Her back teeth ground together. It took all her willpower to subdue her frustration with him. "I'm sorry. I really do have to work."

"I know your boss—the new owners of the resort. I could get you some time off." There was a gleam in his eyes. Was it a hopeful look?

She shook her head. "I need to get back to work."

It was only then that she noticed him turning his head and taking in the view of the long line, waiting to have their sketches done. "I understand."

And yet he continued to stand there. Why was he being so obstinate? Had he never been turned down before? And then it came to her that no one would turn him down. Well, that was, no one except her.

Secretly, she was tempted to learn more about this prince. If she had met Istvan under different circumstances—if she hadn't known his true identity—she would have liked him. And that right there worried her. She couldn't fall for the enemy, because her father had trusted the royal family and look where that had gotten him—dead in what should have been the prime of his life.

He should go.

And yet his feet didn't move.

Istvan was utterly intrigued by Indigo. The more time he spent with her, the more he realized she was unlike any other woman he had ever known. And he had known quite a few during his globetrotting years.

There were times when Indigo looked at him and he thought she might be interested in him. And then there were other times when their gazes met and he could see the hostility lurking in their depths. How could she dislike him? She didn't know him yet. Or was it that she held his lineage against him? She wouldn't be the first person.

Whatever it was that was going on behind her beautiful eyes, he wanted to know the answers. He wanted to walk with her on the beach, and as the water washed over their bare feet, he wanted to learn what made her tick. And then he wanted to talk some more.

Okay, maybe he wanted to do more than talk. His gaze lowered. After all, her lush lips had beckoned to him more than once. *Oh, yes.* He definitely wanted to explore them and see if her kisses were as sweet as the berries he'd had for breakfast that morning.

It wasn't that he lacked for female companionship, but none could compare to Indigo, who insisted on speaking to him as she did everyone else. That was it. He never did like being treated specially—making him stand out from the others. He didn't feel special. Not at all.

And maybe part of that had to do with his uncle. When Georgios had abdicated the throne, it had had a huge impact on Istvan. He didn't want to think about that now. It always put him in a foul mood.

He shoved aside the troubling thoughts as his gaze met hers once more. He had something much more pleasant in mind. He planned to ask Indigo to dinner.

Buzz. Buzz.

He wanted to ignore the phone, but as it continued to vibrate in his pocket, it was impossible to ignore. He knew he wasn't going to like it, whoever it was. He'd bet his crown that it was the palace with some other task that required his attention.

"You should get that," she said, as though relieved to have an excuse to brush him off.

A dinner invitation teetered on the tip of his tongue. But he had a feeling if he were to ask her to dinner right now, she would turn him down, and he didn't want that to happen. Maybe another time would be better—a time when there wasn't a line of people waiting for her attention.

He withdrew his phone and saw that it was indeed the palace. He pressed Decline. But when he glanced up and saw the irritation radiating from Indigo's eyes, he realized it was time for him to move on.

"I'll get out of your way." His gaze lingered on her beautiful face for a moment longer than necessary. And then with reluctance, he walked away.

Buzz. Buzz.

When he checked his phone's caller ID, he found it was the palace...again. Whatever they wanted must be important.

With a resigned sign, he pressed the phone to his ear. "Prince Istvan."

"This is the queen's secretary," the older woman said in a measured tone. "The queen would like to remind you that this weekend we are hosting a formal dinner for Spain's dignitaries."

And yet another reminder of the responsibilities awaiting him at home. But this royal regatta was his responsibility, too. It was being held in memory of his uncle. And since he seemed to be the only family member who wanted to remember his uncle, there wasn't a chance he was leaving Ludus Island before the festivities were concluded.

"You may tell the queen that I'll be unavailable this weekend."

"Yes, Your Highness. And the queen would like to remind you that Monday afternoon you have an appointment to sit for your portrait."

The thought of sitting there for the royal artist, who didn't know how to smile, much less make light conversation, sounded like a punishment Istvan hadn't earned. He didn't see why the man couldn't work from a photo. But Istvan had been informed that a photo just wouldn't do.

Who would want to sit in an uncomfortable chair for hours while their mind went numb from boredom? But he hadn't felt that way when he'd sat for Indigo to sketch him. Now, granted the caricature didn't take nearly as long, but she intrigued him. And he had a feeling she could carry her end of a conversation if they'd had a bit more time together.

Suddenly his whimsical thought of commissioning Indigo to do his portrait was taking on more substance, especially after viewing some of her formal work. He wondered if she would be up for a trip. He would definitely make it worth her time.

"Tell my mother I'll make time for the portrait, but I plan to do it on my terms."

"Your Highness?" There was a note of a question to the secretary's tone.

Istvan chose to ignore her inquiry. "I must go." And with that the call was concluded.

He had been butting heads with his parents for years now. They wanted things done their way—the way they'd always been done. He wanted change. He wanted the monarchy to act with compassion.

Once his father had let it slip that Istvan was just like his uncle—thinking the dynasty should change according to the people's whims. But as soon as the king said it, he'd retracted the words. He told Istvan that he would never be like Georgios—he would never walk away from his responsibilities—because he'd raised him different. He'd raised him to be a true king.

CHAPTER FOUR

AT LAST, HER shift was over.

Indigo stifled a yawn. Thanks to the prince's insistence on a second sketch, she'd had an endless line of excited subjects. And they'd all had questions about Istvan—questions Indigo did her best to discourage.

She flexed her fingers. Her entire hand ached. She repeatedly stretched her fingers wide apart, trying to ease the ache in them. It only helped to a certain extent. If she had known her sketches were going to be in such great demand, she might have negotiated for a per-sketch fee on top of her base pay.

She folded the easel, grabbed her supply caddy and started toward the resort. With evening closing in, the beach area had quieted down. Everyone must be inside getting cleaned up for dinner. Indigo's stomach rumbled at the thought of food. She hadn't had time for lunch today. She couldn't keep up this pace. If it continued, she might have to mention to Hermione about hiring another artist.

"Indigo." Hermione, the resort's manager, waved as she rushed to catch up with her. "How did the day go?"

Indigo wasn't sure how honest to be with her boss about the overwhelming line of people. On the other hand, it was job security. "There were people lined up all day."

Hermione smiled. "I've been hearing lots of good things about your work. We'll have to discuss extending your time at the resort."

"Thank you." Indigo wasn't sure how that would work out going forward. She had a lot of hopes and dreams relying on her upcoming gallery show. Still, it was like her father used to tell her—*don't take for granted what is in hopes of what may be.* "That sounds good."

"So the prince has taken a liking to your work." Herm- ione sent her a reassuring smile. "That is huge praise. He's very particular about what he likes."

Indigo should be pleased with this compliment, but it just made her feel more uncomfortable. And she didn't want her new friend to think she was tripping over herself for the prince. "I… I didn't do anything for him that I haven't done for the other guests."

"And that's what makes it even more special."

Ding.

Hermione pulled her phone from her pocket. She read the message on the screen and then sighed.

Indigo hoped it wasn't bad news. Hermione had been kind to her. Indigo liked to think they were becoming fast friends. She appreciated how Hermione had taken a chance on hiring her when neither of them had known if the idea of caricatures would be a hit or a miss with the resort guests. Lucky for Indigo, her fun sketches had been met with great enthusiasm. And now she wished she could think of a way to pay Hermione back for believing in her.

"Is there something I can help with?" Indigo asked.

Hermione glanced up from her phone. Her fine brows were drawn together as though she were in deep thought. "Um…no. Thanks. I've got it."

Indigo didn't believe her. "I'd like to help if I can. After all, my shift is over."

Hermione sent her a hesitant look. "If you're sure." When Indigo nodded, Hermione said, "I wouldn't ask, but there's a snafu with a shipment at the dock, and on my way out of the building, I forgot to drop off some papers at the gallery."

"Okay. Let me take the paperwork to the gallery. It's on my way out."

Hermione withdrew a clipped stack of papers from her black leather portfolio. "Here you go. Everything is there that they'll need for the shipment." She then gave Indigo

JENNIFE FAYE 37

specific instructions on where to take the papers and whom to hand them to. It all seemed very straightforward and easy enough to handle.

"You're getting rid of an exhibit?" Indigo had been to the gallery many times. She loved to admire the various artworks. She hoped someday to have one of her paintings displayed in such a prestigious gallery.

Hermione shook her head. "We have agreements with other galleries. We exchange various pieces. This time we're loaning out *Clash of Hearts*."

Indigo remembered the piece because of its vibrant colors from hot pink to silver. It had been created of conjoined hearts of varying sizes that were repeated over the entire canvas. "It's a beautiful piece."

"Thank you. I was the one to acquire it." Hermione smiled brightly. When her phone dinged again, she said, "I better get going. Are you sure you don't mind doing this?"

"Not at all. I'll see you tomorrow." She gave a little wave before turning toward the resort.

Once inside the resort, the plush carpeting in the wide hallways smothered the sound of her footsteps. The resort was quiet. It was a lot like walking through a museum with its many art pieces, not only in the gallery but also displayed on the many hallways.

She found herself referring to it as a commoner's palace. But then again, why shouldn't the resort be fashioned after a palace, since its founder was once a king—a king who stepped aside to let his brother take over. In the process, King Georgios not only gave up his crown but he also lost his country and his family.

And though the Ludus Resort had every amenity imaginable and looked magnificent, it still wasn't a home. Both the former king and Indigo's father had died without ever being able to reclaim what they had loved and lost—their homeland. And for that she felt so sorry for both of them.

She approached the entrance of the Ludus Gallery. The large glass door silently swung open without much effort. The gallery was divided between the large front section with its tall white walls that gave the space a wide-open, airy feel and the back section that was the opposite, with black walls and spotlights used to highlight the gallery's headliner.

In this case, it was the Ruby Heart that was the shining star. Indigo had seen it once before, but it had been in passing because the gallery had been so busy. But today the gallery was quiet. It would give her a chance to admire the precious stone for as long as she wanted.

She approached the glass case. The stone was quite large. It was much too big to ever be worn as a piece of jewelry. The many cuts looked to have been very carefully planned, and each picked up the light, making it sparkle as though it were actually alive and full of energy.

She noticed a sign that displayed background information about the stone. Just as she was about to lean in closer to read the words, she heard someone behind her.

"It's beautiful," the smooth, deep voice said.

Indigo didn't have to turn around to know who was behind her—Prince Istvan. Not sure what to do, she continued to stare at the magnificent jewel. "Yes, it is."

"And yet it pales in beauty compared to you." His voice was so soft that it was as if the words had caressed her.

Heat gathered in her chest before rushing up her neck and setting her cheeks ablaze. Thank goodness she wasn't facing him.

She swallowed hard. And then hoped when she spoke her voice didn't betray her. "I've never seen a gem so large."

He moved next to her. "Did you read the legend attached to it?"

Her heart pounded. Her mouth grew dry. "Um, no. I was just about to do that."

"Let me." He leaned toward her as he focused on the

display. "'The legend of the Ruby Heart. If destined lovers gaze upon the Ruby Heart at the same time, their lives will be forever entwined.'"

Lovers? Suddenly a very hot and enticing image of her and Istvan entwined in each other's arms filled her mind. She gave herself a mental shake, chasing away the temptation. Why, oh, why had she stopped here? She should have just dropped off the papers and left. Then she could have avoided this awkward moment.

"Hmm…" The sound rumbled in his throat for a moment, almost as though he were a Cheshire cat eyeing up his prey—in this case, that would be her. "I wonder if they might be referring to us."

It felt as though the air-conditioning had been turned off and a blowtorch had been lit in her face. Her mouth went even drier as she struggled to swallow. "I'm quite certain they are mistaken in this case." How she got those words out and did not melt into a puddle on the floor was utterly beyond her. "I should be going."

The only problem was that he was standing between her and the hallway she needed to access to reach the business office, where she was to drop off the papers.

"Having second thoughts?" he asked.

When she glanced at him, she saw the amusement dancing in his eyes. "Not at all. You just happen to be standing in my way."

With an amused smile plastered on his undeniably handsome face, he stepped out of the way. "I look forward to our next meeting."

His words made her heart flutter. She tried to tell herself that it was just casual flirtation, but there was this look in his eyes. Other men had looked at her that way, so she recognized it. It was a look of attraction—a look that said he was interested in taking their relationship to the next level. Her heart went *thump-thump* in her chest.

The prince is interested in me?

She moved quickly toward the privacy of the little hallway. The distance from the prince didn't stop the heat from gathering in her chest and rushing to her face. She resisted the urge to fan herself.

She came to a stop in front of an open door. The sign on the door read Museum Curator. This was the right place. She rapped her knuckles on the doorjamb.

"Come in."

She stepped inside and noticed a messy desk off to the side. A middle-aged man with reading glasses perched on the end of his nose glanced up from a computer monitor. "Can I help you?"

"Yes. Hermione asked me to drop these off." She held out the clipped papers.

"Oh, yes. I was waiting for them." He accepted the papers. "Thank you."

"You're welcome."

It was time to leave, but she hesitated. Was the prince still in the gallery waiting for her? The thought sent her heart racing. She told herself it was the anxiety of dealing with his incorrigible flirting again. Nothing more.

"Was there something else?" the man asked.

"Um…" She quickly weighed her options. "Is there another exit?"

The man arched a brow in puzzlement. "There's the back exit. In the hallway, go to the right. And then make another right. It will take you to the loading area."

"Thank you."

She just wasn't ready to face the prince again. Not yet. She turned right just as the man had instructed.

Her steps were quick as she moved through the hallway. When her hands touched the metal door handle, she pushed it open. She breathed a sigh of relief. She'd escaped. But escaped what?

She wasn't prepared to answer that question. She shouldn't have let Istvan get to her. If she let her guard down with the handsome prince, it would lead to nothing but more heartache. She'd already had enough of that to last her an entire lifetime.

CHAPTER FIVE

THE GRAND RACE was about to begin.

It was the following afternoon, and Indigo couldn't deny that she was a bit curious about the regatta. She'd never been to a boat race before. And just as the prince had predicted, her line of guests had dissipated as the magical hour neared. Even Adara, the resort's concierge, had stopped by to let her know it would be all right for her to take in the race.

What would it hurt? After all, it wasn't like she was going there with the intent to see the prince. She was going because it was the biggest event on the island and everyone was going to watch the boat race, leaving her nothing else to do.

With her art supplies secured in a locker at the resort, she made her way to the area of the beach where the race was to start. However, she stood at the back of a sea of people. There was no way she'd make it to the front. And from back here she wouldn't be able to see a thing.

She glanced around, looking for a better vantage point. Just south of where she stood were cliffs. She didn't know if she could make it up there, but she'd give it a try. And so she started walking at a rapid pace.

When she found a trail that appeared to lead to higher ground, she followed it. It was a bit rugged and steep at times. Her sandals were not ideal for this trek, but that didn't deter her. And when the trail finally leveled off, she noticed a small clearing, and in the distance was a cliff.

She wasn't the only one to have this idea. Other people were gathered there. Some of the people she recognized as employees of the resort. She wondered if they were supposed to be working, like her. Still, if there were no people at the resort needing anything, why not indulge?

She made it to an open spot along the stone wall. At last, she could see the boats. In fact, they weren't that far away. And Prince Istvan's boat was easy to spot, with its host of flags. The top flag was a deep purple with a gold crown, signaling that there was a member of the royal family aboard.

A loud horn blew. Was this to signal the start of the race? Indigo was curious to see if Istvan would win. His boat was the same length as the others. She wondered if there were limitations on the boat size.

The boats started their engines and then moved into position. Since there were too many to line up in a single line, she assumed each boat had some sort of tracking device to keep track of its time.

And then she spotted Istvan standing behind the wheel of his boat. He was shirtless—again. If she were to paint him—not that she had any plans of doing such a thing— she'd be inclined to included his impressive chest and those six-pack abs. She subdued a laugh when she thought of the horrid looks such a painting would receive from the royal family.

As she continued to stare down at Istvan, he turned. His gaze scanned the crowd, and then it was as though he'd singled her out. His gaze paused. And then he waved. Surely he couldn't be waving at her. As everyone around her raised their hand to wave back, she resisted. It was a small resistance, but she had to prove—even if only to herself—that she was strong enough to resist his charms.

The horn blew again. The prince took his seat. Her gaze strayed across a digital clock at the end of the dock. Red numbers counted down from ten. And then with a third and final blow of the horn, the boats took off with a roar and a spray of water.

She watched as the prince guided his boat into the lead. Something told her it was where Istvan was most comfortable. And then the boats moved out of sight. From what

she'd heard from the people she'd sketched, the race en-
circled the island. And until they returned, there was nothing here to see.

She followed the trail back down to the resort, where she
nearly bumped into one of Prince Istvan's security detail.
The man was quite tall. She had to crane her neck to look
at his face. And then there were the dark sunglasses that
kept his eyes hidden from the world.

"Sorry," she said. "I didn't see you there."

"Ms. Castellanos?"

"Yes." What did he want with her?

"This is for you." He handed her a small envelope before walking away.

She stared at the sealed envelope. It took her a moment
to figure out what must be inside…the prince was insisting
on paying her for the sketches, even after she'd told him it
went against resort policy. Although the extra money would
help her mother, she just couldn't keep it. She didn't want
to lose her job at the resort.

But she was curious to see how much the prince valued
her work. That couldn't be against the rules, right? She
slipped her finger in the opening of the envelope and then
carefully released the flap.

She reached inside and pulled out a folded slip of paper.
This certainly wasn't a check. Disappointment assailed her.
So if the prince wasn't attempting to pay her, what did he
want?

She unfolded the paper and began to read.

Meet me at the Whale-of-a-Time Suite. 6 p.m.

That was it?

She turned the paper over to see if he'd written more. He
hadn't. What in the world was this about? Was this his attempt to ask her to dinner—or something more intimate?

Either way, it wasn't working for her. Besides if he knew who she was, he wouldn't want anything to do with her. And then she realized what she intended to do—stand up a prince. Who did such a thing?

The answer was easy…someone who knew the truth about the royal family of Rydiania. They were cold and ruthless. How many times had her father told her so while he drowned his sorrows in scotch?

And so on her way back to retrieve her art supplies, she passed a wastebasket. She paused. Was she really going to do this?

And then she heard the echo of her father's words: *Don't trust a royal.*

I won't, Dad. I remember.

She dropped the note into the trash and kept going. Prince Istvan would soon realize that he couldn't have everything he desired—and that included having her.

He sat alone.

Istvan checked the time. Again.

She was late. He had no patience for tardiness. It had been drilled into him since he was a young boy that you should be early for occasions. Apparently Indigo didn't believe in that bit of logic. As of that moment, she was thirteen and a half minutes late.

This did not bode well for hiring her to do his formal portrait. The painting had to be completed on a specific deadline as stipulated in the contract he'd had drawn up. The Treasury Department ran by a strict timeline. If he were smart, he'd give up on the idea of having Indigo paint his portrait.

Still, he hesitated. Maybe something had had happened to her. Maybe she had been unavoidably detained. The thought that something might have happened to her bothered him.

He signaled for Elek, his most trusted guard. When the

man approached him, Istvan asked, "Did you personally hand Indigo the note?"

The man clasped his hands together as he leaned down. "Yes, Your Highness."

"And did she read it?"

"I do not know, sir. I was called away before she had a chance to open the envelope."

"Well, something must have happened or she would be here." He stood, sending the chair legs scraping over the floor. He was no longer Interested in eating. "We must check on her."

"Your Highness?" Elek looked confused.

"We'll go to her room. Find out what room she's in."

"Yes, sir." Elek pulled out his phone and placed a call.

Istvan began to pace. Something must be terribly wrong or she'd be here. The thought of anything happening to the pretty artist bothered him more than he was expecting.

Elek returned. "She's not staying at the resort."

Istvan sighed. "Of course she's not. She's an employee. I should have thought of that. Do you have her home address?"

Elek nodded. "They didn't want to give it to me, so I had to mention your name."

"It's fine." He would do what it took to make sure Indigo was all right. "Let's go."

Elek didn't immediately move.

"What?" Istvan was anxious to get to the bottom of what had delayed Indigo.

"Are you sure about this?" Elek didn't speak up unless he felt it was in the prince's best interest. "You could try calling her instead."

"Did you get her number?" When Elek nodded, Istvan said, "Well, let's have it."

He reached for his phone and quickly dialed the number. It rang and rang. And then it switched to voice mail.

"Hi. I can't answer the phone right now. I'm probably working on my next masterpiece. Just leave your name, number and a brief message, and I'll get back to you as soon as I can." *Beep.*

Istvan disconnected the call. He wasn't interested in leaving a message. He wanted to know why she'd stood him up. The thought pricked his ego. He'd never been stood up. There had to be a serious reason. And he wasn't going to rest until he knew what it was.

Because the more he thought of Indigo—and he found himself thinking of her quite a lot lately—the more certain he was that he wanted to know more about her.

She didn't appear to be easy to win over. She certainly wasn't swayed by titles. And that's what he admired about her.

If she were to paint his portrait, she would breathe some freshness into his image, just as he wanted to breathe freshness into the monarchy. He recalled the long talks he'd had with Uncle Georgios about the state of the monarchy. Though they didn't agree on everything, there was one area where they both were in agreement—the monarchy needed to change.

And Indigo was his first step in showing the world that when it was his turn to step up to the throne, he would do things differently. So he had to find out what was keeping her.

CHAPTER SIX

SHE COULDN'T STOP thinking of him.

Why would a prince ask her to dinner?

Indigo had absolutely no answer for that—at least none that she was willing to accept. Because there was no way someone like him would be interested in someone like her. No way at all.

And if he thought they were going to have a quick island romp before he flew off to his palace, he could think again. Even if his family hadn't destroyed hers, she was never one for a quick fling. It just wasn't her thing.

"Indi, do you know where I left my book?" her mother called out from the living room.

"Give me a second and I'll look for it."

Indigo had arrived home from work a little while ago. She'd grabbed a shower and switched into a summer dress. Her little two-bedroom apartment didn't have air-conditioning, and the dress was light and airy.

This summer was unusually hot. The first thing she'd done upon arriving home was to open all the windows. The fan in the living room was already on for her mother.

Indigo glanced in the bedroom mirror. Her hair was still damp from her shower, but it wouldn't stay that way for long. She twisted the long strands and pinned them to the back of her head.

And then she headed for her mother's bedroom. Her mother had been reading a historical series about Scottish highlanders. Her mother read a lot of different things, from romances to cozy mysteries to biographies. Now that her mother's health was failing and she couldn't get around the way she wanted, she said she liked to escape the walls of their apartment through the words in a book.

Indigo glanced around her mother's small bedroom. There were stacks of books everywhere. Some new, a lot old and there were magazines added in. "What did you say the title was?"

Her mother called it out and then added that it should have been on the side of the bed. It was then that Indigo was able to spot it.

She carried it to the living room. "Here you go. Do you need anything else?"

"I don't think so. Why, are you going somewhere?"

"We need groceries." And there was no way she could unwind right now. Every time she closed her eyes, the image of the prince was there. A walk might help. "Is there anything special you want?"

"I have a list on the counter. There's not much. Just a few things." Her mother frowned.

"What's wrong? Are you in pain?"

Her mother shook her head. "I'm fine." She smiled, but it didn't reach her eyes. "I just feel horrible that I've become such a burden to you."

"Mama, don't ever think like that. I love having you around." And she meant it. She would be lost without her mother in her life.

Her mother's eyes filled with unshed tears. "How did I get so lucky to have such a wonderful daughter?"

Indigo shook her head. "I'm not special."

"Of course you are. And as soon as I have a place to move where I can get by on my own, you'll be able to have your life back. You should be out dating, not staying home, looking after me."

"Mama, I love you. I know you want your independence back, but until that happens, I love having you here."

A tear splashed onto her mother's pale cheek. "I love you, too."

Indigo knew how important it was to her mother to live

on her own once more. It's part of the reason she'd taken the job at the resort. Between that income and hopefully the money she would make at her very first gallery showing, she'd have enough money to get her mother into an assisted living center.

The problem was that this was her first gallery showing. She had absolutely no idea how well her paintings would sell. But she wouldn't give up. She'd do whatever it took to make sure her mother was happy.

Knock-knock.

She wondered who that could be. Perhaps her aunt was stopping by to visit. The sisters were really close. In fact, they were best friends.

"Are you expecting Aunt Aggie?"

"No. But you know she drops by whenever she gets a chance. And she did mention that she had a new book to loan me as soon as she finished reading it. Maybe she finished it sooner than she expected." Her mother's face lit up.

Indigo stepped into the small foyer and opened the door. For a moment, the world stood still. There, standing before her, was Prince Istvan. Her heart lodged in her throat. *What in the world?*

She blinked. She had to be seeing things. Her pulse raced. There was no way he was on her doorstep. But after she blinked twice, he was still standing before her.

"Indigo, we need to talk." His voice was deep, with a heavy accent.

"Indi, send your aunt in," her mother called from the other room.

Indigo didn't want her mother to see the prince and get upset. So she closed the door in the prince's face. "It's not Aunt Aggie." She struggled to sound normal. "Just someone who knocked on the wrong door."

"I hope you helped them."

"I did." She reached for her purse. "Now I'm off. I'll be home a little later."

"Okay. I'm going to read some more."

When Indigo opened the door again, the prince's brows were drawn into a formidable line, while irritation showed in his eyes. Obviously he wasn't used to people closing the door in his face. But to be fair, she wasn't used to people tracking her down at home.

She raised her finger to her lips to silence him until the door was shut and they were a few steps away. Then she paused and turned to him. "How did you find me?"

He paused as though he hadn't been expecting that question. "I had someone ask at the resort for your address."

"And they just gave it to you?" She would have to speak with Hermione.

His lack of a response meant he was accustomed to getting any information he needed. She should have known. If you were royalty, the rules didn't apply to you.

She huffed and crossed her arms. "Why are you here?"

"I want to know why you missed dinner. Did you have an emergency?"

"No." Why would he think that? In the next breath, she realized he wasn't used to being turned down. "Now, I need to be going."

"We need to talk."

She shook her head. "If this is about dinner, I can't."

His dark brows rose high on his forehead. "It doesn't have to be dinner. I would just like a moment of your time."

She tilted her chin upward until their gazes met. "And if I say no, you'll just go away."

Frustration shimmered in his eyes. He wordlessly stared back at her, letting her know he wasn't going anywhere until he had his say.

Tired of the staring game, she said, "I'm going to the market. If you want to walk with me, you can have your say."

"You want me to go grocery shopping?" His voice held a surprised tone.

"It's up to you." She turned and began walking.

For a moment, she heard no footsteps behind her. Was it possible he'd finally given up? She ignored the sense of disappointment that came over her.

And then she mentally admonished herself for having any sort of feelings where the prince was concerned. Because even if he was drop-dead gorgeous and persistent, in the end, he was a royal. And even though she was a Rydianian by birth, she'd promised herself as a child that she would never claim her heritage as a Rydianian citizen. As an adult, she'd never traveled to her birthplace. She preferred to focus her energy on the here and now versus what had once been.

"Wait up." She heard rapid footsteps behind her.

She didn't slow down. What was so important to him? She couldn't deny that she was curious. But she wasn't curious enough to turn back.

He fell in step with her. "How far away is this market?"

"Afraid of a little exercise?"

"Not at all. But these shoes aren't the best for walking long distances."

She glanced down to see he wore a pair of sand-colored loafers. "You don't have to walk with me."

"I want to." He settled a ball cap on his head and obscured his eyes with dark sunglasses. "Listen I'm sorry for overstepping."

The fact he realized that even a prince could overstep impressed her, but she still wasn't ready to let down her guard with him. *Don't trust a royal.* Her father's words echoed in her mind. He'd repeated them countless times over the years. It left an indelible impression.

"The market is only a couple of blocks away." She wasn't sure if it was her attempt at making peace or her way of dissuading him from following her.

The thing about Prince Istvan that worried her the most was his way of confusing her. She knew she should see him as the enemy. And yet there was a part of her that was curious about Istvan. Why was he going out of his way to speak to her? It wasn't like she was rich or famous. And she certainly wasn't a royal descendant. In royal terms, that would make her a nobody. So what was his interest in her?

"Are you this hard on all the men who try to ask you to dinner?" The prince's voice interrupted her thoughts.

"Only the princes." She couldn't believe she'd made that little quip until the words passed her lips.

"I see. So if I was someone else, you would have consented to dinner?"

She turned her head so that their gazes would meet. "You can never be anyone but who you are—heir to the throne."

"Ouch. You make that sound akin to a deadly disease."

His choice of words made her think of her father. In his case being close to the royals had been exactly like a deadly disease that in the end took his life. It might not have been at their hands, but they couldn't deny the role they'd played in his untimely demise.

They continued walking in silence because she had nothing nice to say to him. When she thought of her father and how he'd been treated after a lifetime of duty and devotion, it made her furious.

When she reached her destination, she turned to him. "The walk is over."

She pulled open the door and stepped inside the small market that she knew like the back of her hand. She visited the Samaras Market numerous times a week because she liked to cook with fresh vegetables. Since her mother had been diagnosed with heart failure along with some other health conditions, Indigo had made it her mission to help her mother in every way she knew how, including a vegetarian diet filled with fruits and vegetables. In the end, they both felt better.

She grabbed a basket and moved toward the fresh produce to see what they'd gotten in that week. All the while, she could feel Istvan's gaze on her—following her. He certainly was persistent.

When she picked up some tomatoes, he said, "Those don't look ripe. You might want to try the ones up higher." He pointed to some other tomatoes. "They look like they'll be more flavorful."

She couldn't help but smile at the prince offering her shopping advice. "Istvan, do you really expect me to believe you do your own shopping?"

"Who's this Istvan, you speak of? My name's Joe. And I shop here all the time." He grabbed some tomatoes and placed them in his own basket.

He had a basket? He was shopping, too? Her gaze jerked around to meet his. She couldn't believe he was working this hard to get her attention.

Perhaps it wouldn't hurt to play along for a little bit. "So, Joe, how do you feel about zucchini?"

He shrugged. "I'm neutral on the subject."

"I see. And how about olives? Do you prefer black or green?"

"Green, for sure."

She couldn't resist the smile that pulled at her lips. "Are you planning to follow me through the whole market?"

"Who, me?" His voice held an innocent tone. "I'm just here to do a little shopping."

She honestly didn't know what to make of him. One minute he was infuriating, with the way he took advantage of his royal status, and the next minute he was acting like he was a normal person who was just trying to create some sort of bridge between them.

Secretly she was swooning just a little. After all, what

woman didn't want a prince tripping over himself to impress her? Not that she was going to let on to him that his actions were starting to work on her.

As they made their way through the market, making small talk about various items, she noticed the puzzled looks the other patrons were giving them. Maybe because he was wearing sunglasses inside. Between the glasses and the dark ball cap, it was harder to make out his identity.

Or maybe it was his security team that had given him way. But when she glanced back, she noticed his entourage was nowhere to be seen. Was it possible he'd told them to remain outside?

"Why are you doing this?" she asked.

"Just like you, I need a few things." He scanned the pasta before adding his selection to his almost-full basket.

"And what exactly are you going to do with all that food once you buy it?"

"Eat it, of course." His tone was serious as he moved onto some jarred sauce.

She rolled her eyes. Was he always so obstinate? She couldn't help but wonder what it'd be like to spend the evening with the prince. Not that she was planning to do it or anything else. But it didn't mean she couldn't wonder about these things.

He was certainly going through a lot of bother to speak with her. And the funny thing was he never said a word about what he had on his mind. As the minutes passed and their baskets grew full, her curiosity was getting the best of her.

But by then they were at the checkout with a fresh loaf of bread topping each of their baskets. The bread was still warm from the oven. As she inhaled the aroma, her mouth watered. They were definitely having it for dinner. Her mother loved fresh-baked bread dipped in seasoned olive oil.

He let her check out first. When the checker told her the total, Istvan said, "I've got it."

She frowned at him. "No, you don't."

He looked at the checker. "You can just add it to my order."

Her gaze swung around to the checker. "Don't you dare." Then she reached in her wallet and produced the appropriate amount of money. She held it out to the checker. "Here you go."

The young man shrugged his shoulders before taking the money. He quickly counted out her change. And then Indigo turned a challenging look to Istvan.

He was wearing a smile. "You are unlike anyone I've ever known."

She didn't think she was that unusual. "Because I like to pay for my own groceries?"

His gaze held hers. And when he spoke, his rich voice dropped down a tone. "No. Because you are fiercely independent, very stubborn and utterly enchanting."

Her stomach dipped. Why exactly was she resisting spending more time with him? In that moment, the answer totally eluded her.

CHAPTER SEVEN

THIS WAS BETTER than a dinner date.

Wait. Had that outrageous thought really crossed his mind?

Istvan gave himself a mental shake.

He had never been grocery shopping before, but if it was this entertaining every time, he wouldn't mind doing it more often. But something told him it wouldn't have been half as much fun without Indigo.

She was as stubborn as she was beautiful. And the more he was around her, the greater the challenge became to work his way past her cool exterior. He'd seen the way she'd looked at him at the beach, and he knew the attraction went both ways. But for whatever reason, she was fighting it.

Once he paid for his groceries and they stepped outside, he offered to carry her groceries. To his surprise, she let him. It was the first thing she'd let him do for her. It was to the point where he almost thanked her for letting him carry her groceries. Then he realized how ridiculous that sounded and instead said nothing.

"This has been an interesting trip to the market," she said. "But I must know what brought you to my door."

So she was curious. Good. That was a step in the right direction. He was pleased to know his banter had actually produced the results he wanted.

"I tried to call, but you didn't answer."

"That was you?" When he nodded, she said, "When it said the caller ID was blocked, I figured it was a spam call."

"Spam? I've been referred to a lot of ways. Some good, some not so good. But I've never been called that."

An awkward silence ensued before she asked, "And what was so important that you had to see me?"

"I have a proposal for you."

She glanced over at him. Suspicion blazed in her eyes. "Dare I ask what sort of proposal?"

"I think you'll like it."

"I won't know until you tell me."

He cleared his throat. Surely even she wouldn't turn down this proposition. Then again, he was finding that he wasn't able to predict Indigo's reactions. It's part of what he liked so much about her. "I would like to hire you."

Her fine brows rose. "Hire me to do what? Cook for you?"

"Hmm... Now that you mention it, that's not a bad idea. Maybe we'll have to negotiate that later." He sent her a teasing smile. "Right now, I'd like to commission you to do my formal portrait."

She stopped walking. She was quiet, as though she were digesting his words. "You want me to paint you?"

"Yes."

She stared at him like he'd suddenly sprouted a third eye. Then, in a calm voice, she said, "No."

She'd turned him down? Really? Suddenly his amusement over her stubbornness turned to agitation. Fun and games were fine for a bit, but this was serious business for him. Did she have any idea how many artists had vied for the honor of painting his formal portrait?

He had to try again. "Don't you realize this would make your career? You could name your price after this. You could take on any project."

"I do. And the answer is still no."

He knew Indigo was different and did things in her own way. The other thing he knew about her was that her art was very important to her. So then, why would she turn down this prime opportunity?

Perhaps he hadn't explained it well enough. "This portrait I'd like to hire you to do would be high-profile. It will be my official portrait. It will be used for postage stamps, currency and who knows what else."

"That's nice for you, but the answer is still no."

Was it his imagination or had her pace picked up? Was she trying to get away from him? But why? The more he was around her, the more the questions came to him. "Why are you so ready to turn down such a great opportunity?"

She stopped and turned to him. She leveled her shoulders and lifted her chin ever so slightly. "I know you aren't used to being told no, but I have other obligations."

"Move them." It wasn't until the words were out of his mouth that he realized how much he sounded like his father. And that wasn't a good thing.

"No." She glared at him.

This conversation had most definitely taken a wrong turn. He swallowed hard. "My apologies. That didn't come out right. I meant to say that if there's anything I can do to make this an option for you, all you have to do is say the word. I think your work is exceptional, and it has a freshness to it that I'm looking for."

A myriad of expressions filtered over her face. She could say more with her eyes than with her lips, which were currently pursed together.

As the strained silence lingered, he grew impatient. "Will you do it?"

"No." She resumed walking.

At this point he should turn and walk away. With anyone else, that's exactly what he would do, but there was something special about Indigo—*erm, about her work.*

He'd give it one last try and then he was done. If fame and worldwide recognition wouldn't do it, perhaps money would work. "I can pay you." And then he mentioned a large sum of money. "Imagine what you could do with that money."

Her steps slowed. She was still moving—still not saying

anything—but he knew he had her attention. She stopped and turned to him. "You can't be serious."

"Of course I am."

She didn't say no this time. In fact, she didn't say anything as she resumed walking, presumably to give his offer serious consideration.

She suddenly stopped. Then slowly she turned to him. "Why me?"

"Because I like your style. It's original, and it has depth to it."

"I'm sure your family already has an artist chosen to do your portrait."

"Don't worry about my family. I'll take care of them." He was certain his mother would fight him about this, but in the end, he would win. After all, he was heir to the throne. His parents would have to get used to the idea that he didn't plan to do things the way they wanted them done. "So you'll take on the project?"

She hesitated. Her gaze moved down the sidewalk as though she were weighing her options. But what was there to consider? He didn't know anyone who would pass up this opportunity, not to mention the small fortune he was willing to pay.

They began walking again. He was starting to think there was more to Indigo's aversion to him than just playing hard to get, but how could that be? It wasn't like they'd ever met before. Maybe she had something against rich people. But if that was the case, she wouldn't work at the Ludus Resort. He was overthinking this. Maybe it was as simple as her being nervous around a crown prince. But she sure didn't act nervous—at least not since their first meeting.

Indigo was a puzzle, and he longed to figure out how all the pieces fit together. And this trip to his kingdom would provide him with that opportunity. So long as she agreed to go with him.

When they came to a stop in front of her apartment building, he asked, "What do you say?"

"I can't just take time off from my new job at the resort." She worried her bottom lip.

"Don't worry about the resort. I'll take care of it. Your job will be safe."

Her eyes momentarily widened. Then she said, "That's right. You're friends with Hermione." Her gaze studied his. "I'll need twenty-five percent up-front."

She wasn't afraid to negotiate for what she wanted. Good for her. "Done."

"And the remainder upon completion of the portrait."

"Done." Then he held his hand out to her. "Shall we shake on it?"

Her gaze moved to his hand. She hesitantly placed her hand in his. He immediately noticed the smoothness of her skin. As her fingertips slid over the sensitive skin of his palm, sparks of attraction flew between them. A current of anticipation zinged up his arm and set his heart pounding. Oh, yes, this was going to be the most amazing adventure.

She withdrew her hand far too quickly, breaking the connection. He instinctively rubbed his fingertips over his palm as the sensation of her touch faded away.

And then recalling the contract, he retrieved it from Elek and then held it out to Indigo. "Here's a formal agreement. Read it over, sign it and bring it with you. My car will pick you up first thing Monday. Six a.m. sharp."

She accepted the papers. "To take me where?"

"To my private jet. Don't worry. We won't start working Monday. You'll have time to settle into your suite of rooms at the palace."

"The palace?" Confusion showed in her eyes.

"You surely didn't think we'd be completing the portrait here, did you?"

"I, uh, hadn't considered that this would include travel." She frowned.

"If you haven't been to Rydiania, I can promise you that it's beautiful. And while you're at the palace, you'll have access to its amenities."

She shook her head. "I can't."

"Can't what?" Maybe it was him, but he was having a difficult time understanding her today. "Enjoy the amenities?"

"All of it. I'll do the portrait, but it has to be here."

He breathed out a frustrated sigh. He was tired of all the barriers she kept putting up. He'd tried being congenial and generous, but his patience was now razor-thin. They made a verbal agreement, now he expected her to hold up her end of it.

Maybe it was time he be frank with her. Nothing else seemed to be working. "I don't know what is going on with you, but we have an agreement. I expect you to fulfill it. Be ready to go Monday at 6:00 a.m." When she opened her mouth to argue, he said, "I have witnesses to our verbal contract." He gestured to his security team. "Don't push me on this."

Her eyes narrowed. "Now your true colors come out."

He wasn't sure what that meant, but he was beyond caring at this point. He handed over her groceries, plus his own. "Here you go. I will see you tomorrow."

She glanced down at the bags. "But these are your groceries."

"I've lost my appetite. Good evening."

Then he turned to find his car waiting for him. He climbed inside and closed the door. All the while he asked himself why he bothered. If she was that opposed to working for him, why push the subject? Was it his ego? Or was it something more?

In that moment, he didn't want to dissect his emotions. It was enough that she seemed to have finally resigned herself to the fact that they were leaving on Monday. He had a feeling sitting for this portrait wasn't going to be boring. Far from it.

Had that really happened?

She'd agreed to work for the prince?

Indigo replayed the events in her mind as she let herself into the apartment. As she passed the living room, she found her mother had dozed off with her reading glasses on and an open book now resting on her chest.

The money the prince was willing to pay her for the portrait would be enough to get her mother moved into the assisted living center that her mother had chosen. It would make a world of difference to both of them. Her mother would no longer feel like such a burden to her, which wasn't the truth as far as Indigo was concerned. But it was what her mother thought and felt that was important.

With her mother having round-the-clock help, it would give Indigo the freedom to do what she needed to do to expand her career. Her first step in that direction was the gallery showing coming up in two weeks.

That meant she had two weeks to do the preliminary work for the portrait of the prince. It should be enough time. She just hoped he knew that an oil painting would take much longer. It was necessary to allow the paint to dry between layers. It could take her four to six weeks to complete the project. And that would be pushing it, because she had other obligations.

Indigo put away the groceries, including those the prince had given her. Though she opposed handouts, in this case she didn't believe in things going to waste. Then she prepared a selection of vegetables in a light marinara and served it over pasta.

She shared dinner with her mother, who regaled her with what she'd read in her book. Her mother loved books more than anything, but she wasn't opposed to bingeing on a good television series. It was whatever struck her mother at the moment.

"Mama, I need to talk you." She hoped what she had to say wouldn't upset her.

Her mother leaned back in her chair, having finished her meal. Her oxygen cannula helped her breathe. These days it was her constant companion. "You look so serious."

"It's nothing for you to worry about," Indigo said. "It's just that I had this amazing opportunity come up, and I was hoping to take advantage of it."

"It sounds exciting. I'm assuming this has something to do with your gallery show."

She shrugged. "I don't know. We'll see."

Suddenly her mother gave her an idea or two. She could make this trip work for her in more than one way. Though it was too late to put together any more pieces for the showing, it wasn't too late to start on new pieces for the next show. And from what she'd heard from her father and now the prince, Rydiania was one of the most beautiful countries in all of Europe. She might be able to get some photos and sketches that she could work from later. She tucked the thought away for future use.

"What is the opportunity?"

There was no way she was telling her mother the truth. She didn't want to upset her. "I'm going to be traveling around a bit—doing some research for some future paintings."

"When are you leaving?"

"I need to leave Monday. Will that be a problem?"

Her mother frowned. "Sweetie, I don't want to hold you back. That's why I would like to live on my own again."

"And I have good news there. I think we'll be able to get you moved into assisted living when I get back."

Her mother's eyes filled with hope. "What? But how?"

"I've been working with the finances, and between what you have and what I have or will have very soon, we can afford to get you into the place you chose."

Instead of the excitement she expected to see on her mother's face, she frowned. "This isn't what I wanted."

"You don't want to move?" For months, it was all her mother had been talking about.

Her mother shook her head. "It's not that. I just hate having to rely on you. I hate that you have to pay for me to move. It's just not right."

Indigo got to her feet and moved to her mother's side. She knelt down next to her. "You aren't asking me to do this. I'm doing this because I want you to be happy. And I know living here isn't the same as you having your own place. I love you, Mama. Please let me help you with this."

Tears shimmered in her mother's eyes. "How did I get so lucky to have a daughter like you?"

"I'm the one who is lucky to have you." She gave her mother a hug.

When Indigo pulled back, her mother asked. "How long will you be gone?"

"No longer than two weeks, because I have the gallery showing."

Her mother nodded and smiled. "I can't wait to go. I'm so proud of you."

"Thanks, Mama."

It never ever got old hearing that her mother was proud of her—though there were times when Indigo didn't think there was much for her mother to feel proud about. If her mother knew what Indigo was about to do in order to come up with the money for her mother's new living arrangements, she was quite certain her mother would be disappointed in her.

"Did you speak to your aunt yet about stopping by while you're gone?" her mama asked.

"I wanted to speak to you first." And then she remembered all the food in the fridge. "I already stocked the kitchen. It should keep you for a little while. And there are leftovers from tonight."

"I'm not an invalid," her mother insisted.

Her mother was right, but Indigo also knew it didn't take a lot to tire her mother. "I just don't want you overdoing things, is all."

"I won't."

"Famous last words." Indigo sent her mother a smile. "Now what can I do for you before I go?"

"Well, you took care of the shopping, and I just got a new shipment of books and I'll take care of calling your aunt. It'll give her a chance to tell me what's been going on in her life. I think she might be dating someone, but she hasn't told me his name."

"Maybe she's not ready to talk about him yet."

"But she's my sister. She's supposed to tell me everything. I live vicariously through her."

Indigo had known for a long time that her mother had no intentions of finding love again. Even if she wasn't dealing with heart issues, she said that she'd had her one great love and that was enough for her. Indigo wondered what it would be like to have a love like her parents had shared.

Indigo was beginning to wonder if there was a love out there for her. Not that she was looking, because right now she didn't have time for romance. She had too many other responsibilities.

Her mother carried her dishes to the kitchen. Her steps were slow and small, but she didn't let that stop her.

Indigo hated seeing her mother being just a shadow of the strong woman who had buried her husband and raised her teenage daughter alone while working as a reporter. Her mother had been such an amazing role model until her health made her slow down.

And now it was Indigo's turn to do everything she could to make her mother's life as comfortable as possible. Part of that included giving her mother back a semblance of independence—even if it meant going back on a promise to her father to never step foot in Rydiania.

CHAPTER EIGHT

SHE COULDN'T BELIEVE she'd agreed to this.

At exactly six o'clock that morning, a black sedan had pulled up in front of her apartment building. There were no flags to reveal that its passenger was a foreign dignitary. And the windows were tinted, hiding the occupants from her aunt's curious view as she'd passed by on her way into the apartment.

Aunt Aggie paused on the doorstep next to Indigo. "Is the fancy car waiting for you?"

Indigo attempted to act casual. "Yes. I'm off to the airport." Her fingers tightened on the handle of her suitcase. "Thanks for helping out Mama."

"You don't have to thank me. I'm more than happy to help out. Good luck with your project." Aunt Aggie sent her a bright smile, as though she knew what Indigo was up to.

But that wasn't possible. Her gaze moved to the dark sedan to make sure Prince Istvan was still inside. She breathed easier knowing he was hidden from sight behind those dark tinted windows.

"Thank you. I should be going." After a quick hug, Indigo made her way to the waiting car.

The driver got out and opened the door for her as well as took her luggage to stow in the rear. To Indigo's surprise, Istvan wasn't waiting for her inside the sedan. According to his driver, the prince had other matters to attend to and would meet them at the private airport.

Istvan was indeed waiting for her outside the hangar. The crew was ready to go and in no time, they were in the air.

A few hours later, Indigo lounged in a leather seat of the private royal jet, where she'd been staring out at the blue sky. In the rear, the prince's security detail was seated. They were so quiet it was easy to forget they were there.

She glanced over to the side to find Istvan sitting across the aisle with his laptop resting on a table in front of him. He had an earpiece, and he talked in a fast, low voice. His fingers moved rapidly over the keyboard. She couldn't help but wonder what had him so preoccupied. Was it royal business? Or something else?

Whatever kept him so busy had given her time to come to grips with the reality of the situation. She stared out the window at the blue sky dotted with a few puffy white clouds. The earth looked so far away as they grew nearer to her birthplace.

Her palms grew damp as she envisioned coming face-to-face with the king and queen. The idea didn't appeal to her. Not at all. There had to be a way to avoid them. She just needed to give it some more thought.

Ding.

Indigo glanced toward the front of the cabin. She noticed a small seat-belt sign was lit up. This must mean they'd already arrived in Rydiania. She glanced over at Istvan to see if he'd noticed the alert.

"I don't care. I've got other obligations. We'll discuss this later." He withdrew the earpiece and placed it in his pocket. Then he glanced in her direction. "I'm sorry about that."

"No problem." And she meant that sincerely. She wasn't sure what they would have discussed during the four-plus hours they'd been in the air.

"The palace isn't happy that I was away. There's a lot to catch up on."

"I can't even imagine." Which was quite true. When she was a young child, back before her father had been exiled, he had come home late at night after she'd gone to sleep. On the rare times he was home early, he'd tell her tales of the royals. She'd been so young at the time that she'd thought they were fairy tales, but as she grew older, she realized many of the bedtime stories her father had told her had been grounded in reality.

"I take it this is your first visit to Rydiania." His voice interrupted her trip into the past. "I'll see that you have a tour. After all, we can't have you locked away painting the whole time you're here."

"I don't mind working the whole time." The faster she finished her preliminary work, the sooner she'd get back to Greece. And even though her aunt was keeping a close eye on her mother, Indigo didn't want to be gone too long. Since the death of her father, she and her mother had grown even closer than before.

"I insist," Istvan said in a firm tone. "All work and no play, makes Indigo a dull girl."

The fact he knew that saying totally caught her off guard. It sure didn't seem like something a royal would know. It seemed... Well, it seemed so normal. Kind of the way it'd felt when they'd visited the market together.

But Istvan wasn't normal. He was a royal. And not just any royal—a Rydiania prince. And no matter how hand-some he was or how kind he could be, she couldn't forget that he was one of them. Only she wasn't like her father—she wasn't going into this blind. She knew how cutthroat the royals could be. And armed with this knowledge, she was protected from being hurt by them.

"Buckle up." His voice drew her from her thoughts.

"Um...what did you say?"

"We're about to land. You'll need to fasten your seat belt."

"Oh. Right." Heat rushed to her cheeks, as he'd once more distracted her. She couldn't let that happen again. She had to stay focused.

After fastening her seat belt, she turned her head to the lush landscape. The green was periodically dotted with towns. She really wouldn't mind exploring the area. The last time she'd been outside Greece had been to paint in Italy. Her portfolio had needed some diversity, and the trip to Venice had been quite successful.

A smile tugged at her lips. For so long, she'd struggled to get her art career off the ground. Her father had told her to be more practical. Her aunt had tried to hire her at her hair salon. The only one who had believed in her becoming a success had been her mother. She had told Indigo numerous times that she could become anything she set her mind on.

And now, after this assignment, she'd be able to request high fees for her portraits. And her art would go for large enough figures that she'd be able to maintain her mother's care indefinitely. The thought reaffirmed her determination to make the most of this trip.

As the plane began its descent, Indigo gripped the arms of her seat. The plane shook as it hit turbulence. Her body tensed as her fingers dug into the armrests. *We'll be fine. We'll be fine.*

All of the sudden, a warm hand covered hers. She glanced over to find Istvan gazing at her.

He sent her a reassuring smile. "We're almost on the ground."

She nodded, not trusting her voice. And then her gaze darted back toward the window. The fact she'd flown at all was a bit of a miracle. But she'd learned from her father, who had let the world get the best of him, that she couldn't follow his lead. She had to be strong and face life's challenges if she wanted to make it in this world.

"Are you okay?" he asked.

She nodded.

"Was it bad?"

Her gaze swung back around to him. "What?"

"The plane incident—was it bad?"

How did he know? It wasn't like she ever talked about

it. In fact, she didn't really want to get into it. But part of overcoming her fear was talking about it.

"It could have been worse." It never escaped her that her life had been spared that day. "I... I was in a near crash a few years back."

He gave her hand a reassuring squeeze. "That would unnerve anyone."

"At first I didn't want to fly ever again, but I realized if I wanted to follow my dreams, flying would be a part of it."

"That was very brave of you."

She shrugged. She didn't feel brave. She felt silly for being afraid to fly, even if she overcame the fear little by little each time she stepped onto a plane.

"I was on a flight home from London." In her mind's eye she was back on that plane. "It had been the usual flight, with the inevitable delay taking off, but then everything settled down. The plane wasn't full, so I had no one beside me and I could relax. I was so anxious to get home. I wanted to tell my mother all about my art classes." It was right when her art career had started to take off.

"That's a long way to go for art lessons." His voice was gentle and not judgmental. It was though he had said enough to prod her to keep telling her story.

"It isn't far to go when you have a rare opportunity to learn from one of the best artists in the world." And then she dropped the name of a well-respected painter and glanced at Istvan to see if he recognized the name.

His eyes widened. "I understand the reason for your trip. Obviously, like me, he saw the true magnificence of your work."

His compliment made her heart beat faster as heat rushed to her cheeks. Was Istvan serious? As she gazed deeply into his blue eyes, she forgot what she'd been thinking. When she realized she'd been staring into his eyes too long, she lowered her gaze. His hand was still covering hers. It made her heart *tap-tap* even faster.

She needed to focus on something besides the prince. She swallowed hard as she prepared to finish her story. "I was gazing out the window, enjoying the sunshine and blue skies. The next thing I knew, there was a strange sound that I later learned was a bird strike, and the engine went out."

The memory of the fire and smoke was so vivid in her mind—just as it had been in her nightmares for a long time after the event. Maybe other people wouldn't have been affected by the event, but she'd felt like she'd been given another chance at life, and she'd promised herself she wouldn't squander it.

She could feel his gaze upon her. "I… I didn't think we were going to make it out alive. Suddenly the plane started to descend quickly. Too quickly."

"No wonder you aren't comfortable on a plane."

"In the end, our amazing pilot made an emergency landing. It was a rough landing, but I was never so happy to step on solid ground in my life."

"And yet you didn't let it stop you."

"I know what happens when you let setbacks and events stop you from living your life." Now why had she gone and said that? She wasn't going to share the tragedy that had befallen her father.

Just then the plane shuddered once more. She turned her head to the window and found they were on the ground. She could at last breathe a bit easier.

The prince withdrew his hand from hers, leaving a noticeably cool spot. "We have arrived."

While the plane taxied to a private hangar, Istvan gathered his things and placed them in his attaché. All Indigo had to grab was her sketch pad that still held nothing but blank pages. Usually she spent her downtime sketching ideas for a new painting, but she'd been utterly distracted on the flight. She told herself it was the flying and not her company that had her distracted.

As the plane rolled to a stop, she glanced out the window to find a dark sedan waiting for them. This time the sedan was larger, and the country's flags adorned the front of the vehicle. A gold crest of the royal family was emblazed on the door. This vehicle was here to whisk them off to the palace.

Her stomach sank down to her heels. "I don't have to stay at the palace," Indigo said. "I'd be fine staying in the village."

Istvan arched a brow. "You are refusing to stay at the palace?"

"I'm just saying that I would be more comfortable staying in the village. I… I'd get a chance to take in the community and the sights."

He studied her for a moment. "If I didn't know better, I'd think you were trying to get away from me."

She was busted. "If that's not acceptable, just say so."

He shrugged. "I'm not going to make you stay at the palace. You just need to be available to work on the portrait starting tomorrow."

"I will."

They moved to the now-open doorway. A man wearing a dark suit and a serious expression stood at the bottom of the steps, waiting to greet the prince. "Your Highness, did you have a good trip?"

"Yes, I did." Istvan glanced over at Indigo as she joined them. "Jozsef, this is Indigo. She's going to be painting my portrait. Indigo, this is Jozsef, my private secretary, who keeps my calendar manageable."

Jozsef's brows ever so briefly lifted before he resumed his neutral expression. "Your Highness, you should know the queen has hired her own artist."

"I'll deal with the queen later. Right now, Ms. Castellanos would like to have accommodations in the village. Could you find her something appropriate?"

"Yes, sir." Jozsef stepped away and made a phone call.

"You didn't have to make him do that." Indigo didn't want to be an imposition. In fact, she was hoping to make her presence less known by staying the village.

"It's no problem. It's Jozsef's job to handle these matters." When they approached the car, the driver opened the door for him. The prince stood back and gestured for her to get in first.

She did as he requested. The interior of the sedan was done up in black, just like the outside of the car. But on the seat in gold thread was the royal family's crest. And the leg space was more generous than in a normal car. There was even a small bar in the back of the front seats and a dividing window to give them some privacy.

When the prince climbed in the back seat and settled next to her, the space seemed to shrink considerably. His arm brushed hers and sent a cascade of goose bumps racing down her arm.

She moved over. The door armrest dug into her side. When she glanced over at Istvan, she found amusement dancing in his eyes.

"You don't have to press yourself against the door." He closed his door. "There's plenty of room for both of us."

The problem was that sitting back here with him was cozy. Too cozy. And she was increasingly aware of how attractive he was, with his broad shoulders, muscular chest and long legs. Her heart pitter-pattered. She swallowed hard.

She needed to remain professional. She laced her fingers together in her lap. "You do understand that I can't complete the painting in the two weeks I'll be here."

He nodded. "I understand. Do you want me to sit for you tomorrow and you can sketch me or something?"

She shook her head. "I'd like to observe you going about your normal day, if that would be possible."

His brows rose high on his forehead. "You want to watch me work?"

She nodded. "If possible."

"It's certainly possible, but it sounds boring." He sent her a smile.

She noticed the way his lips parted, revealing his straight white teeth. There was a dimple in his cheek that made him even cuter. And when the smile reached his blue eyes, they twinkled.

She subdued a sigh. No one had a right to be that handsome. And try as she might not to like him, she was failing miserably. She'd found absolutely nothing to dislike about him. Was it possible he was nothing at all like his parents? Hope swelled in her chest.

"So why did you hire me if the queen already has someone to do your portrait?"

"Because it's my portrait, and I want to pick who paints it. My country needs a fresh approach. I'm hoping with your help they will see me in a new light and not part of the same old regime that has been running the country in the exact same manner for much too long."

Wow! She really had misjudged him, hadn't she? Her hope was so great that it surprised her.

It wasn't like she was going to let herself fall for him. Not a chance. But she hoped he was different for, um, his country. Yes, that was it. His country could use new leadership. Because it didn't really matter to her personally if he was the same or different. Not at all.

CHAPTER NINE

PERHAPS THIS HAD been a miscalculation.

Istvan had noticed how Indigo made sure to leave a lot of space between them, whether it was on the jet or now in the back seat of the car. What had made her so jumpy around him?

He wanted to ask her, but he didn't dare. As it was, their conversation was finally getting her to relax a bit. And he didn't want to stop talking because the more she relaxed, the more he saw the part of her that had first attracted him to her. Not that he was expecting or even wanting anything to come of this arrangement—other than an impressive portrait that would put his unique stamp on his upcoming reign.

"You just need to tell me what you'll need while you're here," he said.

"Need?"

"Yes. What art supplies will you need?"

"Oh. Okay." She reached in her purse and pulled out a slip of paper. She held it out to him. "Here you go."

He was duly impressed that she was this organized. He glanced down at the list. "I'll see that these items are brought to you."

"Thank you."

Tap-tap.

Istvan opened the window. Jozsef stood there. He leaned down and spoke softly into Istvan's ear. There was no room available in the village. It would seem Indigo would be staying at the palace after all.

He put up the window and turned to Indigo. "It would appear there's a wedding celebration in the village and all the rooms are taken."

"Oh." Disappointment showed in her eyes.

Just then the car engine started, and they began to move. Istvan leaned back in his seat. "Don't worry. You'll like the palace. It's a cross between a home and a museum."

She smiled at him.

"What did I say that was so amusing?"

"I've just never heard anyone describe their home as a museum."

He shrugged. "It has a collection of art from the past and some from the present. Every time a foreign dignitary visits the palace, they feel obligated to bring a gift. So there's quite a collection. Except in my wing."

"You have your own wing of the palace?"

He nodded. "It's one of the benefits of being the crown prince. My siblings all share a wing. And then my parents have their own wing. And that leaves one wing for visiting guests."

"And here all I have is a two-bedroom apartment. It could probably fit in just one room in the palace."

When she sent him a playful smile, he let out a laugh. The more she relaxed, the more he liked her. She reminded him of his younger sister Cecilia. They were both free spirits and full of energy. He had a feeling if they had a chance, they would be fast friends. And then maybe he'd have an excuse to see Indigo again.

She wanted to hate Rydiania.

She wanted it to be the ugliest place on the earth. But instead, she found it to be one of the most beautiful places she'd ever been.

Indigo stared out the window at the tall green trees lining each side of the smooth roadway. When the trees parted, there was a lush meadow with a large pond. Upon the placid water were ducks—a mama and seven ducklings. Inwardly she sighed. If she didn't know better, she'd swear Istvan had created this scene to impress her—not that he had any reason to want to do such a thing.

And yet Indigo felt as though they were driving through a watercolor painting. This wasn't fair. There had to be something about this place that she hated.

Her gaze hungrily took it all in. The roadway wove through the country, and for a moment she felt like she was on holiday and had just landed in paradise. Then she decided that the problem with this place was that it was too rural, with its endless green grass, its abundance of wildlife and array of wildflowers. After all, that stuff was nice if you were an outdoorsy person, but she preferred the hubbub of neighborhoods and shops.

And still she kept her face turned toward the window, memorizing all she saw. She told herself that she kept staring because the alternative would be facing Istvan. She wasn't ready for that. Sketching his striking image with his kissable mouth was one thing, but dealing with him on a personal level was quite another.

"What do you think?" he asked.

Did he know her thoughts had drifted back to him? Totally impossible. She just had to keep her wits about her. She couldn't let him know how easily he distracted her.

She gave a small, nonchalant shrug. "It's great if you're a nature fanatic."

He let out a laugh. "I take it you're not into nature."

Why did he insist on making conversation? It wasn't like they were going to become friends. This was a business arrangement. Period. At the end of these two weeks, they'd never see each other again. She'd return to Greece to complete the portrait and then ship it to him. And yet she found herself wanting to talk to him, because he made it so easy to carry on a conversation.

She shrugged. "Honestly, it's beautiful. I'm just used to spending time in a more urban setting."

He nodded. "I understand."

She felt as though she'd said something wrong. She hadn't meant to. "But if I loved a more rustic life, this would definitely be a lovely place to live."

"Have you always lived in Athens?"

She turned her head toward him. "You don't know? I mean, I figured you ran a background check before hiring me."

"Of course. It's a matter of practice for all hires, but that doesn't mean I actually reviewed the entire report. I just made sure you weren't a criminal. And my private secretary rang your employer. Was there something you were expecting me to see?"

She shook her head. She wasn't ready to dredge up the past. "As far back as I can remember, I've lived in Athens."

"That's a long time."

"Hey, did you just call me old?"

His brows rose. "What?" Worry reflected in his eyes. "No. Of course not."

She sent him a playful smile. Who knew it was so easy to undo the prince's calm, cool exterior? "Uh-huh."

"Do you have a lot of family?"

"I have my mother. My father, well, he died when I was a teenager." Why had she gone and brought up her father? She never discussed him with anyone but her mother. And even then it was about his life, never his death.

"I'm so sorry."

She shrugged off his sympathy, refusing to acknowledge the pain she felt when she thought of the life that had been cut much too short. "It was a long time ago."

"Do you have any siblings?"

She shook her head. Tired of talking about herself, she decided to turn the tables. "And how about you? Any siblings?"

"I have three sisters."

She tried to imagine him as a child with three younger sisters chasing after him. "Your childhood must have been interesting."

He sighed. "You have no idea. My sisters can be a handful. You'll get to meet them while you're here."

"I look forward to it." Did she? Or had she just uttered those words out of habit? She wasn't sure—she wasn't sure about a lot of things lately.

She turned back toward the window. The car wound through the lush valley. Indigo found herself captivated by the majestic scenery. Her fingers twitched with the need to reach for her pencils and sketch pad. But there wasn't time. All of nature's beauty passed by the window far too quickly. Instead she reached for her phone to snap some photos.

Istvan cleared his throat. "I like to think that Rydiania is one of the most beautiful places on the planet. I hope you'll get a chance to do some exploring while you're here."

The idea appealed to her, but she needed to remain focused on her work. "We don't have much time together. I really need to do the groundwork for your portrait."

He nodded. "I understand."

The car slowed as it approached a more urban area. She gazed forward, finding high-rises and a sea of concrete buildings. *A city? Here? Really?*

But then the car turned to the left and completely diverted around the city. "We're not going to visit the city?"

"You sound disappointed."

She shrugged. "I'm just curious to see what a city in Rydiania looks like, especially one that is surrounded by a forest."

"I'll make sure we plan an excursion so you can explore. There's an arts section to the city that I'm sure you'll be interested in. But right now, I'm expected at a meeting at the palace."

"Of course." It was far too easy to forget that he was a

prince and not just a commoner, like herself. She would have to be more careful going forward.

A peaceful silence settled over the car as it carried them closer to the palace. She had to admit that she was curious to see it in person. The pictures she'd seen online were striking. She wondered if it was really that impressive or if the pictures had received some touch-ups.

More houses came into view. They were separated by expansive property. Most yards were meticulously cared for with short grass, trimmed bushes and brightly colored flowers from yellow to pinks and reds.

They slowed to a stop and then merged into a single roadway that wound its way into a small village. It was filled with what she imagined were tourists. Some had brochures in their hands. Others had their phones out and were snapping pictures of the rustic storefronts.

This place, with its many unique shops and amazing aromas, from buttery cinnamon to herbs and vegetables, permeated the car. Indigo found herself inhaling deeply. "Something sure smells good."

Istvan smiled. "Oh, yes, there are many wonderful places to eat in the village."

Her stomach rumbled in agreement. "I'll definitely keep that in mind. Is the palace far from here?"

"Not at all. In fact it's just on the other side of the village."

Her stomach knotted. Even though she had agreed to come here to help her mother, she felt as though she were betraying her father. Would he understand her decision? She hoped so.

The car slowed, drawing Indigo's attention. She focused on the very tall wrought iron gate in front of the car. Guards in deep purple uniforms with black hats stood in front of the gate. To either side of the gate were black guard shacks that were much more than shacks, because no shack looked that nice.

With precise movements that must have been practiced for many, many hours, they moved in unison and swung the giant gates open. As the car proceeded along the smoothly paved roadway, Indigo's heart raced and she clutched her hands together.

And there before them stood a gigantic palace. It was built out of a light gray stone. Impressive turrets stood at the corners. Atop the palace fluttered a purple-and-white flag. The car swung around and pulled to a stop beneath a portico. The doors were swung open by gentlemen dressed formally in black-and-white suits.

"Welcome to my home." Istvan sent her a reassuring smile.

She opened her mouth, but no words would come out. What was she supposed to say? *It's beautiful?* Because, well, it was the most magnificent *home* she'd ever seen. Or was she supposed to be unimpressed, as this was the home of the people who had hurt her father so deeply? She pressed her lips back together. Nothing felt quite right.

And so she was quietly led up the few steps to the red runner that led them inside the palace. No matter how much she wanted to hate this place, she couldn't deny the flutter in her chest as she took in its magnificence. *Just... Wow!*

If she hadn't seen all this for herself, she never would have believed it. Because the pictures online didn't come close to doing the palace justice—not one little bit.

It was like stepping into the pages of a storybook—the kind her mother read to her when she was a child. Sunlight streamed into the round foyer through a giant glass dome three stories up from where they stood. The sun's rays lit up the room and gave it a glow. It was though she were standing in a very special place.

"Indi, are you coming?" Istvan called from where he

stood on the grand steps that were lined with a deep purple carpet that led to the second floor.

"Indi?" It was the first time he'd called her that, and she wasn't sure how she felt about him using the nickname.

He smiled. "Has no one ever called you that?"

"Um…yes. My friends do."

"Good. It suits you. I'll show you to your room."

As she made her way up the steps, she couldn't help but wonder what had just happened. Was the prince saying he wanted to be friends with her? If so, how did she feel about him taking such liberties? But was it worth her getting worked up over a nickname? Probably not.

Istvan didn't have airs about him like she'd imagined a member of a royal family having. He was down-to-earth. And dare she admit it…if he were anyone else, she would be totally into him.

Still, he was the crown prince of the country that had played a role in the loss of her father. She couldn't ever let herself forget that, no matter how sexy she found his smile or how she could let herself get lost in his dreamy eyes.

When she smiled, she stole the breath from his lungs.

He hadn't felt this alive and invigorated in a long time.

Istvan was certain he'd made the right decision to bring Indi here. She was like a breath of fresh air in this stodgy old palace. He needed someone like her around to remind him of how things could be in the kingdom if the harsh traditions that had been carried on generation after generation were to be replaced with a gentler and more modern way of doing things.

He was going to be the change for his family. He knew his radical ideas would be met with resistance. He just hoped he had the strength to see change brought to this country that was stuck in the ways of the past.

And his first way of showing his country that his reign

would be different—that *he* was different—was in his formal portrait. Indi would take his idea of change and make it a visual statement.

They climbed the many steps and paused at the top. He wanted to give Indi a chance to look around and gain her bearings. Not everyone was used to living in a palace. Even though he had grown up within these massive walls, he realized it didn't hold the warmth and coziness that other homes did. He supposed there were trade-offs for everything in life.

His three sisters strode toward them. What were the three of them doing together? On second thought, he didn't want to know. Their eyes lit up when they noticed Indi at his side. In fact, they hardly paid him any attention. He groaned inwardly. His sisters could be quite overbearing when they thought he was interested in someone. Not that he was interested in Indi in a romantic way. At this point in his life, he didn't have time for a relationship.

The three princesses came to a stop in front of him. Gisella and Beatrix were dressed in blouses, pants and heels, while his youngest sister, Cecilia, wore a light blue skirt that barely made it to her midthigh and a pale-yellow halter top.

"Who's your friend?" his eldest sister, Princess Gisella, asked.

He glanced at Indi, who looked curious to meet the princesses. "Indigo, these are my sisters." He gestured to the left. "This is Princess Gisella. She is the oldest. Next to her is my youngest sister, Princess Cecilia. And next to her is Princess Beatrix."

"It's nice to meet you all," Indigo said.

His sisters all wore their well-practiced smiles. They could be so friendly and welcoming when they wanted to be, but they could also become defensive and freeze out people. He had absolutely no idea how they were going to react to Indi. He hoped they would give her a chance.

And then his sisters all spoke at once. Each fired off

questions at Indigo, who looked surprised and overwhelmed. His sisters could be like a force of nature when you had to deal with all of them at once—at least that's what his father often said. And Istvan had to agree with him.

"Stop!" His firm tone drew his sisters' attention. "Let Indigo get situated before you bombard her with questions."

Gisella narrowed her gaze on him. "Does Mother know about this?"

"No." He chose not to add any further explanation.

Gisella crossed her arms and frowned at him. "She's not going to like you bringing home an unexpected guest."

His other sisters nodded in agreement.

"She's not a guest. Not like you're thinking. Indigo is an artist. She's here to paint my portrait."

Surprised looks filtered across all the princesses' faces. So they really thought he was bringing home a girlfriend for his family to meet? That would be the last thing he would do with someone he was romantically interested in. His family could be intimidating on a good day, and on a bad day, well… He didn't want to think about it.

"Is that true about you being an artist?" Cecilia asked.

Indigo nodded. "It is. We met when I did a sketch of your brother."

"That sounds interesting," Beatrix said. "Where was this?"

"Stop," Istvan said. "Indigo is tired from traveling."

"Istvan, is that you?" the queen's voice trailed up the staircase.

He turned to the stairs, expecting to see his mother, but she was still downstairs. "Yes. I'm home."

The click of heels on the foyer's marble floor could be heard approaching the stairs. He turned back to his sisters. All he saw was their backs as they all headed in different directions. So much for them helping him manage his mother so she didn't frighten Indigo away.

He leaned over to Indigo and said softly, "Don't worry."

"I'm not." Her tone was firm as she straightened her shoulders.

Most people were intimidated when they first met the king or queen. That didn't appear to be the case with Indigo. Interesting.

"Istvan, there you are." The queen stepped onto the landing.

He turned his attention to his mother as she headed toward them. She wore a conservative navy dress with white trim, and near the neckline was her diamond-and-amethyst royal brooch in the shape of a crown. Both of his parents wore their pins daily. He was supposed to wear a similar one since he was heir to the throne, but he found it pretentious. He picked and chose the days he wore his royal pin.

"Hello, Mother." He stepped forward and gave her a feathery kiss upon the cheek.

"It's about time you returned."

He noticed how her gaze moved to Indi, and instead of a surprised look, she assumed her well-rehearsed smile. He knew that smile. It was one of duty that never reached his mother's eyes. She used it as a shield to hide what she was really feeling.

And since he had not advised his mother that he would be bringing home a visitor, he was certain she had been caught off guard—something she hated. His mother liked to know about everything before it happened.

"Mother, I'd like to introduce you to Indigo Castellanos of Athens, Greece. Indigo, I'd like to introduce you to Queen Della."

He noticed how Indi froze. She didn't smile. She didn't do the customary curtsy to the queen. She didn't move. It reminded him of their first meeting. Maybe he should have given her a heads-up on what was expected when first meeting the king or queen. But he'd been distracted by Indi's presence and his excitement to spend the next couple of weeks with her.

An awkward moment passed before the queen said, "Welcome."

He noticed the muscles of Indi's throat work. "Thank you for having me in your…home."

The queen continued to study Indi.

"Mother, I've hired Indi…um, Indigo to paint my formal portrait."

This time his mother couldn't hide her surprise. Her penciled brows rose. "We already have an artist. He's done other royal paintings."

"Not this one." His voice held a firmness. He wasn't going to change his plans. If he backed down now, his mother would always walk over him and his plans. He couldn't be an effective ruler that way.

The queen's eyes grew dark, but when she spoke, her agitation was veiled. "The king is looking for you."

"Is he in the blue room?" It was his father's favorite room in the palace. Though it wasn't the king's formal office, it was the room he used most to conduct his business.

"Yes. He's expecting you to meet with him immediately."

He was not going to abandon Indigo, whose face had gone distinctly pale. "I will see Father shortly." And with that he turned to Indigo. "Shall we?"

Indigo continued to stare at the queen, but he wasn't able to read her thoughts. To say their first meeting hadn't gone well would be a total understatement. The queen turned and made her way down the steps. Indigo watched until she was out of sight.

He gently took ahold of her arm. "Shall we?"

She blinked and looked at him. "What?"

He grew concerned about her. "Are you all right?"

She nodded. "I'm sorry. I…uh, was lost in thought for a moment."

He wasn't sure he believed her. By her pale complexion and the gaze of her eyes, it was almost as though she'd seen a ghost.

Indie walked beside him. Maybe he was just overthinking things. After all, they'd had a busy day of travel, and then meeting the queen without any forewarning or guidance on their customs must have caught her a little off guard. He would have to do better in the future.

CHAPTER TEN

THAT HADN'T GONE quite as she'd thought.

Many times over the years, Indigo had imagined one day facing the king and queen of Rydiania. In none of her fantasies had she stood there silently. That was the second time she'd been rendered silent upon meeting a member of the royal family. What was wrong with her?

She wasn't one to keep quiet when something bothered her. So then why had she been so quiet upon meeting the queen?

Maybe it was the fact that she had hoped the queen would recognize her—that she'd apologize for banishing her father, for ruining his life. Not that Indigo ever really thought any of that would happen.

There was a bit of satisfaction in the fact that the daughter of the man who'd been banished from the kingdom was now an invited guest of the palace. Yes, indeed, it felt good. Although it didn't come close to offsetting the pain and destruction that the royal family had caused hers. And for what? So they could eliminate any threat to them claiming the throne for themselves?

She'd felt a rush of so many emotions on her first night in the palace that she'd begged off on joining the royal family for dinner. She pleaded a headache, which wasn't far from the truth. A tray of food had been sent to her room.

The following morning, Istvan had given her the grand tour of the palace. Her favorite rooms had been the library, with its many bookcases and comfy couches, and the conservatory, with its walls of windows and dozens of plants.

Others would probably have been awed by the throne room or the flag room, but they did nothing for her. She was actually curious about the kitchen, but the tour didn't include that room. She wondered, if a royal got hungry in the middle of the night, did they slip down to the kitchen to get a snack? Or did they have someone to do it for them? She decided it was probably the latter.

As evening settled on her second day in the palace, she was alone in her room. She turned around, taking in the spacious room that could easily fit her apartment. Right now, her home seemed a million miles away. She'd just spoken to her mother, who was enjoying Aunt Aggie's company. Indigo missed them both.

It was time to dress for dinner. She decided to shower. It had been a long day, and a shower would make her feel refreshed. Istvan had said he would be by to pick her up at seven.

She wasn't exactly sure how to dress. Obviously jeans and a T-shirt were out. And so she picked a peach-pink maxi dress. She blew her long hair dry and then pulled it up into a ponytail, pulling loose curls to soften her face.

As for makeup, she didn't usually wear much, which was probably odd considering she was an artist. But she very rarely wore heavy eye makeup or bold lipsticks. Tonight she would do what she normally did. The more she stuck with her usual routine, the more relaxed she'd be.

She applied foundation, followed by powder. She indulged in some glittery sand-tone eyeshadow and mascara. And on her lips, she applied a frosted beige gloss. Okay, so maybe it was more than her normal, but it wasn't too much. She wondered what Istvan would think.

As soon as she realized that she cared at all what he thought of her, she banished the thought. She was here for work, nothing more.

Knock-knock.

Her heart started to race. She sensed Istvan standing on the other side of the door. And suddenly this evening was feeling much more like a date than a business dinner.

Perhaps she should have opted for the jeans, but even she knew that would be utterly unacceptable for dinner with the royal family.

"Coming." She glanced in the mirror one last time.

Considering she was having dinner in the palace, she realized her outfit was a bit on the casual side. Perhaps she should have brought something more formal, but then again, she didn't really own anything fit for palace living.

She moved to the door and opened it. Standing on the other side of the door was Prince Istvan. She could tell he had recently showered, as his dark hair was still a bit damp.

Wow! She swallowed hard. His collared shirt had the first few buttons undone, giving the slightest glimpse of his tanned, muscular chest. Her gaze skimmed down to his dark jeans. Jeans? So the royals did wear jeans around the palace, just like normal people. *Interesting.*

"Are you ready to go?" He smiled at her.

So she'd been busted checking him out. Her mouth grew dry, and she struggled to swallow. She had to keep it together. She didn't want him to know how much his presence got to her. That wouldn't be good. Not good at all.

"Yes, I am. I hope I'm dressed all right for dinner." Now, why had she gone and said that? It wasn't like she was looking for approval from anyone.

His smile broadened. "You look beautiful."

His compliment made her heart flutter in her chest. "Thank you."

He presented his arm to her. "Shall we?"

She considered ignoring the gesture, but she didn't want to be rude. So far on this trip Istvan had been nothing but kind and generous. He was making it impossible to dislike him. In fact, she was starting to wonder if she had been wrong about him. The thought startled her.

Instead of guiding her to the front stairs that they'd used

when they'd first arrived, he turned and headed in the opposite direction. It must be the back way to the dining room.

Her stomach shivered with nerves. Perhaps she should have pleaded another headache in order to get out of this dinner, too. Yes, that would have been a good idea. Would they believe she had a headache for her entire visit? Probably not.

They descended a more modest set of steps. Her stomach was full of butterflies. There was no way she was going to be able to eat. Not a chance.

When they reached the landing, instead of heading into the center of the palace, Istvan led her to an exterior door, where a guard bid them a good evening.

"I don't understand," she said. "Aren't we having dinner in the palace?"

He pushed the door open to a warm summer evening. He paused to look at her. "Is that what you want?"

"No." The word popped out before she realized it.

He smiled at her. "I didn't think so. I have something else in mind."

She should probably ask about the alternate plan, but she decided it didn't really matter to her. If it meant not having to sit across from the king and queen, she was fine with whatever he planned.

The late-summer sun hung low in the sky, sending splashes of pink and purple through the clear sky. Rydiania certainly had the most beautiful sunsets. Just as she was about to mention it, Istvan came to a stop next to a low-slung cherry-red convertible.

He opened the door for her. "I thought you'd like a ride to dinner rather than trying to walk into the village in those."

She glanced down at her heeled sandals. When she'd chosen them, she'd thought she would be walking down the stairs to the palace's dining room. Her gaze lifted to meet his. "You're right. They aren't good to walk long distances in."

"No problem. I haven't had this car out for a spin in a while. So it'll help us both."

She lowered herself to the buttery-soft leather seat. Istvan closed her door, and then he circled around to the driver's seat. It was then that she noticed just how compact the interior was, because when Istvan settled in his seat, his broad shoulders brushed up against hers. Just the casual touch set her stomach aflutter. She slid closer to the door. It was best to keep her distance—at least whatever distance the car allowed them.

He didn't seem to notice their contact or the fact that she'd moved away from him. If he did notice, he certainly didn't let on. Well, if he wasn't going to be affected by their closeness, neither was she.

She focused her gaze straight ahead as he started the car. The engine purred like a fine-tuned machine. Then the tires rolled silently over the paved drive. There was nothing about the palace that wasn't pure perfection, from the manicured green lawn to the impeccably trimmed bushes to the stunning flower gardens with purple, red and white blooms. Quite honestly, no matter what she thought of the royal family, she couldn't deny that she felt as though she were driving through a painting.

"You seemed really interested in the village when we passed through it," he said. "I thought we would dine there. But if you would rather, we could drive into the city. It isn't that much farther."

She would like to explore the city, but that would mean more time alone with Istvan in this impossibly small car. And if she were to lean her head to the side and inhale deeply—not that she had any intention of doing such a thing—but if she were to do it, she knew she would smell his unique masculine scent mingled with soap. Her pulse started to race. It was quite an intoxicating combination. Again, she wasn't going there. Not at all.

"The village is fine." Did her voice sound funny? A little deep and throaty? She swallowed hard. "It…it's beautiful here."

"I agree but then again, I might be a bit biased."

When she glanced over at him, she noticed the smile that hinted at his perfectly white, straight teeth. It was just one more thing that was perfect about him. Not that she was keeping track.

"I'm surprised you spend so much time away from here." She needed to keep the conversation going in order to keep her thoughts from straying.

She could feel his gaze briefly flick to her. "You've been checking up on me?"

"Uh, no. I mean, I just wanted to know a little more about you before I took the assignment. And the internet showed that you travel quite a bit."

He was quiet for a moment, and she started to wonder if he was going to respond. It was obviously no secret that he traveled all of Europe regularly. The press covered his every move—and every single woman he dined with. She ignored the uneasiness she'd felt at glancing at the picture of him with all those beautiful, glamorous women. It also made her wonder why there wasn't press surrounding the palace or lining the street as they made their way into the village.

"I do like to travel." He didn't expand on his reason for being out of the country so much.

The car slowed as they entered the village. The roads were narrow, with vehicles parked on either side. They stopped numerous times to allow people to cross the road. Indigo couldn't help but wonder if the people recognized the prince's car. After all, there were no royal flags on the hood or gold coat of arms on the doors as there were on other royal vehicles.

If the villagers did recognize the car or him behind the wheel, they didn't let on. Sure some smiled and waved, but it wasn't any different than if an ordinary citizen such as herself had stopped for them. Interesting. Even more interesting was that Istvan didn't expect any royal treatment. He was definitely different than she'd imagined. But how different? That was still to be determined.

A relaxing dinner.

And a chance to spend some one-on-one time with Indigo.

Istvan was quite pleased with himself for coming up with a legitimate excuse to avoid a stuffy, strained meal with his parents and siblings. He was certain to hear more about hiring a "nobody" to do his formal portrait.

He'd already been given disapproving looks, not only from the queen but also from the king when he'd met with him before picking up Indigo for dinner. His father wasn't happy with him. Not all. And then his sister Gisella had sighed at him and asked the same question she always asked him: *Why can't you just do your part?*

His sister made it sound like he should just go along with whatever his parents expected of him. That was never going to happen. He was not a yes man. Never had been. Never would be.

His intent was to bring about a more modern Rydiania. Though the more he strove to move in that direction, the more resistance he encountered. Was he the only one that realized if they didn't loosen the reins, their position as leaders of the kingdom would be in great jeopardy?

He slowed for a car just pulling out and then proceeded into the now-vacant parking spot. "Anything you are particularly hungry for?"

Indigo shook her head. "I'm curious to try some of the local cuisine."

"Then you've come to the right place. No other place cooks Rydianian cuisine quite the way they do here."

"It sounds like you come here often."

"I do." He noticed how her warm brown eyes briefly widened. "I try to spend as much time in the village as possible."

"Isn't that difficult? You know, with you being the prince and everything. Don't people constantly want pictures and autographs?"

He shook his head. "It's a small village, and the locals all know me. There's no need for them to treat me different. I don't expect it, and they know it. But when the tourists spot me, it can get a bit lively. Thankfully, the village usually quiets down in the evening, when most tourists return to the city."

"Interesting."

"You sound surprised."

"I am. I just—I don't know—thought you spent all your time in the palace."

"My parents do—for the most part. But I don't see how you can govern a country appropriately when you aren't out among the people finding out what's important to them. Come on." He climbed out of the car.

By the time he rounded the front of the car to open the door for Indi, she already had it open and was standing on the sidewalk. He couldn't help but smile. He loved her independent spirit. She didn't stand on traditions or formalities. He needed someone like her in his life—someone to remind him that he wasn't all that different from the people of Rydiania.

Not that he was planning to keep Indi in his life. He knew her life was back in Greece. And his future was all about the next steps for him to step up as king. Even though he'd been groomed for the position ever since his uncle had abdicated the throne, it was still a daunting challenge.

As they strolled along the sidewalk, villagers smiled and

said hello in passing. Most of the people were familiar faces to him.

"They're all so nice," Indi said.

"They definitely are." He felt lucky to be a part of this village. It wasn't the same for him in the big city. He only traveled there with heightened security. Here in the village, his security hung back a bit.

Indi gazed at the quaint shops lining both sides of the street. "This village is so cute. I want to grab my pad and pencil to sketch out the scenes."

Her enjoyment of the village pleased him. He pointed to a shop on the street corner. "See that place? They bake the most amazing cinnamon rolls with a buttery frosting. It practically melts in your mouth." He moved his finger to the left. "And over there is a bookstore with every genre imaginable. There are so many bookshelves that it's like making your way through a maze." He continued to provide details about the many storefronts.

"I'm already falling in love with this place." She glanced around the village with big eyes, like those of a child who was set loose in a great big toy store.

They turned a corner. Right across the street was something he knew would spark Indi's interest—an art gallery. He waited for her to spot it.

Indi gasped as she came to a stop. "You have an art gallery, too?"

"We do. Would you like to have a look?"

"I definitely would." She hesitated. "But we have plans for dinner."

"Plans are made to be changed." He wasn't in any hurry to see the evening end—even if his father wanted to have a meeting about new responsibilities that were being transferred to him. All that could wait. Right now, he was more interested in getting to know Indi. He wanted to know everything about her.

She turned to him. "You'd really do that?"

"I would. Let's go."

"As tempting as that is, I'm afraid that if I go in there, we'll miss dinner completely."

"No problem. I'll just have them prepare some takeaway meals."

Surprise lit up in her eyes. "Are you always this accommodating to your portrait artists?"

He let out a laugh. "No. Definitely not."

She smiled at him. It was a smile that started on her glossy lips and lifted her cheeks until it reached her eyes and made them sparkle like fine gems. It swept his breath away. And for a moment, his gaze dipped back down to her mouth. He wondered what she would do if he were to lean over and press his lips to hers.

He had gone into this arrangement intent on keeping things businesslike, but now he was wondering if that had been an error on his part. It had been so long since he'd enjoyed someone's company this much. Perhaps they could mix a little business with a whole lot of pleasure. Oh, yes, that sounded perfect.

He started to lean toward her.

"Istvan, look at that!" Her excitement drew him from his thoughts.

He immediately straightened and gave himself a mental shake. What was he doing? Indi didn't strike him as the casual-relationship type. If she were, it would have happened by now. And he didn't want to do anything that would end up hurting Indi. She was too kind, and in her eyes he saw pain. Someone had hurt her in the past, and he didn't want to do anything to add to that.

He looked to the left and spotted what had gotten Indi so excited. Moving slowly up the road was a horse and wagon. It wasn't an uncommon sight.

"Some of the local farmers believe in doing things the

old way." Much like his father believed change had no place in Rydiania. "They bring their goods into the village in their wagons."

"I love it." She retrieved her phone and snapped some photos.

While she watched the chestnut mare, Istvan watched her. He had a feeling his life was going to be a lot emptier when she left next week.

"Istvan?" Indi sent him a puzzled look. "Did you hear me?"

"Sorry. I was just thinking about—" he hastily grabbed the first excuse that came to him "—a meeting I'm supposed to have later this evening."

Her brows drew together. "We don't have to go to dinner if you have someplace else to be."

"Don't you worry. I'm exactly where I want to be." He sent her a reassuring smile. And then he presented his arm to her. "Shall we go have a bite to eat? It's just a little farther."

She hesitated, and then she placed her hand in the crook of his arm. "Let's do it."

"Maybe tomorrow we can come back so you can explore the gallery to your heart's content." And then he recalled that his calendar was busy the rest of the week. "On second thought, we'll have to do it next week. I just recalled that we'll be hosting some important guests the rest of the week."

"Oh. I understand. I could return to Greece if this isn't a good time to work on the portrait?"

"No. Stay. We'll make it work. I just won't be able to make any excursions until after our guests have departed. But then I promise a trip to the gallery."

She turned her head and lifted her chin until their gazes met. "I'd like that."

There was this funny feeling in his chest—something he'd never experienced before. It was a warm sensation that radiated from the center outward. And when she turned away, he wanted to draw her attention back to him. Yet he resisted the urge.

He had to stay focused on the preparation for the transition of power—on establishing his own working relationships with influential businesspeople in Rydiania. His father's health wasn't the best, and they wanted to transfer power while he was still in physically decent shape. To wait until he was frail would put the kingdom in peril. No one wanted that.

But Istvan wasn't anxious for the transition to happen. He had a lot of mixed feelings about it. First, he hated that his father was ill and had to step down. Second, he wasn't sure how he felt about his parents looking over his shoulder while he was on the throne. He knew they wouldn't approve of the changes he wanted to bring to the kingdom—the changes the kingdom needed to see it through another century and beyond.

He halted his thoughts as the restaurant came into sight. A carved red-and-black sign hung above the door.

"L'Artiste Bistro." Her voice held a note of awe. She turned to him. "What's it like?"

He pulled the door open for her. "See for yourself."

She rushed inside to have a look around. Her eyes lit up as she took in all the art, from the mixed-media wall hangings to the busts on pedestals to the plants that were also works of art.

"This place is like a museum." She continued to glance around.

"I thought you would like it. The owner is the sister of the man who owns the art gallery. They decided to combine their talents, and L'Artiste Bistro was born."

"I love it." She smiled brightly.

At that moment, the maître d' spotted them and rushed over to seat them. Instead of requesting his usual table in the back corner of the restaurant, where he was less likely to be spotted by tourists, Istvan decided to sit in the center of the restaurant, where Indi would have a better view of all the art.

After they were seated, she continued to take in the vast amount of artwork. "I feel like I should get up and tour the restaurant."

"Feel free, to but you might want to order first."

She shook her head. "I don't think so."

"Why not?"

"Because…" She glanced around at the other tables. "I don't want to make a scene."

"It's okay. You won't be the first or last to admire the fine artwork."

"Maybe I will after dinner."

As they were handed menus, he realized he was no longer hungry—at least not for food. His gaze strayed over the top of the menu to Indi, who was busy reviewing all the wonderful dishes being offered.

The only thing he desired in that moment was to learn more about the intriguing woman sitting across from him. She was like a real-life work of art, from her silky hair that made his fingers tingle to reach out and comb through her loose curls to her delicate face that he longed to caress. And then there were her lips—*oh, that mouth*. It begged to be kissed. And if there wasn't a table sitting between them, he might have done exactly that.

CHAPTER ELEVEN

THE FOOD WAS DIVINE.

The decor was amazing.

But the company was sublime.

Indigo couldn't believe she admitted that about Istvan. He was supposed to be the enemy, but the more time she spent with him, the more she found herself enjoying their time together.

He was fun. He was thoughtful. And he was compassionate.

How was it possible Istvan was part of a family that could so coldly and meanly disown their own family member, as well as the staff? It baffled her. There was a lot more to Istvan than she'd ever imagined possible.

And there was the fact that he'd brought her here to do his portrait. In his world, she was an unknown artist—an untested talent. And yet he was willing to stand up to his parents and insist on using her services over those of an established artist. It was the biggest compliment anyone had ever paid her.

The evening had gone by far too quickly, and now they were driving back to the palace. She glanced over at Istvan. In the glow of the dash lights, she watched as he skillfully worked the manual transmission as though it were an extension of his body. He maneuvered the sports car easily over the winding road. With great effort, she forced her gaze straight ahead. She didn't want to be caught staring at him.

And then they were pulling into the palace drive. She suppressed a sigh that the evening was over. She wanted to hear more about him, about his travels. Throughout dinner she had been busy answering his questions about her career and how she'd ended up at the Ludus Resort.

At first, she'd been hesitant to tell him too much about herself. She'd thought it would make her feel vulnerable. But Istvan was very laid-back, yet appropriately engaging. He didn't make her feel awkward. Talking to him, well, it was like talking to an old friend.

As the car slowed and they moved toward the back of the palace, she chanced another glance at him. He was a complex man. He was more than a prince, a brother, a dutiful son and an heir to a throne. He was caring and funny. He could even make jokes about himself. Somehow she couldn't imagine his mother laughing at herself—not a chance. She wondered if the king was more like Istvan.

The car pulled to a stop beneath a big tree. "And we're home."

She let out a small laugh.

"What's so funny?"

"You describing this grand palace as a home."

He arched a brow. "Is it not my home?"

"I suppose. But when I think of a home, I think of someplace not so grand and definitely not so large. I mean, you could fit four, no, maybe eight or more of my apartment buildings inside the palace walls."

He shrugged. "I had nothing to do with its construction."

"But you don't mind living there—even though it's more like a museum than a home?"

He was quiet for a moment, as though giving her question due consideration. "I guess it's just what you are used to. I was born and raised here. For a long time, it was all I knew."

"And now that you've been out in the world, if you could choose something different for yourself, would you?" She knew it was a bold question to ask the crown prince, and maybe she should have refrained from asking it, but she was really curious about his answer.

"I don't know." His voice was so soft that she almost thought she'd dreamed it. But then he shifted in his seat and his gaze met hers. "I don't have the luxury of imagining a different life. My destiny was determined before I was born."

In that moment, she felt sorry for him, which was totally ridiculous. Why should she feel sorry for someone who had every imaginable luxury at his fingertips?

But there was this look in his eyes that tugged at her heartstrings. Before she could decipher its origins, he blinked and the look was gone.

In a soft tone, she said, "It's not fair. You should be able to choose your future."

He took her hand in his own. His thumb stroked the back of her hand, which did the craziest thing to her now-rapid pulse. "You're the first one to say something like that to me."

In that moment, she saw the man behind the title. He seemed so relatable. Because he wasn't the only one living a destiny that had been thrust upon him. She too was fulfilling the destiny left to her by her father—she was taking care of her mother by coming to this country, by facing the very people who had put her family on this painful course in life. But she didn't want to think of that now. It had no place in this magical evening.

As she gazed into Istvan's blue eyes, she was drawn to him. Neither of them had wanted these responsibilities, and yet neither of them could turn their backs on their families. In essence, they were trapped in their roles in life—his preparing to rule a kingdom, and her doing whatever it took to care for her mother.

His gaze dipped to her lips. Her heart *thump-thumped*. His hold on her hand tightened. And then she felt her body leaning toward him.

Between the erratic heartbeats, reality got lost. The reasons that kissing him was a terribly bad idea were lost to her. The only thing she needed to know was what it was like to be in Istvan's embrace—to feel his lips upon hers.

The breath lodged in her lungs as anticipation thrummed in her veins.

It felt as though time had slowed down and sped up all at once. One moment she was lounged back in her seat, and the next she was leaning over the center console into his strong, capable arms.

His warm lips pressed to hers. He didn't hesitate to deepen the kiss. His tongue traced her lips before delving past them. A moan emanated from him. It was though he needed this kiss as much as she did.

Her hand landed on his chest. She immediately appreciated the firm muscles beneath her fingertips. *Mighty fine. Mighty fine indeed.*

With the stars twinkling overhead, it was as though they were in their own little world. She didn't want this moment to end. When it did, she knew it would never happen again. And that made her all the more eager to make it last as long as possible. In fact, she wished this kiss would never end.

Her body tingled from head to foot. It'd been a long time since she'd made out in a car. But it wasn't like this could happen in the palace, with so many people around from the staff to the queen hovering about. And definitely no one could know of this very special moment.

This stolen kiss would be both the beginning and the ending. Her heart squeezed with the bittersweetness of the situation. As the kiss deepened, she noticed that he tasted sweet, like the berries and champagne of their dessert. Her hand moved from his chest and wrapped around the back of his neck. Her fingertips combed through his thick hair, and a moan of delight swelled in the back of her throat.

They came from different worlds. He might not have directly banished her father, but assuming the role of crown prince meant he was willing to go along with his family's ruthless behavior.

She pulled back. *What am I doing? Being a traitor to Papa's memory.*

He blinked and looked at her. Confusion reflected in his eyes.

"That shouldn't have happened." She didn't wait for him to say anything as she yanked open the car door. She jumped out. She wasn't even sure she closed the door as she rushed across the parking lot.

"Indi, wait!"

She kept moving. She couldn't face him now. She had no idea what she'd say to him. The kiss had been mind-blowing, but it was so very wrong. As much fun as they undoubtedly could have together, it would lead to nothing but heartache when it was over.

She headed for the back of the palace. She just wanted to go home—her home. Her modest Greek apartment with her comfy bed and pillow, where she could hide away from the world, at least for the night.

But she wasn't afforded that luxury, as she had signed a contract to do this portrait.

She was let into the palace by one of the uniformed guards. Thankfully he recognized her. The last thing she wanted to do was have to explain her reason for being there—or worse, wait for Istvan to get her past security.

She rushed up the back stairway and prayed she wouldn't run into anyone. As luck would have it, when she reached the top of the stairs, she practically ran straight into the queen.

Indigo's heart launched into her throat. With effort, she swallowed. "Excuse me, ma'am. I didn't see you."

The queen's gaze narrowed. "Obviously. Do they not teach you manners where you come from?"

Indigo's shoulders straightened into a firm line. A smart retort teetered on the tip of her tongue. And then an image of her mother in her new apartment came to mind, and she swallowed down her indignation. Her mother had taught her that if she didn't have anything nice to say, sometimes it was best to say nothing at all. Though Indigo didn't necessarily subscribe to that way of thought, in this particular moment it was probably sage advice.

With gritted teeth, she did the slightest of curtsies. "Your Majesty."

The queen studied her as though making her mind up about her. "You know it won't work."

Indigo's heart rate accelerated. Did she know about them kissing? Impossible. They'd been hidden in the shadows of a tree. And somehow she didn't see the queen spending her time spying out windows. But that didn't stop the heat of embarrassment from blooming in her cheeks.

Not sure what the queen was referring to, she said, "Excuse me?"

"Trying to win over my son. You are a nobody—a wannabe. While he is royalty. He is the crown prince, and when he marries, it will be to someone of the finest upbringing with a grand lineage. He will not marry some commoner—some foreigner."

Indigo opened her mouth to protest the part about her being a foreigner. She was very much a Rydianian. But what good would that slight clarification do? And worse, it might make it seem like she was truly interested in Istvan, when nothing could be further from the truth. She pressed her lips together firmly.

Still, Indigo inwardly stewed about being called a foreigner. Both sides of her family had lived in Rydiania for many generations until the queen and king had abruptly forced her family from their home. The thought left a sour taste in the back of her mouth.

"Heed my warning. It's best you leave here. The sooner, the better." Then the queen snorted before lifting her chin and making her way in the opposite direction from Indigo's room.

Indigo's steps were quick and heavy as she made it to her room. How dare that woman look down her nose at her? At least she hadn't abandoned her family or forced them from the only home they'd known, like the royals had done to Istvan's uncle, King Georgios.

When she reached her room, Indigo stepped inside and let the door swing shut with a little more force than normal. In that moment, she didn't care if she made a scene. She was so over dealing with the royals.

If only she was over Istvan, too. The problem was the kiss had awakened a part of her that she hadn't known existed. It was the passionate part of her that was willing to suspend her rational thought in order to appease her desires—and she desired Istvan. A lot.

She flopped down on the huge four-poster bed with a wine-colored comforter and about a hundred different-shaped pillows. Okay, maybe there weren't that many, but there were a lot.

Tap-tap.

"Indi, can we talk?"

Her heart thumped. Her initial instinct was to rush to the door and throw it open. She desperately wanted to see him again. But then what?

Would she throw herself into his arms? Or would she do the queen's bidding and warn him away? She was torn.

Tap-tap.

"Indi, please."

She needed time alone. And so, with great regret, she said, "Go away."

Her breath caught in her throat as she waited and listened. A moment of silence passed, and then the sound of his retreating footsteps could be heard.

What was she going to do? At this particular moment,

she had no idea. She'd never expected to feel anything for the prince. And now that his kiss had awakened a bunch of emotions in her, she didn't know how to react.

What had he been thinking?

The truth was that he hadn't been thinking. Not at all.

He'd been acting out his desires. Ever since he'd spotted Indi at the Ludus Resort, he couldn't help but wonder what it'd be like to hold her in his arms and kiss her. And then once he'd gotten to know her better, his desire only grew.

Istvan sighed. Now that he'd given in to that driving desire, he'd royally messed things up. He clearly recalled the wide-eyed stare she'd given him after she'd pulled away from him. The memory tore at his gut. And then the way she'd fled from the car. She hadn't even stopped to close the door, that's how much she'd wanted to get away from him.

But why? That's the question he could not answer. No other woman had ever reacted that way after he'd kissed her. So what was so different about Indi?

His phone buzzed. He withdrew it from his pocket and found a testy message from the king's private secretary. Istvan was late for his meeting with the king, and his father was not happy.

With a groan of frustration, he made his way downstairs. Thoughts of Indi would have to wait until later. And then he would come up with a plan of how to fix things between them. Because surely there had to be a way to repair the damage that had been done. He just couldn't contemplate losing her friendship. She had brought a light to his life that he hadn't known he was missing. And without her, he feared being plunged back into the darkness.

He came to a stop outside his father's office. He straightened his shirt, leaving the collar unbuttoned. Then he opened the door and stepped into the outer office of the king's secretary, who worked ridiculously long hours, just as his predecessors had done and those before them. The bald gentleman with gold wire-frame glasses glanced up from his computer monitor. The relief immediately showed in his eyes.

He briefly bowed his head. "The king is expecting you." He scurried to his feet. "Wait here." He disappeared inside the king's inner sanctum only to return a minute later. "The king will see you now."

Istvan was escorted into the king's office. "Your Majesty," the secretary said. "Prince Istvan has arrived."

The king nodded and then with his hand gestured for them to be left alone. The secretary backed out, never turning his back to the royals. And then the door softly snicked shut. They were alone.

"Your Majesty." Istvan bowed to his father as he'd been taught when he wasn't much more than a toddler.

His father was seated behind his desk. There was a mountain of papers on his desk. The king hadn't migrated to computers with the rest of the world and still preferred paper.

"Sit." The king's tone was terse.

Istvan moved to one of the two chairs in front of the large oak desk. He knew he was in trouble, but that didn't bother him nearly as much as having Indi run away from him. He wondered what she was doing right now. So long as she wasn't packing to leave, he had a chance of fixing things. He hoped.

"You seem distracted," his father said. "I take it you've been spending your time with that woman."

"You mean Indigo. And yes, I took her to dinner in the village."

The king's brows rose. "Since when do we entertain the help?"

"She's not the help." The words came out faster than he'd intended. "Indigo is an artist that I've commissioned to do my formal portrait."

The king leaned back in his chair and steepled his fingers. "You've been away from the palace a lot lately. That needs to stop."

Istvan settled back in his chair. He refused to let his father think his disapproving tone or frown bothered him. In truth, Istvan didn't like being at odds with his parents, but they always assumed they were right and their decisions should be followed without question. The older Istvan got, the more their self-righteousness and immediate dismissal of his opinions grated on his nerves.

"I've been very busy on those trips." Istvan struggled to keep his rising temper at bay. "It's not like I was on vacation. I've been drumming up support for the We Care Foundation."

"That needs to stop."

Istvan couldn't believe his ears. "What must stop?"

"You will no longer work on that foundation."

"But I'm the one that founded it." He'd started it after little Jacques, a child from the village, came down with rare disease and his parents struggled to keep their jobs and spend time at the hospital. Istvan had felt the need to do something to help families in similar circumstances.

"Give it to one of your aides. Or better yet, let the staff of the foundation handle it."

Istvan's fingers tightened on the arms of the chair. "That won't be happening."

The king's brows knitted together, creating a formidable line. "You're refusing?"

Istvan sat up straight. "This project is personal to me, and I intend to continue overseeing it. Now, if there's nothing else—"

"There is one other matter. The woman you brought here. She needs to go."

Istvan's anger bubbled to the surface. "The woman has

a name. It's Indigo. And she's not leaving until she's fulfilled her contract."

"Istvan, I don't know what's gotten into you, but this is unacceptable. When your king gives you an order, you are to follow it without question."

"When my king's requests are more reasonable, I will take them into consideration." And with that he got to his feet. He gave a brief bow of his head, and then he turned. With his shoulders ramrod straight, he strode to the door.

He couldn't get out of the office fast enough. He was afraid if he stayed he would say something he would regret. And that wouldn't have done his foundation a bit of good. Because whether Istvan liked it or not, the king had the power to shut it down. That thought didn't sit well with Istvan.

When he was young, he'd believed everything he was told—that the king and queen always knew what was best, that the king and queen had been placed at the head of the kingdom by God, and that everyone should follow the direction of the king and queen without question.

But then his beloved uncle, who had been king, stepped down from the throne. Istvan had never understood his uncle's choice to give up the crown. After all, if you were chosen by God for such a mighty position, how could you possibly walk away from it?

And then there were the actions of his father after he'd become the new king. He'd banished his own flesh-and-blood brother from the kingdom. By royal decree, Istvan's uncle could never step foot on Rydianian soil again. And it was not only his uncle but his uncle's Immediate staff. They were all cast out of the realm.

For a six-year-old, it was a lot to take in. Istvan hadn't seen the crown quite the same way after losing his favorite uncle. And when he was forbidden to make contact with Uncle Georgios, Istvan had promised himself that he would track down his uncle as soon as he was old enough to travel alone.

It hadn't been until he was eighteen that he was able to escape his security team and travel to the Ludus Resort, where he was reunited with his uncle and he met his uncle's wife. It had been awkward at first as he'd had many questions for his uncle about the past—a past that his uncle hadn't been so willing to discuss.

The closer Istvan got to assuming the crown, the more he wanted to make changes. He knew his parents would be horrified. In fact, if the king and queen knew he envisioned more of a democracy for the kingdom, they wouldn't step aside and let him take over. Of that he was certain.

And the other thing he was certain of was that Indigo wasn't going anywhere until his portrait was completed. She had a contract, and if it came to it, he intended to enforce it. He just hoped it didn't come to that.

CHAPTER TWELVE

OH, WHAT A KISS.

Indigo yawned again. And again. She'd tossed and turned for a large portion of the night. Even her morning shower hadn't wakened her the way it normally did.

Countless times she'd replayed the kiss with Istvan. And though she wanted to put all the blame on him, she couldn't do it. She'd wanted to kiss him, too. She'd tried to remember who'd made the first move. Or had they moved at the same time?

She supposed it didn't matter now. The kiss was an undeniable thing between them. And she had no idea how to deal with it. Did they talk it out? Did she explain why it couldn't happen again? Or did she pretend it had never happened? Like that was possible.

During the wee hours of the morning, she'd recalled the Ruby Heart and the folklore about how lovers viewing it together would be forever linked or some such thing. Last night, she'd let herself believe some sort of spell had been cast over them and that's why they'd given in to their desires. But in the light of day, she realized how ridiculous it sounded and reminded herself that she didn't believe in folklore or legends.

Showered and dressed, she glanced in the mirror. She'd put on a little more makeup today than she normally would have in order to hide the shadows under her eyes. And there was her hair...should she wear it up? Or down?

This was her third day in Rydiania. It was time to get to work. She glanced at the antique clock. It was seven-thirty. She had to hurry. She wanted to arrive early for the prince's first sitting so she could set up for the portrait. And then she'd have a private word with Istvan about why they needed to pretend the kiss had never happened.

She grabbed her supplies and headed for the door. The problem was that she had no idea where she was headed. She had to stop and ask someone, who had to make an inquiry of someone else, before she was directed to a vast room. The only piece of furniture in the entire room was a single wing-back chair. She couldn't tell if the room was always devoid of furniture or if it had been cleared for the portrait.

The room was too small for a ballroom and yet too large to be a sitting room. But the exterior wall was nothing but big windows. The other three walls were done with white wainscoting on the bottom, while the upper walls were done in a cool brown tone. Sconces were spaced throughout, with various framed nature photos showing the seasons from winter to autumn.

And then she realized where she was—the conservatory. She hadn't immediately recognized it with it being devoid of furnishings. It was such a beautiful room. If this was her home, she'd turn this room into her studio, as it was filled with natural light.

She positioned the chair closer to the windows. She wanted to be able to pick up every nuance of Istvan's handsome face. She knew no matter how long she lived that she would never forget him or the kiss they'd shared. But she couldn't let it distract her. She was here to do a job—a job that would secure her mother's care and independence.

And that was the reason she'd decided to act as though the kiss hadn't happened. It was the only way they were going to move beyond it. She could do this. She could act like that kiss hadn't rocked her world.

"Good morning."

She immediately recognized Istvan's deep voice. She swallowed hard, straightened her shoulders and turned. She forced a smile to her lips. "Morning."

"I stopped by your room and was surprised to find that you were gone already."

"I wanted to get here early and set up. I know you don't have much time, with your guests arriving today. This is a wonderful room to work in. The large windows are perfect. And I hope you don't mind that I moved the chair. I mean, I could put it back, but I thought the lighting was better over here." She pressed her lips together to stop her rambling.

Istvan stepped up to her. "It's fine. Whatever setup you want works for me. But is that really what you have on your mind?"

Her gaze moved to his. Her heart pounded in her chest. *Just pretend the kiss didn't happen.* "I… I think it would be best if we focus on the portrait and nothing else."

Istvan didn't say anything for a moment. "So you just want to act like last night never happened?"

"Yes." She kept her arms at her sides, resisting the urge to wring her hands.

"Are you sure you can resist the temptation?" He arched a dark brow.

What was he trying to say? Did that kiss mean more to him than a passing flirtation? Of course not. After all, he was a prince. And she was, what? An artist. She certainly wasn't fit to be his…what? Girlfriend? Nervous laughter bubbled up inside her. She quickly stifled it.

"I can resist." Two could play at this game. "But can you?"

"I'm not making any promises."

She narrowed her gaze. "If you want me to complete this portrait, you can't be distracting me."

He planted his hands on his trim waist. "Did you just call me a distraction?"

"You know what they say…if the shoe fits."

She couldn't tell if he was flirting with her or just having fun. Perhaps it was a bit of both. Whichever, it was still better than the tension of last night. The flirting she could handle. It was the kissing that totally tripped her up.

He smiled and shook his head. "Are you ready to get started?"

She glanced around at the armchair and her easel. Suddenly this setting just didn't feel right, at least not to get started. "How about I just follow you around today? You know, while you're working or whatever."

"Who am I to argue? I've got a lot to catch up on from when I was on Ludus Island."

"Then lead the way and I shall follow."

He arched a brow. "You're sure about this? Because I have to warn you that it'll get boring."

"Don't worry about me. Just act like I'm not there."

"That would be impossible." He sent her a warm smile that caused a flutter in her chest. "But I shall do my best."

She grabbed her bag with her supplies and slung it over her shoulder. On their way out the door, they passed an older gentleman with white hair. He was dressed in a dark suit, and he had an easel in one hand. Another artist?

Her gaze moved between the two men. They seemed to know each other. Her curiosity was piqued. Was this man her replacement? She hadn't even done her first sketch and she was already being let go.

She recalled the queen's insistence that the palace's artist would do the prince's portrait. Indigo had thought Istvan would stand up to his mother and tell her what he wanted, but it appeared that once more the crown had won out.

Inside, Indigo was totally crushed. She hadn't known until that moment how much she'd been looking forward to completing such an important project. She could hang her entire artistic future on this one assignment. And now it was about to end before it even began.

"Your Highness." The man bowed. When he straightened, he said, "I am here to work on your portrait."

She caught the older man staring at her. Disapproval showed in his eyes as he took in her white-and-yellow summer top paired with jeans. Then he lifted his nose ever so slightly and turned his attention back to the prince.

What was it with this man to turn up his nose to her? Her body stiffened as angry words clogged her throat. She'd had just about enough of everyone in this palace thinking they were better than her. Not even the prince had treated her so disrespectfully.

Although the prince had apparently caved in to his mother's wishes, and now she was out of a job. Her jaw tightened as she resisted throwing accusations at the prince in front of an audience. Why would he continue to string her along?

"I won't be sitting for the portrait today." Istvan's voice drew her attention. "I have business that requires my attention."

The older man momentarily frowned but quickly hid his reaction. "Yes, Your Highness."

After they'd moved some distance down the hallway for some privacy, she stopped walking. "What's going on?"

Istvan paused and turned to her. He wore a sheepish expression. "I may have forgotten to mention that I am having two portraits done."

She frowned at him. "If you no longer wanted my services, all you had to do was say so."

He shook his head. "It isn't that. I still want you to do my portrait."

She crossed her arms. "Why, when you already have the palace's artist doing one?"

He stepped closer to her. She took a step back. He sighed as he raked his fingers through his hair. "You don't understand what it's like with my parents. When they want something, they don't stop until they get it."

"Why keep me here when you know you'll end up using the other portrait?"

"That's not my intention. But in the meantime, it's easier to appease my mother."

Indigo didn't like what she was hearing. Istvan was giving in to his parents. And to her way of thinking, that meant he condoned their decisions. The thought left a bitter taste in the back of her mouth.

If she'd had any second thoughts about abruptly ending their kiss, she no longer did. She couldn't trust Istvan. He was one of them—no matter how much she wished he was different. He was the prince of Rydiania, now and always.

CHAPTER THIRTEEN

A WEEK HAD passed since she'd arrived at the palace. The last several days, the royal family had hosted the country's business leaders, leaving very little time for Indigo to observe the prince.

She'd resorted to taking photos of him. She promised herself that she would delete them as soon as the portrait was complete. She would not keep them and stare at them, wondering what might have been had they met under different circumstances.

And now the moment she'd been dreading had arrived. Dinner with the family.

When Istvan had mentioned it, he'd made it sound so normal. Indigo knew having a meal with his family was anything but normal. Her stomach shivered with nerves.

She wished they could slip away to dine in the village again. The small town was so laid-back and the people so welcoming. It was everything the palace wasn't—warm and inviting. But then again, their dinner in the village had ended with them kissing, so maybe that wasn't such a good idea.

She felt as though she were going to dine with the enemies. How could two people who were so cold as to cast out their own relative, not to mention his loyal staff, have a son who was so friendly and seemingly caring for others?

Indigo sighed as she stared at her selection of dresses. She didn't know which to choose. Istvan had said not to worry, that it was going to be a casual family dinner. She glanced down at her jeans and cotton top. Definitely too casual.

Knock-knock.

"Come in." She expected it to be Istvan checking in on her.

When the door opened, a young maid appeared. Indigo had met her before, but for the life of her, she couldn't remember her name. "Hi."

The young woman smiled. "I am here to see if I can help you prepare for dinner."

"Help me?" she mumbled to herself. Suddenly she worried that she'd totally misunderstood this dinner. Perhaps she needed a few more details. "Uh, come in and close the door."

The young woman did so. "How may I help you?"

It was best to get the awkward part over with first. "I'm so sorry, but I can't recall your name."

"It's Alice, ma'am."

"Please, call me Indigo."

"Yes, ma'am… I mean Indigo. How can I help you?"

"I'm not sure what to wear to dinner. The prince said it will be casual, but I'm not sure which dress to wear." She held out her top two choices from the wardrobe. One was a white summer dress and the other was a little black dress that could be accessorized to make it fancier.

The maid eyed both choices. Her expression was devoid of emotion, leaving Indigo at a loss as to what Alice was thinking.

"May I suggest something else?" Alice asked.

Indigo could use all the help she could get so she didn't embarrass herself in front of the royal family. Not that she was trying to impress them, because what they thought didn't mean a thing to her. But what Istvan thought was starting to matter to her. She didn't want to do anything to ruin this evening for him.

"Yes, please." She couldn't help but wonder what Alice had in mind.

"I'll be right back." Alice disappeared out the door.

Indigo hung up the dresses. She felt so out of place here, where casual wasn't even casual. She wondered if it was too late to plead a headache again. At this rate, it wouldn't be a lie.

This was not going to go well.

Istvan had had a sinking feeling in his gut ever since his mother had insisted on a family dinner that evening—in-

cluding Indi. He'd warned his mother to be on her best behavior where Indi was concerned. His mother didn't take
well to warnings, but he wasn't about to have her drive
Indi away.

When the king had overheard the conversation, he'd told
Istvan that he was overreacting. After all, it was a family
dinner, not an inquisition. Istvan wished he had a normal
family and not one that was constantly worried about protecting their public image.

Istvan stepped in front of the mirror to check his tie. He
adjusted it just a little. Then he buttoned the top button on
his suit jacket and headed for the door. He hoped Indigo
was ready. Being late to dinner wouldn't go over well with
his very punctual parents. Though his youngest sister was
notorious for being late.

He wanted this first meal with his family and Indigo to
go well. As much as he didn't want to admit that his parents' opinions mattered to him, they still did. And if they
just gave Indigo a chance, he was certain they would see
there was something special about her.

He made his way to Indi's door and knocked.

"Come in."

He opened the door and stepped inside. When he caught
sight of Indi, her back was to him. It appeared she was struggling with the zipper on her dress.

He paused to take in her beauty—some of her hair was
pulled up and held with sparkly pins while the rest fell past
her shoulders in long, elegant curls.

"You're just in time. I need help with this zipper."

His gaze lowered to the smooth skin of her back. His
pulse picked up. He moved across the room. He reached for
the zipper and gave it a tug. It didn't move.

"I think it's caught on some material."

Before he could work on loosening the zipper, she spun

around. Her eyes were wide with surprise. "I thought you were Alice."

"Sorry to surprise you." He waited, wondering if she would send him away.

Her gaze moved to the closed doorway and then back to him. "I don't want to be late for dinner." She turned back around. "Do you think you can fix the zipper?"

"I can try." He had to admit that most of his experience was with lowering zippers, not pulling them up.

When his fingertips brushed over her smooth skin, it sent his heart racing. He tugged at the zipper. It refused to move.

His gaze strayed to the nape of her neck. If he were to lean forward and press his lips to that one particular spot, he wondered what sort of response it would elicit from her. The idea was so tempting that he couldn't resist. He leaned closer.

"Is it broken?" Indigo spun around.

His face was only a couple of centimeters from hers. The breath hitched in his throat. His gaze caught and held hers. He noticed how she didn't back away. In fact, she didn't move as she continued to stare at him with desire evident in her eyes.

His gaze dipped to her glossy lips. They were oh, so tempting. And then his vision lowered to the place on her neck that pulsated. That was where he would start. *Oh, yes.*

His hands reached out, gripping her rounded hips. He lowered his head slowly. She didn't move. He inhaled the sweet scent of primrose that reminded him of a cool spring evening with a bit of tangy, fruity sort of twist that was mingled with the hint of vanilla. Mmm…what a heady combination.

When his lips touched her smooth skin, he heard a distinct hiss as she sucked in air. Her pulse beat wildly under his lips. Her heart wasn't the only one beating wildly.

He began kissing his way up her neck to her jaw. It was

slow and deliciously agonizing. He couldn't wait to pull her close and claim her lips beneath his. And if that little moan he heard in Indi's throat was any indication, she was enjoying this moment as much as he was.

Knock-knock.

He heard the click of the doorknob and the slight squeak of the door hinge. A gasp sounded behind him.

With the greatest regret, Istvan pulled away from Indi. As he drew in a deep, calming breath, his gaze strayed across her mouth. Frustration knotted up his gut.

With great restraint, he placed a pleasant look on his face and turned to find the maid with pink-stained cheeks.

"I'm so sorry," Alice said. "I should go."

"No. Please stay," Indigo said. All the while she avoided looking at Istvan. "The zipper on my dress is stuck and, um…the prince was trying to free it, but it won't budge."

So that's what he was doing? He smiled. Just then Indigo's gaze met his, and he let out a laugh. She might be ready to deny the chemistry sizzling between them, but he knew the truth. And this wasn't the end. It was merely a pause—to be continued later.

Had that really happened?

Had she been kissed by the prince? Again?

Indigo's heart raced every time she recalled his hot breath on her neck and the delicious sensations he'd sent cascading throughout her body. If they hadn't been interrupted, she wondered just how far things would have gone.

When his lips had pressed to her skin, reality had spiraled out of reach. All she could think about was how amazing he'd made her feel and how much she wanted more—so much more.

But that couldn't happen. His future was here in Rydiania, and she shouldn't be here. The truth was they were never, ever supposed to mean anything to each other.

Going forward, she couldn't let her guard down around him. The prince didn't seem to mind playing with fire, but she for one didn't intend to get burned. She'd already lost enough in this lifetime. She wasn't about to lose any more— including her heart.

With her zipper fixed, she was ready for dinner. She stepped out into the hallway, where Istvan was waiting for her. This was the first time she was able to take in his appearance, in a navy-blue suit and white dress shirt with a boring blue tie. Her imagination stripped away the proper shirt and tie to reveal his tanned chest. As soon as the thought came to her, she halted it.

Her mouth grew dry, and she swallowed hard. "I'm ready... I think."

He sent her a slow smile that lifted his mouth ever so slightly at the corners. "Don't worry. This is just a casual family dinner. And if you need further assistance with your zipper, I'm available."

"Istvan, stop." Heat flamed in her cheeks.

"I'm just offering to help."

"Thanks, but no. You've helped quite enough. The whole palace staff is going to think we're having some wild affair."

He gazed into her eyes. "And would that be so bad?"

"No. I mean, yes." She exhaled a frustrated sigh. It was best to change the subject. "You said this dinner was to be casual, but my understanding of casual doesn't include formal attire."

"Ah...but see, that's where you're wrong. This is formal casual. Formal attire would be a tux and a gown."

"Sorry. I'm not up on my royal fashion trends."

"Then stick with me. I'll show you how it's done." He presented his arm to her.

She hesitated, but at the moment her legs felt a bit wobbly. The last thing she needed to do was to take a tumble down that long flight of stairs. And after all, it was just a hand in the crook of his arm. It wasn't like having his lips pressed to the sensitive part of her neck.

In that moment, her gaze dipped to his mouth—oh, that amazing mouth. She wondered at all the wonderful things he could do with it. Not that she would ever know, but it didn't keep her from wondering.

"That will have to wait until later." His voice drew her from her errant thoughts.

She lifted her gaze to meet his. She'd been busted day-dreaming. Heat rushed to her cheeks and made them burn. She should glance away, but she didn't.

She leveled her shoulders and tilted her chin upward ever so slightly. "That will never happen again."

"You said that before, and yet look at what just happened." He led them toward the grand staircase.

"That was your fault."

"I didn't hear any complaints. I wonder what would happen if I were to kiss you right here and now."

She stopped and yanked her hand free. "Don't you dare."

"Oh, but I would dare." His eyes twinkled with mischief.

"If you think I can't resist you just because you're a handsome prince, think again." *Wait.* Did she just admit that she thought he was handsome? Inwardly she cringed, but outwardly she refused to acknowledge her faux pas.

"As much as I'd like to continue this debate with you, we can't be late for dinner."

She was relieved to put an end to this awkward conversation. "Agreed."

"Shall we?" He once more held his arm out to her.

This time she accepted his gesture. She refused to acknowledge the way being so close to him made her heart beat out of control. *Nope. Not going there.*

She couldn't remember where the private dining room was in the palace. There were just so many rooms that it could easily be converted into a high-end hotel. Not that

Istvan would ever consider it. Still, it was so big just to be a private residence. She couldn't imagine ever calling this place her home.

As they made their way down the grand staircase, she imagined the foyer filled with formally dressed partygoers. Okay. So living here might have its benefits. The parties must be out of this world. Not that she would ever get to attend one with Istvan.

Her gaze moved to him. Her heart pitter-pattered. He was certainly the sexiest date—*erm, escort*—she'd ever had. And there was a part of her that was really curious to know how far things would have gone if they hadn't been interrupted. She quelled a sigh.

Once on the main floor, he guided her to a hallway that led toward the back of the palace. Their footsteps were muffled by a long red runner. The halls were so wide that it felt strange for her to refer to them as hallways. They were like huge, long rooms with a lot of closed doors to each side. And in between were couches—the kind you'd be afraid to sit on, because they looked like pieces of art. In addition, there were ornate pieces of furniture as well as priceless statues and large ceramic vases.

"Something catch your interest?" he asked.

She shook her head. "I'm just taking it all in."

"There's a lot to take in." That was an understatement.

He stopped in front of a set of double doors and turned to her. "Are you ready for this?"

Her heart started to pound. Her palms grew damp. And her mouth grew dry. This would be her first time meeting the king—the man ultimately responsible for the demise of her father. That thought ignited an old flame of anger. She would not let him intimidate her.

Every muscle in her body tensed as she turned to Istvan. "Let's do this."

He sent her a reassuring smile. "Let's."

Istvan grabbed both of the gold door handles. He swung both of the doors wide-open. Her heart leaped into her throat. She felt as though she were walking into the lion's den.

On wooden legs, she passed by Istvan and entered the room. She was pretty certain she was supposed to follow him, with him being a prince, but, ever the gentleman, he let her go first. Although she wasn't sure he'd done her any favors as every head turned in her direction.

Silence fell over the room. Her fingernails dug into her palms. *You can do this. You can do this.* She continued to repeat the mantra.

The king looked like an older version of Istvan, with gray temples and a close-trimmed beard that was peppered with gray. The man didn't smile. His gaze seemed to study her. All the while her insides shivered with nerves. What was he thinking? Did he see a resemblance to her father? Impossible. Everyone said she favored her mother.

"Father," Istvan said, "this is Indigo. She's a remarkable artist, and I've invited her to the palace to do my portrait."

The king's intense gaze never moved from her, though when he spoke it was in reply to his son. "I'm not used to you bringing the hired help to the dinner table."

"Indigo isn't hired help. She's a talented artist and my friend."

Indigo's back teeth ground together. Would it be wrong to tell the king what she thought of him? Probably. And it would definitely have her out of a job. The thought of what this job meant to her mother's quality of life was the only thing that kept her quiet.

She continued to hold the king's gaze. If he thought she was going to glance away or bow, he had another thought coming. There was only so far she would go to keep this job.

"Welcome." The king's voice lacked any warmth.

She couldn't tell if he was always cold or if it was just her presence that brought out his frosty side. "Your Majesty."

"Let's get you seated," Istvan said.

When her gaze surveyed the table, she found two available seats. They were not side by side, like she'd been hoping. Instead they were at opposite ends of the table. One was by the king. The other was next to the queen. Indigo groaned inwardly. Why exactly had she agreed to this dinner?

"She can sit down here," the queen said.

And so the decision was taken out of her hands. All the while the three princesses watched the scene unfold. Whatever their thoughts about the situation, they weren't revealed on their faces. Indigo wondered if that blank stare was something taught or if it was inherited.

Her stomach was tied in a knot as she took a seat to the queen's left while Istvan took a seat to the king's left. At least she could glance in Istvan's direction now and then. But the table was so long that trying to make any conversation with him was nearly impossible unless she wanted to yell.

The meal was slow, and the timings appeared to depend on when the king finished each course. When he was done, the table was cleared, whether others were done or not. Indigo didn't figure this out until the third course. Needless to say, she didn't finish the first two courses.

Conversation was sparse around the table. She wondered if the silence was due to her presence or if it was always this quiet.

At last, the queen asked, "So how exactly did you present yourself to my son?"

Was the queen even speaking normal English? "I didn't *present* myself to him." Was it so beyond the queen's thinking to imagine her son might seek out female company all on his own? "He stopped by my umbrella for a sketch."

Twin lines formed between the queen's brows. "An umbrella?"

Indigo went on to explain her position at the Ludus Resort. The queen listened, as did the princesses, but the men were involved in their own conversation. Each time she glanced in Istvan's direction, he appeared absorbed in his discussion with his father.

"My son wanted you to draw a cartoon of him?" Disapproval rang out in the queen's tone.

"It's a caricature. And it's not exactly a cartoon. It's an exaggerated drawing."

"I don't understand why he'd want you to do his portrait. This portrait is very important. It can't be a cartoon. Thank goodness I've had the forethought to schedule the palace's portrait artist."

Indigo's pride bristled at the queen's disdain over her artistic skills—skills the woman hadn't even witnessed. "I've studied art my whole life. I grew up with a paintbrush in my hand. I am capable of much more than caricatures."

"So your family is in Greece?" the queen asked, dismissing what Indigo had just said.

"Yes. My mother is there."

"It's just the two of you?" When Indigo nodded, the queen said, "Then you must be anxious to return."

"Actually, I am. I have…" She hesitated. She didn't want to share her gallery showing with the queen just to have her make a snide comment about it. "…a job to return to."

"I understand. That sounds important. I'll see that you are on the next flight back to Greece."

Wow! Talk about a bold brush-off. But the queen wasn't the first difficult person she'd had to deal with. And she wasn't going to be rushed off. Not a chance.

"Thank you, but my job here isn't complete yet." She placed her fork on the table. Her appetite was long gone. "Please excuse me. I have some phone calls to make."

There was a gasp from one of the princesses as Indigo got to her feet. With her head held high, she moved toward the door, skirting around the waitstaff as they carried in the main course. She didn't dare look at Istvan. She didn't want to see the disapproval on his face. He should just be happy that she hadn't said what she was really thinking.

She kept putting one foot in front of the other. This assignment wouldn't be over soon enough. She couldn't wait to get out of this kingdom—away from these people.

She was almost to the stairs when she heard her name being called out. It was Istvan's voice. She didn't slow down. She didn't want to talk to him right now.

He must have jogged to catch up with her, because the next thing she knew, his hand was on her arm. "Indi, wait."

She stopped at the bottom of the steps and turned to him. "I know you want me to apologize, but I'm not sorry. Your mother... She's..." She groaned in frustration.

"I know. And I'm the one who's sorry. I thought my parents would act better than that." He rubbed his neck. "I didn't mean to make you so uncomfortable. Let me make it up to you."

She shook her head. "I'm just going to call it a night."

"But you haven't had much to eat."

"I'm not hungry. Good night."

She continued up the steps. She could feel Istvan's gaze upon her, but he let her go. She wasn't good company tonight. She needed to call home and remind herself why she was staying here when all she wanted to do was leave.

CHAPTER FOURTEEN

THINGS WERE NOT going well.

Sure, his meetings that morning had been productive.
And he was starting to catch up on the work that had piled
up while he'd been away on Ludus Island, but it was Indi
that had him worried.

Ever since she'd found out that he was having two portraits done, she had been unusually quiet and her sunny
smile was missing. It was though a big, dark cloud was
hovering over them. And last night's disaster of a dinner
hadn't helped matters.

He was quickly finding that he never quite knew where
he stood with Indi. One moment everything was fine. They
would be laughing and talking. The next moment she was
looking at him like he was the enemy. He just wanted to
find some common ground where they could begin to trust
each other.

As his meeting with his secretary about next month's calendar concluded, he could see that Indi was utterly bored.
He'd even caught her hiding a yawn not once but twice. It
was time for a new plan.

"I'm sorry that took so long," he said.

She waved off his comment. "No problem. I got a lot
done."

He'd seen her pencil move over her sketch pad throughout his meetings. He was very curious to see what she'd
been up to. "May I see?"

She clutched her sketch pad to her chest. "No one sees
a work in progress."

"But that isn't even the portrait."

"It's the groundwork. You'll have to use some patience."

Throughout his meetings, he'd been distracted by Indi's

presence. He'd worked hard to hide his interest in her, but he couldn't hide it from himself. He became quite impatient—to make her smile, to hear her laughter, to feel her lips pressed to his. He jerked his errant thoughts to a complete halt.

What was he doing? There had never been anyone in his life who could utterly distract him. And yet somehow Indi had gotten past his carefully laid defenses to make him care about her. The revelation stilled the air in his lungs.

That wasn't possible. He was just overthinking things. He had to be careful, because with him being the crown prince, he didn't have the liberty to get involved with just anyone. When he got serious about a woman, she had to be the right woman. How many times had his parents told him that?

His future queen had to come with the right background. She had to be perfectly cultured, beautiful and submissive to the authority of the crown.

Though Indi was the most beautiful woman he'd ever known, she was most definitely not submissive—far from it. She had a mind of her own, and she wasn't afraid to speak her opinion—though she did pick and choose the times she shared what she was thinking.

Enough. He needed a distraction. In fact, perhaps it was time for them to go to lunch. He was thinking of heading into the village and perhaps taking time for a visit to the art gallery. He was certain that would return the smile to her face. He grabbed his phone and texted his secretary to arrange a showing at the gallery that afternoon.

Even if they couldn't have anything more between them than what they had today, it didn't mean they couldn't be good friends—genuine friends. He had enough people in his life that told him what they thought he wanted to hear. Indi didn't do that. She told him the truth whether he liked it or not. He needed her in his life. She grounded him.

With the meeting concluded, he checked his phone and

found the answer he wanted from the gallery. He got to his feet and rounded the desk. "I have to meet someone in the village. Would you care to join me?"

Her eyes lit up for the first time that day. "I would like that. Would you mind if I made a detour to the art gallery?"

"Not at all. I actually had that in mind, too." He smiled at her.

She didn't smile back. "Let me just grab my purse from my room."

"I'll meet you out on the drive."

And then she was gone. She might not have smiled yet, but he was certain she wouldn't be able to refrain when they got to the gallery. He grabbed his phone and made a call to confirm that they were on their way. Hopefully it'd get him back on Indi's good side.

Excitement flooded her veins.

This village was where she was born—where her father and mother were born. She never thought she would see this place in person. And now she was here walking through her past—a past she'd been too young to remember.

Still, she felt as though she were at last at home. She knew that wasn't the case, but it just felt like…well, like she belonged. And she would have if it hadn't been for Istvan's family. She'd still have her father, and perhaps her mother's health wouldn't have failed.

She gave herself a mental shake. Instead she focused on her memories. After they'd moved to Greece, her father used to tell her about the village. She strove to recall those stories.

Her father would talk about a fountain in a small square. She wondered if she could find it. "I love the village. Are there any piazzas?"

"There's a town square not far from here."

Excitement pumped through her veins. "Does it by chance have a fountain?"

"It does. Would you like to see it?"

She nodded. "I would. I love exploring old towns."

In a few minutes they were in the old town square. There were a few two-story buildings on each side. They were all colorfully painted. And the second stories had small balconies. She couldn't help but wonder if these were the original colors. If so, she might be able to find the exact building where she was born.

"I just love the colors. Were they always this color?" She tried to sound casual as her gaze took in the older buildings that held so much character.

"I think so. At least as far back as I can remember."

This made it easy for her. She moved to stand next to the fountain. Her gaze took in the sidewalk café, the bakery whose buttery scent made her mouth water and the florist with bright, colorful blooms filling the big picture window. And then her gaze landed on an indigo-blue building.

Her gaze lifted to the small white balcony and the windows of the second floor. That had been her parents' home. It was the place where she'd taken her first breath.

A rush of emotion came over her. She blinked repeatedly. She had to keep it together in front of Istvan. She didn't want him to know that this place—this country—meant anything to her. She wouldn't give him or his family that power over her.

"Indi, did you hear me?"

She blinked and turned to him. "What did you say?"

"I asked if you want to have lunch here?"

"Yes. I'd like that."

And so they made their way to the cute outdoor café. She remained quiet as she was overcome by so many emotions from seeing her home to standing next to the sexiest man that she'd ever known. When he looked at her, it was like he could see straight through her. And then there was the way her heart pitter-pattered every time he smiled at her.

As they waited for their meals, she said, "I love it here."

"I do, too. I learn a lot from the villagers."

"What sorts of things do you learn?"

"That the village needs a children's after-school program."

"And is that something you're interested in starting?"

"It is." He toyed with a red swizzle stick resting on the white tablecloth. "I've already set up a children's foundation. It provides free accommodations for the parents of sick children and also provides a modest allowance to help with lost wages while their child is sick."

She was stunned into silence. *Wow!* There really was another side to him. And she was mighty impressed. "Your parents must be so proud of you."

"Not exactly. My parents and I have different views of what my responsibilities should be as the crown prince. They want me to do things the way they've always been done."

"And what do you want to do?"

"I want to change things. I think change is vital to the survival of the royal family. And more importantly, I think change is vital to Rydiania. Without keeping up with the changing times and investing in technology, we will fall very far behind the other European countries."

"And while you are worrying about all that, you're running a foundation to help sick children and their parents?"

He nodded. "A three-year-old from the village became very sick. Treatment was in the city. With the parents being there for their son, they weren't able to keep up with their jobs, and they eventually lost everything. I didn't know about it until after they'd lost their jobs and home."

"Talk about making a tough time even worse."

"Agreed. So the foundation is also promoting job protection while caring for a sick family member, but the king won't make it law, because it will change the way things have always been done. When I am king, it's one of the first things I plan to do, whether my parents agree or not. I guess I'm more like my uncle than anyone ever realized."

And then their food was delivered to the table, which was a shame, because she wanted to know what his last comment meant. She suspected he was referring to the uncle who had abdicated the throne. Was Istvan thinking of abdicating, too?

Just as quick as the ridiculous thought came to her, she dismissed it. First of all, he didn't have a throne to abdicate. He was still the crown prince. And he had all these wonderful plans for the country. A person who was thinking of walking away from the crown wouldn't be making plans.

Still, the more she learned about the prince, the more intrigued she became. Something told her if it was up to him, his uncle wouldn't have been cast out of kingdom, along with his most trusted staff and their families.

CHAPTER FIFTEEN

LUNCH FOR TWO at an outdoor café.

The delicious meal had done the trick.

When Indigo smiled, Istvan relaxed. At last things between them were good once more. And he wanted it to stay that way. They only had four days left together. It didn't seem nearly long enough.

With the bill paid, they headed on their way. He made a quick stop by the bank to discuss some foundation business. Indigo opted to wait outside. She seemed to have fallen in love with the village. He had to admit that it was quaint but held its own unique charms.

His business didn't take long. When he exited the bank, he found Indigo sitting on a nearby bench. She had a book in her hands and was so captivated by the words on the page that she didn't hear him approach.

He cleared his throat. When she glanced up at him, she had a distant look in her eyes. He smiled. "Did you find something interesting?"

"I did." She gathered her things and stood. She turned the cover of the book so he could read it. "I've been reading about the history of this village. It has quite an illustrious history, from wars to royalty."

"So you like it here?"

"If you mean this village, I love it."

"Me, too."

He'd never felt such a closeness with anyone—even when Indi was miffed with him. But he had a surprise for her that he was hoping would make up for the earlier upset.

"Are you ready for your gallery tour?" he asked as they began to walk.

"I am." She smiled brightly at him.

They walked in a peaceful silence. Each of them was lost in their own thoughts. He was thinking about how much it had bothered him when Indigo believed he'd broken his word to her. He'd felt horrible about the misunderstanding.

And if he had been that bothered by her being upset with him, how was he going to cope when she flew back to Greece on Friday? He wanted to ask her to stay longer, but how long would be enough?

His thoughts halted when they reached the big white building that was home to the Belle Galleria. "We have arrived."

"I can't wait." A bright smile lit up her face. Then her gaze moved to the glass door, and the smile slipped from her face.

"What's wrong?"

"The gallery's closed today."

"Don't worry. We're having a private showing."

Her eyes widened. "You arranged this?"

He nodded. "I did. I know how important it is to you."

"Thank you. But you shouldn't have." Her gaze lowered. "I feel awful that people had to come in on their day off."

He could tell she wasn't used to people making a fuss over her. "It's all right. I made sure they were adequately compensated."

Just then someone approached the doors. They unlocked them and pushed them open. As Indi stepped inside, he thought of the other surprise he had in store for her.

The gallery was painted white with a slate-gray floor. The walls were covered in canvases, while vitrines were strategically placed throughout the large room. Within the lighted glass cases were smaller artistic pieces. Some were pieces of jewelry, and others were delicate structures constructed of wire or wood.

Istvan had visited the gallery many times. He found it peaceful and relaxing. And so he followed Indi around, letting her set the pace. She was unusually quiet as she took time to study each piece of work. He wanted to know what she was thinking, but he didn't want to interrupt her process. He was content just to watch her quietly.

Every now and then she'd make a comment. He listened and observed. By touring the gallery with Indi, he was able to see the art with a totally new appreciation.

And then she came to a stop. He almost ran into her.

She gasped. "It's mine."

He didn't have to look to know what she'd stumbled across. This was his other surprise. "I wanted to share your caricature with others."

Her eyes were filled with confusion. "I thought you wanted to auction it off."

"Ah…yes. I still plan to do that with the second sketch. But this is the first sketch you did for me. After I had it framed, I decided to loan it to the gallery."

"So it's not for sale?"

He shook his head. "Definitely not."

"Oh."

"Not everything in the gallery is for sale."

"How do you know the difference?"

He motioned for her to follow him back to the prior room. He approached a portrait of a lush, colorful garden with a dog hiding in a bush. Then he pointed to the bottom right corner of the frame. "See this red tag?" When she nodded, he said, "This means the piece is still available for sale."

"I understand."

"For the most part, they have the sale items together and the nonsale items in a different room."

"You seem to know a lot about the gallery."

He nodded. "I've known the owners for years. They're the reason I started the We Care Foundation."

"I don't understand."

And so he told her of Jacques and his health problems.

"He was the three-year-old I mentioned earlier. His parents lost their jobs because they were caring for their son. I'd known them previously from the village and wanted to help. When they said they wanted to start their own business, I was all for it."

"So you started this art gallery for them."

He shook his head. "Definitely not. I wouldn't have had a clue of how to go about it. I just made start-up funds available to them so they could make their dreams come true. They've since paid back the loan. And now my foundation makes similar loans to other struggling families."

"That's fascinating. You're doing such amazing work that helps so many people."

"My family thinks my sole focus should be on preparations for becoming king one day."

"But you're doing that by caring for the citizens. I would think that's what a good king would want to do."

He shrugged. "When my uncle abdicated the throne, the whole country experienced unrest, from riots to staging a plot to steal the throne. I was very young then, but I remember the fear that rippled through the palace. I'd never seen my parents so scared before. At one point, we were driven from the palace in the dead of night because of security issues. We went into hiding in the countryside. My mother changed after that. She became a lot more serious, and her thoughts are always about protecting the crown."

"I didn't know that."

"Why would you?"

She was quiet for a moment. And he sensed there was something she was keeping from him.

When she didn't answer, he asked again, "Why would you know that? You're from Greece."

"I didn't see any reference to the unrest in the history book I just bought," she improvised.

He nodded in understanding. "I'm sure it's in there. You just haven't gotten to it yet."

"Your Highness, I was hoping to catch you before you left." An older woman with short dark hair and a smile that warmed her face approached them. She bowed to the prince.

"Esme, it's so good to see you." Istvan stepped forward and gave the woman a quick embrace. When he stepped back, he asked, "How is Georges?"

"He is doing good. He's at home today. He's remodeling the house. He keeps telling me it's almost done, and then he finds something else to work on." She shook her head. "As long as he's happy, I suppose I can put up with the mess. At least for a little longer."

"And how is Jacques?"

Her smile broadened. "He got a clean bill of health at his last appointment. He's growing up so quickly. He'll be sorry he didn't get to see you today, but he is helping his papa." Esme's attention turned to Indigo. "And who do we have here?"

"Esme, I'd like you to meet Indigo." His attention turned to Indi, who was wearing a friendly smile. "Indigo, I'd like you to meet the owner of this gallery, Esme Durand."

The two women greeted each other, and when Indi stuck out her hand for a handshake, Esme did what she always did—she pulled her into a hug.

When Esme pulled back, she said, "I knew when Istvan brought that sketch to the gallery that there was more to it than liking the piece of art, which, by the way, is excellent. You wouldn't believe how many offers I've had to buy it."

Color flooded Indi's cheeks. "Thank you."

Istvan nodded in agreement. "I am so impressed with her work that I've hired her to do my formal portrait."

Esme's brows rose. "That's quite an honor." Her gaze moved between the two of them. "You make such a cute couple."

"Oh, but we're not," Indi said.

"You're not a couple?" Esme looked confused.

"We're friends," Istvan offered. Though he couldn't help but think of the legend of the Ruby Heart. Were they destined to be together?

As soon as the outlandish thought came to him, he dismissed it. There wasn't a chance. Indi didn't even want to admit that the kiss they'd shared was more than a spur-of-the-moment action. But he remembered how her body had trembled with desire when he'd kissed her neck.

Ding.

His phone interrupted his errant thoughts. "I need to check this." He withdrew his phone from his pocket and read the screen. "I have a meeting at three. I'm sorry, but we need to be going."

Indi nodded. "Of course." She turned back to Esme. "Thank you for opening the gallery for us. I really enjoyed getting to stroll through it. Your pieces are beautiful."

"I hope you'll come back and bring some of your own artwork. I'd love to display it for you." Esme hugged Indi again.

As they walked away, he said, "I hope you're not upset with me for lending them my sketch."

She shook her head. "Not at all. I'm just surprised you think it's good enough to display for the public."

As they walked toward the exit, he said, "I think you are wildly talented and you are about to impress the art world with your talent."

Pink stained her cheeks. "You don't have to say that."

"I know. I said it because I meant it."

Once out on the sidewalk, he turned toward the palace, and she said, "We're walking back?"

"Is that a problem?"

"No. Uh… I just thought you were in a hurry."

"Why waste a summer afternoon? There's time to walk.

And between you and me, if I'm a few minutes late for the meeting, they'll wait."

"I suppose you're right. After all, you are the crown prince." She didn't smile.

He felt as though that had come out all wrong. "I didn't mean it the way it sounded. I don't throw my position around. I just meant that I won't be more than a couple of minutes late and they would wait."

He hadn't explained that sufficiently. They continued to walk in silence. There was something about Indi that made him feel a little off-kilter. And it felt like there was something she wanted to say, but she was holding back.

They were passing by a small park on the edge of the village. Trees and bushes were strategically placed on the walkways. Sunshine poked through the leafy canopy as a gentle breeze swept past them.

He wanted to make sure things were all right between them before they reached the palace. "Let's stop here."

She glanced over at the quiet park before turning her gaze back to him. "What about your meeting?"

"This is more important."

Worry showed in her eyes. "What is it?"

He guided her to a park bench. They sat down and he turned to her. "What's wrong?"

She shrugged. "Nothing."

"That's not true. I've had the feeling something was bothering you all day. What is it?"

"I… I just didn't know that you'd decided to go with the palace's artist."

"And I explained that it's just to pacify my mother. When the formal portrait is decided, it will be yours that I choose."

"You can't say that. You haven't even seen it yet."

"No, I haven't. But I know what you're capable of, and I know you'll breathe life into the painting. You'll give my image a different perspective, and that's what I want people to see—I want them to know that when I'm king, I'll bring about change."

Whimper.

He paused and glanced around. "Did you hear that?"

"Hear what?"

"Shh… Listen."

Whimper. Whimper.

Istvan stood and glanced all around. He didn't see an animal anywhere. Could he have imagined it?

Indi stood next to him. She too glanced around.

Not sure if he'd really heard anything, he asked, "You did hear that, didn't you?"

She nodded. "What do you think it is? Are there wild animals around here?"

"There are, but I don't think you have anything to worry about. Whatever it is sounds hurt."

Ding.

When he didn't make any move to grab his phone, Indi asked, "Don't you need to check that?"

He shook his head. "It's just another reminder about the meeting."

She nodded in understanding. "You should get going. You don't want to be late."

He didn't hear any sounds now. And he had no idea where the sound had come from, so he should return to the palace. When he turned to leave, he noticed Indi wasn't beside him. He glanced back. "You're not coming with me?"

She continued to look around. "I think I'll stay here and look for the animal."

"But what if it's a great big bear?" He raised his hands like claws and bared his teeth.

She elbowed him. "You just told me I have nothing to worry about."

Whimper. Whimper.

"There it is again," Indi said. "Can you tell where it came from?"

Istvan was already moving in the direction of the sound. He was headed straight for an overgrown bush near a tree. The closer he got, the louder the whimper became.

He honestly wasn't sure what to expect. He sure didn't want to find a bear cub, as he knew the mama wouldn't be far away. Wildlife abounded around the village and palace with the mountains in the background. But no matter what lay in the bushes, he had to attempt to help it.

Indi moved up beside him.

"What are you doing?" he asked.

"Helping."

"Get back. We don't know what we'll find."

"I'm not going anywhere. You check this side and I'll check the other side."

He watched as she moved around the bush. And then he did the same thing on his side. He stared intently into the shadows between the little leaves, but he couldn't make anything out.

"It's okay," he said in a soft voice. "I'm just going to help you."

"Istvan, over here."

He moved as fast as he could, not knowing if Indi was in trouble or not. When he rounded the giant bush, he found her down on her hands and knees, flashing the light on her phone Into a hole.

"What is it?" he asked.

"A puppy. It's trapped in the hole. Every time it tries to climb out, it falls. We have to help him."

Istvan dropped to his knees. He leaned forward and placed his hand down the hole, but he couldn't reach the puppy, who continued to whimper.

Istvan lay flat on the ground. He gently inserted his arm

in the hole. His fingers moved, hoping to feel fur. Still nothing. And then there it was.

He moved his upper body, trying to lower his hand just a little farther. Just enough to wrap his fingers around the puppy's chest. *Just...a...little...farther.*

With a great big sigh, he pulled his arm back. "I can't quite reach him. I was so close."

Frustration knotted up his gut. He rolled over onto his back, expecting to see Indi, but she wasn't there. He sat up and looked around. He spotted her off in the distance.

"What are you doing?" he called out to her.

She rushed back to him with a large, flat rock in her hand. She used it to start dragging the soil away from what must be a rabbit hole, if the bits of fur surrounding the opening were any indication.

He searched around for another rock. With a rock in hand, he joined her. Together they dug at the ground, widening the opening.

He had no idea how much time had passed before he once again lay on his stomach and lowered his arm into the hole. There was no longer any whimpering. He hoped they weren't too late.

He lowered his hand into the hole. He moved slowly, not wanting to hurt the puppy or send it farther down the hole.

And then his fingers once more touched the soft fur. He gently wrapped his fingers around the pup. Very slowly he began to lift.

When the black-and-white puppy was freed, it blinked its blue eyes and stared at him with a sad look. Istvan smiled at him.

Indi ran her fingers over its back. "It's okay, little one. You're safe now." She glanced at Istvan. "What should we do with him?"

"We'll take him home. He needs water, food and a bath."

"Home? As in the palace?" She looked at him with surprise written all over her face.

"Sure. Why not? Let's go. I'll have my secretary notify someone in the village of the hole. It'll need filled in so no other animal falls in it. And I'll have them get out the news about the puppy so the owner will know where to find him."

He was so relieved to have been able to rescue the puppy. He didn't even want to think about what would have happened if he hadn't suggested they stop in the park to talk. And then he realized they hadn't quite finished their conversation.

As they walked quickly toward the palace, he asked, "Are we okay?"

Her gaze met his. "We're good."

"You're sure?"

She smiled at him. "Positive."

He expelled a small sigh of relief. One problem solved—and now another one to contend with. The puppy was docile in his arm. He hoped that wasn't a bad sign.

CHAPTER SIXTEEN

HE'D NEVER HAD a pet in his life.

And suddenly this orphaned puppy was so important to Istvan. Maybe it was because he knew how it felt to lose part of your family. His thoughts briefly strayed to his uncle—the man he'd had a closer bond with than his own father.

Maybe in part it was the fact that he could help the puppy. He could do it himself. He wanted to save the puppy and nurse it back to health. He wanted to feel needed instead of merely being a showpiece of the palace.

They entered the palace through the front door. He wasn't going to waste time walking to the side entrance, which was normal protocol unless they were welcoming guests.

Once in the foyer, Indi asked, "Have you ever had a puppy before?"

"No. But I'm sure I can figure it out." He noticed her lack of agreement. "Maybe you could help me."

She nodded. "I used to have a dog. His name was Charlie. He was big and friendly."

He was relieved to hear that at least one of them would know what they were doing. He took the stairs two at a time until he realized Indi was having problems keeping up with him. He slowed down for her. When he stopped in front of his suite, Indi rushed to open the door for him. Once they were inside, she pushed the door shut.

"He needs water." Indi turned in a circle, searching the spacious room for something to use as a water bowl.

Istvan moved to the seating area and grabbed a dish from the end table. He handed it to her. "This should do."

Indi gaped at him and then looked at the dish. "But this is an antique."

"It's a bowl." He didn't care how old the dish was as long as it held water. "You can get water in the bathroom."

She moved toward the bathroom and soon returned with a bowl of water. She set the bowl on the floor as he placed the puppy near it. When the creature didn't move to drink, Indi dipped her finger in the water and then dabbed his nose. His pink tongue came out and licked his nose. She did it again. And soon the puppy was drinking out of the bowl—in between dribbling water everywhere.

"I'll start the bath." She started toward the bathroom. At the doorway, she paused and turned back to him. "Do you think there's some baby shampoo in the palace?"

"I don't know, but I can find out."

"What about food?"

"I'll have someone get us some puppy basics from the village."

Indi nodded in agreement before slipping into the bathroom. He placed a call to his secretary, requesting baby shampoo as well as other puppy supplies.

A couple of minutes after ending the call, there was a knock at the door. *That was really fast.*

"Come in." Istvan really didn't want to deal with another visitor. He had more important things to do. He picked up the puppy and held it close to his chest, oblivious to the dirt on its coat.

The door opened, and Gisella stepped into the room. Upon spotting the puppy, her eyes widened. "So it's true."

"If you're referring to this—" he gestured toward the dog "—then yes, I have a puppy."

His sister crossed her arms as she stared across the room. "You know Mother won't approve."

"I know." And that wasn't going to change his mind. The only way he was giving up the little guy was if his owner was located. But he didn't want to think about that now.

"What are you going to do?"

"Keep him."

His sister, being a rule follower, frowned at him. "Why do you always have to cause trouble?"

He was confused. "How is having a dog causing trouble?"

"Isn't it enough that you're the crown prince? You always seem to want more. How much is enough for you?" And with that she spun around and stormed out of the room, almost running into his other sisters.

It appeared news of the puppy had quickly made it around the palace. Beatrix and Cecilia rushed into the room, ignoring him in their excitement to fuss over the puppy, who didn't seem to mind their attention.

"Can I hold him?" Cecilia pleaded with her eyes. "Please."

Istvan shook his head. "He's too dirty."

"I don't mind." She held out her hands for the pup.

He gently handed over the puppy. "Be careful with him."

Cecilia frowned at him. "Of course."

"What are you going to name him?" Beatrix asked.

He kept his attention on the puppy. "I don't know. We haven't discussed it."

"We?" There was a singsong tone to Cecilia's voice.

He ignored his sister's insinuation. "Indi—erm, Indigo was with me when we found him in the park."

"You just happened to be in the park together?" Beatrix looked at him expectantly, like he was going to confide some great love affair.

"It isn't like that," he said.

"Isn't it?" Cecilia asked. "We've all seen the way you look at her."

"Especially Mother and Father," Beatrix interjected. "You have them really worried."

Indi stepped back in the room. "Did I hear someone?" Her gaze landed on his sisters. "Oh, hi."

His sisters greeted her. He didn't want them to say anything further and upset Indi, so he said, "They were just leaving," and gave them a pointed look.

Once they were alone again, Indi said, "The bathtub is ready."

Knock-knock.

This time it was one of the household staff with the requested shampoo.

Istvan lifted the puppy until they were eye to eye. The puppy's blue eyes stared at him, and Istvan felt a protective feeling that he'd never experienced before. "It's okay, little fellow. We're just going to clean you up a bit. And then we'll get you fed."

He lowered the puppy to his chest as he followed Indigo into the bathroom. There were a couple of inches of warm water in the tub, and when he placed the puppy in the water, the puppy wasn't quite sure how to react.

Indi put some baby shampoo on her hands and rubbed them together to suds it up. Then she set to work washing the puppy. "You know, if you plan to keep him around, he's going to need a name."

He definitely wanted to keep the puppy, but he also had to slow down and realize that he might have a home. He might have a family that was frantically searching for him.

"Maybe we should wait on that until we post some notices in the village and see if he has owners that are searching for him."

"But we can't just keep calling him 'the puppy.'"

"Okay, what do you have in mind?"

She studied the puppy for a moment. "It should be something proper, if he's going to be a prince's dog." She paused as though sorting through names in her mind. And then her eyes widened. "I know. You could call him Duke."

Istvan's gaze moved from her to the dog and back again. His parents would have a fit over the name, but that didn't deter him. "I like it." He glanced at the pup. "What do you think, Duke? Do you like your name?"

The puppy just gave him a wide-eyed stare before he stood up and shook, showering them with soap suds. They glanced at each other and laughed.

Since Indi had come into his life, things had been changing. She was showing him that it was all right to go after what he wanted. And as he looked at her, he realized that he wanted her. But he knew it could never work—not with him here in Rydiania and her back in Greece, where her mother lived.

Where were they going?

The following evening as darkness fell over the kingdom, Indigo settled back against the leather seat of Istvan's sport utility vehicle with Duke in her lap. The puppy was in surprisingly good health. Even the veterinarian in the village had been surprised by his appetite and energy. And so far no one had claimed him. They made sure Duke was always with one or both of them, as he wasn't housebroken and they'd already had to clean up a few accidents. And then there was the fact he liked to chew on things—most especially Istvan's shoes. He definitely kept them busy.

But earlier in the day, when Istvan sat for his portrait, Duke had fallen asleep on his lap. While the other artist fussed about the dog's presence being most inappropriate, Indigo thought the scene was precious. And if the portrait hadn't needed to be proper, she would have included Duke. The puppy gave Istvan an authentic quality. And she felt herself falling for both man and dog.

Now all three of them were off on an adventure. She had been surprised when Istvan hadn't opted to take his sports car. But she supposed if she had an entire fleet of vehicles to choose from, she would mix things up every now and then, too. Though she couldn't imagine having one sports car, much less a selection of top-of-the-line vehicles.

As Duke slept on her lap, her gaze moved to Istvan. She noticed how his long fingers wrapped around the steering wheel. Her gaze followed his muscled arms up to his broad shoulders—shoulders that she longed to lean into as his arms wrapped around her. A dreamy sigh escaped her lips.

"Did you say something?" Istvan's voice interrupted her daydream.

"Um…no." Heat swirled in her chest and rushed to her cheeks. Needing to divert the conversation, she said, "It's a beautiful sunset. With all the oranges, pinks and purples, it makes me long to pull out my paints and put it on canvas."

"Not tonight. I have something else in mind."

"But we already passed the village. Where are we going?" And then she thought about her arrival here and their drive from the airport. "Wait. Are we going into the city?"

"Perhaps. Would you like that?"

She sat up a little straighter. "I would. I mean, while I'm here, I might as well see as much as I can. Where are we having dinner?"

"It's a surprise."

Her thoughts slipped back to her dinner with the royal family. It had been so stressful that she wasn't sure if she'd even eaten, and if she had, she couldn't remember what it tasted like. She could definitely do without a surprise like that one.

Her hand moved over the puppy's soft fur. "Will any of your family be at this dinner?"

"No. Definitely not."

She breathed easier. "That's good."

It wasn't until the words were out of her mouth that she realized her thoughts had translated to her lips. The breath caught in her lungs as she waited for Istvan to respond. She hoped her slip hadn't ruined the whole evening.

"I agree. I'm really sorry about the other night. It won't happen again."

Her pent-up breath whooshed from her lungs. "It's not your fault."

"But they are my family. And if I had known my mother was going to be that way, I never would have agreed to the dinner."

The SUV slowed as it entered the city. Duke stood up on her lap and put his tiny paws on the door so he could peer out the window. The streets were busy, but the prince's escort stayed with them. One vehicle was in front and one in back. Even if they had to run a red light, the caravan stayed together.

"I noticed you're able to move about the village without your escort, but not so much in the city."

"Don't let them fool you. I always have protection. The risk in the city is a lot higher. I can't move about here without bodyguards next to me."

"That must be rough. I can't even imagine what it's like having people watching my every move."

He shrugged. "You'd be surprised what you can get used to. But where we're going, we'll have some privacy."

"That's good, because I doubt many restaurants are going to be happy when we walk in with Duke."

Istvan reached over and petted the puppy. "You never know. He might win them all over."

"You mean like he did with us?"

Istvan smiled. "Exactly."

Woof-woof.

They both laughed at Duke's agreement.

They made their way into the heart of the city. She couldn't help but wonder where the art district might be. She'd love to visit it. But then again, she didn't even know what Istvan had planned for this evening. She just hoped her dress would be appropriate.

She'd chosen one of the dresses that had been delivered to her room the evening before. This time she'd selected a midnight-blue lace minidress. Its stretchy material fit snugly against her hips and waist. Her arms and shoulders were bared by the halter neckline. She'd matched it with her heeled sandals.

"Are you sure you won't tell me what you have planned?" she asked, not that there was anything she could do about her outfit now.

"No. But we're almost there."

The vehicle slowed as the lead car put on its turn signal. They were turning into an underground garage. Interesting.

They parked, and then they stepped into an elevator with two of his security detail. A key-card swipe and a button push had them heading for the top floor. Since she didn't know what kind of building this was, she didn't know what would be up there. She could only assume it was a restaurant with a beautiful view.

The doors whooshed open. They stepped out into a nondescript hallway, and as she glanced around, she noticed there were four doors, numbered one through four. Istvan started for the door with a gold number one on it.

Istvan opened the door and then turned back to her. "Come in."

With Duke in her arms, she passed by him. She got the slightest whiff of his spicy cologne, and for the briefest moment, she considered stopping and leaning in close to him to breathe in that most intoxicating scent, but as quickly as the thought came to her, she dismissed it. She had to keep her wits about her. Letting herself fall for the prince would lead to nothing but heartache.

She didn't know what she expected to find when she stepped through the door. Instead of a sparse modern apartment, she found skylights and greenery. There were plants throughout the large, open room.

She turned back to him as he stood near the now-closed door. "Where are we?"

"This is my new penthouse. I had it completely remodeled."

"It's amazing." Her gaze moved back to the two large couches and handful of comfortable-looking chairs. "It's nothing like the palace."

"No. It's not. And that's the way I like it."

"I didn't know you liked plants this much." Duke began to squirm in her arms.

"I like being outdoors. So I thought I'd bring the outdoors inside."

"Do you mind if I put Duke down to explore?"

"Not at all. I had them stock the apartment with puppy supplies. Where I go, he will go."

She released Duke's leash and then put him on the floor. While the puppy explored, she walked around the room taking in all the details, from the hanging plants to the marble animal statues. Even with so many plants in the room, it still didn't feel crowded. There was plenty of room for a party or just for Istvan to kick back on the couch and enjoy his gigantic television. And off to the side was a modern kitchen that looked as though it had never been used.

In the corner of the kitchen were silver bowls with Duke's name on them. And next to the couch was a box of puppy toys. Indigo smiled. Even when she was gone, she knew Duke would be well cared for and loved. Istvan would see to it.

"How long have you had this place?" She moved toward the wall of windows.

"The remodel was just completed. I've never actually stayed here. In fact, you are my first guest."

She ignored the way her heart fluttered in her chest. She

turned to him and found him approaching her. "Thank you for sharing this with me."

"I'm happy to have you here. Please, sit down."

She sat on the couch and found that not only was it nice-looking but it was also comfortable. When Istvan sat in one of the chairs, there was an air of relaxation about him. The worry lines smoothed from his face, and he looked so at home.

She reached into her oversize purse and withdrew a small sketch pad and pencil. She couldn't resist capturing this moment. And though she knew she could easily snap a photo of him on her phone, it just wouldn't be the same.

"What are you doing?" he asked.

She flipped open the sketchbook, and soon she was moving the pencil over the paper in rapid movements. "I just want to capture this moment."

"Wouldn't you rather eat? I have dinner planned for us out on the balcony."

"In just a moment." Luckily, she was quite skilled with sketches, so this wouldn't take long.

She couldn't pass up the peacefulness written all over his face. He never looked like this when they were within the palace walls. This place was good for him. She was glad he'd found a home away from home.

And this sketch was for herself. With only three more days in Rydiania, their time together was drawing to a close. She wanted something to remember him by—the real Istvan, the man who wasn't bothered by getting dirty to save a puppy, who didn't yell when his dress shoes had tiny bite marks.

That wasn't the man she'd expected to find within the palace walls. He also wasn't the man she'd expected to break through the wall around her heart. He was a man of many surprises.

CHAPTER SEVENTEEN

DINNER WAS DELICIOUS.

The company was divine.

And Duke had worn himself out exploring the penthouse and had fallen asleep in his new bed, giving them some alone time.

The meal had been served out on the balcony. Istvan smiled across the candlelit table at Indi. She seemed to enjoy the food, though he noticed she didn't eat it all.

"Was everything to your expectations?" he asked.

"The meal was delicious. There was just so much of it."

She got to her feet, reached for her wineglass and then moved to the edge of the balcony. He joined her there. Quietly they watched as the last lingering rays of the sun sank below the horizon.

She turned to him. "You have such a beautiful view."

He gazed deep into her eyes. "I couldn't agree more." But it wasn't the sunset he had on his mind. He reached out to her. The backs of his fingers brushed over her cheek. "Indi, I—"

"We should go inside." She jumped back as though his touch had shocked her. "It's getting cool out."

Really? Because he thought it was rather warm. But he didn't argue the point as he followed her inside.

Once inside, Indi moved to the sectional sofa with deep red cushions while he checked on Duke, who lifted his head, yawned and then went back to sleep. Istvan joined Indi on the couch. He still felt as though the disastrous meal with his parents was standing between them, like a wall that he wasn't able to scale.

But he refused to give up the idea of bridging the gap. There had to be something he could say, something he could do, something that would recreate the closeness they'd once shared.

He turned to her. "Indigo, talk to me."

Her gaze met his, but her thoughts were hidden behind a blank stare. "What do you want to talk about?"

He realized that it was up to him to start this conversation. "I'm sorry things haven't gone well with my family."

"Stop apologizing. I don't hold it against you. And, by the way, I really like your sisters."

"You do?" When she nodded, he said, "Gisella can be a little intense."

"That's just because she cares about you."

"So if it's not my family, why do I feel like you keep putting walls between us?"

She turned her head and gazed into his eyes. "Are you happy?"

She was avoiding his questions. He shrugged. "I don't know."

"That's not a very positive response."

He suddenly felt uncomfortable with the direction of this conversation. No one had ever asked him that. "I've never allowed myself to consider the question. My future was mapped out for me even before I was born."

"You don't have to do it. You don't have to become the king—not if it won't make you happy."

He sat up straighter and stared at her. "Are you telling me to walk away from the crown?"

"Of course not. I'm telling you not to make yourself miserable. Find a way to be happy, whether it's here at your penthouse or inside the palace walls. If you aren't happy with your choices, you won't be of any help to those around you."

He'd never thought of it that way. But he did know one thing that made him happy. He gazed at Indi. His gaze dipped to her lips before moving back to her eyes, which reflected her own desire.

"Kissing you would make me happy." He leaned in close to her and claimed her lips with his own. Her kiss was sweet, like the wine they'd been drinking. And it was so much more intoxicating.

He knew this moment—this night—wouldn't be enough time with Indigo. He didn't know how he'd do it, but he wanted to see her after this week. There had to be a way to get her to stay here in Rydiania.

When his arms wrapped around her to draw her close, her hands pressed on his chest. And then, to his great disappointment, she pulled away from him.

"This…" She gestured between the two of them. "It can't happen."

He expelled a frustrated sigh. "There you go again putting up a wall between us. Why do you keep fighting the inevitable?"

"Because your family has a habit of getting rid of the people that don't fall in line with their expectations." She said it so matter-of-factly that it caught him off guard.

"What?" And then he realized what she was referring to. "You mean the way they treated my uncle."

A frown pulled at her face. "It wasn't just your uncle. There were a lot of other people that got hurt when your parents threw them out of the country—expelled them from the only homes they'd ever known."

He was surprised by her level of emotion about something that had happened when they were nothing more than kids. "You must have learned a lot about my uncle while reading that book you bought in the village."

"I didn't learn any of this from a book." Her voice was soft and held a note of…what was it? Was that pain he detected?

As the darkness closed in around them, he longed to be

able to look into her eyes. "Indi, tell me what's going on." He reached out, taking her hand in his. "What don't I know?"

Her gaze searched his. "You really don't know, do you?"

"No. Or I wouldn't have asked."

She paused as though gathering her thoughts. "I'm Rydianian."

He was confused. "But you're from Greece."

"We moved to Greece when I was very young. But I was born in the village that you love so much."

And suddenly the pieces fell into place. "That's why you wanted to find the village square."

She nodded. "Our home was in the square overlooking the fountain."

"Why didn't you tell me before now?"

"At first I thought you knew exactly who I was from the background check. By the time I realized that you didn't know, we were already here, and I couldn't afford to lose the contract. I'd already spent the money to get my mother into an assisted living unit."

"Whoa! Slow down." He had the feeling he was still missing something big. "Why would I have fired you if I knew you were born here?"

Her gaze lowered. "Because of who my father was."

A cold chill came over him. "Who was your father?"

Her gaze rose to meet his. Unshed tears shimmered in her eyes. "He was King Georgios's private secretary. When your uncle was banished from the kingdom, so was my father. He lost everything."

Istvan got to his feet and moved to the window. He combed his fingers through his hair as he digested this news. Never again would he read just the highlights of a background check. He suddenly felt like he understood Indi so much better and why she kept putting up barriers between them.

"I'm sorry I didn't tell you sooner." The soft lilt of her voice came from right behind him.

A rush of emotions plowed into him. Anger at her for keeping this from him, anger at himself for not pushing harder when he sensed she was keeping something from him, anger at his parents for wrecking more lives in order to preserve the crown. And then there was sympathy, because he, too, had had his young life turned upside down when his favorite uncle was gone with no explanation and he was forbidden to speak of him.

And then he realized how hard it must have been for Indi to come to Rydiania and then to face the king and queen. He couldn't imagine what that must have been like for her, but he knew what strength it took. He admired her more than he ever had before.

He turned to her. "I'm sorry for what you and your family endured."

The apology was small in light of the magnitude of the damage that had been done. He longed to reach out to her and pull her close, but he hesitated, not wanting her to pull away again.

Her pain-filled gaze met his. "You don't have to apologize. You did nothing wrong. You were just a child at the time."

"Your family moved to Greece?"

Indi nodded. "My mother had some distant relatives there. My father, well, he never liked it there. He was never the same after we left Rydiania. He started to drink. And then one day when I was a teenager..." Her voice trailed away as tears slipped down her cheeks. "I..."

He heard the pain in her voice from dredging up these memories. "It's okay. We don't have to talk about this."

This time he did pull her into his embrace. He wanted to absorb all her pain and agony. In that moment, he would have done anything to make her feel better, but there was nothing he could do but stand there and hold her. He'd never felt so helpless.

Indi pulled back and swiped at her damp cheeks. "I came home and found he'd killed himself." Fresh tears splashed onto her cheeks. When she spoke her voice was rough with emotion. "When he was banished from the palace, from the life of service that had been passed down to him from his parents and grandparents, he lost a piece of himself. He... he was never whole again. It broke my mother to watch the man she loved disintegrate before her eyes, and there was nothing she could do. I can't imagine loving someone that much and then feeling so helpless."

"I'm so sorry."

She gazed at him with bloodshot eyes and tearstained cheeks that tore at his heart. "You lost someone you loved, too."

Even in her moment of great pain, she was able to offer compassion. He was in awe of her. She was the kind of queen Rydiania needed, but now he knew there was absolutely no chance of that ever happening.

He wrapped his arms around her, wanting to protect her from the pain, the horrific memories and even from his parents. They could never find out about Indi's past, because if they did, they'd banish her—the same thing they'd done to her father—in order to keep them apart.

When Indi lifted her head to look at him, he dipped his head to reclaim her lips. Her arms snaked their way around his neck, pulling him closer.

He'd never felt so close to a person. Now that the wall was gone between them, he didn't want to let her go. He wanted to make the most of this night.

This time he was the one to pull back. "Indi, stay here with me."

"You still want me after everything I told you?"

"I do. More than ever. But do you want me?"

She immediately nodded, and desire flared in her eyes. "I do."

He swung her up in his arms and carried her down the hallway to his room. He moved to the king-size bed.

He gazed down at her—wanting her so very much. "Are you sure?"

"I am." She reached out, hooking her fingers through the belt loops on his pants, and pulled him toward her.

Once he was next to her, she pressed her lips to his. This was going to be a night neither of them would ever forget.

CHAPTER EIGHTEEN

THIS PROJECT WAS going better than she'd imagined.

In fact, she was enjoying herself a lot.

Since last night, she couldn't stop smiling. She couldn't prevent what was going to happen in the future, but she could savor each moment she had left with Istvan. Even though it was already Wednesday and her plane was to take off on Friday evening, she intended to make the most of the time they had left.

Istvan had been so sweet and caring after she told him about her past. She had finally decided that he was nothing like his parents, or at least he hadn't given in to those unsavory traits.

When he'd held her and kissed her, he'd revealed to her the vulnerable side of himself. She was glad he had the penthouse, where he could escape and just be himself.

She lifted her gaze from the portrait, where she'd begun to paint his image. She intended to give him an approachable expression—one that hinted at his vulnerabilities but also showed his strength. It would be her greatest piece of work.

Indigo sat on a stool in front of the canvas. She glanced past the easel to Istvan, who sat casually in the armchair next to the window with the sunshine streaming in. He was her favorite subject ever.

Woof-woof.

Duke had decided he'd been held quite enough. He was busy chewing and chasing his toys about the big open floor.

Every time the puppy made a noise, the artist next to her would let out a disgusted sigh. How could anyone dislike a puppy? Especially when one was as cute and loving as Duke.

When they'd arrived at the palace that morning, Istvan's

secretary had told him that Duke's owners had been located. The family was honored that their dog's puppy had become part of the royal family. She'd seen the relief in Istvan's eyes when he learned that Duke was officially his, and she'd been happy for both of them.

She continued to work, excited to see the final product, because try as she might, the finished portrait was never exactly how she initially envisioned it. Sometimes it was better, sometimes not. Then her gaze moved to the older man, who frowned as his hand moved rapidly over his canvas. He was very focused. Yet when he found her staring at him, he glanced over at her with a scowl. *Yikes.* Talk about a man feeling insecure about his abilities. If he was comfortable with his skills, he wouldn't care that she was there.

"I need a break." Istvan stood and stretched. "We'll pick this back up this afternoon."

The other artist continued to work while she put down her pencil. She lowered the cloth over the canvas to keep Istvan from sneaking a look. There was nothing about this piece that she was ready to share with anyone.

She glanced over the canvas to see Istvan gesturing to her to join him. She was more than happy to spend some more one-on-one time with him. After their night at his penthouse, she felt closer to him than she had any other man in her life.

"I was thinking we should take Duke for a walk in the garden," he said. "What do you think?"

"I think that would be lovely." Then she lowered her voice. "But what about him?" She gestured over her shoulder to the other artist.

Istvan whispered in her ear, "I think he has plenty to work with."

"Perhaps you're right." As they made their way into the hallway, she asked, "How about we have a picnic lunch in the garden? We can soak up some sunshine while Duke runs around."

"I think it's a great idea. I'll have the kitchen pack up a lunch." He reached for his phone and placed a quick call. When he put his phone in his pocket, he said, "It's all been arranged."

"Thank you." She was tempted to kiss him, but she refrained, as they'd both agreed to avoid any public displays of affection around the palace. Why did life have to be so complicated?

It was a perfect summer afternoon.

But Indigo was what made the day all bright and shiny.

Istvan wasn't ready for this picnic lunch to end. Even Duke had run around and barked so much that he'd worn himself out. He was now stretched out against Istvan's legs taking a puppy nap.

Everything had changed between him and Indi last night. And it was so much more than their lovemaking. They'd learned to trust each other with everything. He'd even dare to say she was the closest friend he'd ever had, but he knew that wasn't a fair assessment, because they were so much more than friends…though he wasn't ready to put a label on it. He just wanted to enjoy it as long as he could.

Ding.

He sighed. "I'm beginning to hate that sound."

"Just change the ringtone." Indi gathered the leftovers.

"No. I mean, I hate that it reminds me that I have obligations when all I want to do is stay here with you." He glanced around to see if anyone was watching. When he didn't see anyone, he gently grabbed her wrist and slowly drew her to him.

"Istvan, what are you doing?" There was a playful smile on her lips. "We agreed on no public displays of affection."

"But there's no one around." He pressed his lips to hers.

This was what he would think of on future summer afternoons. Because in this moment with Indi and Duke, life was perfect. He was fulfilled.

Ding.

He groaned as Indi pulled away. She let out a sweet and melodious laugh.

"How can you laugh?" he asked with a frown. "It's not fair that I'm being drawn away from this to go sit in some tedious meeting."

"It's not that bad." She smiled at him as he continued to frown.

"Yes, it is. And it's your fault."

"My fault?" She pressed a hand to her chest.

"Yes. You showed me what I could be doing, and now my business pales in comparison."

She let out another laugh. Her eyes twinkled with happiness. "Well, I'm sorry if I did all that."

"You should be." And then he leaned forward and stole another quick kiss. When he pulled away, he said, "I needed something to tide me over until this evening."

She arched a brow. "Who says you are going to get more of that later?"

He sent her a pouting look. "You wouldn't deny me such pleasure, would you?"

She pursed her lips as though considering his plea. "I suppose not, but we have to go. Now."

With great regret that their leisurely lunch had to end, he helped her collect the remaining things. Then the three of them headed back into the palace. He hoped he didn't have to make any important decisions that afternoon, because his mind would be elsewhere as he counted down the minutes until he could see Indi again. In the meantime, Duke would keep her company.

CHAPTER NINETEEN

HER FEET WEREN'T even touching the floor.

Indigo smiled brightly as they entered the palace. It seemed so dark inside compared to the sunny gardens with their radiant blooms. She'd previously done some sketches and snapped photos of the garden so she could do some paintings when she got home.

Duke wiggled in her arms. Now that he was well-fed, he was a ball of energy. But they'd agreed it was best to carry him through the main parts of the palace where they would likely run into the king or queen.

They'd almost reached the stairs when the queen called out to them. "Can I see you both in the library?"

It wasn't so much a question as an order. Indigo inwardly groaned. The very last thing she wanted to do now was to make nice with the queen. But as Istvan sighed and turned, she did the same.

Once they were inside the library, the queen turned to one of the house staff that had just brought her a cup of tea and said, "Would you leave us? And close the door on the way out."

The older woman quietly nodded and did as she was bidden.

The queen was unusually quiet, and that worried Indigo. She was probably going to complain about Duke running through her flower gardens and trampling a few low-lying stems. As though he sensed he was in trouble, the dog settled in her arms.

The queen looked pointedly at Istvan. "Do you know who this would-be painter is?"

"I know everything I need to know about Indi."

The queen's eyes momentarily widened at his use of the

nickname. "I don't think you do, or you wouldn't be rolling around in the garden with her."

Indigo gasped. They had been spied upon. She felt invaded that someone would try to ruin a private moment between her and Istvan.

"We weren't rolling around." Istvan's voice took on an angry tone.

"Regardless, she's been lying about who she is."

"I know who she is," Istvan said calmly.

"No, you don't. Her father was banished from the kingdom."

"I know." Istvan's body tensed as though he were in a struggle with himself to hold back his anger.

This time it was the queen who gasped. "But how could you spend the night with her? You are putting the crown at risk by getting involved with her. You are a prince. She is no one."

Indigo now knew what it felt like to be invisible. But she had something to say. She stepped forward.

"The prince isn't putting anything at risk," Indigo said in a steady voice, though she felt anything but steady on the inside. "We are friends. Your son never led me to believe it would be anything more. And I would never make trouble for him."

The queen gave her a stony look. "If you came here hoping for some sort of revenge—"

"Mother, stop. You are insulting Indigo and making yourself look petty in the process."

Della's eyes narrowed. "Istvan, I suggest you remember that you are speaking to the queen."

The two stared at each other as though waiting for the other to blink. Indigo felt bad that she was responsible for creating this turmoil between Istvan and his mother. She needed to do something to help him.

"I am going back to Greece," she uttered. "Today."

This ended the stare-off between the two as they both looked in her direction. There was a gleam of victory in the queen's eyes while there was sadness in Istvan's.

"I'll make the private jet available," the queen said.

It was on the tip of Indigo's tongue to thank her, because her parents had raised her to have manners, but she decided the queen wasn't worthy of manners, not when she was so willing to hurt her son.

"Don't do this," Istvan said.

Knock-knock.

"Come," the queen said.

It was Istvan's private secretary. He bowed. "Pardon, ma'am. The king has sent me. The prince is late for a meeting."

This was Indigo's cue to make her exit. She headed for the hallway. Istvan rushed to catch up to her. He fell in step with her.

"Don't you have a meeting to attend?" she asked.

"I can't go to it until I'm sure you aren't leaving."

"It's for the best."

He didn't say another word until they reached his suite, where Duke's belongings were, including his kennel. She placed the puppy inside, and he moved to his puffy blue bed. Once Duke was secure, she straightened.

She sensed Istvan standing beside her. She wished he'd just go to his meeting and not make this more difficult. Because she had absolutely no idea how she was going to say goodbye to him. Especially now that she'd fallen head over heels in love with him.

Ding.

Ding.

Ding.

Istvan sighed. "This is important business or I wouldn't leave. Just wait for me and we can discuss it."

And then he leaned in and kissed her. Her heart lodged

in her throat, as she knew this would be their final kiss. Because every fairy tale had an ending, and this was theirs.

The meeting took forever.

But in the end, an agreement was reached with the local farmers. And life would continue in the kingdom as it always had.

Istvan rushed to his suite, hoping to find Indi there playing with Duke, but the puppy was still in his crate playing with a stuffed fish. He immediately dropped it upon spotting Istvan. He barked to be let out.

Istvan paused long enough to fuss over the pup quickly and put on his leash. It was time for him to be walked. They moved down the hallway to get Indi for the walk.

Knock-knock.

"Indi?"

He knocked again, with no response. As an uneasy feeling settled in his gut, he opened the door. The dresser was devoid of Indi's sketch pads.

No. No. No.

His whole body tensed as he rushed over to the wardrobe and swung the doors open. The only clothes inside were the dresses he'd bought her. Everything else was gone. Indi was gone.

It felt as though the air had been sucked out of the room. He stumbled over to the bed and sank down.

Why didn't she wait? Why?

"Istvan?" It was Gisella's voice.

He scrubbed his palms across his eyes and drew in a deep breath, hoping when he spoke that his voice wouldn't betray him.

"What do you need?" He kept his back to her as he bent over and picked up Duke.

"I heard about Indigo." He waited for her to agree with

their mother about Indigo being trouble, but instead his sister said, "I'm sorry. But you know it has to be this way."

He turned to her. "Does it have to be this way?" He shook his head. "I don't think so."

"What are you saying?" Concern laced her voice.

"Would you be happy if the only thing you had in your life was the crown?"

"Of course." There was sincerity in her words.

He lacked that conviction. He'd always believed there were more important things in life than being crowned king. Indi was one of those things.

"How can it be enough for you?" He felt he was missing something.

"How can it not be enough?" She studied him as though she were concerned about him.

"Maybe the problem is that you should be the heir."

"I wish." And then she glanced down at the envelope in her hand. She held it out to him. "Indigo left this for you."

On wooden legs, he approached his sister. He wasn't sure he wanted to know what the note said, but he couldn't help himself.

He accepted the envelope, and his sister moved on. He slipped his finger under the flap and yanked, withdrawing the slip of paper.

I'm sorry I couldn't wait. I knew if I saw you again that you would talk me out of leaving. Your mother was right about one thing—you are the crown prince. You have to focus on the future. You will be the best king ever. The people of Rydiania need you. I will never forget our time together, but we both must move on. Me with my gallery showing and you with your need to help others. I wish you all the best.
    Indi XOX

PS Kiss Duke for me
PSS I'll send you money for the dress.

After reading her letter, he was certain of one thing—his future was with Indi. He didn't care what it cost him. They would be together again. Because he loved her. He'd loved her since the first time she'd sketched him. He couldn't imagine his life without her.

CHAPTER TWENTY

LIFE HAD CHANGED.

She had changed.

Indigo had been home for a few days, and nothing felt the same. Her mother had just moved into the assisted care facility, and she was happy that her mother was finally where she wanted to be. And when her mother inquired about Indigo's melancholy mood, she blamed it on jet lag and the fact that she was going to miss her mother. Neither was a lie.

She hadn't had the heart to work on the portrait of Istvan since she'd been home. She knew she couldn't put it off forever, though. Istvan had wired the remainder of her fee the day after she left Rydiania. Was that his way of cutting ties with her?

She wasn't sure. But she'd kind of been hoping for a phone call from him, and none had come. It was really over. The thought weighed heavy on her mind.

But not tonight.

Tonight was her long-awaited gallery showing. She was so excited.

She'd opted to wear the blue dress from her night in the city with Istvan. It was the only dress she'd taken that he'd given her. And she'd already sent him the money for it, but without a price tag, she'd had to guess at the value.

"Are you enjoying yourself?" her agent, Franco, asked her.

She nodded. "It's great. How did you get the press to show up?"

"I didn't. I thought you arranged it."

She shook her head. "It wasn't me."

"Well, however they found out, it's a good thing. By tomorrow, everyone in Athens will know your name. And it's only up from there."

Franco got a little overexcited at times, but she appreciated his enthusiasm. She wouldn't be a household name like Jackson Pollock or Georgia O'Keeffe, but if her name became known in the art world, her dreams would be achieved.

Suddenly there was a commotion near the front of the gallery. Flashes lit up, and excitement moved over the crowd.

"What's going on?" she asked Franco.

"It seems a celebrity has shown up."

"Who?"

"I don't know. I sent out some invites but didn't hear anything back."

And then the crowd parted and Istvan was there, larger than life in a dark suit with a white dress shirt sans the tie, but he was accessorized by the sweetest puppy in his arms. Her heart pounded. What were they doing here?

"Duke!" Indigo rushed forward and fussed over the pup, who licked her face in return.

"Don't I rate a greeting?" Istvan asked.

A hush fell over the room as cell phones were pulled out to film the moment. Inwardly Indigo groaned. Why was he here in public with her when he knew it would stir up trouble for him?

She forced a nervous smile and then did something she'd never done before. She bowed. "Welcome, Your Highness."

"Indi, you don't need to do that," he said softly.

"I do," she whispered. And she straightened. "May I show you around?"

He nodded. "I'd like that."

And so she walked with him through the gallery. All the while she wondered what he was doing in Greece. She knew what she wanted him to say to her, but she also realized it was an impossibility. As they moved agonizingly slowly through the gallery, all she could think about was getting him alone so they could speak frankly.

When they neared the office, she signaled for him to follow her. Her heart pitter-pattered. He was so close and yet so far away.

When the door closed, she asked, "Can I hold Duke?"

He handed the puppy over.

With the dog in her arms, it kept her from reaching out to him like she longed to do. She ached to feel his kiss again, but she knew that was all in the past.

"You shouldn't be here," she said as the puppy wiggled.

"There's no other place I'd rather be." He stepped closer to her and took Duke from her. Once the puppy was on the floor, Istvan stared deep into her eyes. "I've missed you."

Her heart thumped so loudly it echoed in her ears. "I… I missed you, too. But you shouldn't be here. The press is going to make a big deal of this."

"Let them. I don't care."

He was talking nonsense. "Of course you care. You have to care. You're a prince. And not just any prince, but the crown prince. You can't just walk away from that."

He stepped closer, wrapping his hands around her waist. "I can and I did."

She shook her head, unable to accept the gravity of the words he spoke. Maybe she'd misheard him over the pounding of her heart. "Istvan, this—" she gestured between them "—isn't going to work out. You have your life, and I have mine."

"That's where you are wrong. Because where you go, I will go."

"You can't." How was he not hearing her?

"Can you look into my eyes and tell me that you don't love me?"

Really? This was what it was going to take to make him see reason—to realize that their future wasn't together. But when she stared into his bottomless eyes, she saw the future—their future.

No. No. No. She couldn't let this happen. She couldn't let him give up his future, his destiny, his family. He couldn't sacrifice all that for her.

"You can't do this." Her voice wavered.

"Yes, I can. Don't you understand that without you, I am nothing?"

"Without me, you're a prince—the future ruler of Rydiania."

"I'd much rather be the prince of your heart."

She swooned just a bit. He was saying all the right things. How was she supposed to reason with him when he was being impossibly sweet?

"Istvan, please, be reasonable. What are you going to do if you aren't a prince?" The thought of him being anything but a royal totally escaped her.

He frowned at her. "Do you think I have no other skills?"

"I, uh…" Heat engulfed her cheeks. "Of course you do. I didn't mean it that way. I'm just, well… I'm caught off guard."

The smile returned to his perfectly kissable lips. "Indigo, it is done."

"What is?" Her voice was barely more than a whisper.

"I have stepped down as heir to the throne. Gisella is going to be the future queen. She always should have been the heir. She believes the crown comes first—above all else."

Indigo couldn't believe what she was hearing. She went to step back and ended up stumbling over her own feet. Her entire body was in shock.

Why was he saying all this? What did it all mean? Why would he do this? The questions swirled in her mind at a dizzying pace.

Istvan wordlessly helped her over to the desk. When she

turned to look at him, she noticed a calm serenity in his eyes. He was at peace with this decision.

"You can't do this," she begged. "Go back. Tell them you had a moment of delusion and you didn't mean any of it."

He shook his head. "I can't do that."

"Why not?"

"Because I meant every single word I said before I departed that palace."

Her mouth gaped. This couldn't be happening. She had to be imagining the entire conversation. Yes, that was it. This was nothing more than a dream. When she woke up, all would be back the way it should be—with Istvan at the palace and her at her apartment.

"Indigo, did you hear me?"

She pressed her lips together and nodded. "But you can't give up your family for me. You'll regret it, and I couldn't live with the guilt."

"Indi, relax. I'm still a part of the family."

"You are?" She was relieved but confused.

He nodded. "Because I wasn't crowned, there was no need to banish me. By royal decree, I was removed from the line of succession."

"But you're still a prince?"

"I am."

"Thank goodness. I didn't want you to end up like my father or your uncle."

"Not a chance, with you in my life."

"But why would you do this?"

"Because I love you—I love the person you are, and I like the person I am when I'm around you. So unless you can tell me that you don't love me, I plan to be wherever you go."

Happy tears blurred her vision. She blinked them away. "And if I tell you that I don't love you?"

"Then I will take my broken heart and go live like a hermit in a hut on the top of a mountain."

She smiled and shook her head. "I can't see that happening."

"Neither can I, because I love you, Indigo, and I know you love me, too."

The happy tears returned and splashed onto her cheeks. "I do love you."

As he drew nearer to her, she knew in her heart that this union was right for them. Because she was a better person with him in her life. And now that she'd had a glimpse of the love and happiness they could have together, she couldn't imagine her life without him in it. He was the prince of her heart, now and always.

EPILOGUE

Ludus Island, September

THE LAST FEW months must have been a dream.

There was no way reality could be this good.

Indigo felt as though she was walking on clouds. After her gallery showing, her artwork had been selling as fast as she could produce it. And the amount the pieces were selling for was more than she'd ever imagined. It was enough to guarantee her mother would be able to stay in her assisted living apartment indefinitely.

With Istvan's portrait complete and hanging in the palace, Indigo was working on pieces for a new gallery showing. This time, with the help of her agent, she'd been able to land a spot in Paris. Every time she thought of how far her career had come, butterflies fluttered in her stomach.

Then there was the fact that she had her very own Prince Charming. How lucky could a girl get?

Ever since Istvan had removed himself from the line of succession, the king and queen had started changing their ways. Not only was Istvan still part of the family, but they'd welcomed Indigo as well. It wasn't a warm, fuzzy relationship, but the hostility was gone, and now she could visit the village where she'd been born without worrying that it would cause problems for Istvan.

These days Istvan split his time between Ludus Island, where he had a long-term suite at the resort, and his penthouse back in Rydiania. She was hoping that soon they could spend more time together, because she missed him when he was gone, but she had her mother here in Greece and she wanted to be close to her.

Istvan had texted her earlier that day and asked her to meet him at the resort, yet when she arrived at his suite, he wasn't there. When she texted him, he asked her to meet him out on the patio. She wondered what he was doing out there at this hour.

When she reached the doors that led outside, Istvan was standing on the patio waiting for her. "Hello, beautiful."

"Hello yourself." She rushed to him, lifted up on her tiptoes and pressed her lips to his. She'd never grow tired of his kisses. Much too soon, she pulled away. "So what are we doing here?"

"I have something to show you."

"You want to show me something out there? In the dark?"

He smiled at her, making her heart flutter in her chest. He took her hand in his as they started to walk. "Have I told you how much I've missed you?"

She gazed into his eyes. "Not as much as I've missed you."

The still-warm sea breeze brushed softly over her skin. There were a few couples lingering and enjoying the sunset. She had to admit that the sky was worthy of a painting.

She glanced at him. "Did you want to watch the sunset?"

"Yes. But not here. I have something else in mind." He continued walking across the patio and down the steps to the lit walkway that led to the beach.

He was acting very mysterious tonight. And she was dying to know what he was up to. She didn't have to wonder for long, because soon the beach came into view. With a vibrant orange, pink and purple sunset in the background, there were votives on the beach. Their flickering lights spelled out Marry Me.

Indigo gasped as happy tears blurred her vision.

When she turned to Istvan, he dropped down on one knee. "Indigo, I knew there was something special about you from the first day we met."

"But I don't even remember speaking to you. I was so caught off guard by your presence."

"You didn't have to say a word. It was just your presence that made me curious to know more about you."

She smiled at him. "So it wasn't just coincidence that you ended up at my umbrella for a sketch?"

"Definitely not. I made sure to inquire about you."

She smiled. "You did, huh?"

"Oh, yeah. I wasn't letting you get away."

"I think you're rewriting history. All you wanted from me was my artistic skills."

"That's what I wanted you to believe. And for a while, I tried to tell myself that, too. But there was no denying the way you made me feel. You gave me the courage to go after what I wanted—the life I wanted. And I want to share that life with you."

He withdrew a ring box from his pocket and held it out to her. "Indigo, you have shown me that love is accepting and tolerant. You've helped me find the courage to step out of the destiny I was born into to create the destiny I desire. I love you, and I can't imagine my life without you in it. Will you be my princess?"

She blinked repeatedly, but it was too late. The happy tears cascaded down her cheeks. "Yes. Yes, I will."

He straightened and then slipped the diamond solitaire ring adorned with heart-shaped red rubies on her finger. As soon as she saw the ring, she realized what he'd done.

"So you believe in the legend of the Ruby Heart, huh?" she asked.

He shrugged. "Seemed to work for us. And from what I heard, it worked for Hermione and Atlas."

As she admired the ring, she said, "I wonder who will fall under the spell of the Ruby Heart next."

"I don't know, but if they are as happy as we are, they'll be the lucky ones." He wrapped his arms around her waist and pulled her close.

"How happy are you?"

"Let me show you." He lowered his head, claiming her lips.

Fairy tales really did come true.

* * * * *

COMING SOON!

We really hope you enjoyed reading this book.
If you're looking for more romance, be sure to
head to the shops when new books are
available on

Thursday 4th
August

MILLS & BOON®

Coming next month

PREGNANCY SHOCK FOR THE GREEK BILLIONAIRE
Kandy Shepherd

"I don't need a DNA test," Stefanos said.

"But I—"

"I don't believe you would lie about something so important."

She looked up at him, unable to stop her eyes from misting with tears. "Thank you Stefanos, that means a lot. I...I...can't tell you how much it means." Frantically she scrubbed at her eyes with her fists. "Not crying. I'm really not. It's just that I feel so unwell, and I'm so tired, and I'm overwhelmed and... and I'm terrified." Despite her every effort to suppress them, she burst into full on sobs.

Stefanos immediately drew her into a hug. He had broad, accommodating shoulders and he wrapped his arms around her and let her cry.

Finally, she sobbed herself out. Her breathing evened out except for the odd gulp and occasional sniffle. She stilled, wishing she could stay there forever and not have to face him after making such an exhibition of herself. It was humiliating.

That had been one of her grandmother's expressions when Claudia had lost her temper or started to cry, or as a teenager had had too much to drink. Grandma Eaton had had quite a lot to do with her and Mark's upbringing when her parents had been really busy at the pub. Apparently Claudia, as a child, had quite often made an exhibition of herself and had to be reprimanded. No wonder she'd grown up tamping down on strong emotions and determined to present the best possible view of herself to others.

Finally, she reluctantly pulled away from Stefanos, feeling like she was leaving a safe haven. She looked up at him and was relieved to see kindness, not criticism in his eyes.

"I'm sorry, I didn't mean—" she started.

"Do you remember what I said about not saying 'sorry'? You have absolutely nothing to be sorry about." He wiped a damp strand of hair away from a face in a gesture that was surprisingly tender.

"Your shirt! Oh no, there are damp patches." Ineffectually, she tried to dab them away with the sleeve of her wrap. "Luckily I wasn't wearing makeup, so no mascara stains at least."

"Just salty tears," he said, sounding more than a touch bemused. "They'll dry."

"But…but that nice linen fabric could be rumpled. Let me iron your shirt, it's the least I can do."

"There is absolutely no need to do that, Claudia."

"If you're sure, but it's no trouble and—"

"What I want you to do is tell me why you're terrified of having a baby."

Continue reading
PREGNANCY SHOCK FOR THE GREEK
BILLIONAIRE
Kandy Shepherd

Available next month
www.millsandboon.co.uk

MILLS & BOON

THE HEART OF ROMANCE

A ROMANCE FOR EVERY READER

MODERN

Prepare to be swept off your feet by sophisticated, sexy and seductive heroes, in some of the world's most glamourous and romantic locations, where power and passion collide.

HISTORICAL

Escape with historical heroes from time gone by. Whether your passion is for wicked Regency Rakes, muscled Vikings or rugged Highlanders, awaken the romance of the past.

MEDICAL

Set your pulse racing with dedicated, delectable doctors in the high-pressure world of medicine, where emotions run high and passion, comfort and love are the best medicine.

True Love

Celebrate true love with tender stories of heartfelt romance, from the rush of falling in love to the joy a new baby can bring, and a focus on the emotional heart of a relationship.

Desire

Indulge in secrets and scandal, intense drama and plenty of sizzling hot action with powerful and passionate heroes who have it all: wealth, status, good looks…everything but the right woman.

HEROES

Experience all the excitement of a gripping thriller, with an intense romance at its heart. Resourceful, true-to-life women and strong, fearless men face danger and desire - a killer combination!

To see which titles are coming soon, please visit

millsandboon.co.uk/nextmonth